In a world where everyo... legend says magic itself craves a mate. Legend says those with opposite magics have the greatest chance of forming the unbreakable Bond it desires.

A.B. Cerise is an obsessive-compulsive pop star with the ability to turn invisible. He's an out bisexual with absolutely no belief in Bonds. He has a love-bruised heart, thinks dating in the spotlight is a hassle at best and a nightmare at worst, and has no intention of going through it all over again.

Matthew Hellman-Levoie is the NHL's number one goalie prospect, the youngest in a hockey dynasty, and one of the rare few who can see the unseeable. He's a straight man who wears his heart on his sleeve, has grown up searching for a Bond, and dreams of finding the love of his life.

Their magic is magnetic. Their touch is electric. They're the textbook case for Bonding. But legend never said anything about what to do when sparks fly between people opposite in more ways than magic.

THE MAGIC

BETWEEN

Stephanie Hoyt

A NineStar Press Publication

www.ninestarpress.com

The Magic Between

ISBN:

First Edition, February, 2022

Also available in eBook, ISBN:

CONTENT WARNING:
This book contains sexual content, which may only be suitable for mature readers. Depictions of homophobia/biphobia in sports and entertainment media.

For all the bisexuals out there—this one's for you.

Prologue

@kim_martinez
Flight's delayed :/ AMA

@marygrace
@kim_martinez over/under on Bonds being real?

@kim_martinez
@marygrace Under one for sure. IF THAT.

@docdulosis
@kim_martinez do you think traditionalists will ever stfu??? Like, are we EVER going to get to a point where I can use the elements to light a candle in public without someone clutching their pearls like I've done something indecent???

@kim_martinez
@docdulosis Unforch, no. But I DO believe one day Displaying won't carry the same weight many people still give it, and that seeing people use their magic freely will be as commonplace as Healers using—and frankly being expected to use—theirs to help regardless of who's around.

@meganlafleur
@kim_martinez omg this is so embarrassing I'm supposed to be meeting my boyfriend's family soon and if they approve of me, they're going to Divulge but I can NEVER remember all the different magics. PLEASE tell me you have a trick for remembering what's in each category!!!

@kim_martinez
@meganlafleur ooof I wish I had some mnemonic device up my sleeve but the best I can do is link you to this old listicle* of mine! Good luck!

*Listicle is available to read in the Index on page 403.

Chapter One

Two years ago

EXCLUSIVE: Source Confirms AB Cerise Is a Known Charmer Despite Conflicting Reports He Vanished on Stage Last Night

AB Cerise Joins Long List of Celebrities to Come Down with the Frits This Summer

13 of the Wildest Tweets About What Happened at AB Cerise's Concert Last Night

How Often Do the Frits Cause Invisibility Blips? We Asked a Magicologist About AB's Stage Disappearance to Find Out

Now

AB Cerise is a disaster. He's an obsessive-compulsive ball of barely checked anxiety surrounding his Invisibility being discovered and used against him. He has no rational reason for it. None at all. The fear is annoying, unreasonable, absolutely nonsensical, considering the whole world is full of magic. Like, AB knows no one would care about him being a Concealer beyond him cracking after years of dodging the particularly bold interviewers' questions of where he falls on the list of categories.

But the real kicker, what makes this obsession of AB's so much worse, is the absolute lack of proof to support the possibility of someone being able to manipulate him and his Invisibility just by Knowing he is. In fact, his Invisibility has always been tied to his emotions, so the obsessive way he fixates on being controlled and the compulsive way he avoids ever turning Invisible only further destabilizes his magic. Again, AB knows this. He does.

When it comes to magic, AB is his own worst enemy, but he can't stop. He's spent nearly five years in therapy, and he's still plagued by the same insidious hell his mind has created for optimal torture. His intrusive thoughts are a terrible inconvenience that AB has spent an inordinate amount of time wallowing over, but despite her best efforts, AB can't accept what Dr. Barnes says. Her end goal, since the beginning, has always been for AB to publicly Divulge and rob his intrusive thoughts of their power. Unfortunately, AB can't even think about Divulging without breaking out in a cold sweat.

But therapy hasn't been a useless waste of time. He is trying and he *is* making progress. Sort of. He hasn't made as much progress as he should, but he's made enough. He can now stay present when he's anxious, no longer getting lost in his emotions to the point he has to run off and hide before he Conceals in front of people he's never Divulged to. Hell, AB even survived a strange, and frankly traumatic, case of the Frits from two years ago that resulted in him Concealing the moment he stepped on stage at a sold-out Madison Square Garden.

Sure, the whole ordeal led to a spike in anxiety, a tightening of the grip the fear of being Known and controlled had over him, but the very thought never got the best of him. He never turned Invisible because of it. Which, in AB's opinion, is a significant achievement, considering how Displaying in front of tens of thousands of strangers would've been a catastrophic, debilitating event at the start of his therapy journey.

AB thinks about going Invisible often. Thinks about the only indication he even had the Frits was the split second of spontaneous Concealment. About the two full weeks he spent monitoring for other symptoms that never appeared. About his Invisibility always coming with a spark and how the sensation at the Garden was wild and electrifying. How much *more* exhilarated he was on stage—as if the dial had been turned all the way up, maxed out. But mostly, AB thinks about the random times the same sensation has prickled beneath his skin while he wanders New York City—fast and intense but never as substantial as the one at the concert, never enough to bring on the Frits, not even a tiny blip of Invisibility.

He's at brunch, smiling awkwardly as people recognize him on his mimosa-soaked trek to the bathroom, when the same electricity makes another appearance. This time, the sensation is accompanied by a sharp tug at his heart, and AB knows, deep in his bones, Invisibility will be inevitable no matter how hard he tries. He speeds to the bathroom; thankful the sensation doesn't reach its peak until after the door shuts; annoyed as he checks to find his hand the same transparent purple he always is while Concealed.

Personally, AB thinks a lap full of mimosas is enough inconvenience for the day, but the universe doesn't seem to agree. Not only can he not push the Invisibility down, but when he leans against the door to stop anyone else from coming in, and lets out a soft, frustrated groan, something clatters to the ground in front of him.

Because of course someone was already in here. Of course, AB couldn't be spontaneously Invisible in peace. Of course, he already ruined his chance of getting out of the way without making a noise. Of course, this guy is staring at AB with wide bewildered eyes.

Wait.

Back up.

No.

That's not possible.

"What the fuck?"

Is AB shrieking? He's definitely shrieking. But... "You can see me! You can see me? Can you see me?"

Not only can this absolutely beautiful man—no, this *bro*—see him, but he's staring at AB with absolute wonder in his eyes. He opens his mouth but then shuts it with a click of his teeth; instead, he looks AB up and down with such a methodical intensity AB begins to fidget. AB wouldn't consider himself a blusher, but every sweep of this guy's eyes leaves AB burning. His gaze settles back on AB's face before speaking, and when he does, AB thinks he must be hearing things— there's no way.

No.

Possible.

Way.

"Uh, what?"

Mr. Omnivision over there—because what else could he be?—purses his lips, then repeats, "I know this sounds ridiculous, but I think you're my future Bondmate."

AB might be short-circuiting. What the actual fuck! This guy, this gorgeous guy with his ridiculous sweatpants and his ridiculous backwards snapback and his ridiculous smile, can't possibly be standing in front of him claiming they're Bondmates. At brunch. While AB is covered in mimosa. This has to be fake.

Did he make an enemy of an Illusionist who's messing with him? Is he seeing things? He must be seeing things. This guy has to be an Illusion.

"I can assure you I'm real," Mr. Omnivision says, looking at his pants with bemusement before stepping forward with his hand outstretched. "Hi, I'm Matthew."

Oh, great. He's been thinking out loud.

AB knows he's being rude—can faintly hear his mother's voice chastising him in the back of his mind—but he can't stop staring. Despite his awful outfit, which AB has apparently insulted to his face, Matthew is stunning. He has dirty-blond hair and a ridiculously strong jaw and a dusting of freckles. Which really isn't fair—freckles are his kryptonite. How could he not stare?

"This isn't going the way I've always imagined."

Matthew drops his hand and awkwardly rocks back on his heels. The downward slope of his mouth knocks AB's brain back online.

He thrusts his hand out. "Shit. Sorry for staring. And insulting you. I'm AB."

"You also called me gorgeous, so I've decided to think of it as balancing out," Matthew says, his mouth quirking as he takes AB's hand.

AB is making a fool of himself, and he'd absolutely die of embarrassment if shit didn't get downright weird when he takes Matthew's hand in his. Simultaneously, bright golden light bursts from where their palms meet, and AB pops back into view.

"What the fuck?" AB squawks, snatching his hand away.

Even after breaking contact, the heat of Matthew's hand burns against AB's skin, and while he's no longer Concealed, none of the electricity produced by their touch has dissipated. Instead, they're encased in an invisible crackling bubble of it, as if the light of their handshake shocked the air surrounding them.

"So, that was weird," Matthew says, after AB fails to add anything constructive to their conversation. He bites his lip, an indecipherable emotion flickering across his face, and then adds, "Uh. I kind of have to go? But I'm serious about what I said. And considering all of this—" He motions between them, pointedly staring at AB's hand. "—I'm hoping you'll give me a chance to explain?"

"Wait, what?"

"Uh, like, can I...maybe get your number or...shit."

Matthew fidgets with his hat, the tips of his ears burning. "Look, I don't live under a rock. I know who you are and how this could...I don't know, come off as some sort of ploy to get your attention? You mentioned this could be an Illusion, which I'm not, obviously, but I absolutely understand if you're not comfortable giving me your number, but I'd really like to explain myself when we're not in a bathroom and my impatient friends aren't ten seconds away from storming in here to drag me out. Or maybe your email? Or—you have Twitter, right? Who doesn't have Twitter? Well, I don't have Twitter, but uh...Instagram? Or if you're into face-to-face chats we could agree on a time and public place to meet up again? I'm running out of ideas here. What else is there?"

Matthew blushes, turning his sun-tanned skin an adorable shade of ruddy pink, and all AB can focus on are the freckles, darker on his nose than anywhere else. He's staring again. Or maybe he never stopped staring, and really, AB should be mortified, but this has been such a strange encounter he doesn't think Matthew can judge him. He's running through all the ways entertaining Matthew's declaration is a terrible idea, how he clearly caused the one thing AB is so obsessed with happening, how he should be running far, far away, when everything clicks into place.

"Were you, by any chance, at my concert when I played Madison Square Garden a couple years ago?"

Matthew furrows his brow. "Yes, but what does—wait. It wasn't actually the Frits? You think I caused your Concealment? Or, well, our magics Reacting made you Invisible?"

"Wait, sorry... How can you possibly tell what type of Concealer I am?"

"A guy's got to keep some secrets," Matthew says with a slow, crooked smile. "Maybe I'll tell you one day."

The smile tips him over, and AB makes a decision Carson might actually murder him for.

"I'm not sure about Bondmates, but you're certainly affecting my magic. Which intrigues me almost as much as it pisses me off. So yeah, give me your number."

AB unlocks his phone and brings up a new contact page, then hands it to Matthew. "I'll text you once I've decided whether or not meeting up with you is a dangerous idea or just recklessly irresponsible."

Matthew snorts when he reads the name AB put him in as.

AB shrugs. "Well, aren't you?"

Matthew's face is dazzling when he smiles. "Yeah, you got me there."

Chapter Two

On their fifth birthday, Matthew's grandmother sat him and Maddie down and told them the legend surrounding different magics. She started with the facts. Magic is energy. Magic has different forms. Some magic is stronger, some is rare, but everyone has some coursing through them. Magic is mysterious and befuddling and can't always be explained.

She told them about the way some people's magic Reacts strangely when encountering others. The most common is an electric shock, so easily mistaken as static. Sometimes the spark is big enough to create a visible burst. Rarely, electricity can be produced when the proximity of two magics charges the surrounding area. She told them there is no universally agreed-upon explanation as to what causes the Reactions, but from what experts know, the greater the difference between magics, the greater the Reaction.

As a result, a widely accepted belief emerged about only two magics being different enough to be classified as True Opposites, and how no Reaction will ever be greater than one between an Omnivision and a Concealer. She told them how Divulging and Displaying conventions have limited the study of Reactions, but from what evidence they do have, no Reaction has ever occurred between two identical forms of magic.

Matthew's grandmother said the only prevailing theory—the one found all throughout history, even before the Revelation, and in all different cultures—is magic craves a mate. Legend says the Reactions are due to the attraction between magics. Says the stronger the Reaction, the more likely a Bond is to be formed. Says once a Bond is formed it can never be broken. Legend says a Bond creates a magic of its own. Says the new magic allows the pair a greater understanding of each other, and once formed, there is no connection more profound.

Legend says a great deal, but Matthew always thought the most important one was about Bonds being formed by love.

Unlike Maddie, who lost the wonder surrounding Bondmates somewhere around seventh grade, Matthew has never stopped hoping for the possibility. At five, he was certain he'd be blessed with a Bond because he was an Omnivision and Omnivisions have a True Opposite. At thirteen, his confidence began to waver as he discovered how rarely Bondmates have been recorded, how few people truly believe them to be real. At seventeen, he started dating his first serious girlfriend, and Bonding faded into something far less pressing.

But throughout it all, Matthew never stopped dreaming. He imagined an instant connection. He imagined a lot less swearing and a lot more certainty. He never once considered his future Bondmate could be a guy. Because no matter how much his grandmother said love comes in all forms and Bonds can too, Matthew has spent the last sixteen years dreaming about a girl he'd one day marry. But now, as he looks at the satiny purple stain on his palm, Matthew wonders what else he got wrong about Bonding.

"What's up with you?" Zeke asks once they've made it back to their apartment. The tone of his voice, and the way Oliver is biting back a smile, suggests he's been dying to ask the entire way home. "You've been staring at your hand like it's the eighth wonder of the world since we left the restaurant."

"I think I met my actual, very real, potential Bondmate?"

Zeke groans but Oliver looks intrigued. "You don't seem so sure? This is the fifteenth time you've told me your magic Reacted to someone else's, and you haven't sounded so unsure since the very first. What gives?"

Zeke holds his hand up to Matthew. "Wait, before you get started..." He directs his attention to Oliver, his eyes comically wide. "You're joking right? Because I thought the four I've been here for were outrageous enough."

Oliver shrugs. "Middle school was a confusing three years. Matthew and his quest for a Bondmate was no exception."

Zeke shakes his head as they move to the living room. "For your sake, man, I hope this is the real deal. I don't know how you've put up with this hopeless romantic for so long."

"I wouldn't say I'm *hopeless*."

Oliver ignores Matthew. "You'd be surprised by how boring things were when he was in Michigan. At some points I found myself *missing* Matthew mistaking static electricity for a Reaction."

"Hey! You know all of those weren't static!"

"But you admit some of them were?" Oliver counters.

Matthew shrugs. "*Perhaps.*"

Oliver smirks, as if Matthew *did* agree, and Zeke rolls his eyes as he makes a show of getting comfortable. He flops down on the couch and kicks his feet up on the coffee table. Oliver settles in on the other end, leaving Matthew to take the chair, and Zeke rolls his hand through the air, nodding at Matthew. "Okay, I'm ready. You can proceed."

"If I have your permission..." Matthew says, and Zeke's grin grows. "Do you two remember when we were all at AB Cerise's concert together?"

Zeke and Oliver glance at each other, confusion written all over their faces.

"Of course," Zeke says eventually.

"And do you remember how I said I felt weird?"

"Yeah," Oliver hedges. "Because you were being inundated with things—"

"Yeah, no," Matthew cuts in, stopping Oliver before he starts his well-meaning, but annoying, speech about how normal it is for Matthew to be overwhelmed by all the added visual input created by the sounds and magic of thousands of people in one place.

Matthew can admit the dull ache behind his eyes occasionally kicks up to an actual headache when things are too loud. He's gotten used to the pain while playing hockey, and he knows he has to focus on staying calm, centered because the headaches turn debilitating when he's wrung out and emotional, but he's never felt like he was going to buzz out of his skin the way he did two years ago. He'll never forget the current running through his veins, the way it lit him up like a conduit, how it burned through him in a way that should have been painful but wasn't. Nor will he forget the few times he's felt the same prickle of electricity while roaming the city and how identical it was to the heat sparking through him as AB opened the door today.

His roommates' doubt can't sway him. Matthew is sure. "It wasn't the magic causing it—it was a Reaction to my potential Bondmate."

Zeke looks skeptical. "You're telling me in a venue of more than twenty thousand people your magic was Reacting to the magic of one specific person? How could you possibly know? I know they're not the most common, but there could've been any number of Concealers at the concert. Hell, if the legends are true, you could've been Reacting to a shitload of magics—all varying degrees of different than yours—at the same time. How would you know in such a huge crowd? No offense, man, I truly adore you, and I hope one day you find the love you're looking for, but I don't think Bonds can really happen. And I'm *positive* you can't know whose magic was making you feel off two years ago."

"Obviously all the rest never went anywhere, and I'll gladly admit I was mistaken, but I'm telling you—this is it. I felt the same exact wave of electricity running through me today as I did at the concert and brunch was nowhere near the level of MSG. Not even close."

Oliver's tone is flippant, but the dulled blue of his voice betrays his true concern. "If you've got the Frits again, you have to go stay with Maddie. Last time was awful and I'm not taking care of you again."

"I don't have the Frits! You guys are the worst listeners— constantly interrupting me."

Oliver has the decency to look apologetic, but Zeke shrugs. "If you'd get to the point faster…"

"I'm going to remember this the next time you ask me to run through flashcards with you. Anyway! What I've been trying to say is when I went to the bathroom before we left, I felt the same way as before, but this time it was accompanied by a very visceral tug at my heart. And next thing I know, the door's opening and I'm dropping my phone because there's one very Invisible man standing against it. One who may or may not have been going into shock over me being able to see him."

"Same," Oliver mumbles.

"Wait," Zeke cuts in. "You think this guy is your Bond-mate?"

"Yeah," Matthew says. "I mean, if I wasn't sure with the whole magnetic pull thing, I'd definitely be convinced by what happened when I introduced myself. We shook hands and there was an honest-to-god golden burst of electricity and then *bam!* He's Visible again. And now, I've got his handprint on my palm, and it doesn't seem to be fading. So yeah, your doubts don't hold much weight with me any-more."

"As if they ever did," Oliver laughs.

"Fair," Matthew says. "But he *has* to be my future Bond-mate. There's no other explanation. This is the real deal, guys."

Out of all the Reactions Matthew has had, a handprint has never been left on his skin. The mark not fading has to mean this is his chance. It has to. He doesn't know what he'll do if the smear of color isn't a sign a Bond is imminent, if it turns out to be another dead-end Reaction.

Neither Oliver nor Zeke can see the mark, and Matthew is sure Zeke will challenge him because of it, but after all their interrupting, Zeke and Oliver are silent.

Oliver gathers his thoughts first. "So, to clarify, you think your Bondmate is going to be a man?"

"Yeah. A complete shock. I know."

Oliver's brows knit with confusion, but Zeke's smile couldn't be any broader. He looks absolutely delighted as he says, "I take back everything I've ever said. This is going to be good."

Matthew narrows his eyes. "Oh, you're on board with Bonding now? Just like that?"

"Of course not," Zeke answers. "Not really. It's going to take a lot more than an Omnivision seeing a spark to convince me Bonds are real."

"Really? Not even the handprint?"

Zeke shrugs. "Maybe if I could see it."

Matthew rolls his eyes and Zeke lets out a small, amused huff of air. "Come on, Matthew, people's magic Reacting to each other is verifiable enough, but Bonding? It's been hundreds of years since anyone even said they Bonded. What I really want to talk about here is how you're completely un-fazed by meeting *a guy* while he was fully Displayed."

"Why wouldn't I be chill?"

"Maybe because you've been imagining this grand love affair basically your entire life, and within a moment, you've given it all up," Oliver suggests.

Zeke turns to Oliver with an amused, almost smug grin. "Unless our baby's finally having his very own bi revelation."

When he turns back to Matthew, his expression is far more serious than Matthew expected. "Is this your moment? Has this guy sparked an awakening for you? Are we about to lose our token straight friend?"

"Uh. No. I think I'd know if I was into dudes." Oliver opens his mouth and Matthew cuts him off. "Yes, I *know* people can realize in all phases of life. But I don't—I'm not into him. Well, no, I'm very into finding someone my magic Reacts to this strongly, but I'm not attracted to him."

Matthew is comfortable enough with himself to admit AB is attractive. Maddie has been a fan of AB since he was nothing but a kid their age posting covers on YouTube. Matthew can still remember all the lyrics to "Dangerous" from hearing it a million and one times the summer before he started in the NTDP. He's seen enough photos and been cajoled into watching enough videos to know what AB looks like. Matthew doesn't need to deny AB's good looks—he knows what they are. But the same can be said for knowing Oliver and Zeke are handsome. Matthew recognizing the physical attributes of other men doesn't change Matthew's sexuality—he's still straight.

"And you're not disappointed by this?" Oliver asks. "Not even in the slightest?"

"I don't think so?" Which is a bigger surprise than his future Bondmate being a guy, actually. "Maybe briefly on the way home but not really. Not anymore. I think I'm more shocked about how far off I was in my imagination."

Oliver purses his lips. "Are you *sure* this isn't a queer thing?"

"Yes," Matthew says.

"I'm sorry," Oliver says. "But I'm having a little trouble wrapping my head around this when you've been a one-and-done kind of guy since you and Tori decided going to college on opposite sides of the country was too hard. You've been on *maybe* three second dates in the last two years."

"And?"

"And!" Zeke scoffs. "You're suddenly changing your entire MO because some guy put a mark on you! You do see how this is all a little gay, right?"

Matthew crosses his arms. "Okay, first, I'm pretty sure you've both told me before platonic Bonds could be possible."

"Yeah," Oliver says. "When we were trying to get you to go on second dates with girls you were obviously into but didn't React to! And you literally never listened!"

"And now I am!"

Oliver gapes at him, no words coming out.

"You're a real piece of work, Matthew." Zeke shakes his head. "But if this is the real damn deal, and I'm definitely not saying it is, I'm reserving judgment until you two make it past the one-month mark, but if it is real then, hey! You'll never have to worry about self-sabotaging your love life again. Can't really use the 'I'm waiting for my Bondmate' excuse as a reason the relationship won't work out when you've already got one."

"Eh," Oliver says. "I'm not so sure 'hey, this is my platonic Bondmate who I share a deep and magical connection with' is going to be any better for his love life than refusing to date someone he doesn't React with."

"Maybe if Matthew was into guys, but I think it's a nonissue since he's straight. He and Maddie have the spooky Twintuition, and come on, can a Bond really be any different?"

"I'd think they have to be a little more intense if no one believes in them but Matthew," Oliver says.

"Don't forget his grandmother," Zeke says.

"You two are the worst," Matthew huffs.

"And yet you love us," Zeke says.

"Much to my dismay," Matthew says.

Zeke rolls his eyes. "Are you going to tell us about this guy? Because I've got some questions."

Matthew nods, motioning with his hand for Zeke to continue.

"First: Where does he stand on Bondmates? Second: Did you even mention Bondmates? Usually, you're a babbling mess by now, but you've been pretty tight-lipped. Come to think of it, does this guy even have a name?" Zeke looks utterly horrified. "Oh god, Matthew. Please tell me you got his name."

"Of course, I got his name," Matthew says, affronted.

"Which is what?" Oliver prompts.

"Uh, A—" Matthew starts to tell them but then reconsiders. "Abe. His name is Abe."

He's not sure why, but telling them AB is the guy he met makes him a little queasy. He wants to say he keeps AB's name to himself because he doesn't know what an incredibly famous celebrity would think about Matthew telling people about their encounter. He wants to think he was being considerate. But later, when he's back in his room, desk and hands covered in pastel smears of pinks and blues and purples, trying desperately to capture the ethereal beauty of AB's complex purple—Concealed, yet visible to Matthew—he realizes he doesn't want to share either.

Chapter Three

Meeting someone who has now led to AB Displaying twice should, logically, send AB into an obsessive spiral. AB wants to believe his disastrous encounter with Matthew not triggering a tailspin is a real testament to his own progress. He wants to say this proves Dr. Barnes right when she insists nothing about his intrusive thoughts is rational, and thus, he shouldn't try to reason with them as if they are. He wants to say he hasn't been thinking about texting Matthew since he got back from brunch. He wants to say he's a reasonable, self-preserving kind of man. He wants to say he wouldn't willingly put himself in a situation where he might exacerbate his own anxieties.

But see, AB is not that man. AB is a reckless fool when met with a pretty face, and well...Matthew has one hell of a pretty face.

Honestly, it's a certified miracle AB makes it two weeks before he cracks. He knows texting Matthew isn't a good idea. He knows nothing good will come from opening this door, but AB is so grossly intrigued by Matthew's ability to *see* him. Not even Derek, an Immune, can tell the difference between AB as he is and AB Concealed. And the way Matthew looked at him in the bathroom, as if AB was magnificent— no, AB was doomed from the start. He might as well give himself credit for holding out this long.

They've just finished soundcheck for the sixth show on this leg of the tour, and AB is once again staring at Matthew's contact page. His fingers itch with the need to act. He either needs to delete the number and eliminate the temptation (impossible—he has it memorized), or take the plunge already.

AB does neither.

He calls Gabby instead. If anyone in the world can talk some sense into him, it's the girl he's known since birth.

The phone rings once. "What do you want?"

"Hello to you, too, Gabs."

"Of course, it's always good to hear from you," she says. "But let's not kid ourselves here; you hate talking on the phone and would rather send me novel-length texts to avoid it, so I know this isn't a casual call. You either want something or something has gone terribly wrong. Spill."

"I maybe need a little advice."

"Advice?"

"Yes, I do believe that's what I said."

"Oh god, what did you do? If you're calling me for advice, it means you want permission to do reckless shit."

"First, I don't have a reckless bone in my body."

Gabby makes a derisive noise.

"And second," AB stresses, "*I* didn't do anything."

"I don't believe you for a second," Gabby says. "But go on; you have my undivided attention for however long you need."

"Okay, so, on a scale of one to ten, how possible do you think Bonding is?"

"Oh god," Gabby says again, her laughter barely concealed.

"Just answer the question, Gabrielle!"

"If you're Gabrielle-ing me, maybe I should've grabbed snacks for this. What the hell have you gotten yourself into here? This is shaping up to be the most interesting thing to ever happen to you, isn't it? But to answer your question: I'd say a three. Most info we have is so fantastical and romanticized it doesn't seem real at all. Like an Atlantis situation, you know? Clearly a work of fiction but taken as fact by some people. But I'd also be lying if I said a couple don't deviate enough from the general formula to make me wonder sometimes. Kind of like Bigfoot, I guess."

"Hold on; you still think Bigfoot is real?"

"Oh, fuck *off*! You still think Santa Claus is real!"

"Because he *is*!"

"How can you believe in Santa but not Bigfoot?"

"Because our moms haven't left out a present from Santa since you came home crying in fifth grade when Darren Blake told us we were too old to still believe in silly baby stuff. And yet, every year until we turned eighteen, we woke up to stockings full of candy our moms didn't leave us."

"I don't know, AB; I still think those were from them."

"Why would they admit they left all the other gifts and then continue to pretend Santa was real? That makes no sense."

"So, what, Santa skipped over us until our parents stopped? That doesn't make any sense either!"

"I don't know, Gabby! It's magic! Maybe there's a reimbursement process."

"Okay, I'm sorry. Wait a goddamn minute. You're pulling the 'it's magic' card on Santa, but you don't believe in Bigfoot?"

"Wouldn't it have been *found* by now?"

"The exact same could be said for Santa! If magic's involved, why couldn't it keep itself from being seen?"

"Are we deciding Bonding *could* be real, then? Is that what you're getting at?"

Gabby sighs. "Fuck if I know! The only time I've *ever* thought Bonding didn't sound like a straight-up fairy tale was the one about those two women in the French Revolution or whatever. So, I really don't know. If it *is* possible, it's rare as hell. Like, rarer than Immunes rare. So yeah, a three. A three is all I can give it."

"Okay. What about how they claim magic can React to someone else's?"

"Claim!" Gabby scoffs. "AB, I know you're busy in your own little world, but you can't be *that* out of touch!"

"Has it happened to you?"

"Nope," Gabby answers, with an exaggerated pop of the *p*. "Doesn't mean it hasn't to other people, though. Besides, I'm a Convenient. As a Big Four, you'd have a better chance anyway. Is that why you're calling? Did baby get his very first Reaction?"

"Yeah, partially."

"Go on."

"Well, do you remember two-ish years ago when we thought I had the Frits?"

"Yes," Gabby says, a sudden hardness to her voice. "As if I could ever forget the audacity of Steven reaching out to me! Like he had *any* right to be upset you wanted him to sign an NDA. How could you ever trust him not to blab about your Invisibility being the real cause after the shit he pulled?"

"Moving on," AB says, heart still aching at the mere mention of Steven. "Turns out I was right to worry about it not being the Frits."

"What do you mean? Are you saying a *Reaction* made you Invisible?"

"Seems so. The guy I met today said he was at that concert."

"Since you're not in a complete panic, I take it he didn't make you Invisible this time?"

"Oh, no, he totally did. But I was in the bathroom when it happened, so no one else saw it go down."

"Okay, wait, wait a second," Gabby says after a long beat of silence. "How hot is this guy?"

"Why must he be hot?"

Gabby snorts. "Because there's not a chance in hell you'd entertain the idea of being near someone who could make you Invisible if they weren't."

She's not wrong. "He's a solid eleven, Gabby."

Gabby laughs, light and airy, and god, does AB miss her.

"You are so predictable. You see a pretty face and suddenly everything you've ever known goes straight out your ears."

"You think it's a terrible idea for me to text him?"

"Depends, really."

"On?"

"What exactly happened. Because look, as much of an accomplishment it is for you not to have run scared from this guy, I'm unsure putting yourself in a situation where you could get attached to him before you know if he'll make you Conceal again is a good idea. When would you even be able to test it?"

"Not until the end of August."

"That's more than a month, AB."

"So then, don't text him."

"I'm not saying you can't text him," Gabby says. "But I *am* surprised you're considering any of this."

She's right. Of course, she's right. Entertaining the idea of seeing Matthew again is reckless even by AB's standards. But he can't stop thinking about the way Matthew's hand felt in his, electrifying and far too hot, but neither painful nor unpleasant. Even now, weeks later, AB can feel the faintest impression of it. He doubts Matthew's right about Bondmates, but he can't deny what happened. He can't deny there's something about Matthew's magic affecting AB's own. And the more he thinks about it, the more he needs to see if it will happen again, needs to see if Matthew is going to be a problem for him in the future.

"Listen, Gabby, not only could he see me, but from how he was looking at me it was more than Concealment not working on him, like he could *see me*—"

"Wait, you met an *Omnivision*?"

"What did you think we were talking about here?"

"I don't know! I thought—I mean, this makes more sense. Okay, well, now I see why you're being more rash than usual. True Opposites. Wow."

"Bonds still aren't real, Gabs."

"I mean, maybe not. But this guy pulled you into Invisibility. I've never heard of such a huge Reaction. And you were saying something else happened, right?"

"Yeah," AB says. "But listen. You have to promise not to laugh because I know how unbelievable it sounds."

"Babe, come on," Gabby says. "Even combined, Immunes and Omnivisions don't make up 1 percent of the population. And yet Derek's in your band, and you met this guy in a bathroom. Your track record with the unbelievable is remarkable. Just tell me."

"When we shook hands, there were honest-to-god *sparks,* and then I was Visible again."

"Oh, wow. That's...yeah."

"This making you speechless might be enough reason to text him on its own."

"Unfortunately, if you were expecting me to be the voice of reason here, I'm now fully on board and want to see how this pans out. If Bonds aren't real, maybe he'll at least tempt you to renege on your self-imposed dating ban."

"I don't want to date him!"

"Are you sure?" Gabby says, laughing. "Because this is the first person you've actually shown an interest in since you went all 'Dating in the public eye is too hard, breakups are inevitable, I am doomed to be loveless.'"

"All those things are still true," AB says.

"Not sure you can blame being loveless on fame when you're not even trying. But regardless, he's *also* the first guy you've wanted to see again since Steven's little stunt."

"Unsure I'd call it a stunt," AB mutters.

"Don't see why you insist on giving him the benefit of the doubt. He broke your heart once, which was bad enough, and then he came back for seconds. He's an asshole."

"Yeah, yeah," AB says. "Add it to the list of reasons not to date."

"What you and Steven did was not *dating*. So, you can't compare anything to it. But I'm not trying to fight your stubborn ass on this dating thing—if you say you're not going to date the guy, I believe you'll self-sabotage enough to not date the guy."

"Wow."

"But if you're serious," Gabby says, "you're going to need to be upfront with him. Because *you* might not be into Bonding and you might be well accustomed to making yourself miserable in terms of love—"

"Wow!"

"Are you or are you not setting yourself up to get attached to someone you refuse to date all because the press couldn't shut up about you and Chloe's breakup?"

"You know that's not the only reason I don't want to date anymore," AB says.

"Minus Steven, all your reasons are basically in the same vein. But whatever. I'm not having this argument again. You don't listen, and you refuse to talk to Dr. Barnes about your issues with being perceived wrong by strangers, which I understand, really. I'd hate to have people talk about me the way they talk about you, but until you can ignore your press, I know this argument is futile."

"I'm glad you've finally accepted my decision," AB says.

"Don't sound so smug. Once school starts and I'm back to procrastinating, there's nothing stopping me from making you a detailed PowerPoint on why your reasons are shit."

AB snorts in laughter. "Well, if there will be a Power-Point..."

"But as I was saying, before you distracted me—"

"How did I—"

She raises her voice to speak over AB. "As I was saying! If you're hell-bent on not dating him, you need to be upfront about it when you contact him. He believes in Bonding, babe. I can't imagine he's expecting a friendship from this."

"He'd be lucky to have me as a friend. I'm great."

"You're all right," Gabby says. "But seriously. You called for my advice. And if you've made up your mind, which you so clearly have, then yeah, that's my advice. Tell him you're not looking for anything romantic. Oh, and please don't give Carson and the rest of your team a heart attack by meeting up with this guy in a place where everyone can see before you know if you'll Conceal again. Because you might not be ob-sessing right now, but I know you, AB, and you're not going to stay this way forever. And there's only so many times you can rely on the Frits to cover a Concealment."

"Yeah, good point," AB says. "Guess I'll have to invite him over when there's a break from tour."

"I think inviting a stranger over definitely falls into the 'giving Carson a heart attack' category."

"Won't really be a stranger in six weeks, will he?"

"Oh my god, look at you! Trying to make a new friend," she coos. "I'm so proud of you."

"Did I miss the part where I don't have friends?"

"I love them all dearly, but your personal assistant and bandmates are not what I mean."

"What about—"

"Neither are Heath and Mary Ann. And *especially* not Chloe. You need people outside the industry. People who aren't your ex. People you can come home to."

He has to admit, it would be nice for AB to know more people who are in New York more often than he is—who might be able to see him off when he leaves instead of coming along with him. But...that sounds a lot like wanting... No. He can't even entertain the thought. There's too much in his life working against a relationship.

"I'm not going to date him, Gabby."

"Mm."

"I'm not!"

"And I totally believe you!"

Chapter Four

Matthew isn't naive enough to think he'll hear back from AB right away, but with each passing day he grows more and more discouraged. He hides his disappointment as best as he can, but as two weeks approaches, Matthew can't shake the despondency. He's lost his best chance at Bonding, lost it before he even really had it, and Matthew has to move on, figure another way out, find someone else no matter how much he *wants* it to be AB.

"Okay," Maddie says, perching herself on the armrest of his chair. "'It's your birthday and you can cry if you want to' *only* works when you're not a twin and you can be emo without ruining your sister's vibe."

"I'm not crying."

"Might as well be with all this negativity you're infecting me with."

"Good thing it's not actually our birthday yet," Matthew says.

Maddie rolls her eyes. "Close enough, asshole."

But as she complains, she sends a concentrated burst of her own happiness through him—something she's so much better at than him—and Matthew laughs as the giddy bubbles cut through his melancholy. "Thanks."

"No problem," she says, pressing a shot into his hand. "Birthday cake vodka for the big day."

"How gross is it?"

"Disgusting." Maddie wrinkles her nose. "But it's going to be nothing compared to what Finn and Nolan are concocting in the kitchen. Your friends do not respect taste buds. At all!"

"Oh god," Matthew says, gagging at the cloying taste of the shot and the thought of what those two could be making.

"Okay, now come on, it's almost our birthday. I'm outlawing sulking over your boy for the rest of the night."

"He's not my boy," Matthew grumbles.

"Right, my bad. But your 'potential boy you've been pining over since we were five' is such a mouthful."

"You're such a pain in the ass. Oliver and Zeke were a lot less argumentative about it not being like that."

"Oliver and Zeke are cowards," Maddie says with a satisfied smile. She waves her hand in the air when Matthew starts to argue the point, cutting him off. "Besides, as your twin, I get to push you to self-examine harder than they do and here's the thing, little bro—"

"You were born three minutes before me!"

"Here's the thing, little bro!" she says again, loud enough to draw Oliver's attention away from Sara. He raises his eyebrow and Maddie waves him off. Her gaze dips back down to Matthew, and she drops her voice. "Much to my dismay, I've always been worried about your love life, and this apparently isn't the point I stop. I was so happy when the years you spent pining for a stranger didn't get in the way of you loving Tori. And I know how angry you were when you realized there was never going to be a Bond for the two of you and how much *worse* it was for you when you accepted loving someone who wasn't a Bondmate only for it to *still* not work out. I felt all of it with you, Matty. But you've been letting this potential Bondmate get in the way of your happiness for the last two years. You've used it and the failure of your relationship with Tori as reason to hold out until the perfect, strongest, best-case Reaction came along, and now it has! And instead of going for it, instead of seeing if this is what you've been waiting for, you're refusing to accept you might be into dudes after literally telling me he's the most beautiful thing you've ever seen."

"As in his *colors*!"

"Yeah, okay," Maddie snorts.

"I think I would know if I had the hots for men. I've sure seen enough of them growing up! Don't you think I would've found at least one of them attractive by now?"

"Maybe you're late to realizing you did. Or maybe," Maddie says, "athletes aren't your type."

"Whatever. I'd tell you I'd keep an open mind, but he's not going to text me anyway, so it doesn't even matter."

Maddie pats his shoulder, a small smile pulling at the corners of her mouth. "Let's see if we can find you a candle to put on this little liquid birthday cake your friends are working on."

"You want me to wish for him to text me back?"

"Couldn't hurt, could it?"

And apparently, she's right, because maybe half an hour after they ring in their birthday, Matthew's phone vibrates in his pocket.

Before he's even swiped the message open, Maddie slings her arm around him, smug as can be, "I'm always right."

But Matthew can't even muster up his usual irritation over her gloating. Not when a pleasant warmth unfurls in his chest, drowning out all other emotions as he reads AB's text.

He still has a chance after all.

Chapter Five

AB doesn't text Matthew until he's back in his bus bunk for the night. Not because he doesn't know what to say, or because he thinks Gabby's right about him wanting to date, but because his band is made up of four busybodies with far too much interest in his love life. If they found out about Matthew, they'd be even worse about trying to get him to date the guy than Gabby.

Mr. Omnivision

Sat, Jul 18, 11:31 PM

> Okay Matthew convince me Bonds are real

Uhh it's my birthday and everything I say is right

> Well HAPPY BIRTHDAY but unfortunately that's not going to cut it

What about: my grandma says they are?

> While the grandma card is cute it's still unconvincing

But I WILL give you one whole point for trying

I think the grandma card should get me at least two points! She makes a very compelling argument

An argument I have no knowledge of!!!

And one you're not SHARING WITH ME

But I'll give you half a point extra because I do love grandmas

And it IS your birthday

How gracious of you

But to answer your question: it just makes sense to me. Magic is all over the place and we know it can react to other kinds in close proximity, so why wouldn't it be true? If the legend says Reactions happen and they do, then why wouldn't it be possible for Bonds to happen too?

Aren't legends usually based in some fact

You believe in Reactions but not in the possibility of Bonding?

Tbh I thought Reactions were fake until I met you too

Wait really? You've never Reacted with anyone?

> Nope! You were a pretty impressive first if I do say so myself Mattycakes!

Mattycakes??? I felt a little guilty I told my people your name was Abe but I think mattycakes absolves me

> ABE???? Do I look like an ABE TO YOU??

In my defense, it's not exactly easy to come up with an alias on the fly for someone with initials for a name! AND I didn't know what either of the letters stood for! AND!! I figured you might not want me to broadcast who you were before you made up your mind about me and unfortunately Abe was the only logical conclusion. Especially after the A was out of my mouth

Warmth flutters in AB's chest, pulse stuttering. Gross. This was definitely a mistake. He thought he could do this. He thought he could talk to Matthew, tell him they couldn't date, make a friend, but no. Matthew is cute *and* considerate. Totally unacceptable. He didn't want to acknowledge her before, but Gabby was right—he does have an awful tendency of getting attached. And can he really afford to get attached to someone who's going to bail on him the second he realizes Bonds aren't real? What a disaster he's gotten himself into here.

AB shoves his phone under his pillow and tries to forget all about Matthew and his silly little fairy-tale beliefs. But a night of sleep does nothing to quell his unease. If only Matthew weren't into Bonding, if only AB weren't so fucked up when it came to relationships, if only this could be a casual fling he could wash his hands of once he had a taste. If only Matthew hadn't texted him back nearly an hour after AB stopped responding; if only he weren't still feeling the heat of Matthew's hand against his own; if only Matthew weren't so goddamn beautiful.

If only AB weren't so curious.

If only.

Mr. Omnivision

Sun, Jul 19, 1:16 AM

I'm sure I haven't convinced you Bonds are real but I do have a question of my own if you don't mind. Are you against the idea of Bonding or do you just not believe it's real?

9:55 AM

Mostly the latter. Idk if I'm against it really but doesn't it sound a little boring to you?

How is magic doing cool magical shit boring?

Well when you put it like that!

There's no other WAY to put it!

Fine maybe bore is the wrong word but don't you think it takes the wonder out of love for magic to be pushing us together? You don't think it sounds like FATE???

I think you're looking at it the wrong way here. Nothing I've seen says magic can affect how people feel about each other. It's more like it gives us more to connect with.

To me, it's another thing to build a relationship on, like having something in common
or being attracted to each other. You
wouldn't say two people being attracted to
each other means they'll fall in love one day,
would you?

No I guess I wouldn't

See!

Look I get it. No one around me other than
my grandma really believes in this stuff, so
I'm totally used to the skepticism. But nothing I've read, and I've done a lot of reading
on this lol, says the way we feel for each
other comes from the Bond. It only ever says
the Bond comes from our feelings, like we're
def still the masters of our own fate

Hmm. What about it not being broken? Doesn't it seem a little weird we
could end up hating each other but
still be connected FOREVER?

Just because the effects of the Bond can't
be broken doesn't mean we couldn't tell
each other to fuck off

Which I'd definitely do

Good to know

But yeah, assuming the Bond really can't be
broken I don't think that'd be too bad. It's
not much different than how you always
carry around the memories of someone you
loved before. This way just has magic

AB doesn't know if it's better or worse for him that Matthew says he's okay with their feelings disappearing but the Bond remaining. On the one hand, it gives AB hope Matthew won't ditch him when his dream goes belly-up. But on the other hand, if Matthew isn't going to inevitably leave him, if he might stick around regardless, AB will have to work even harder to not get attached—a responsibility AB doesn't want.

Ok you've convinced me

I really thought it'd take longer

Oh don't get ahead of yourself here! It's gonna take waaaay more than our little magic act to change my mind on Bonding

But you asked me to let you explain yourself and I'm still curious so I figure we can meet up the next time I'm home if you're REALLY up for the challenge of hanging out with someone who's only around half the year

And who knows! This could be the start of a grand adventure even if Bonds aren't real

I think I'm up for the challenge. Though if I'm right and we DO Bond, you owe me fifty bucks for the skepticism

Ok I'll take that bet

But if I'm right I want an extra large iced coffee and one of those fancy little opera tortes as payment

Think you can do that?

I actually think I've seen a recipe for one in my nana's cookbook. If it turns out you're right, I might even get her to help me make it

Ooooh

What do I have to do to get nana's homemade dessert BEFORE we figure out this Bonding thing?

I'll get back to you

Boooo

Also I have an addendum! If we end up hating each other one day I get New York

ALL of New York? I think we'll have to negotiate if it gets to that point

Fine I guess that's fair

But all jokes aside I do have a couple conditions you should know before we commit to this little quest of yours

And what would those be?

If it turns out I keep Concealing when we React we won't be able to hang out in public because I really can't afford that happening again and we won't always be lucky enough to be in a bathroom by ourselves

Fair enough. What's the second?

This is a friendship

We can't fall in love

Chapter Six

Matthew can't stop reading "We can't fall in love." He's so fixated it takes Maddie shaking his shoulder to drag his attention away from his phone.

"Abe?" Maddie asks, arching a brow.

"Yeah."

"Did he tell you to fuck off?" Maddie asks.

"No, he wants to be friends."

"I'm confused," Maddie says. "Friends is what you wanted. Why do you feel like you've been sucker-punched in the ribs? I'm not digging this at all, to be honest."

"It's nothing," Matthew says.

Maddie purses her lips. "Doesn't seem like nothing. But I'll allow it."

Matthew huffs a laugh. "How kind of you."

"It is! You know I'm a nosy bitch. If we weren't waiting for Mom and Dad at this very fancy restaurant, I'd totally be wrestling your phone out of your hand."

Matthew's fingers flex instinctively against his phone and he's suddenly thankful for his mother's choice of locale.

"Are you sure you don't want to talk about it?"

"Yes, Maddie," he says. "I'm fine."

"Sure."

"I never told him I was straight, okay! And now he's said we can't fall in love, which, okay, but I don't know how to tell him, and I feel like I should apologize for coming on the wrong way," he says in a rush, the tightening in his chest caused by the words *can't fall in love* loosening a little.

"Only you'd tell someone he was your Bondmate and not specify it was platonic," Maddie says, the laughter in her voice bubbling through their link as well, successfully lifting his mood.

"I didn't think it was necessary!"

But heat creeps up the back of his neck at how ridiculous it is he didn't realize any mention of a Bond might sound romantic to someone who didn't already know Matthew was straight. Though, it probably doesn't matter since they ended up on the same page anyway.

"Honestly, this could've been a disaster if the guy wasn't pulling a *Walk to Remember*—which let's be real, didn't work in the movie either—but since he doesn't want to date, he's given you a perfect opportunity to clear this up. All you have to do is say not falling in love won't be a problem since you're straight."

Her face gives nothing away, but an inkling of doubt curls through their link on the last word. He appreciates the show of restraint and the advice. Because she's right about how easy clarifying his intentions should be. This is in no way a problem. This is what he wanted.

His unease with AB's request must stem from unin-tentionally leading AB on. Matthew not being able to shake this is nothing more than guilt over accidentally expressing a non-existent interest. That's all. Not falling in love with AB is going to be a cakewalk. He has nothing to worry about. Really.

Except clearing the air does nothing to stop the pounding in his ears.

No worries there, I'm straight. Sorry that
wasn't clear

> Huh definitely thought you were
> looking for some grand love affair
>
> But this is probably for the best tbh
>
> I'm not in the market for a relation-
> ship atm and I really wasn't trying to
> break your heart

His heart somersaults. Nothing about this should be up-setting. Matthew is straight and AB isn't looking for love. They're a perfect match for a platonic Bond, but Matthew's ears never stop roaring. He should be delighted AB decided to give friendship a chance, touched by AB's willingness to give him a shot before he knew Matthew was straight, before he knew Matthew wasn't expecting AB to be his True Love. But somehow, knowing this information makes his heart pulse hot and uncomfortable, leaving him on edge. He doesn't understand this new emotion in the slightest, but maybe he's concerned he won't be interesting enough to keep AB around. Maybe he's worried the curiosity AB has sur-rounding their magic will wear off and all Matthew will be left with is the memory of what could have been.

Maddie furrows her eyebrows, before her face smooths out into this knowing expression, her understanding rever-berating through him, and Matthew expects her, almost wants her, to tell him what she's thinking. He expects her to name this *thing* roiling inside him, to call him out for this mysterious emotion torpedoing their link. But she doesn't push, and despite having absolutely nothing to worry about, despite this being exactly what he wanted, Matthew is left to wonder when the anxious swirl in the pit of his stomach will dissipate.

By the end of their lunch, the promise he and AB made no longer slices through him, and Matthew decides any dread he felt reading those five words was the last stage of letting go of a dream he's had since he was five. His distress had nothing to do with AB and everything to do with needing to process more than two years' worth of missed opportunities.

AB texts in waves—silent for days at a time until suddenly he's sending Matthew a question at midnight, each one sparking a conversation that lasts deep into the night.

He starts small.

> Favorite flower

I don't have one

> No you have to if we're going to be friends!

Continues with first-date small talk.

> Kinda messed up you know all about my singing career but haven't offered up what you do with YOUR time

Did you expect me to randomly interject your game of twenty questions with "I'm an art student at Columbia and the hockey team's goalie"???

> OBVIOUSLY! And tbh your brunch attire should've clued me in to you being an athlete

> That's my bad

Moves on to what all Matthew knows about AB.

> Do you have a favorite song of mine?

Probably dangerous but everything on the
radio is catchy as hell

> Part of me is offended you only know
> my radio hits but tbh it'd be weird if
> you were a super fan lmaaaao.

As the days pass, the questions don't stop coming and
AB never seems to get bored. July bleeds into August, and
Matthew realizes he was off base to worry he might not be
the type of person AB would want to be friends with.

Except, the realization doesn't eliminate Matthew's need
to impress AB. In fact, the more attention Matthew gets from
AB, the more a single notification from him sends Matthew's
heart skipping.

Mr. Invisible

Sat, Aug 22, 12:14 AM

> Okay Matthew I have some ques-
> tions for you

You always have questions for me. Why
don't I ever get to ask any questions?

> Because you can look me up online
> duh

I'm not going to look you up online

> Not even to see what AB stands for?

Figured you'd tell me if you wanted me to know

Oh bless

A boy's gotta keep some secrets

Maybe if you stick around long enough I'll tell you

Why wouldn't I stick around?

I'm unconvinced you'll be satisfied with a platonic Bond

I think you'll be surprised

But if it doesn't pan out? You really think you'll still want to deal with this life?

I said I was up for the challenge

Not to show my trust issues too early but I won't believe you until your name is in the tabs with mine and fans are bombarding your Instagram comments

My Instagram is private

Okay you know what! That actually did make me laugh

Please don't take it personally tho

I'm just Like This

It's fine

It's not but thanks

Anyway! My questions!

1) favorite cake 2) what is the worst birthday gift you could get and 3) when I get you that will you hate me?

I know this is going to offend you but I'm not a huge cake fan

You're right I AM offended

What do you want instead?

For what?

For your BIRTHDAY asshole and if you say it's not your birthday any-more I WILL gently smash a cake in your face the next time I see you

I usually prefer pie but no, I wouldn't hate you. It would just be an extreme waste of money if you got me any gift at all

Oh you've made a terrible mistake here

There are so many things I can give you without spending any money at all

Despite the weeks of texting, Matthew spends the last few days before AB returns a nervous, anxious mess. He still hasn't told anyone about Abe being AB Cerise, unsure how Maddie and his roommates will react to knowing the person Matthew is set to Bond with is their favorite pop star, unsure if knowing AB's real identity will make Maddie more or less inclined to believe him when he says he *doesn't* have a crush on AB.

So, when Friday afternoon comes along and he heads out to test whether their magic is going to be more detrimental than Matthew ever imagined, Matthew doesn't really have a response for Zeke when he tells him AB is just some guy and he shouldn't be so nervous. Because AB is way more than *some guy*, both in terms of who he is to Matthew and who he is to the world.

And, okay, Matthew isn't a stranger to famous people. He's met a few over the years. But most of them, especially the ones he's had more than a brief encounter with, have been other hockey players. But see, when his father is Andre Levoie, Hall of Famer and one of hockey's most awarded players, it's hard to compare those experiences to spending time with AB Cerise at his house, of all places. AB is internationally famous and gets far more media attention than his father, or his grandfather, or any other hockey player combined, and the truth is, Matthew's not sure he has enough in common with AB to hold a conversation in person without making a fool of himself.

But then he thinks of Aleisha, the Illusionist he had the greatest Reaction with before AB, and how he blew his chance with her without a hint of fame involved. How he'd been so nervous after their first meeting, so caught up in how this could be *it*, he didn't text her for nearly a week. How when they finally did go out, the conversation had been stilted and one-sided because he couldn't stop thinking about screwing things up. How he ended up embarrassing himself *because* he couldn't stop overthinking his every move. How he never heard from her again because he'd been such miserable, boring company.

Somehow being capable of fucking up all Bonds is what calms Matthew's nerves, and by midafternoon he's standing outside a pink house with cherry-red doors in the Upper West Side, nervous, but mostly confident. He and AB already have six weeks of friendly communication under their belt. He's far better prepared for this than he was with his date with Aleisha. He can do this. Really.

Still, he stands in front of AB's door for a full minute, reminding himself if AB thought he was boring—and Matthew was quick to learn AB is *so easily* bored—he would not have invited him over.

When he does ring the bell, a burly dark-haired man with narrowed, mahogany eyes answers the door immediately.

"You're Matthew?"

"I am."

The man doesn't respond, and the shimmery brass aura of his magic surges as the man's stare intensifies. Matthew doesn't know what magic this guy has, but Matthew is being examined, pulled apart, and laid bare. The hairs on the back of Matthew's neck stand up under the scrutiny, but he doesn't give in to the urge to fidget. Matthew doesn't need to know what the magic is to know this is some type of test he shouldn't fail.

"Carson, give it up!" AB says from somewhere behind the door. "Did you get a good read off him or not? I would like to see him and test another theory sometime this century."

Finally, Carson cracks a smile and steps aside, the glow of his magic subsiding. "Come on in, Matthew. It's nice to meet you, but I must warn you, he's a real piece of work, and you may end up regretting this decision."

"Carson!"

Carson turns to AB, directing Matthew's attention to where AB's leaning against the wall to the right of a set of French doors, right outside the line of sight of the entryway. He's wearing midthigh-length cutoff jeans and a threadbare white shirt reading Let Boys Be Feminine in faded pink letters, and the only word Matthew's brain supplies is *soft*.

"Are you saying I'm wrong?"

AB's mouth twitches, but he doesn't give in to the smile. "I'm an angel, you ass."

Carson snorts as he pushes the French doors open. "I'll keep that in mind the next time you try to run off in a shitty disguise in a foreign country."

"I did that one time!"

"One time too many," Carson calls over his shoulder as he walks off, leaving Matthew and AB alone in the foyer.

With Carson gone, AB shifts his attention to Matthew, and when he smiles Matthew is struck by how beautiful AB is and how far out of his league AB would be, if this were the Bond he'd expected.

"Well, Matthew," he says, his smile turning mischievous. "How's it feel to pass the most important test of your life?"

"Is Carson's vibe check or you not going Invisible more important?"

"Since I'm not my mother, Carson's is only a plus but, yes, the Invisibility thing. How boring would it be if the only thing we could do together was hang out here? You'd never last—I'd get very cranky, and you'd think I was the worst."

His words are light, gently self-deprecating, but Matthew doesn't miss the discoloration of AB's violet voice—he really does believe Matthew will get sick of him. But AB doesn't give him time to reply, the color of his voice lightning bright when he says, "But if I did my job right, you'll think I'm the worst after you see what I got you for your birthday."

"It can't be that bad."

AB motions for him to step through the doors, and Matthew's breath catches. There, with the same satin quality as the mark on Matthew's hand, is the sunny yellow stain of Matthew's hand on AB's palm.

"Uh, Matthew?"

Matthew drags his attention back to AB's face, ignoring the urge to reach out and examine his hand. "What?"

AB's eyes gleam with curiosity. "This is the face you were making when I was Invisible. So, I assume my hand's doing something remarkable."

"I have your handprint on my hand, and you've got—" He reaches out on instinct, stopping midair, ears flushing. "Uh, there, on your palm, is my handprint. Or well, I think it's mine. Since I have yours."

AB checks his hand, unseeing, and his eyes narrow in disbelief. "I left a handprint on your skin."

"Yes."

"Okay, well, come on," he says, thrusting his hand forward. "Let's see what other cool, magical shit happens this time."

Matthew takes AB's hand, and as before, pressing their skin together is like touching a frayed wire—hot and electrifying—and though the light their touch produces isn't gold, a similar tangle of purple and yellow lightning dances around their joined hands. And when they pull away from each other, the marks on their hands glow golden.

"Huh," AB says, looking at his hand.

"Can you see it now?" Matthew asks as the gold of AB's handprint shifts back to purple on his palm.

"Not anymore, but for the three seconds it was gold, yeah."

"Strange."

"Strange, unfair, basically the same thing, really," AB says, smile dimming as he continues. "Though as cool as this lightning magic looks, it might make going out in public together more difficult. Imagine the headlines if people got a picture at just the right moment! Do you think they'd go with Bonding? Oh god, are you Known? Would people be able to extrapolate my magic based on yours?"

The muted quality to AB's color when talking about Matthew not sticking around is nothing compared to the decayed violet of his voice now. Once again, Matthew has the urge to reach out and touch AB, but now is not the time. Honestly there may never be a time where Matthew can lay a comforting hand on AB's arm if these sparks cause such anxiety.

"I'm Known to quite a few people, yeah. You know, with hockey and all," Matthew says, stomach twisting uncomfortably. "Is that going to be a problem?"

AB picks at the already chipped purple polish on his nails.

"No, it's fine. I just—I have a whole thing about being Known," he says with a derisive sort of laugh.

As a Big Four in sports, Matthew has gotten used to Divulging to people because of the Enhancement Cap, but he knows everyone isn't as cool with people Knowing. But still, the spoiled browning purple of AB's voice, and the tightness around his eyes, suggests this is far more than thinking of magic as a personal thing. And okay, maybe Matthew isn't blowing it by second-guessing himself, but this day is taking a turn.

"I don't think people will go straight to Bonding," Matthew says, trying to course correct. "Not when people rarely believe in the possibility."

"Right," AB says, the purple of his voice brightening.

"And they might go to True Opposites as an explanation, but I've also had a spark Reaction with an Illusionist and you know, there's two Concealments so, I mean, it would stay speculation unless you confirmed it, right?"

"Right, sorry. I uh—well—it's nothing, really. Never mind," AB says, dismissing the thought with a flick of his wrist. "This isn't ideal, but it's not a problem. We can work with this, right?"

"At least you're not turning Invisible?" Matthew tries, unsure what the best response here is.

AB grins, the tension in his shoulders seeping out a little. "Yeah, I really think spontaneous Invisibility might've been an actual deal breaker. But I guess for now we just have to be sure not to bump into each other while we're out. Can't be too hard, right?"

"Right," Matthew agrees.

But at the kitchen table, AB places a trick-candle-lit cherry pie in front of Matthew, the sparks of their arms brushing together sending a warm, comforting heat through his entire body, and Matthew realizes maybe this won't be as easy as he thought. And when AB sits across from him, unveiling a mound of his own cherry-themed merchandise, with a delighted twinkle in his eyes, and a sharp curve to his mouth, Matthew realizes how fucked he really is.

He *wants* to reach out and touch AB. He wants the magical heat coursing through his veins as their skin meets, wants the sparks dancing around the point of contact, kissing his skin like a gentle flame.

He wants, but he cannot have.

This is going to be a platonic Bond, and he needs to stop letting his mind wander to things he would've wanted with a romantic partner when AB made it clear this is a friendship. Matthew doesn't actually *want* AB in a romantic way; he only wants the magic to course through them again. Once he adjusts to this, once he gets used to forming a Bond without the same physical intimacy he was expecting, the longing to have AB's hand on him will go away.

Time is all he needs. Everything is fine.

This desire will pass. He'll get used to not being able to reach out for AB like he does with his roommates and his teammates.

And if he can't, well...wanting physical contact with your friend isn't a declaration of love. Matthew has nothing to worry about there.

Chapter Seven

Gabalicious

Fri, Aug 28, 8:23 PM

HOUSTON WE HAVE A PROBLEM

> Oh NO did you go Invisible when he came over??

IF ONLY

At least then I'd know what to do

> AHA! You DO want to date him

Maybe a little bit :(

> Then please FOR THE LOVE OF GOD AND ME drop the dating ban and charm his pants off

There will be no charming his pants off because he's STRAIGHT and I really am not on the market

> He's what now?

You read that right!

When did you find this out?

When you finally convinced me to text him

AB..........that was more than a month ago. Why didn't you tell me?

Because it's irrelevant

It's not irrelevant if he's going to be another Steven

He's not going to be another Steven because he's actually straight

And if you fall in love with him anyway?

He's not going to be around long enough for me to fall in love

You can't believe that

I do!

Shit for brains! You have SHIT for brains!! People who believe in Bonding aren't going to give up so easily

You really think a straight guy who believes in Bonding is going to stick around to waste his once in a lifetime never going to be broken Bond on someone he can't even fuck

I'd hope someone who believes in Bonding is looking for more than sex, you dipshit

Okay point

But still

When we don't Bond what's going to keep him around? Especially when you throw my chaotic schedule in the mix

> Doesn't it take a while to Bond?

Fuck if I know

> I'm pretty sure it does and I don't think relying on him to ditch you before it's obvious what's going to happen with the Bond is a reliable way to not fall in love

Either way I'm not going to fall in love

We made a deal

> Right because promising not to fall for each other always works out in the movies

Good thing this isn't a movie

> Look, I'm not going to talk you out of making a new friend, especially when there's cool magic involved. But you need to be careful. You fall quick and you fall HARD and not wanting to date because you're being stubborn and NOT BEING ABLE TO because the guy's literally not into you are two different miseries

I'll be fine Gabby

He's not my type anyway so I'll eventually
get over his pretty face

And he'll eventually decide he'd rather have
a romantic Bond

I'm sure of it

★

A prickle of electricity goes up AB's spine the moment they walk through the entrance of their usual bar. His back stiffens and he instinctively checks his hand to make sure he's still *there*. If he's not Invisible...but there's no way Matthew could be here.

What would be the odds?

Far too slim to happen, right?

Right.

Except while Carson leads AB, Derek, and CeCe through a crowd of bodies to the back of the bar, AB can't shake the feeling that Matthew is here. The electric current running through him is identical to the one from yesterday while he was waiting for Matthew to step through the door, the same one from when he met Matthew at brunch.

But it's fine. Really. The music is loud and CeCe's plastered against his back, pointing over his shoulder, and laughing in his ear. "She's got a crown! Who got her the crown?"

There's a large horseshoe sectional in the back corner of the bar they love to commandeer for their group, and in the center is Reina with a gaudy costume crown and a neon purple boa around her neck. Her birthday isn't until Friday, but he'll be back in Houston by then and Zoe, the band's biggest partier, insisted they celebrate together. Once Lupe pointed out they've been celebrating their birthdays as a team for the last three years, there was really no way to convince Reina to go out without him.

When they join them at the table, the girls are already on the right side of tipsy. CeCe immediately grabs for one of the obscene number of shots laid out on the low table in front of the couch and downs it before flinging herself at Lupe. The two of them burst into a fit of giggles, and when they pull apart, CeCe settles next to Lupe, leaning against her side and using her shoulder as a pillow. AB doesn't miss the way Derek makes a choked noise in the back of his throat; nor does CeCe by the way she looks up at him with feigned innocence. When Lupe turns to say something to Zoe, who's sipping at a bright-pink drink on Reina's other side, AB tries not to laugh as Derek mouths "Fuck you" to CeCe. She ramps up the innocent act, batting her eyes and mouthing "Love you" as Derek flops down by her side.

Carson grabs the beer Zoe is holding out for him and then finds a high-top table close to the couch, angling his body so he can stand sentry as people approach. Zoe passes him a shot and slings her arm out over the back of the couch and AB folds in by her side.

"Your pocket is accosting me," Zoe says as the buzzing of his phone goes beyond one new notification.

He slips his phone out and chokes on the sickly-sweet birthday cake vodka as he reads the texts—apparently the odds are much higher than he thought.

★

Mattycakes 🎂

Sat, Aug 29, 10:07 PM

Okay here's the thing: it's my best friend's birthday and he just saw you walk into the same bar we're at and if it's chill with you I'm going to come over and ask if you'd tell him happy birthday.

We never talked about it again and I don't even know how to break the news to them that the guy they're all a fan of is my Bondmate. So if you're down with it please play along while I pretend I've never met you lol

If it isn't chill, just have Carson tell me to fuck off before I come up. I won't mind and Oliver will get a kick out of me embarrassing myself anyway

This is not what Gabby had in mind when she told him to be careful, nor is Matthew already referring to him as his Bondmate a good indicator he'll end up ditching AB. But this is for someone's *birthday*. What harm will it do to interact with him for a fleeting moment in a crowded bar? None at all. AB will say hello and happy birthday, and then he can go back to keeping Matthew at arm's length, pushing him away until he realizes AB is not the Bondmate for him.

Yeah all right but if you break I hope you can come up with a reasonable explanation for how we met that isn't the truth lmao

Because I've only told Gabby about this and would rather not explain this whole situation to a bunch of drunk people

AB hasn't even put his phone back when he catches sight of Matthew heading their way. Carson appears to have noticed as well, turning his attention to AB with a raised eyebrow. AB nods, and Carson relaxes a little, making no further move to intervene.

"Incoming, babes," Zoe says to the table, an excited lilt to her voice. "We've got some lookers coming our way."

Reina follows her gaze, face lighting up as she sets eyes on Matthew and his friends. "Let me guess, we're doing the free drinks tally?"

"Obviously," Zoe says. "When do we not?"

"You know the rules, AB; you don't count," Derek adds.

"Which I still think is unfair," AB says by rote, even though he's fully expecting Reina and her purple boa to draw in more free drinks than him anyway.

Zoe pats AB's thigh. "Don't worry, babe; Reina doesn't count either."

"Hey," Reina pouts. "It's my birthday!"

"It's *almost* your birthday," Zoe corrects, as if the distinction matters. "Which is why you don't count! Birthday girls always get more drinks."

"What if you and AB compete against each other?" CeCe suggests. "Let's see if birthdays win out over fame."

"Ooooh, I want to see this one," Lupe says. "Reina's already up two, AB."

"No, not fair! You can't count the ones before the tally started."

"It's her birthday," Zoe and Lupe say at the same time.

Reina sits back, victorious, and laughs when AB heaves a sigh. "You literally just reminded her it wasn't her birthday! These rules suck."

Out of the corner of his eye he sees Matthew approaching, and he has to bite the inside of his cheek to keep a straight face. He thought for sure Matthew would be the one to give them up, but clearly, he overestimated his own ability to keep his cool. Which, really, he should have known better. In what world is AB good at lying? In what world is AB capable of being chill? Certainly not this one.

"No," Zoe whines. "Why'd the others stop? AB, fix this."

"What am I supposed to do about it?"

"Ask them to come over here, obviously," Derek answers and AB can't help but laugh.

"Y'all could do it yourselves," he says right as Matthew steps up to them.

He has his hands in his pockets, a gesture AB is beginning to suspect is associated with Matthew's nerves, and when they lock eyes AB bites down harder on the flesh of his cheek to not say his name in greeting. A fool. AB is a complete fool for thinking he could pull this off.

Matthew rocks back on his feet, and AB finds solace in Matthew's nervous tics—maybe he's not the only one who overestimated how easy this would be.

"So, here's the thing. Uh, my friend turned twenty-one today, and he's maybe a little in love with you," Matthew says, his whole face lit up by a shit-eating grin. "And I was wondering if you could tell him happy birthday right quick. I mean, my friend Zeke—" Matthew motions back with his thumb, and AB follows, looking back at his friends, noting their obvious disbelief. "—paid for dinner and my twin's got a tab going for all his drinks, but I'm thinking 'happy birthday' from his favorite pop star might take the cake. Would you mind helping me win the birthday gift game?"

Okay. Maybe Matthew's nerves weren't about giving their secret away. Maybe he's playing it up for his audience. Maybe AB is the only one who's struggling right now.

Matthew worries his bottom lip between his teeth and ducks his head. The dim light of the bar illuminates Matthew beautifully, making his offensively long lashes glitter as he, honest-to-god, bats them at AB. "I mean, if it's too much trouble, I could buy you a drink for your inconvenience."

Holy shit. If AB didn't know any better, he'd think Matthew was *flirting*. Thankfully, his surprised snort at the show Matthew's putting on here is drowned out by Zoe's and Reina's groans and the chaotic sound of CeCe cackling into Lupe's shoulder.

"Don't worry," Lupe soothes. "You're still up by one, Reins."

AB never takes his eyes off Matthew, too caught up in the whole ordeal of this, but apparently his hindbrain is functioning normally enough to snipe, "Technically, I'm winning."

Matthew furrows his brow in an endearing show of confusion, and AB wants to know if he's *always* been this charming or if the alcohol has already addled his perception. "Sorry, that was for Reina. But yeah, bring them over. I don't mind."

Matthew turns to motion his friends forward, and Zoe elbows him in the side. "I swear if you don't get them to stay..."

Extending this interaction further than needed is a terrible idea, but if Matthew can pretend to flirt, then AB can take him up on his offer. One drink won't make this any more of a risk or any less of a game. "And even though it's no trouble, if you're still offering, I wouldn't mind a drink and a name."

Matthew's gaze snaps back to AB, his friends walking up utterly forgotten. He looks shocked and for a moment his smile slips, but he regains his composure quickly. With his crooked smile back in place, he once again radiates self-assurance, but AB can still see the red tips of Matthew's ears as he says, "Oh, uh, I'm Matthew. And if you want, I can definitely get you a drink. For sure."

Matthew introduces Maddie first. She's tanner than Matthew, with golden hair, big, hazel eyes, and thick, perfect eyebrows, and despite their differences, AB doesn't need to be told they're twins. They carry themselves with the same casual confidence and have the same crooked smile, and AB is overwhelmed by how stunning they both are. In fact, Matthew apparently surrounds himself with gorgeous people because Zeke and Oliver are no less striking.

Zeke has dark-brown skin, tightly coiled hair, and an immaculate black beard, much fuller than Derek's but not as thick as Carson's. He is almost as tall as Matthew, carries himself with the same confidence as the twins, and from this distance AB can make out an adorable line of three small moles on the bridge of his nose. Like Zoe, Oliver has ivory skin and silky jet-black hair, and while his demeanor doesn't demand the same attention as the others, his features certainly do. He has a sharp jaw, sharp eyes, sharp cheekbones, and a sharp, gold septum piercing. He and Zeke have almost identical round glasses, and despite AB's mind's preoccupation with *not staring at Matthew*, he can't help but wonder if they bought them together.

AB comes to the horrific realization he's already attached to Matthew as he makes introductions. AB isn't going to fall in love—he's not—but watching Matthew light up as he talks to AB's second family, outgoing and animated as he speaks, drives home how hard it will be when Matthew does bail on him. He needs to shut this down. He needs to stop letting himself fall for Matthew's charm. He needs tonight to be the last time he sees Matthew for a while.

"Excuse my friend here," Zoe says, slinging her arm around AB and jostling him back to the moment at hand. "He gets a little tongue-tied in front of pretty people."

"Oh my god," AB groans into his hands.

"Sorry about them," AB says, taking note of the way Matthew's mouth turns up in a faint smile. "Everyone here has two missions in life: music and being the bane of my existence."

"It keeps you grounded," Lupe says.

"Yeah, babe," Derek chimes in. "Can't let your head get big with fame."

"Right." AB rolls his eyes, turning his attention to Oliver. "You turned twenty-one today?"

Oliver looks a little shell-shocked, but he manages a nod, and Matthew slings his arm around Oliver's shoulders. "He's the last of us. Our baby."

Oliver rolls his eyes and dislodges himself from under Matthew's arm, the annoyance of his actions undercut by his soft smile. Somehow, Matthew's smile grows even larger.

"Something we have in common, then." AB says, motioning to himself and then his group of friends. "I am very much the baby of this group. So, from one baby to another, happy birthday."

Finally, Oliver cracks a smile, and AB's pleased with himself. "Are you having a good time?"

"Uh." Oliver's smile apparently can't weather being asked a direct question. He blinks back at AB in an amazing imitation of an owl, and Matthew and Zeke duck their heads together in a horrible attempt to hide their laughter while Maddie makes a valiant effort to keep an even tone as she answers AB.

"In Oliver-speak, that means yes."

"Good, great," AB says as Zoe says, "Okay, babes, grab a seat."

She pushes her weight against AB to make him move, and when he does, she presses her hand against his back, guiding him to stand. "Your friend here owes our boy a drink, and we've got plenty of birthday vodka to go around. Might as well take advantage of it while they're gone."

Zeke and Oliver look to Matthew with expressions AB can't place, and Maddie steps in behind Oliver so only Matthew can hear when she speaks. The only acknowledgement her statement gets from Matthew is rolled eyes and pursed lips.

Oliver still looks a little shell-shocked as he walks forward, gingerly sitting down in AB's vacated spot, and though there's room for Zeke and Maddie on either end, Reina scooches in closer to Lupe and pats the couch. "Zoe and I don't bite. Come, sit."

"Unless you're into it," Zoe says. "And then we'd be happy to oblige."

"I'll keep that in mind," Maddie says, taking the seat between Reina and Zoe, directing her attention to Reina. "Is it your birthday too?"

"Did the crown or the boa give me away?" Reina asks.

AB doesn't think he's paying attention to Matthew—focused instead on the way his friends so easily fit themselves into AB's group—but Matthew's movements act as a magnet for his eyes. Before Matthew's hand reaches AB's shoulder, he has regained AB's attention. Matthew drops his hand and nods his head toward the bar, moving to the side to let AB lead the way. At the bar, their shoulders brush, and though their skin doesn't make direct contact, the touch sends heat coursing through him. His heartbeat doubles at how close they could have been sparking in public, but the warmth of the graze is pleasant enough to cut through the resurgence of anxiety.

Matthew leans slightly over the bar to get a bartender's attention and then turns his gaze back to AB. "What do you want?"

"Not birthday cake vodka."

"Way to narrow it down, man."

"Surprise me," AB says.

Matthew shakes his head. He rests an arm on the bar, leaning against it to where he's still angled toward AB and while he waits for the bartender to approach, someone squeezes in at AB's side. The skin of the newcomer's directly on his own is cold and vacant compared to the press of Matthew's heat through his shirt, and AB hates how much he wants to feel Matthew's skin on his for real.

"Hey, you're that singer, right? The one with that song always on the radio?"

The blond next to him doesn't elaborate, and AB's not annoyed because some drunk guy at a bar doesn't know his name or the songs he sings. But Matthew is a low-burning fire next to him, and the guy's question makes Matthew shift farther away, and while the heat lingers, it's nothing like before. And if its absence didn't annoy AB, the way he *misses* Matthew's heat would. Fucking hell.

"Yeah," AB says, making a concentrated effort not to let his frustrations show. "I might be one of those singers."

The guy laughs. It's a nice, vibrant sound coming from a nice, handsome face, and this could have been a nice, amusing moment to rehash later if the guy didn't open his mouth to speak further. "You're super hot. Can I get you a drink?"

AB stares back in shock. He gets offered enough free drinks to (obviously, unfortunately, unfairly) disqualify him from their group tally, but most of them come in the form of overeager recognition and flattery about his music. He can't remember the last time someone who recognized him came onto him, especially not right out the gate. AB isn't sure if he's annoyed or amused by this guy's boldness, but then the guy's mouth twists in this smug, expectant kind of way, and irritation wins out.

"Uh, sorry, I'm not in the market for another drink right now. Got a lot back at my table and am waiting for one right now. Thanks for the offer, though."

The guy looks put off for a moment, but then his mouth turns up at the corners. "Let me get the one you're waiting for, then."

By now, Matthew has their drinks, and the warmth returns as he leans into AB's space to hand him a cherry-red drink. When AB turns his attention back to the stranger at his side, his face has fallen, the laughter in his eyes has died out, and there's a hardness to his smile. "I see someone got here first."

"Oh uh," AB says, uncomfortable with this guy's whole... thing. "No one got to me first. But seriously, thank you for the offer. I hope you have a good night."

AB turns to leave and the guy grabs his wrist, fingers tightening as AB tries to pull away.

"I would've had a better night," the stranger says, a hard edge to his voice, "if you didn't waste my time and told me up-front you were here with someone."

AB snatches his hand away, temper rising. "Not my fault you didn't take my first no as an answer."

AB pushes past the guy, their shoulders knocking as he does, and AB can already imagine the headlines tomorrow, odds high on this guy going straight to a tabloid about how much of a dick AB is. What a fucking disaster.

Matthew presses in close against AB as they walk away, and for one brief moment, he doesn't worry about Matthew's heat calming his nerves.

"Does that happen to you a lot?"

"Uh, no?" AB answers.

"Was that supposed to be convincing?"

Matthew's so close AB brushes against him as he shrugs. "It happens sometimes. I mean, Carson never lets them get their hands on me, but he'll be glad to know I'm self-sufficient enough in a pinch."

They're not too far from the table now, so AB slows his step and turns to get a look at Matthew. He expects to see him laughing, or at least a little amused by AB making it on his own, but Matthew is none of those things. The look on his face causes AB to stumble. Matthew looks irritated, angry, maybe even a little territorial. But the latter makes no sense; AB must be misinterpreting his expression. This is only their third time seeing each other; how would AB know? He's nowhere near an expert on Matthew's micro expressions.

Matthew must catch on to AB's bewilderment. "He was being a dick. I don't understand how you stayed so calm."

"Easy enough. I never want to give a stranger a bad impression," AB says. "Though, if I'm honest, I did a pretty miserable job of being calm there, and I won't be surprised if he's already concocting a story about me being a sleazy celebrity with too big of an ego or some ridiculous shit. He was def giving off those vibes, don't you think?"

Unfortunately, the truth doesn't ease Matthew's irritation at all. So AB does what he would do with any of his friends; he playfully pats him on the chest, amused when Matthew's irritation bleeds into shock as his gaze drops to where AB's hand was a second before.

"I find your concern charming," AB says. "But being aware of my public perception is part of the game. And I do try not to piss people off even when they're pissing me off."

"Sounds miserable," Matthew says.

"Why do you think I gave up dating?"

Once again, AB's self-deprecating levity falls flat, and Matthew's face only clouds over further. And if AB didn't know better, he'd think Matthew was upset about AB no longer dating. But being bummed about AB's love life makes even less sense than the flash of *whatever* from before. AB is reading way too much into things. Matthew is a nice, kind person, who wants nice, good things for his friends, and him being put off by the rather unfortunate side effects of AB's job has nothing to do with Matthew being interested in AB.

Despite his best efforts, he wants to be liked by Matthew, so he's seeing it in everything, and he needs to stop. He needs to see Matthew as a *friend*. He needs to keep himself from getting any further attached to yet another man who will never want him the same way. Keeping his relationship with Matthew superficial until he runs along to find another Bondmate is the only thing preventing extreme disappointment.

Chapter Eight

They celebrate Reina's birthday all the way until last call, and as the morning dwindles into noon, AB wakes to the aroma of espresso and baked goods.

"How are you hungover?" Reina asks, as AB opens his sticky, sleep-hazy eyes.

"Ugh." He forgot he was treating Reina to a spa day today. "Time?"

"I never tire of your verbose morning communication." She checks her watch. "It's ten till noon. When'd you book us for?"

"One." AB grabs the espresso she's holding out for him, downing it in one gulp, and motions for the croissant on his nightstand. "You didn't have to go out for this."

"I didn't. Went downstairs this morning for some coffee, and Carson had a box full of them."

"Look at this special treatment," AB laughs. "Carson never brings me sweets after a night of drinking."

"I mean, you're still eating them, aren't you?"

"Yes, but did he get them for me? No! He got them for you because you're his favorite."

"If 'favorite' and 'bonded over dealing with you' are synonymous, then, yeah."

"Oh, shut up. You both adore me."

Reina sits down on the side of AB's bed, quiet and contemplative as he enjoys the first few bites of an almond croissant. She watches him carefully, sipping slowly from the chipped cat mug she keeps in his cabinet, but doesn't say anything while he eats. AB chews slowly, under the assumption he's in for some sort of interrogation when he's done.

As suspected, when AB puts the last bite of his croissant in his mouth, Reina sets her mug on the table and turns to sit fully on the bed, cross-legged and facing AB. "Sooo, Matthew."

"What about him?"

"What about him? What about him, he says! You two were thick as thieves last night. Did you get his number?"

"Uh." Reina's the most perceptive person AB has ever met, and she's not even magically inclined to it. He's never been able to successfully lie to her before, and today will be no different.

"What? Why do you look like you sucked on a lemon? What are you keeping from me?"

Attempting to keep this to himself is futile, but he still tries. "Nothing! It's nothing."

"Aww, no. You were trying to devour him with your eyes last night; tell me you didn't fumble getting his number. Is that why you're making the lemon face? 'Cause you flopped?"

"No. I...do have his number."

Reina narrows her eyes. "Uh, weird way to phrase it. What am I missing here?"

"It's really not a big deal, but I've met Matthew before."

"Wait? What?"

She looks genuinely confused, and AB doesn't understand why he didn't let her believe he got Matthew's number last night. Why he didn't leave it at them meeting at a bar under normal circumstances. Why he can't ever lie convincingly.

He throws the blanket off and climbs out of bed. "I need to take a shower. But yeah, we didn't meet last night. We've been texting since July."

Reina grabs his wrist, stilling him. "Wait, hold the fucking door. *July*? That was two months ago! You can't drop this kind of bombshell, and then skip off to hide in the shower. I will cancel our nail appointment if you don't fess up."

"You can't cancel the nail appointment I'm treating you to!"

"I can and I will," Reina says, crossing her arms.

He throws his arms up in defeat. "Fine! We're friends. But I'm not looking to date, and he's straight. So, whatever you thought you saw last night, you didn't."

Reina wrinkles her nose. "But the *vibe*, AB."

"You can't not believe someone when they say they're straight because you think the *vibe* is queer."

"Fine. So, he thinks he's straight."

"Reina!"

"Okay, change of plans," Reina says, surprising him by not fighting her point. She scrolls through her phone and then puts it to her ear as she points him toward his closet. "I want to day drink on the roof while listening to you tell me this ridiculous story while we soak up the nice weather. We'll get our nails done this evening. Get dressed. I'll make the margaritas."

She's on the phone with the salon and walking out of AB's room before he has a chance to protest. Ten minutes later they're on the rooftop terrace, sipping margaritas with their feet dipped in the giant, inflatable pink flamingo pool CeCe got him as a housewarming gift.

"So, what's the deal here, AB? How do you already know Matthew, and more importantly, why were y'all pretending you'd never met?"

"Remember when I spilled mimosa all over myself at brunch? The one before we left for this last leg of the tour?"

"Vaguely," Reina says. "What the hell, AB? Two months is an absurd amount of time to keep this from literally every person you were with last night!"

"Not everyone," AB says, averting his gaze as Reina narrows her eyes at him. "Carson's met him."

"Okay," she says, voice deceptively calm. "Why hide it, then?"

He takes a large sip of his margarita and sets it down. "I'm going to tell you something, and you need to not freak out about it."

"Oh god, what did you do?"

"Why is everyone always asking me what I did? I didn't do anything!"

"Because if Carson's met him, I assume Matthew's not some sort of freak. So again, what's going on? Should I be worried?"

"I swear it's not a big deal," AB says. "You're going to make it a big deal because that's what you do, but it's not actually one."

"If you mean looking out for you, then, yes. That's what I do."

"There's nothing to look out for here. But...our magics Reacted, and I went Invisible. That's all."

"What do you mean 'went Invisible'?" Reina's voice is shrill. "Like when you had the Frits? There and back in a second, but not necessarily long enough to be anything other than an illness? Because it's not a super-common symptom but plenty of people *have* gone in and out of Invisibility when they have a bad enough case. My cousin was Invisible for an entire day a couple years ago when he got it. The only reason people knew he was in the room was because he was also stuck projecting a frog Illusion."

"Well, it wasn't a long time, but it was longer than at the concert. And speaking of, he was there, so we think our magic probably caused it and not the Frits."

Reina sinks down in her lawn chair. "How does this keep getting worse? I started this conversation thinking you might be interested in dating again, and now there's a guy out there who can make you Invisible! Next thing you're going to tell me is you met the one Omnivision in all of New York, and there's no way we can write it off as the Frits if the story gets out."

"I mean, in a city this size? No way Matthew's the *only* one in New York."

Reina nearly splashes herself with margarita in her haste to fully sit up and look at him properly. "What the fuck? You've got to be shitting me, AB. Why didn't you *tell* any of us? Holy shit, holy shit, how am I supposed to not worry about this? Did he sign an NDA? Tell me he signed a fucking NDA!"

"No! What, you think I carry an NDA in my pocket? Come on, no."

"Okay, well, we need to get him one. I'll call Sara right now."

AB grabs her phone off the table between them before she can get her hands on it. "We're not calling Sara! And there will be no NDA! Can you chill for five seconds? Let's— can you turn personal assistant off for a minute and listen to this as a friend?"

Reina settles back, tentatively relaxing. "Okay. But to be honest, friend-Reina also thinks he needs to sign an NDA. Two months is a long time to keep a secret but not necessarily long enough to know if you can trust him. Hell, you had Steven—"

"That's not the same."

"Maybe not, but—"

"He's not going to go to the press with my magic," AB says, a little surprised by his own confidence. "He told his friends my name was *Abe* because he wasn't sure I'd be cool with people knowing before I decided to text him back. His own twin doesn't even know about me yet!"

"Okay...fine. That's a start. But I'm still unsure he won't decide to blab his mouth to anyone who will listen if you decide not to date him."

"Straight, Reina. He's *straight*. You don't have to worry about him 'revenge leaking' my magic to the press because he's straight, and as I've already established, he's very considerate."

"Are you sure?" Reina asks.

"That he's a considerate—"

"No, not about his character," Reina says with a roll of her eyes. "About being straight. Are you *sure* he's straight? Because you two were getting along quite well last night. And I don't think I was the only one who saw how he was looking at you. Maddie, his twin, right? Right. Spent her time flirting with Zoe and watching you two interact out of the corner of her eye."

"Matthew says she's a fan. She was probably curious or whatever."

"She wasn't watching *you*," Reina says. "She was watching the way Matthew was looking at you."

"You can't know which of us she was looking at."

"I mean, I definitely can," Reina says. "I'm perceptive."

"Not infallibly so, though," AB says. "Besides, who goes around clarifying they're straight to the person they think they're going to Bond with?"

This time Reina does spill margarita on herself. "Way to bury the fucking lede!"

"I was getting to it!"

"Not fast enough! I can't believe you kept this from me for nearly two whole months. I'm impressed. Do you think he's right about Bonding? The Reaction must've been intense if you even gave him the time of day considering your position on Bonding and your anxieties about being Known."

"The Reactions the first day were intense, but our magic didn't React the same on Friday, or yesterday, so I assume it was a first-time meeting kind of thing and won't happen again. Probably. The only concern I really have—and I'm trying not to let it get in the way of this because I actually like Matthew's company even though getting close to a straight man I'm attracted to is a terrible idea—is our skin creates a little electricity when we touch."

"And you're telling me you don't think Bonding is real?"

"No, I don't," AB says, amused by Reina's dreamy expression. "Reactions are real, but a strong one doesn't mean Bonding suddenly is."

"For an artist, you are surprisingly unromantic," Reina says with a pout.

"Not believing in Bonding doesn't make me unromantic!"

"Whatever," Reina says. "You two are totally going to Bond."

"We're not," AB says. "He's going to find some girl he Reacts with and give up on this little platonic experiment of his."

"It's cute you think he's not into you."

"Shut up," AB whines. "He's not. Besides—"

"You're no longer dating, blah blah blah. I remember. But I know chemistry when I see it, and you two have it in spades."

"We're friends, Reina."

"Mhm." Reina's mouth twists into a small, delighted smile. After a beat, her face softens with pride, and AB's chest aches at the sight.

"I'm really impressed with you," she says, voice painfully earnest.

AB's throat feels tight, and he has to look away to hide the tears pricking his eyes. "What for?"

"Because you're being reckless about magic," Reina says.

"I thought my recklessness was my worst quality," AB asks, looking over at her with what must be a ridiculous grin.

"Oh, it definitely is," Reina says. "But I'll allow it in this one situation."

Chapter Nine

AB wasn't always obsessed with the idea of being Known. He was never as free with his magic as Gabby, who went through a phase when they were seven where she flaunted her Calming ability to win any argument at recess, but he wasn't like this. He wasn't preoccupied by *what* would happen if he did Divulge. He just...didn't want to share it with people.

But that was before he ran into Steven and all they managed to do was stare at each other. Before the electric sensation of Invisibility coming on forced him to run to the bathroom, praying the Invisibility would hold off until he got there, that the space would be empty and safe for him to Conceal. That was before a quick errand for his mother burrowed itself into his memory, a ticking timebomb waiting to demolish his brain.

He didn't even get a week before it blew up. He'd been eating breakfast two days after his run-in with Steven, when this thought first popped into his mind. *What if Steven made me Invisible? What if Steven controlled my magic to get out of talking to me?* He brushed it off at the time. He knew Steven had no control over him, knew his emotions at seeing Steven got the best of him as they had so many times before, knew no one could make him Invisible outright. He repeatedly told himself only he could control his magic, refuting the thought each and every time with the same rationale until he was opening for the biggest boyband in the world, and everything got insurmountably worse.

By summer, his popularity had skyrocketed, "Dangerous" was all over the radio, and there wasn't a single day *"What if anyone I Divulge to can control my Invisibility?"* didn't pop into his mind and completely sidetrack his day. The only true reprieve was his time on stage, where the incessant, angry buzz of his obsession dropped away, and he was able to enjoy himself fully, with no caveats.

He has no idea how he made it through an entire tour with only one incident, but two nights before the end, it got so bad he couldn't pull himself out of Invisibility long enough to go on stage. He was forced to pretend to have a serious, and unseasonal, case of the Frits preventing him from performing, and the concert went ahead with no opening act. It had been such a low moment for him AB let his mom convince him to go to therapy. Eloise spent weeks researching therapists who specialized in obsessive thoughts which was how he ended up flying to New York City the Sunday after Thanksgiving for his first session with Dr. Barnes, the leading specialist in Pure O.

Eventually, he and Dr. Barnes moved to Skype to accommodate for distance and AB's schedule, but the first meeting had been crucial in managing this obsession. AB was unable to open up about anything, and Dr. Barnes used her truly impressive skills to lead him in the strangest game of twenty questions until she could sum up what brought AB to her office without him saying a single thing. Without her Empathy allowing her to read his unsaid emotional responses, AB probably would've gone on suffering much longer—too afraid to vocalize what he was thinking lest he give another person he didn't trust power to control him.

Two instances of staying Visible while Matthew's around shouldn't be enough to convince AB spontaneous Concealment won't happen again. The fact he and Matthew could spark up at any moment and lead AB's fans right to what his magic is should turn the ever-present buzzing of a bee his obsession usually is into a full-blown swarm. AB knows the novelty of Matthew being able to see him will only last so long, so it shouldn't come as a surprise when the other shoe finally drops.

Still, when he wakes up on Monday with a cold dread pressing down on him, telling him he's risking everything by talking to Matthew, he's caught off guard by how fast the obsession takes hold, how hard it latches into the meat of his brain and drags him into a relapse. He's convinced Matthew's existence in his life will result in AB being Known. He's afraid once they know, the paparazzi will be more aggressive, will try to bait him into Displaying, and is overwhelmed by the prospect of them stopping at nothing to get video of him flickering in and out of Invisibility, stressed at knowing how fast the video would be posted online, stripping him of the one piece of himself strangers haven't been able to consume.

But then, Matthew texts him midafternoon to see if he wants to meet up once more before the semester starts since he might not be able to catch AB before he leaves for Houston, and a flicker of desire permeates the hold his obsession has on him.

"Well, what do you want to do, AB?" Dr. Barnes asks.

AB is thankful she was able to take his call between regularly scheduled appointments, but he hates it when she asks what *he* wants.

"I *want* to not be bothered by this shit anymore. How the hell am I still worrying about the same thing five years later? I'm as obsessed as I've ever been."

"You aren't, though," Dr. Barnes says. "When I first met you, you couldn't even name your magic out loud. At sixteen, you would've gotten a restraining order against a man who turned you Invisible not once, but twice. Sixteen-year-old AB would never even be able to see this person as a viable friend. Five years ago, Matthew would've been nothing but a trigger to avoid at all costs. Your ability to meet him, to engage with him, to develop feelings for him despite your obsession is a monumental step."

"Oh, well, okay," AB says, flustered by Dr. Barnes laying out his progress so bluntly. "I mean, I probably wouldn't have gotten the restraining order."

"Definitely not the part you should be focusing on here," Dr. Barnes says, a hint of laughter seeping into her clinical tone.

"No, but I know what you're going to say next, and I don't want to hear it."

"Enlighten me."

"You're going to tell me if I really want to eliminate the hold these thoughts have over me, I have to stop feeding them with my compulsive avoidance. You're going to say the best way to starve the obsession is to Divulge in one fell swoop and eliminate the ability to avoid, the ability to shroud my magic to the point I'm still capable of worrying about it being discovered."

"Glad to hear you've been listening."

"Look, Doc," AB says. "I know what you want for me, but I'm still unsure I'll ever be able to Divulge."

"Which is fine," Dr. Barnes says. "It's understandable you haven't made it there yet. But I think palling around with someone who makes you put your own desires above the endless what-ifs your mind concocts surrounding being Known is a great idea."

"Then I should keep seeing him?"

"If only the decision was so simple," Dr. Barnes says. "On the one hand, you've come a long way since we started, gotten to the point where you can stay Visible while I'm throwing the worst emotions at you, but there's only so much a controlled session where you have the privacy to fail can do for you, and I think the uncontrolled nature of the magic between you and Matthew will be incredibly beneficial to your mental health journey. But on the other hand, your feelings for him do complicate things."

"How so?"

"Our primary objective here is obviously your OCD, but it would still be ill-advised for me to encourage your entanglement with another man who could use you for sexual exploration only to decide he could not commit to you."

"I'm not going to make the same mistake," AB says. "I'm not going to go down the same path with Matthew as I did with Steven. It's not like that. He's completely and totally straight."

"If you're sure," Dr. Barnes says. "If you have faith in yourself not to make the same mistakes you made several times with Steven St. James, then by all means, go make a new friend."

"This crush will pass," AB assures them both. "I'm not going to fall in love and get my heart broken."

He wants to believe he's not lying to himself; he wants to believe this isn't wishful thinking; he wants to believe this will all pass, but later, he opens the door for Matthew and AB's heart does a gross little stutter, and he isn't so sure.

They eat Thai food at the island countertop, and the large, unmarked paper bag Matthew brought over mocks AB the entire time. It takes Matthew fifteen excruciating minutes to finish his food, and the moment he sets his fork down AB jumps down from his barstool.

"Okay. Now can I see what you brought?"

"It's barely been ten minutes since we got the food," Matthew says, amused by AB's suffering. "There's no way you're this impatient."

"Incorrect!" AB folds his arms across his chest. "I absolutely am this impatient. Besides, I've shown an incred-ible amount of self-restraint here. I'm a very big proponent of instant gratification and hate waiting, and yet here I am, bursting at the seams after waiting patiently, I might add, for you to finish your dinner."

"I don't think you can really call scarfing down your food and then glaring at my bag waiting patiently," Matthew says, finally grabbing it from the edge of the counter.

"Sorry I'm curious about what you brought. I'll make sure to never show interest in anything you bring me ever again," AB says.

"Based on this little display of dramatics, I don't think you'd manage," Matthew says, a satisfied grin dimpling his cheeks.

Matthew has a point there. For all his success in masking his emotions when he's being AB Cerise, he's abysmal at it when his guard is down, and he can just be. Not only is Matthew offensively perceptive, but he's somehow managed to worm his way into being someone AB can't wear a mask around. Frankly, this is shaping up to be far more troublesome than a *crush*. "I don't know what you're talking about. I have a great poker face."

"I have to call your bluff there," Matthew says, taking pity on AB and finally dumping the contents of the bag on the countertop. Out pours a dozen or so tubes of used paints, a large, thick pad of paper with sheets jutting out, and a small, beat-up sketchbook.

"What's this for?"

Matthew rubs the back of his neck, looking at the supplies as he answers. "Uh, I was restocking my supplies for the semester and thought I'd bring some of this stuff over...for your flower dictionary."

"Are you serious?" AB asks, shocked something he mentioned in passing while giving Matthew a tour of his house made such an impression on him.

Matthew's gaze snaps up, looking at AB in bewilderment. "What? Of course."

"You didn't have to," AB says. "I mean, thank you. But I could've picked some stuff up. I would've eventually gotten around to it. You didn't have to give me yours."

"Yeah, but I had this stuff lying around, and now you don't have a reason to procrastinate. Besides, it'll be nice to have stuff lying around if I'm ever struck with actual inspiration for my thesis project."

"Matthew," AB says.

Except, Matthew takes it the wrong way, turning red and spluttering. "I mean, I'm not expecting to be here a lot but—"

"That was a 'this is incredibly thoughtful, and I am surprised you cared enough about my flower obsession to do this' Matthew, not a 'you can't come to my house' Matthew. For future reference."

"Oh," Matthew says, ducking his head a little. "Right."

"You'll eventually get used to the nuances," AB says, for once not thinking of Matthew leaving him for a romantic Bond as inevitable. Which is a problem in and of itself. Because if Matthew's fairy-tale dream of having the perfect romantic Bond doesn't eventually win out, AB is going to have to be a responsible person and cut himself off from Matthew to not be a miserable, pining mess. AB hates having to be responsible.

If only Matthew weren't so cute, and so easily flustered, and so unbelievably kind, then maybe AB wouldn't have this crush slowly but steadily gliding down into an actual sea of feelings. But hey, at least Matthew's straight. At least AB doesn't have to worry about getting his heart toyed with.

Except, Matthew comes over every day after his classes and AB starts to notice things. How Matthew gets this pleased little look in his eyes when AB slips up and calls him "babe" for the first time. How attuned AB is to Matthew watching him out of the corner of his eyes while AB introduces him to the wonders of baking competitions. How his ears burn bright red when AB catches him looking. How Matthew's attention is a weighted blanket wrapped around AB's shoulders, making everything AB says feel important, cared about, no matter how frivolous.

AB can write off most of Matthew's responses to AB's presence as Matthew being enamored with finding his alleged Bondmate. He assures himself Matthew would be this way with anyone he had this sort of Reaction with, that AB isn't special. But convincing himself he is nothing but a poor substitute for the thing Matthew has always wanted becomes much harder when AB sees Matthew the last time before his pit stop in Houston before the next round of tour.

Thursday evening comes with the sinking dread of running out of time, and when Matthew comes over, AB's in an absolute tizzy.

"Hey, Houston," Matthew says, as he joins AB in his room. "Carson tells me you're in panic mode. Should I go?"

"No," AB answers immediately, absolutely ignoring the way Matthew giving him the simplest of nicknames is still causing warmth to curl through him. "I mean, it's probably in my best interest to tell you to get out and let me pack, but you're here already, and I hate packing, and you're not terrible company, so, yes, stay. Please."

"You're right. I am great company."

"Mmm. Don't think that's what I said," AB says, wondering if he can will himself to like Matthew less if he pretends it's already true.

"Oh, it's not? I'm sure that's what I heard."

Matthew smiles, beautiful and bright as always, and AB ducks his head to hide his own. "Whatever. Are you going to stand there all day, or you think you might want to help some?"

"Dunno," Matthew says as he crosses the room and makes himself comfortable in the oversized armchair in the corner by the window. "I spent all week trying to get you to pack and you didn't."

"Oh, is that how it is? I have to do all the work and you're, what, going to sit there and look pretty?"

Matthew blinks up at AB, eyes wide, a slight flush to his cheeks, and then a delighted smile blooms across his lips as he looks himself over. "I do look pretty nice today, thanks."

"Oh god," AB groans, rolling his eyes to mask how thrown he is to see Matthew so pleased by AB's offhand comment he's practically vibrating with it. "If you're not helping, you should at least run through ideas for your magnum opus while you sit there. Can't let you be completely useless."

"Ugh. Why would you say that?"

"Oh, I'm sorry. Did I miss the part where you came up with an idea?"

Matthew throws his hands in the air. "Of course, I didn't! But you inspired me a little—"

"*I* inspired you?" AB interrupts, a gross fluttering sensation taking hold in his stomach. "How?"

"All your flowers," Matthew says. "I've been thinking about doing a mixed media study of—well as you know I haven't gotten inspired enough to figure out a theme or whatever—but regardless I've been spitballing how I can incorporate flowers into my work. I think I want to, like, go real gestural with this shit, so I'm thinking of using flowers as paint brushes or dried petals for texture. I've got to workshop it obviously. But..."

AB stares and Matthew fidgets under his gaze. He rubs a hand over the back of his neck, suddenly sheepish, and AB can relate. This should *not* be having this sort of effect on AB, but Matthew didn't even have a favorite flower two months ago and now he's incorporating them into his art because of AB. He shouldn't be so hung up on this, but for an odd, inexplicable reason, Matthew taking an interest in AB's hyperfixation is what tips AB over into believing Matthew will be around for a while.

"You'll have to show me," he says, heart and mind warring with each other as he realizes, again, how futile it might be to rely on Matthew taking himself out of the picture.

Matthew's face lights up—as if he was concerned AB wouldn't be absolutely delighted by this information—and AB tries to push the dread of knowing he's playing with fire aside to live in this moment, right here, without worrying about the future.

"If I ever figure out what to spend the next nine months of my life creating, of course."

"I'm sure you'll figure it out eventually," AB says. "Oh, hey, I'm actually getting back in the studio next month; we can cry together about having no ideas."

Matthew snorts as he comes to join AB at his bed. "Sounds promising. Oh, look at you. You actually got some more stuff done after I left. You're not nearly as bad at this as you led me to believe."

"Considering I leave for the airport in, like, sixteen hours and I still haven't narrowed down everything I'm taking, I'd say you're trying to flatter me."

AB hates this part of touring. What AB would give to have a suitcase with a direct link to his closet, so he would never have to worry about narrowing down his wardrobe—or worse, forgetting something. He's only going to be gone a little over two weeks this time, but the very idea of packing makes AB want to lie down. It's a truly ridiculous thing to get anxious over, but what can he do? His brain's a piece of shit.

"Wait," Matthew says, disbelief flitting across his face. "Did you sleep on top of all this? Please tell me you didn't."

"And risk unfolding all my hard work from yesterday? No. I slept in Gabby's room."

"Of course, you did," Matthew says, as if this is some unreasonable transgression. "Why didn't you put it all in your suitcase and be done with it?"

"Because then I couldn't see what I still needed. Come on; have you never packed before?"

Matthew shakes his head, the slightest hint of a smile forming on his lips. "I've never packed like this. That's for sure."

"Are you judging my methods?"

Matthew bites down on his smile. "I'd never. Now come on; the faster we get this done, the faster you can calm down."

"What are you talking about?" AB says, circling his face with his hand. "Is this the face of a stressed man? No! I am the perfect picture of serenity right now."

Matthew snorts but doesn't comment further. Instead, he turns his attention to the pile of clothes AB laid out while he was gone. "Do you really need to bring all these? You can't need this many jorts—"

"Okay, first! Let's never say *jorts* again," AB says, snatching the pair of cutoffs out of his hand, and showing off the pockets. "These have rainbow pockets." He picks up another. "These are black." Another. "These—"

"Have a hole in the back pocket because you've worn them too much," Matthew fills in for him, as if a tattered pocket is a personal offense.

"Oh," AB laughs. "I know Mr. I Wear Sweats To Brunch isn't trying to give me shit about clothes."

"But did they have holes in them?"

"In summer, Matthew! In summer."

"Uh, if I remember correctly, weren't you wearing jeans?"

"They were tie-dye overalls! Totally different!"

"Were they not long? Were your legs not completely covered?"

AB throws his hands up. "You're impossible!"

Matthew's lips twitch, a smile forming in one corner of his mouth. "What if I said they were my nice sweats?"

"Oh my god. That's worse," AB says. "I can't believe you." He shoves at Matthew's shoulder. "Go sit over there and look pretty. You're not even helping, and I obviously can't count on you for reliable wardrobe choices."

"Who's the one who folded all this stuff?" Matthew asks, ignoring AB.

"I folded at least five of these things."

"Mm-hmm," Matthew hums. He finishes refolding the shorts they were arguing over before moving on to the next pile, pausing when his fingers brush lace. He's holding a collared white lace shirt, but his gaze is focused on the delicate cream-and-black underwear AB forgot he pulled out.

AB doesn't think he's imagining the flash of heat in Matthew's eyes as color rises on his cheeks, or the tense, choked quality to his voice as he asks, "Aren't those a little itchy? With all the lace?"

"I don't think so," AB answers. "I like the way lace feels."

Matthew clears his throat, reaching around the lace garments to pick up a shirt to fold, but AB doesn't miss the way his blush deepens every time his gaze flicks back to the underwear, or how hard he tries not to look at AB. If he and Matthew didn't know each other, if Matthew weren't familiar with AB's wardrobe, AB might think men wearing socially feminine garments, especially of the lingerie kind, was the source of Matthew's discomfort. But as it stands, AB thinks Matthew might be trying not to imagine AB in the lace.

And isn't that great? Now he's got to deal with the growing likelihood of Matthew sticking around *and* the growing possibility of Matthew being into him. This is too much. There's only so many times AB can tell himself doing something is a bad idea before he gives in to his reckless desire to put pleasure before pain. There is only so long he can cling to all the very real, very valid, very well-thought-out reasons he can't date anyone—but especially Matthew—before his impulsiveness wins out and destroys all his hard-earned forethought.

Chapter Ten

The ground is still wet from rain when AB and Carson land in Houston. The air is hot and sticky, a damp blanket clinging to his skin, and AB is so happy to be home he doesn't even care. Gabby greets them at baggage claim with a tacky sign emblazoned with "Welcome home, bitch!" and AB almost knocks her over in his haste to hug her.

On their way to the car, they pass a little kid with Minnie Mouse ears and a too-big Cerise World Tour Shirt who stares at him with wide-eyed wonder, hand caught midair when AB waves at her. Her little awed face is a big enough slice of pure joy to soften the blow of Gabby asking him about Matthew the second the door shuts.

Gabby's driving with Carson in the passenger seat, but AB can see the profile of her face, and her expression is as irritating as he expected. "So, how are things with Matthew? Have you accepted he's not going to run off the moment he finds someone else he has a good Reaction with?"

"Yes," AB grumbles.

"Wait? Really?" Gabby asks. "Oh god. Your little crush has only gotten worse, hasn't it?"

"I'm working on it," AB says.

Carson snorts. "Don't see how inviting him over every day is 'working on it.'"

"AB," Gabby reprimands. "I thought we talked about not getting attached to another straight boy."

"I said I'm working on it!"

Carson looks back at him, raising an eyebrow, and AB shakes his head, ever so slightly, but still, Gabby catches on.

"Wait, what are you two hiding?"

"Nothing," AB says.

"Okay, liar," Gabby says. "But you're going to get bombarded the minute you step inside the house. You're not going to be able to keep this kind of a secret from our moms while under the same roof. My mom's going to smell the Bond magic on you."

"That's literally not possible," AB says. "And it's not *Bond magic*."

Gabby glances back at him, a smug smile on her lips. "You think she'll care? My mom loves all that romantic shit, and she's going to eat it right up when you eventually break and tell them about Matthew. I can't wait."

And sure enough, not even ten minutes into dinner, Matthew comes up.

"Heard you have a new boyfriend," Lily says after taking a sip of wine, her eyes twinkling.

"What?" AB asks, unsure where she got this morsel of untruth.

Lily sets her wine glass down. "Delivered a baby last week—and during one of my rounds the mom and her sister were talking about you being quite the diva with your boyfriend as you turned down some guy."

Lily rolls her eyes. "Of course, I know not to believe everything people say about you—especially since I've been asked by a couple nurses if you and Gabby are *actually* dating—"

Gabby shudders. "It disgusts me people *still* think I'd date you when you're basically my brother. Have they not learned yet? Especially your coworkers! They get our Christmas cards!"

"Anyway," Lily says, not allowing Gabby to go on her usual tirade about the perils of tabloid journalism, "I know not to believe your press, but Ellie and I were hoping you might be opening yourself back up to dating again. That maybe the part about you being with someone could've been true."

"I was with a friend," AB says. "But I haven't changed my mind about dating."

Eloise sweeps her gaze around the table, attention resting on his, Carson's, and Gabby's demeanors for a second before pressing her mouth together. "What are you three hiding?"

The problem with his bodyguard being his mom's best friend's—and frankly AB's second mom's—cousin is that Carson is always the first one Lily and Eloise turn to when they think AB won't fess up. Thankfully, Carson is immune to Lily's stare. "Don't look at me. They're not my secrets."

Gabby, on the other hand, has no qualms throwing AB in the line of fire. "I only know half the secret. But I'm sure if you ask him about Matthew, AB won't *lie*."

"Matthew is the friend from the bar, then?" his mom asks.

"Yes," AB says.

"And you like him?" Lily asks.

"Unfortunately."

"Why unfortunately?" Eloise asks.

"Because he's straight," Gabby says. "Right, AB? Because surely if he wasn't you wouldn't still be sticking to this ridiculous idea of not dating. Especially when you're already so important to him."

Lily narrows her eyes. "What piece of information are we missing here?"

AB sighs. "He thinks we're going to Bond."

"Oh," Lily says, a dreamy, dazed expression softening her features. "And what do you think about Bonding?"

"I don't believe in it," AB answers. "Obviously."

"But," Eloise prompts.

AB pushes his food around his plate, not looking at his mother. "But he does. And I think maybe he's confused."

"What do you mean?" Gabby asks, the slight edge to her voice gone.

"Nothing, I don't know," AB says because even he isn't so sure. But if he clings to this, maybe he can get rid of these unwanted, completely inconvenient feelings. "I'm worried he might be seeing me in a romantic way or getting caught up in all the Reactions of our magic and seeing me in a way he wouldn't if they didn't exist."

"You think he's into you but not actually into you?" Gabby asks, and she only sounds half-annoyed. AB shrugs, so Gabby turns to Carson. "What do you think?"

"I think he likes AB," Carson says.

Gabby rolls her eyes, impatient. "Yeah, but what *vibe* does he give off?"

Carson looks to AB. "Do you actually want to know this?"

"Go ahead," he says, unwilling to admit he's curious about what Matthew gives off when he's around AB, entirely unsure he'll be able to fold this information into his picture of Matthew and come out on the other side without stronger feelings.

"It's not an exact science," Carson says. "Sure, it's easy to pick up on good intentions versus bad or dangerous ones. But you know, some intentions aren't either and are largely up to my interpretation. But Matthew is a little hard to explain. Or harder than usual. The first day, there were obviously no dangerous intentions coming off him, and his driving intention seemed to be a combination of impressing you, getting you to like him, making you happy."

"Okay, sounds pretty standard for someone who wants to Bond," AB says, a wave of relief and dread washing over him.

There's still a chance he'll change his mind. There's still a chance AB won't have to decide to plunge headfirst into another Steven-shaped disaster. There's still a chance Matthew will do what AB needs him to do and cut their friendship short before AB has learned to love him in a real, lasting way.

"Maybe," Carson says. "But that was only the first day, and yeah, the need to impress you is still there, but he's all over the place now. He's a chaos of desires and confusion." Carson shrugs. "I can't pinpoint what he wants, but I know it's all directed at you. And it's *different* from what he came to the house with, and it gets murkier every time he sees you."

"Well then, I need to stop seeing him," AB says, knowing this is the right decision for the two of them.

"What?" Gabby snaps. "You can't be serious."

"I am!"

"But if he likes you and you like him—"

"He could very well be hung up on the Bond—" AB says.

Gabby's nostrils flare. "You can't really think that."

And he doesn't, not really, but it doesn't stop him from worrying.

"Honey," Eloise says. "Not every man is Steven St. James."

AB's heart rate doubles. "I know."

"Not every man is a teenage boy who runs away when confronted with feelings for their best friend," Lily says, her bright-green eyes fierce with conviction. "You cannot expect every experience you have with a man newly discovering his interest in men to end with him running away scared and never speaking to you again. To leave you to deal with the fallout without another word."

Lily and Eloise don't know the full Steven story. They don't know about the summer after AB's first tour, the summer before Steven's senior year, the summer he came by the house with a bouquet of yellow roses as a peace offering. They don't know about AB learning the taste of Steven's mouth, how he memorized the touch of Steven's hands on his hips; they don't know the way AB thought that summer was the start of something great. They don't know AB was Steven's secret even when Steven's sexuality was not. They don't know the whole story.

But Gabby knows, and yet, she still says, "Matthew isn't Steven. Wouldn't you agree, Carse?"

Unlike Gabby and Dr. Barnes, Carson is the only one who knows where the story picked back up. Carson knows all about the three times Steven came over after AB's breakup with Chloe and even he says, "I would."

He should find solace in Carson's faith but— "It doesn't matter! None of it matters because I'm still not open to dating anyone anymore. Y'all know that."

"Run your reasons by me again," Gabby says, a stubborn set to her jaw. "Because I'm pretty sure they're bad and are only there to make you a miserable pining mess."

"You don't even know if he's actually into me," AB says.

"Let's pretend he is," Lily says. "Let's say you two are on the same page and want the same things from each other. What is keeping you from dating him?"

"A lot of things," AB says.

"Which are?" Eloise asks, because everyone in this house is his enemy.

"Because this life isn't made for dating, Mom! And it's especially not made for bisexual celebrities trying to be seen as bisexual."

"But you had so much fun with Chloe," Lily says. "Even while the two of you dealt with all that."

"It was different with Chloe."

"How so?" Eloise asks.

"Because Chloe was a celebrity too. Chloe knew how it would be. She could handle the way tabloids twisted things, the way my fans would go after her, the way everything can so easily be turned into a story even when it's not."

"Isn't Matthew an NHL prospect?" Gabby asks.

"Yes, but—"

"And I don't know if you've realized this," Carson interjects. "But his dad's kind of a huge deal in hockey."

Gabby's eyes light up. "You never mentioned—"

He didn't realize, not really, but— "Does it matter? It doesn't change anything."

Carson's voice is gentle but firm when he continues. "Doesn't it? I'm sure Matthew is used to being scrutinized. Maybe not on the level of you and Chloe, but he's not some run-of-the-mill college student either, AB. He has to know his way around public perception a little."

"Oh, you think a professional athlete is going to be able to be out?" AB asks, Gabby's Calming effect not strong enough to keep his temper at bay. "You think knowing his way around the media will stop this from being another secret too hard to keep? Another relationship not worth the effort? Another person who will leave me?"

"Chloe didn't leave you," Gabby says. "Y'all decided y'all were better off friends."

"I know! But that's not the point."

"Yes, it is!" Gabby snaps. "Because it's one thing to let your experience with Steven inform your decisions, to make you cautious, but it's unacceptable to let a sleaze ball scare you off relationships entirely."

"I'm not scared," AB says. "I'm *not*. Dating in the public eye is just too much of a hassle, and I don't want to deal with it."

Gabby heaves out a sigh. "But you're still letting outside forces dictate what you do, AB."

"Yes, well, it's the decision I've made. And it's the decision I'm sticking by."

"AB," Eloise starts.

"No, Mom. I'm serious!" He takes a deep breath, embarrassed for snapping at his mom. "I'm sorry. It's just not worth it. I've learned to handle people thinking Gabby and I are dating. I've learned to deal with the conspiracy theorists who think I'm lying about not dating Heath. I've learned to handle the way people still think Chloe was my beard. I've learned to deal with all these things. But the way people talked about me, Heath, and Chloe after the split? It's a miracle the three of us were able to stay friends. I'm not putting myself through all that again. I'm *not*."

"Fine, be like that," Eloise says.

"Seriously?" Gabby asks. "We're all going to let AB set himself up to be forever alone because the world is full of disgusting gossipy vultures? Because he's afraid things might *end?* Because people don't know what the fuck—sorry, Mom—bisexuality is?"

"Gabby," Lily says. "This is his decision."

"Well, I think it's shitty, for the record."

"Noted," Lily says.

Gabby turns to Carson. "Tell him he's being irrational."

"You're being irrational," he says to AB.

"Thank you." Gabby crosses her arms over her chest, satisfied again.

"Does anyone else want to tell me how terrible my decisions are?"

"No," Eloise says. "But I do have a question."

"And maybe I'll have an answer," AB says, pleased when his mother laughs at their old bit.

"You have feelings for Matthew, correct?"

"Yes, but I assume that's not the actual question."

"No, but it's relevant to the actual question, which is: What exactly is your plan here, hon?"

"What do you mean?"

"Well, let's suppose Carson's way off base; let's say this Matthew of yours is not developing feelings of his own. Are you banking on your interest fading with time? Or are you preparing to pine for someone who wants to Bond with you, someone who isn't going to give up on you easily, someone you're unlikely to run off with your trust issues? Are you planning to miserably harbor feelings for him indefinitely?"

"I don't like this question," AB grumbles.

"Mama Cerise has a point," Gabby says. "What are you planning on doing here?"

"Well, I'm still kind of banking on him deciding his time is better spent Bonding with a woman—even if the Reaction isn't as strong."

"So, a horrible plan," Carson says.

"Maybe, but it's the only one I've got."

"Would it not be easier to...stop talking to him?" Lily says.

"Mom! Don't encourage his bad decisions."

"But if he's stuck on not dating him," Lily says, "it's a terrible idea to continue building a relationship with someone his heart is already attached to."

"Cutting your losses now would be smart," Eloise says.

"Are you two trying to, like, reverse psychology me here?"

"No," Eloise says. "We're telling you what the smart thing to do is."

"But I don't want to...do that. These feelings will pass. It's fine."

"Oh my god," Gabby says, resting her head in her hands for a moment. "You better channel your miserable pining into your next album and leave me out of it, then."

"Shut up," AB laughs. "Stop acting like you're not going to try to meddle in my love life."

Chapter Eleven

Matthew doesn't count the number of hours between saying goodbye to AB and hearing from him again. He doesn't. He just has an excellent recall. That's all. So, when AB texts him right as he's getting in bed after a night out with Finn and the guys, Matthew knows twenty-eight hours have passed since they last spoke. But seriously... He. Did. Not. Count.

Houston

Sat, Sep 5, 2:37 AM

Over/under on me leaving Houston with a nose piercing go

Over 90

Was going to say over 80 but you're probably right

Anyway since you're actually up Gabby has run out of patience and wants to know what you look like

Pls send pic at your earliest convenience

If this seems objectifying it 100% is and she
will be judging you based solely on appearance sorry

Please keep in mind I was falling
asleep when you texted

Within the space of taking the photo and pressing Send, Matthew goes from half asleep to wide awake. He's never been shy before, so this shouldn't be any different. But the two minutes he waits for AB to respond drag out torturously, unnerving Matthew, and time seems to stop completely once he does.

From Gabby's lips to your phone: 10/10 good
freckles, nice shoulder

And since it's only fair, here you go

In the picture, AB and Gabby have their heads ducked together, hands joined to make a heart, tongues stuck out. Gabby has a nose ring and bright-green eyes. AB's hair is un-styled, falling haphazardly across his forehead, and his mouth quirks in a gentle grin. Matthew's mind is a sea of white, blank save for the persistent chant building in his ears. All Matthew knows is soft hair, soft eyes, soft, soft, soft. Matthew shakes his head. His skin is hot. He definitely drank too much tonight. He needs to go to sleep. He needs to respond. He needs to take a shower and calm down. He needs to stop staring at this photo.

He doesn't respond. He takes a shower. He dreams of running his fingers through AB's hair. He wakes up thrum-ming and goes for a run until his muscles ache and the only thought in his mind is water, water, water. Later, he saves the picture to his camera roll and refuses to contemplate why it feels like a secret to keep.

But once he's sober and well rested, getting photos from AB doesn't make him feel like he's going to burst wide open.

Which is good, because apparently a switch has flipped in AB's communication style. Or maybe Matthew has finally earned AB's preferred mode of communication—which, to Matthew's utter dismay and pleasure, seems to be photos.

Matthew gets photos of AB's hands. New manicure, new rings, a bruise from clipping a doorknob. He gets pictures of animals. A cat on the porch, a dog on the street, a red panda at the zoo. Of food, of places, of things. Tacos and donuts and kolaches. Murals and botanical gardens and airport signs. Beautiful cityscapes and hotel rooms. Empty concert venues and tour bus interiors. And so. Many. Selfies. AB by himself. With Gabby. With his band. With Carson.

Matthew thinks about saving every single one.

But he doesn't.

Not even three weeks have passed before AB touches back down in America, but regardless, Matthew is embarrassingly eager to see him. Despite AB going silent plenty of times their first month of texting, and his general sporadic replying, Matthew has grown used to hearing from AB at least once a day. So, when he goes silent for two days after landing, Matthew starts to second-guess the depth of their friendship, the dent he's made in whatever insecurity plagues AB and makes him expect Matthew to not stick around.

But Thursday after class, AB texts him "Dinner?" and Matthew decides he should probably stop overthinking things.

★

Matthew is familiar with the way people's eyes narrow as they do a double take, how their faces light up when recognition sets in. He's seen it happen enough times with his father to not be shocked when it happens with AB. He even knows, from the bar on Oliver's birthday, people are more prone to approach AB than his dad. But what Matthew didn't realize, what he's never truly experienced with his father, what he dismissed when AB mentioned it, is how easily Matthew can be pulled into the frenzy of AB's celebrity.

They're at a place a few blocks from AB's house, waiting for the biscuit bread pudding that brought them out in the first place, when Matthew sees the girl. He's felt a little watched since being seated, but he wrote it off as Carson being at the next table over—with them but not quite present. But now, the attention clings to his skin, rough and irritating. He tries not to let it bother him, tries not to *look* to see who's staring. But as the waiter leaves with their dessert order, Matthew catches someone averting their gaze from within the restaurant. He and AB are on the patio but the doors are wide open so nothing really separates them, and once Matthew puts a face to the unnerving clawing at his neck, he can't stop thinking about it.

"I see you've realized we've got an admirer," AB says.

"That obvious, huh?"

AB shrugs, the corner of his mouth going up in a crooked, wry smile. "No, not at all. Your shoulders were totally this rigid before we got here."

"Shut up," Matthew says, picking up one of AB's remaining fries and flicking it at him. "I could be stressed about school."

AB quirks an eyebrow as he eats the fry Matthew threw. His voice is the perfect imitation of interested when he asks, "Are you?"

"I could be."

"Not quite an answer." AB puts his elbows on the table and rests his chin on the heels of his hands, framing his face with his fingers. The full weight of his attention on Matthew is heavy. "Tell me, Matthew, what can I do to help?"

Matthew blinks in surprise. The weight of AB's attention is jarring enough on its own, but with this level of focus between them, Matthew notices a new depth to the color of AB's voice. Most people only have two colors. When magic's in use it appears as a shimmering metallic aura while the sounds a person makes appear in bursts and splashes, varying slightly in brightness and saturation depending on tone and intensity. Over the years, Matthew has noticed some people's magic is the same color as their sounds, and in rare cases, people may have different colors for verbal and nonverbal noises. But Matthew has never met anyone as colorful as AB.

He has the same rose-gold aura associated with all Body magic, the same transparent form of the few Invisibles he's seen in passing, but unlike the others, AB's body isn't a translucent version of his aura. No, an Invisible AB is a vivid, celestial swirl of magentas and blues and purples of every shade—only slightly transparent with Matthew's Vision—and the colors of his sounds are no different. The magenta of his nonverbal noises, the violet of his voice, and the kaleidoscope of blues he emits when he sings are all drawn from the dynamic purple AB becomes while Concealed.

But right here, with his gaze unwavering, AB's words are a deep, majestic purple Matthew hasn't noticed outside the swirl of AB while Invisible, and Matthew doesn't understand what about this moment could change his color so drastically.

"You could do my thesis for me," Matthew jokes.

"Think that might be cheating."

"Maybe so," Matthew says. "But seriously, I *am* a little stressed about school. Or well, maybe not stressed, but disgustingly annoyed."

"Still no luck on coming up with a theme? Or is this a general 'I hate school—please let me out of here before I die' kind of thing?"

"No, not a hate school thing. Though, I'm itching to graduate already. It's the thesis. It's always the thesis. The whole thing is an uninspired disaster, and I can't seem to figure out a way to make it...not suck."

"So, you do have something you're working with? You've come up with more than flowers and mixed media?"

"Barely. I'm trying to do a study of emotion but so far everything is absolute crap."

"I'm sure it's not—"

"No really," Matthew says, stopping AB from going further. "It's all garbage. God, my professor even suggested I narrow down my focus—find one central idea to relate the emotions back to, but I can't even do that right. And I love them, but Zeke and Oliver are absolutely useless at brainstorming ideas."

AB shakes his head. "They can't be that bad."

"Oh, you think so? Their ideas might as well be sucking out the last bits of my creativity. And Maddie's as bad as the team. They've made a sport of bad suggestions. But if you're so sure, I'll send them your way when you start writing again, and you can see firsthand what I'm talking about."

AB's eyes are twinkling, a delighted smile forming on his lips, and then his face falls. Replaced in an instant with a different smile—the one he saw when the guy at the bar was bothering him. Matthew hates it now even more than he did then.

He was so caught up in unloading his frustration he forgot all about the girl who was staring. Unfortunately, she didn't seem to forget about them, and now, AB is whispering a rushed apology as Matthew sees her and a friend approaching their table.

"Hey, Adam," she says.

AB's smile doesn't slip, but his eyes widen for a second, and the color of his voice is acrid as he says hello, and while the fan can't see that, surely, she can see the stiffness in his smile, the vacant look in his eyes. Surely, she can tell AB is irritated.

Matthew certainly can, frustration flaring through him as she goes on like she can't tell. "Sorry for interrupting, but do you think we could get a picture with you?"

"Sure." AB turns the smile up, but it's still nothing like the one from before, nothing like the smile Matthew has been memorizing the curve of.

"Do you think," the other girl says, startling Matthew by speaking directly to him, "you could take the picture? With just the one we'll be out of your hair sooner."

"Oh yeah," Matthew answers after a beat too long of the girl holding out her phone. While the two fans flank AB, Matthew notices AB's smile has returned to normal. His attention locked on Matthew instead of the camera, his eyes once again twinkling with amusement, never dropping his gaze even when Matthew finishes his countdown.

Matthew hands the phone back and AB shifts his attention to the fans. He smiles when they compliment the nose stud he came back from tour with, watches them return to their table with a blank stare, and then begins to laugh. It's low and quiet, but the magenta is brighter than the color of his breath, as bright and vibrant as one of his loud, bursting laughs. "How does it feel to have 'photographer' thrust upon you? It's Carson's favorite part of the job."

"Hmm, I don't believe you," Matthew says, turning his attention to where Carson is watching them with a small, quirk of a smile. "You like being a photographer?"

"It's my favorite part of the job," Carson says with such a straight face Matthew almost believes him.

When Matthew turns back, the waiter is dropping off his bread pudding, but AB doesn't look as pleased as he should.

"What's wrong? Not what you expected?"

"Oh no," AB says. "This is god-tier shit right here."

Matthew raises an eyebrow when he doesn't continue, and AB sighs, suddenly sheepish, the faintest hint of pink on the tips of his ears.

"Ugh, it's ridiculous, really, but I liked that you didn't know what AB stood for and now—" He waves vaguely toward the restaurant. "—well, that's all ruined."

"I won't call you that if you don't like it," Matthew says.

AB huffs. "It's not that I dislike it; it's a perfectly fine name for someone else, but—" He shrugs, his mouth curling in an embarrassed smile. "I don't think it suits me, and I hate when people call me it, but I don't really talk about that publicly, so I can't really blame them I guess."

Matthew purses his lips. "If all you ever go by is AB, I think it's fair to expect your fans to treat that as your name and not think whatever they can find on Wikipedia is something they can refer to you as."

"Maybe," AB says, grinning again. "But I think they think it's affectionate or something."

"Perhaps," Matthew says. He thinks it's inappropriately familiar, but he doesn't want to push AB into trashing his own fans. Instead, he smiles, thinks back to what AB said earlier, and takes a chance. "But look at it this way: I actually only know what the A stands for so really, it's only *half* ruined."

AB's laugh lights him up beautifully, any trace of discomfort wiped away as it burst through him. "A shame for you, really, the B's the best part."

AB's smile is loose and delighted, so much more radiant than Matthew thinks this moment deserves, and for a second, Matthew knows what it's like not to be an Omnivision. Matthew's spent years honing his ability to suppress the stark way he sees sound, but he's never been able to block it out completely. Now, even the faint, muted splashes of sound bursting through the air he's used to seeing are gone. For a moment, all Matthew sees is the pink of AB's smile, the blue-green of his eyes, the fading red of his sunburn. For a moment, there is nothing but AB smiling, and all Matthew knows is *warm, warm, warm.*

Chapter Twelve

"Matthew," AB whines. "You're not even watching."

More than an hour has passed since dinner, and they're back at AB's place, watching yet another baking show—something Matthew quickly realized is AB's favorite pastime—and the warmth he felt before has become a simmering force under his skin.

"I am," he insists. "I haven't turned away from the TV once."

AB turns to Matthew now. His smile is soft, amused, and so, so beautiful and for a moment Matthew wonders—no. He has to stop fixating on AB's mouth.

"Oh, really?" AB asks, his smile growing, and it takes far more effort than appropriate for Matthew to look him in the eye. "Who's freaking out about their cake being undercooked, then?"

"Jonathan."

"Jonathan!" AB repeats and the sound of his laugh is bright and radiant, and Matthew can't remember ever appreciating magenta as much as he does when it's coming from AB's mouth. "There's not even a Jonathan on the show right now! You're ridiculous, you know?"

"I'm ridiculous?" Matthew asks. "I think rewatching the same baking shows over and over again is kind of ridiculous too."

"Admit it, this shit's relaxing!"

"It's all right," Matthew says.

"See, I knew you loved them."

He turns back to the show and Matthew steals another glance. He's sure once he captures the bow of AB's lip on paper he'll be able to stop looking. AB has an aesthetically nice mouth, and Matthew noticing doesn't mean anything—artistic curiosity is all this is.

"Hey," AB says after a beat, "are there any occasions where you say fuck it and go wild with sweets?"

"Are you still hung up on me not trying your bread pudding?"

"No." Matthew raises an eyebrow and AB laughs. "Seriously, more for me. But it did make me wonder. Like, you only ate a couple bites of the pie I got you, and you don't take sugar in your tea, or snack from my candy bowl. And I assume it's, like, an athlete's diet plan kind of thing, but you take the sugar a lot more seriously than literally anything else. So like, is there ever a time you succumb to your sweet tooth like you do with fries?"

Matthew's stomach does a somersault. He didn't think AB was paying so much attention to him, and knowing AB has makes Matthew giddy and warm. He runs a hand over the back of his neck. "Uh. Birthdays. Christmas. When Maddie's being the devil and eating my favorite ice cream right in front of me. But mostly not until the season's ended. You know, when I can really indulge and not have to worry about a sugar crash wiping me out."

"Wait, you have sugar crashes every time you have sweets?"

"No? I don't know, not every time. But enough for me to be conscious of it. If I indulge in moderation—like a little bit of syrup on pancakes or the sugar naturally in things—it's usually fine. But like too much caffeine—I know that's another offense to your sensibilities—it kicks my Vision all the way up, and then when it fades, I'm wiped out. And if I've had too much and it lasts too long, when I come down it's a lot like a hangover."

AB grimaces. "Gross. Magic is such a bitch sometimes."

"I take it you've got something similar?"

"Barring you making me Invisible?"

Matthew smiles. "Yes, excluding me."

"Unfortunately so. It's gotten a lot better since—" AB says, violet souring, and then he shakes his head. "Anyway, it's gotten better. But yeah, if my emotions are too amped on either side—though mostly the negative ones—I'll lose control and Conceal. Thus, me being neurotically afraid of being Known." He turns away from Matthew, mouth turned down as he stares at the TV, eyes unfocused. Then in a smaller, even duller purple, AB says, "It's a whole thing. This thought fully formed in my mind years ago and has never gone away. And even though I know people who Know what I am, can't literally control me, I'm still so scared it will happen." He huffs out a humorless laugh. "It's a mess and I hate it. But I've managed to keep it from getting out this long, even with our little mix-up two years ago. So, whatever."

Matthew's stomach sinks. Leave it to the thing Matthew's been waiting most of his life for to compound AB's anxiety—which is so much worse than Matthew imagined it to be. "I—I'm really sorry about the concert."

AB turns his head to look at Matthew again, his smile small but genuine. "It's fine. I mean, completely un-ideal, but hey, it proved my therapist right about it not being the end of the world. She basically thinks meeting you is the best thing to ever happen to me."

"What?" Matthew chokes out.

AB's smile grows. "Well, not you specifically. But you, as an Omnivision who can destabilize my magic."

"I don't understand."

"Dr. Barnes is all about controlling what I can and confronting what I can't. She's very pro ripping the Band-Aid off and Divulging to the world. She thinks by eliminating my ability to avoid being Known, I'll stop feeding the obsession. Which doesn't really have anything to do with you, as a person, but you as an Omnivision, and you as someone who Reacts with me with a literal lightning show, are basically an embodiment of what triggers me. I don't know, that sounds bad—"

"Uh, yeah," Matthew says, concerned he's not only a nuisance to AB as someone who believes in Bonding but actually detrimental to him.

"Think of it this way, and there's lots of different ways this pure obsession type of OCD manifests, but this is always my go-to one other than my own because my mom's an ob-gyn. But yes, think of it like this," AB says. "Sometimes parents will get postpartum OCD after they deliver; they'll get these terrible awful images of hurting their babies, and it's not uncommon for the intrusive thought to be traumatizing enough for them to start avoiding being alone with their child. But the problem with avoidance, as I've learned from Dr. Barnes, is it's an invisible compulsion. And the thing about compulsions is they don't actually stop the obsession. They feed it. They bring the obsession up more, make the compulsion seem more necessary, more urgent, and on and on, an endless hell-cycle.

"So, in the case of parents, their child is the trigger and being near them helps dim the obsession. And in the case of me and you, our Reactions are one of my triggers and allowing myself to be on the edge of Reacting every time we hang out is good for me in the long run. It helps ease me into the idea of being Known outright, of walking around with every person being a potential subject of my intrusive thoughts. And if I can't avoid the triggers, then the obsession will lose a lot of its oomph. Or so Dr. Barnes says."

AB laughs, and both the sound and color are closer to the ones Matthew's grown fond of than they were before. "It's a lot to take in, and most of the time I don't really understand it either, because how are thousands of triggers helpful, you know? But what I'm saying is please don't worry. I've got my shit under control, and as long as you're patient with me being neurotic about accidentally bumping into you, then we'll be fine. We won't have a problem."

"Okay," Matthew says. "But you'd tell me if I needed to fuck off, right? Like, you have to tell me if my presence is making your mental health worse, okay?"

"Don't worry, Matthew," AB says, a smile blooming across his lips. "You'd know if I didn't want you around."

"Good, that's good," Matthew says, the warmth of knowing AB wants him around cutting through the frost of knowing their magic Reacting is a trigger of his. But only a little.

"I'm serious," AB says, smile faltering. "Despite your terrible taste in hats and your love affair with gray sweats and your refusal to admit you like these baking shows, I do enjoy your company, and that's worth more to me than whether your presence is helping or hurting or whatevering my OCD, okay? And I'll tell you if things go sideways with these Reactions, because you deserve to know, but I'm not going to tell you to fuck off until I don't want you around, until I don't *enjoy* you being around anymore, all right? So, jot that down, mark it in your calendar, do whatever you need to do to believe it because I'm not going to say it again."

Matthew isn't sure if he's more stunned by the sincerity and conviction of AB's response, or the reappearance of the deep, dark purple from dinner. But combined, it's almost too much. AB is so rarely upfront with what he feels, always downplaying it or wrapping it up in an affectionate chirp. He doesn't know what to do with this honesty.

"Yeah," Matthew says after a moment. "I'll put it in my notes app: Dear Diary, today AB told me he likes me. He was a brat about it, but it still counts."

Matthew's heart is still hammering, but AB barks out a laugh, head tipped back, eyes crinkling, and Matthew's succeeded in cutting the tension. "Why were you asking about the sugar, anyway?"

"Oh right!" AB says, sitting up in his excitement. "I was *wondering* because I love to bake and wanted to make sure I wasn't being a complete asshole when I inevitably bully you into doing this thing me and Gabby started with our moms and has now grown into a whole competition we do at the holidays. It involves baking and eating baked things, and if you didn't eat more than a couple bites of candy under any circumstances you'd miss out. And missing out on bread pudding is one thing, but this would be super tragic."

"What's the thing?" Matthew asks, ignoring the way his heart races even faster as AB all but confirms he's accepted Matthew being serious about their friendship and sticking around.

"You ever seen *Cupcake Wars*?"

Matthew nods.

"Right. So, it started with *Cupcake Wars*. I think Gabby and I were eleven, maybe twelve, and we really wanted this one cupcake to win. I don't even remember what the cupcake was, or why we liked it so much, but I remember the winner having a terrible display and we were pissed. Why our rage translated into the need for us to recreate the cupcake, I couldn't tell you. And yes, I know, it sounds ridiculous, but I don't try to understand even my own prepubescent mind— so I advise you not to try either. But anyway, we obviously didn't have a recipe, right, but since when has not knowing what the fuck you're doing ever stopped a really determined middle schooler? So, with the help of our moms we did our best."

"And how good was your best?"

AB grins. "Do you even have to ask? It was obviously a major disaster. But now it's a thing."

"A thing you're going to bully me into participating in?"

"Absolutely. It's super fun and super chaotic. We pick a dessert from whatever show we're watching at the time and try to recreate it without a recipe. When it's only us and our moms there's not really a winner, but Carson became the judge once my career took off and he started spending Christmas with us. And then when I moved into this house, Gabby and our moms started spending the holiday here and we opened it up to the band and Reina, and now it's a no-holds-barred, cutthroat battle where teams are picked, family ties are broken, and anything goes."

"A battle? I'm having a really hard time imagining you trying to sabotage someone."

"Are you calling me soft?" AB asks, and there goes that smile again. Bright and dazzling and so, so distracting.

"Yes."

"The Christmas baking competition is second only to the Christmas Pictionary tournament in terms of us going rabid. Gabby's basically threatened to murder you if you help me get any better at drawing and uneven the playing field."

Matthew's phone buzzes in his pocket, but he ignores it. He's enjoying AB talking about himself too much to break the moment. "How exactly does this little battle of yours work?"

"Ah, see," AB says, his smile turning sharp and daring. "You'll have to make it to December to find out."

"Well, now I have to be," Matthew says, heart skipping.

"I think I could live with that," AB says.

AB's words once again burst through the air in rich, royal purple. Matthew doesn't know what the color means, or why its reappearance stirs something in him, but he has to look away. He takes the moment to check his phone and tries to shake the heat simmering beneath his skin.

Roommates

Thu, Sep 24, 9:27 PM

Zeke

HOLY SHIT! HOLY SHIT! HOLY!!!! FUCK-ING!!!!!! SHIT!!!!!!! MATTHEW!!!!

Oliver

What Zeke means is it's one thing to witness you buying AB Cerise a drink but to see you out to eat with him???? For you not to TELL US ABOUT IT?????

Zeke

WHAT THE ACTUAL FUCK

"Hey, what's wrong?" AB asks. Matthew doesn't know how long he's been staring at his phone, but the look on AB's face suggests it was longer than appropriate.

"Uh, I'm not sure how, but my friends know we were having dinner?"

"And...that's bad?"

"Well, yeah," Matthew says. But AB's face crumbles and Matthew swears he can feel AB's hurt in his heart. "Wait, what? Why are you upset? I thought you still didn't want them to know?"

"What? Why?" AB says.

"Because you never said anything! And I know you don't like Divulging and, like, it'd be kind of hard to keep your magic a secret from them considering how we met."

AB rolls his eyes, but he's smiling again. "That's very considerate, but you could've asked."

"I assumed you'd tell me when I could!"

"And I assumed you already told them!" AB laughs, shaking his head. "We're a couple of fucking disasters. Wow. For the record, though, you can tell them. Like, your sister's been in a group chat with Zoe and Reina since Oliver's birthday! I really thought they already knew!"

"Well, yeah, but...I didn't..." Matthew's mind has been all over the place since then. Maddie having new friends, even ones close to AB, hasn't been a top priority. But now it seems so obvious. Of course, Maddie knows. It's the simplest explanation for why she's been saying "Tell *Abe* I said hi" like she knows he's keeping a secret ever since.

"I didn't think," Matthew finally says. "I thought Maddie was picking up on your name not actually being Abe, but I didn't think she actually *knew*."

"Is Maddie the type to tell your friends before telling you? Or did those fans post a picture of you with me?"

"I don't think it was Maddie. If she was going to be an asshole, she'd do it while I was in the room."

"Ah."

There's something like regret in AB's voice and Matthew doesn't understand. If AB doesn't mind his friends finding out, if he's been operating under the assumption they already did, then Matthew doesn't know why the mood has shifted again. "Am I missing something here?"

"Oh, sorry, no. I'm just being..." AB waves his hand around listlessly. "I've been putting off having this conversation."

Matthew's heart is going to give out. He has no idea what's going on, but AB's colors are washed out and frayed, and Matthew knows it doesn't bode well. "What conversation?"

"You know, the one about the assumptions people make when I'm spotted with someone—especially someone as attractive as you."

"Assumptions," Matthew repeats. He's latched onto "attractive" and can't comprehend anything else AB might be trying to say.

Matthew might be operating at 10 percent, but he can still recognize the sound of frustration when AB sighs. "Look, I get it. Hell, I've been expecting it. Not everyone can hack strangers thinking they're sleeping with someone they're not. It's fine. I understand."

The simmering has turned to a boil. Matthew is burning; bombarded one after another with searing hot images of AB—in the lace underwear, of him flushed and sweating in Matthew's bed, of him hovering over Matthew, his mouth so, so close to his own. This can't be happening right now. This is not the time to be having this montage.

"Okay. I know I said I understand, but you could at least look a little less appalled that people might think we're sleeping together."

Matthew is used to AB's colors belying his actual words, but he's never seen them look like this. They're sharp, jagged bursts of cold, dark purple—the polar opposite of the rich, warm blanket of purple Matthew's started to hope to see.

"I know you're straight and all," AB says, this nasty curl to his lip. "But as far as being linked to people you're not actually dating goes, it could be worse. At least I'm decently hot."

"Jesus Christ," Matthew says. Is his heart in his ears? Where is his stomach? Everything is on fire. "That's not—I'm not *offended*."

Despite the Technicolor movie playing in his mind, Matthew registers the way AB's posture relaxes. He still has a pinch of worry around his eyes, but mostly, he looks like he's trying to figure out some unsolvable equation. It unnerves Matthew, and while AB can't possibly see into his mind and figure out the real reason for his distraction, Matthew is compelled to say anything to get AB to stop staring at him like this. "I know you mentioned I could show up in the tabloids with you. But I didn't— I wasn't thinking of it being a dating thing, and it caught me off guard. I'm sorry."

Which is true, but AB either picks up on Matthew not telling the full truth, or he has more concerns of his own. He sounds so tired when he says, "Right, but I'm bi, so it theoretically creates a larger rumor mill."

"Yeah, okay— Yeah, that makes sense." If Matthew could stop these images for even five fucking seconds and regain his bearings, AB might believe him.

"You know," AB says, still explaining. "Heath got spotted with his cousin once, and some tiny gossip site wrote an article speculating he was Heath's new boyfriend. It ended up getting more traction from Blue Sunset fans dragging them for not fact-checking, but we still had a big laugh about it in the group chat. As for you and me—" Those words alone make Matthew ache, but paired with the way AB's gaze bores into him—as if he's trying to stare his way into some deeper understanding—Matthew has to fight the urge to squirm.

"It should eventually become an annoying but manageable part of life. But—" AB grimaces. "This is why I said we couldn't fall in love. Someone's always picking at something when you're dating, and at this point, I think the hassle of it all outweighs everything else, you know?"

The movie stops and Matthew crashes back to reality, an ice-cold dread permeating every inch of previously too hot skin. "Right. But we're...uh...fine? It's not going to bother *you*, is it?"

"I won't lie and say the momentary influx of people assuming my interest in one gender invalidates my interest in any others won't be annoying *but—*"

The color momentarily dulls but then the vibrancy floods back into it, turning into a bright, playful lilac. "Have you seen yourself in a mirror, babe? There are worse things than people thinking we're together for a couple of news cycles."

The nonchalant way AB flirts, like it's no big deal, because it *isn't*, does nothing to soothe Matthew's dread or put out the fire raging inside him. Instead, the tantalizing visuals make a clambering return, and Matthew is left a cold, hot mess. "No, I meant, are you going to see this as a hassle?"

"Ah, no." AB wrinkles his nose, frowning. "Like I said, the whole thing is a bit annoying, but once they figure out I'm never going to kiss you, they'll usually drop it. Or at least the tabloids will move on to bigger, better clickbaits; the fans might hold out. But none of the attention ever becomes truly unbearable until the breakup, so I've just decided to avoid the whole shebang." He shrugs, like it's nothing, but Matthew's stomach turns as the words burst through the room in an unpleasant greenish-purple Matthew truly hates. AB must not be as fine with avoiding dating as he wants Matthew to believe.

But then, AB's lips turn up ever so slightly, and Matthew can't think past the flutter of his stomach. "Anyway, I can handle it. But if you want to sweeten the pot with some coffee, I won't stop you."

Matthew is so intrigued by the resurfacing of the dark purple, so delighted by AB wanting to continue hanging out, so goddamn flustered by not being able to shake the images of his friend's half-naked body from his very straight mind, he doesn't respond.

AB must misinterpret Matthew's loss of words. He purses his lips and furrows his brow. "But if you can't, I understand. I imagine homophobia in sports might complicate things for you. No harm, no foul if not wanting to deal with all this shit outweighs your interest in Bonding. Like, it's not romantic and it comes with this whole mess? I won't hold it against you when you bail on me."

Matthew doesn't need to see the spoiled lavender stabbing through the air to know AB is lying. It's written all over his face, in his posture, in the clipped sound of his voice.

"I'm not going to bail on you," Matthew says.

AB purses his lips.

"I'm not. Maybe *you* need to jot that down in your notes app."

AB's lips twitch but he doesn't smile. Matthew doesn't need him to, though, not when the deep purple springs forth as he says, "Maybe."

So, what if people might be talking about them when AB's starting to believe he's in this for real? How much can a wildly untrue rumor actually affect him? Homophobia in sports is a massive problem, especially in hockey, but people will stop talking eventually. There's nothing to suggest Matthew's into men. They won't stick. He won't be labeled as anything he's not. Matthew isn't hiding anything. He has nothing to fear. Everything will be fine.

Chapter Thirteen

This night has been far more stressful than Matthew planned, and while he's shaken the images of AB from his mind, he can't shake the feeling they left behind. It doesn't help at all when AB makes himself comfortable while Matthew finally replies to his roommates, insisting he'll explain later. AB lies back against the armrest, stretches out his long legs until his feet are inches from Matthew's thigh, and closes his eyes. His long, dark lashes flutter against the purple-gray bags under his eyes, and each exhale is a delicate wash of magenta. As he waits for Matthew to finish texting, AB's mouth curls in the slightest smile, a dimple forming right outside the frame his three little moles create around the left corner of his mouth. The sight strikes Matthew with an inexplicable ache deep in his chest. It seeps into every part of him until it's unbearable. He's uncomfortable and unsure of what, exactly, he's feeling. He only knows the sensation grows with every breath AB takes.

He can't stand it; he has to leave. He means to leave. Really. But when he offers to go, AB's eyes pop open, and he makes a soft, disgruntled little sound Matthew sees more than he hears, and Matthew can't move. AB's eyes are bright with exhaustion, and each blink is heavier than the next, but his mouth spreads in an easy smile as he asks Matthew how he got into art, and this unnerving, unplaceable pang in his chest only grows. It works its way into his blood, gnaws at Matthew until his already racing pulse pounds in his ears and his thoughts fog over. His brain screams for him to flee, to get as far away as he can from whatever is causing this frantic, desperate energy inside him, but Matthew's body won't budge. He's glued to the spot by AB's curiosity and has no choice but to answer.

No one really asks him about art outside of school; most people tend to ask about hockey—what it's like being Andre Levoie's son, why he decided to be a goalie instead of following in his father's footsteps, why he's held out on going to the NHL, why graduating is so important to him. No one really asks him about his other interests, and once Matthew starts, he can't shut up. AB listens as Matthew explains how his mother is a children's book author and illustrator, how his father was out for half a season when a Healed concussion still resulted in migraines too bad and too frequent for him to keep up with, how he always encouraged him and Maddie to have interests outside of sports as a result, and how those two things combined to make art equally important in their home.

AB's yawns come more frequently, but his smile grows as Matthew tells him about his mother's box of hand-bound sports-themed picture books she made from his and Maddie's childhood paintings. Matthew talks because AB keeps waving off his offers to leave, because he wants to share this part of himself, because it drowns out the beat of his own heart. Despite all this, AB falls asleep sometime between Matthew explaining how every year he and his family skate through splashes of paint until his grandparents' frozen pond is transformed into a work of art and Matthew recounting how long it took to realize he was talented and wasn't only using art as an outlet for stress relief.

While looking at AB's unguarded sleeping expression, Matthew is overcome by how soft AB looks, and the unshakable desire for something he can't put his finger on explodes within him. It's impossible to ignore, and without AB's attention anchoring him in place, Matthew has no reason to stay. He can leave. He can get up and run away from whatever's causing this desperate ache clawing at his insides. He can shove these feelings aside and for a little while longer pretend everything is the same as it was before he met AB.

But on his way out, he runs into Carson, and even without the brassy shimmer indicating his magic is in use, Matthew feels like he's being read. A glint in Carson's eyes as he says good night makes Matthew think Carson understands what this indecipherable thing plaguing him is. Or at the very least, has a better idea than Matthew does. Because at this point the only remotely plausible explanation is Matthew has *feelings* for AB. But that can't be right. Matthew doesn't like men. Matthew is straight. He has to be mistaken. He *has* to be wrong. He has to be.

Despite the hour, despite them both having early classes in the morning, despite Matthew spending the entire train ride home hoping he wouldn't have to discuss AB with his roommates, Oliver and Zeke are wide awake when he gets home.

They'll deny it if he asks, but Matthew has no doubt they've been waiting up for him, especially when Zeke all but jumps out of his seat when Matthew walks into the living room.

"You're home earlier than I thought," Oliver says.

"And you're up later than I expected," Matthew says.

Zeke looks him over, assessing the way he slumps in the chair with an unnerving amount of scrutiny, and purses his lips. "You look stressed? Why're you stressed?"

"Today hasn't exactly gone the way I planned."

"So, you weren't planning on letting us find out from Twitter your so-called Bondmate is one of the most famous men in the world right now?"

"No, Zeke, this isn't how I saw my Thursday night panning out."

Zeke snorts. "Wait, Abe *is* your fake name for AB, right? I don't think I have the emotional wherewithal to handle a love triangle between your Bondmate and an absurdly famous and excruciatingly hot pop star all while waiting to hear back from med schools."

"You don't have to worry about a love triangle," Matthew says. "Even if they were different people—which they aren't— I'm not into guys, remember?"

Matthew closes his eyes. The words already sound like a lie, and he's not ready to see if the color of his voice confirms it.

"You don't sound so convinced, and you're upset about it." Oliver's tone brooks no argument, and his certainty cuts Matthew to his core. Matthew's eyes snap open, and he blanches as Oliver motions to where Matthew is picking at his cuticles. "This is about more than us finding out about AB. This is about what you're feeling for him, isn't it?"

"I—" Matthew squeezes his eyes shut to escape his roommates' knowing looks, but what flits through his mind after is even worse. The image of AB laid out on Matthew's bed, lips parted in a soft sigh of satisfaction, everything tinged pink—his lips, his cheeks, his bare chest—is as vivid as ever. He first woke to a version of this image the night he helped AB pack, but he wrote it off as lingering desire for a romantic Bond mixing with the way his mind went to sex the instant he saw the lace. But as the days passed, and the dreams continued, it's become harder for Matthew to push them away as meaningless.

He presses the heels of his hands to his eyes in a desperate attempt to rid himself of this *fantasy* he's not ready to admit he might want. It doesn't work. He tilts his head back and looks to the ceiling, still unable to face his roommates. "My feelings for AB haven't changed since we met."

Zeke makes a derisive noise, and Matthew lowers his gaze, glaring at him. "What?"

"That doesn't mean much when you've been confused about your feelings since the beginning."

"No, I haven't," Matthew says, but the color of his voice, and the nervous swirl of his stomach, suggest otherwise. Fuck.

Zeke opens his mouth, clamps it shut, and then looks to Oliver, who shakes his head. Zeke purses his lips but doesn't go on.

Oliver waits a beat and then says, "Fine. You obviously don't want to talk about it. Is there anything you *do* want to talk about?"

"No," Matthew says. "Maybe. I don't know. You said you found out on Twitter? What're people saying?"

Zeke softens, minutely. "You're concerned about people talking about you on the internet?"

"Might've helped if I got to tell you guys about all this myself."

"People think you're hot," Zeke laughs. "Does that help?"

"No?"

"Oh god." Oliver grins. "You must be deep in your feelings if you're not getting a kick out of a bunch of strangers thinking you're hot."

"Are you calling me vain?"

"Obviously," Zeke and Oliver say in unison.

Matthew rolls his eyes, but their normal banter doesn't make him any less frantic. "Is that it? Is, uh...?" He rubs his hands over his face, his neck beginning to heat. "Are there...? Have people started to...?"

He can't even ask. He doesn't know why he's so flustered by this or why it's gotten more intense since he left AB. But being in front of his roommates—who found out about this from strangers—makes him sick. There's no way anyone could know what Matthew's been dreaming about, but the mere notion of his fantasies being reflected in strangers' assumptions has gotten under his skin, flaying every piece of him. There's an ache building behind his eyes and his Vision is beginning to fire on all cylinders. The noise of the television is too focused in his periphery, the light is starting to burn his eyes, and he can barely look at Zeke and Oliver because their faces are too crisp, too sharp, too *there.*

The last time this happened, they lost in overtime the first round of the Frozen Four. But he'd been upset and ashamed and angry with himself for not blocking the shot, and this isn't a similar situation. He has no reason to be upset right now. He doesn't even know if people are assuming anything. Rumors are nothing more than a possibility. And even so, he wasn't bothered when Oliver came out in middle school and some classmates started thinking they were more than friends. So, what if strangers might think he's sleeping with a guy? Matthew knows what he is, and he knows what he's not, and if people he doesn't know think otherwise, then what does it matter?

It shouldn't. It doesn't.

Except his heart is racing and his head is spinning and his eyes sting from too much input, and the terrifying truth is: Matthew isn't quite sure what he is anymore. He's refused to examine these feelings, written his aches and desires off as something else for so long, and even though it's so clear now, he still can't accept the truth. He's too scared to admit why this situation is so different from the one with Oliver.

"Matthew," Oliver says, voice full of concern. "You look a little green. What's wrong?"

"Nothing," he says, through gritted teeth. He closes his eyes. Keeping them open hurts too much, makes him nauseous, but there's still bright bursts of color burning behind his eyes, and he needs to go lie down.

"I'm calling Maddie," Zeke says.

"No," Matthew protests. "It's not too bad. I'll be fine once I calm down."

It would be convenient to have Maddie around to take the pain away. God, he wishes she were here to take the edge off this headache, but he's not willing to admit he's this worked up.

With his eyes still closed, and an arm shielding him from the weight of the judgment he's afraid he'll provoke with his concerns, he forces the words out. "Are people thinking we're together?"

"Ah," Zeke says. "I see why this is different than a bunch of rabid hockey fans talking shit about your goaltending."

"You're worried people might think you're dating a guy," Oliver says.

Matthew laughs, a hysterical and joyless sound. He throws his arms out, nearly jumping out of his seat with the force of his own emotions. "No, Oliver. People thinking I'm dating AB is probably the least of my fucking worries right now. I *wish* people thinking I'm dating AB when I'm not was my biggest concern."

"So, we *are* talking about this, then?" Zeke hedges.

"I guess so," Matthew says, settling back into his seat. His head still hurts, but the nausea is starting to abate, and his Vision is starting to settle again. Everything is still a little too focused, but at least he can open his eyes. "Maddie will be pissed she wasn't here, but it's probably what she deserves since she's been pretending she didn't know AB was Abe for weeks now."

"She what now?" Zeke asks.

"She's been talking to Reina and Zoe. Apparently, she knows. Which is why AB assumed you two knew. Which is why he never told me I could tell you. Which is why you found out from the internet and not me."

"I told you she had a secret," Zeke says to Oliver, extending a hand. "Pay up."

Oliver swats Zeke's hand away. "I will not! You thought she was back with Tristan; this is clearly a draw."

"Wait," Matthew says, forgetting his own worries for a second. "Why would you think they're back together?"

"I ran into them having lunch twice last week." He waves his hand dismissively. "But don't change the subject! We can talk about Maddie's secrets later. For now, you have our undivided attention."

"I take it back," Matthew says, rubbing at his temples. "Let's talk about this in the morning. I need to sleep this headache off before I have any sort of self-discovery."

Zeke starts to protest, but Oliver stops him with a hand to the arm. Relief washes over him, but then Oliver speaks. "If we talk about it tomorrow, Maddie will be here."

Oliver's statement stops Matthew in his tracks. He sits back down, frowning. "You'd call her."

Oliver rolls his eyes. "As if I'd need to. I'm surprised you didn't get a call the moment you had to close your eyes because it hurt too much to see." Oliver holds his hand up. "Don't insult me by denying it, Matthew."

"Fine. But that doesn't mean she'll be here in the morning. She does have a life of her own."

It's a hollow excuse and he knows it. Oliver's right—the chance of Maddie sensing his distress is absolute. Not only is she better at picking up on the nuances of emotions, she's told him before how nauseous it makes her when his Vision does this, and she's flooded with his pain. There's no way to keep this from Maddie, but he's not sure he's ready to confront someone who will know, without a shadow of a doubt, he's upset about AB.

"If you're sure, let's bet on it," Zeke says, a sly smile forming on his lips. "If she doesn't show up, we can all go back to pretending you haven't been accelerating headfirst into a sexuality crisis since you met this guy."

Fuck. If Zeke and Oliver have already pinpointed what this is all about without an innate link to his emotions, how can he possibly avoid this conversation with Maddie around?

Right now, with this distance between them, she probably can't tell *why* his emotions are a hurricane, but the moment she steps into this apartment she'll be able to tell. Knowing the why of emotions is usually a lot of guesswork, but sometimes, when they're this intense, it becomes obvious. Maddie won't have to push or pry or guess; she'll know without even trying all his emotions are wrapped up in this thing with AB. At least with Zeke and Oliver, there's some plausible deniability—no matter how small—but fooling Maddie is not an option.

"Good thing I'm not having a sexuality crisis," Matthew says, trying to make the lie convincing. It doesn't work, but he didn't really expect it to.

"Matthew," Oliver says.

His voice is soft and full of understanding, and Matthew wants none of this. He is nowhere near ready to accept what he's feeling, but he can't keep running from it either. He doesn't know what to do. Just thinking about admitting what's changed makes the pain ramp up behind his eyes. With the way things are going, he might pass out from too much input before he even decides what to do. But that would be too easy, and he's not so lucky.

Instead, Oliver grimaces as he looks at his phone, and Matthew knows who it is before Oliver even mouths "sorry."

"Hey, Maddie," Oliver answers, unconvincingly casual. "What's got you calling so late? Is everything all right?" His nostrils flare. "It's not like we haven't been trying! You know he's stubborn as shit. He doesn't *want* to talk about it." Oliver bites his lip. "Can you wait until the morning, at least? Okay fine, I'll tell him you're on your way. But he's not going to be happy about it! Of course, yeah. I'll see you in a few. Bye."

"Guess we don't have to bet on it, after all," Zeke says after Oliver hangs up.

Matthew pushes the heels of his hands against his eyes until the pressure breaks through the ache behind them. It won't take long—she only lives a couple blocks from them—but he hides his face from Zeke and Oliver the entire time. As far as Matthew's concerned, he's allowed to shield himself from their sympathy until Maddie walks through the door.

He's almost convinced himself he can handle this conversation when she bursts through the door, saying, "Matthew, you jackass!"

And then she's there with her hands at his temples, a cool, soothing sensation washing through him and taking the pain away. When he opens his eyes, Maddie is scowling at him. Everything is still as crisp and focused as it was before she got here, but the pain—even the dull ache he's grown so accustomed to—is gone. He's so relieved to be rid of the headache he smiles up at her. "Thanks, Mads. You didn't have to come all this way to act as my Advil, though."

Maddie purses her lips and smacks him upside the head. "As I said. You're a jackass. I'm never letting you keep a secret this long again! I was going to bed! And then here comes Matthew's pain! Making me feel like I've got the fucking flu! You should have never let it get to this point."

"In my defense, this was a sudden onset."

She throws her hands in the air. "Oh my god." She turns to face Zeke and Oliver. "Are either of you buying this? No? Didn't think so." She turns back to Matthew and the fierceness in her eyes is startling. "This was not a sudden onset. You've been on edge since AB left for tour. It's been so bad *I've* been hit with longer and longer bursts of your emotions for weeks now."

She takes a deep breath and throws herself on the couch between Zeke and Oliver. Matthew thinks he's faced the worst of her irritation, but Maddie's face only hardens. "I thought him being back would calm you the fuck down, but apparently that was wishful thinking. Everything's gone to shit now. So, fess up, what happened? What pushed this from being a manageable crush we were all dutifully letting you get over to a panic-inducing shit show?"

"I'm not panicking."

"But you're not denying it's a shit show," Zeke says, and Matthew laughs despite himself.

"I mean, I've felt better."

"I swear to god, Matthew!" Maddie says. "It's almost two in the morning! If you don't get it together and start talking, I'm going to lose it."

"I'm sorry, you coming over here in the middle of the night *isn't* you losing it?"

Maddie's eyes flash and her annoyance burns through him, but Matthew refuses to make this easy for them. He doesn't want to say anything even if they all know what's going on. He's not willing to admit it. He's not willing to face wanting what he can't have. And he certainly can't have AB. Not now, not ever. Because AB doesn't want him. AB isn't on the market. AB doesn't think love is worth the hassle of the pressure and prying of the public. Matthew has barely convinced AB he'll be around come December, let alone the legitimacy of their Bond. How could Matthew ever expect to convince a guy with AB's hang-ups he's worth the time and effort? How can he possibly get AB to return his feelings when Matthew doesn't even understand them himself? No. Acknowledging this or, worse, accepting this as a game changer for his sexuality is useless when nothing will ever come of it.

"These guys have class in the morning," Maddie finally says. "But I don't. I can wait you out until you talk."

Matthew is familiar with these tactics. He knows she's not bluffing. But he's just as stubborn. She can sit here all night staring at him, and his resolve won't waver.

"Maddie, I love you." He stands up, glancing at Zeke and Oliver too. "I love all of you. But I'm not talking about this right now. No." Matthew cuts Maddie off. "I appreciate the concern, and I'm beyond grateful you came over to check on me. Without the pain, I can at least attempt to sort through my feelings. But I'm not sharing them with any of you yet. And you need to accept that, okay?"

Maddie crosses her arms over her chest and presses her lips together, but Oliver nods. "Yeah, okay."

Zeke nods too. "Take your time."

Maddie doesn't give up as easily as the others. She glares at him for a long, agonizing moment in which every pang of her concern and frustration shoots through him. Eventually she concedes, though, face softening as she speaks. "You know we all understand exactly what you're going through right now, don't you? All of us have had this same realization before."

"Yes," Matthew says through clenched teeth.

Even vaguely acknowledging he's fucked up over another man pains him, and Maddie understands—pushing a warmth of sympathy through him.

Despite her efforts to bolster his mood, she lets out an exaggerated sigh, a flare of frustration undercutting the compassion flooding their link. "Fine. I guess it's only fair we let you come to this conclusion on your own. And *I guess* you showed me the same courtesy when I was bawling my eyes out about Robin all the time. So, I'll let you have this one."

"Thank you," Matthew says.

Maddie makes a dismissive gesture with her hand and rolls her eyes. "For what it's worth, I'm not happy about any of this. I was a fool for agonizing by myself when you knew it was about her, and you're being a fool right now. But we all deserve to get our shit together, when it comes to this stuff, at our own pace. So fine. Make my same mistakes."

Her annoyance is extra put-upon, but Matthew knows there's still sincerity in her statement. He remembers how difficult it had been being hundreds of miles away from her and knowing she was supposed to be at homecoming having a blast and instead being hit with a tumultuous mix of anger and confusion and sorrow all centered around her best friend

Robin. He knows Maddie is experiencing something similar about him and AB right now, and unlike him—who had no clue Maddie having romantic feelings for Robin was even a possibility—Maddie *knows* AB is his potential Bondmate. She knows what Bonds mean to him, and she knows when his emotions started changing, and she *knows* meeting AB is what sparked the change.

"How big of you, Madison," Matthew laughs, feeling marginally better despite his emotions still being all over the place. He hopes—for the sake of his heart and his and AB's friendship—this doesn't end up being a Thing. Matthew knows AB makes his heart do weird shit, but as he walks back to his room, leaving Maddie to commandeer their living room as her bedroom for the night, Matthew wonders if he can put a stop to all this with a little more time apart from the source of his problem. Trying is worth a shot, right? Especially since he and AB can never even be a thing. He might as well attempt shaking himself out of this before he goes and falls further for someone he can't have. It's the logical thing to do. Really.

Chapter Fourteen

Matthew's Vision has fully stabilized by the time he wakes up. The familiar ache he always has in his eyes hasn't come back yet, even though he's still seeing more than anyone else can. The bright-blue static the television emits is no longer the sharp dagger of blue from last night, but its brightness still doesn't irritate him like usual. It seems he's still benefiting from the lasting effects of Maddie's Healing. Which is good, because sleeping might have reset his Vision, but it did nothing for his emotions. He's still as raw and untethered as he was when he fell asleep.

Maybe even more so after the dream he had. But he's not thinking about that today. He's going to push all his rogue thoughts aside and finally get his mind under control. He isn't attracted to AB. He doesn't want to date him. He's not developing feelings for him outside of friendship. It's just not possible. It's *not*.

"Morning, Matty," Maddie says, raising her mug to him in greeting as he opens his bedroom door. Zeke and Oliver are long gone, but apparently, he hadn't waited Maddie out by sleeping in.

"Is this you giving me space to come to terms with my shit on my own?"

"Oh, you woke up in a mood," she says, standing to follow him into the kitchen.

"I'm in a perfectly fine mood."

She hops up on the counter and wrinkles her nose. "I think it's cute how you still try to lie to me when I know for a fact you're in a terrible mood."

"Why're you still here, Maddie?"

"There's protein pancakes in the microwave for you."

His annoyance fades slightly. "Thank you. You didn't have to make me breakfast."

She shrugs. "The least I could do after pushing your buttons. Though, if I'm being honest, I was craving them, and I'm pretty sure I'm out of protein powder at my place. So, we both win here."

"Ah, that sounds more like you."

True to her word, Maddie doesn't push him any further. She lets him eat in peace, save for making her one usual dig about how disappointed Papa would be if he saw him using the fake syrup instead of maple. The problem is her silence provides no distraction from what's been on his mind since seeing AB again. Worse still is last night's dream and the excruciating clarity it brought him.

There had been nothing arousing or sexual about the dream, but it left Matthew aching and angry because he finally understands what's made him hold back on accepting what he wants from AB. His dream only made it terribly clear why the possibility of people assuming he's dating AB is any different than people doing the same with Oliver.

In his dream, Matthew had been up for the Calder, and AB was there at the NHL awards too. But he wasn't there as a performer. He was there *with* Matthew—as his date. He was taking pictures with him on the red carpet, and Matthew wasn't afraid of what people might say—he knew people loved them. He knew it wouldn't matter.

Waking from this dream had been more upsetting than the first time Matthew had woken from a sex dream about AB. The first filled him with confusion and shame. He'd never had a dream like that about a friend, let alone about another guy, and if he was still dreaming about AB and his lace underwear days later, if he was having those images flit through his mind while interacting with AB, how could he keep writing them off? How could he keep denying lying in AB's bed with AB straddling his lap was a fantasy Matthew wished to fulfill?

But this dream had been crushing in an entirely different way. Seeing a world where he was out and happy and accepted with AB at his side was far worse than realizing he might be attracted to AB. Because happy gay couples don't happen in the NHL, no matter who his dad is, no matter how many men in his family have played. Having a generational talent as a father doesn't change the fact that men in the NHL don't date other men. Being the fourth Levoie to play in the league won't protect him from the rampant homophobia in the sport he loves. Being Matthew Hellman-Levoie, number one overall draft pick and a hockey legacy, won't matter if rumors about his sexuality do stick, if people start to believe the truth about him.

Matthew can think of maybe a handful of queer men who've played hockey professionally. As for the NHL, there's only one player who's ever come out, and Jonathan Brinkley only did so *after* he retired. Matthew can't be the first in the league to play while out, and he definitely can't be the first to be linked with another man. Even if AB were into Matthew, which he's not, and even if he weren't on a dating hiatus, which he is, Matthew and AB could never be. There's too much in the league working against them. Hell, depending on the market, even his friendship with AB could be seen as a distraction if it got him more individual attention than the team.

"Are you *trying* to bend your fork?" Maddie says, cutting through his building haze of anger. "Or are you white-knuckling it for shits and giggles?"

Matthew drops the fork in the sink. It clatters loudly in the silence, and Matthew knows if Maddie doesn't ask him what's wrong soon, he's going to explode. "Shits and giggles, obviously."

"Right," Maddie says, but she still won't ask. She refuses to pry, and Matthew can't handle it anymore.

"Are you going to ask me what's wrong or not?"

"Oh, I know what's wrong, but you don't want to talk about it, remember?"

"You know I maybe have feelings for AB," Matthew snaps, angry at Maddie for throwing his words in his face. Angry at himself for being so damn stubborn the night before. Angry he still can't commit to saying he likes AB despite it only being him and Maddie. Angry that knowing what he wants won't make it possible to achieve.

"I'm going to disregard your snapping since this is a big life-changing realization," Maddie says, but her hurt still flickers deep in Matthew's chest.

"Sorry." Matthew deflates.

"Whatever," Maddie says, waving his apology off. "Now, do you want to talk about this or not? Because I'm not going to push you, and if you tell me to drop it again but start snapping at me when you're in another snit over it, I'm going to be pissed. If you want to talk, you have to start, Matty. You drew the line and I'm trying not to cross it, you jackass."

"Okay. Let's talk about it, then," Matthew says, leaning back against the counter and staring at the floor, his shoulders slumping with the weight of his emotions. "My feelings aren't the only problem here. This is so much bigger than that."

"Okay, tell me if I'm totally off base here, but this is about his fame, isn't it?"

Matthew doesn't answer, but he does look up from the floor. Maddie's eyes are narrowed. She's assessing him, picking at their link, and trying to work out what's the root of the problem. After a moment, a swell of sympathy and understanding surge through Matthew's chest.

"Ah, this is about hockey."

"Unfortunately."

She nods. "Makes sense why you didn't start truly freaking out until you two got spotted together. Before it was just a mild sexuality crisis—" Matthew snorts and Maddie rolls her eyes. "You know what I mean, mild compared to realizing wanting to date a guy might fuck with your career."

"I don't want to—"

"Okay, let's not do this. You can say you 'maybe have feelings' all you want, but it doesn't take Twintuition to know you *like* him. You think I couldn't *see* your disappointment the night he texted you about not falling in love? Come on; I didn't need our link to know it upset you. So, between you and me, let's stop pretending you don't know what you want because we can't work out a plan to get it if you don't."

"What do you mean? No amount of planning will make this work."

Maddie rolls her eyes. "Your newfound pessimism is killing me." She affects the voice of their mother. "Anything is possible with a plan, my dears."

"What's the plan, then?"

"For starters, you have to accept you like another guy."

Matthew takes a deep breath, steeling himself against a nonexistent attack. "Fine. I like a guy."

"Now we're getting somewhere!" Maddie says, smiling. "Seriously, I'm so proud of you. Admitting it was the hardest part for me."

"If only our coming-out stories could be twins, too."

"I don't know." Maddie grimaces. "I lost a whole best friend over mine, so maybe it's not as rosy as you remember."

"Fuck Robin," Matthew says.

"Fuck Robin," Maddie echoes, but there's no pain present; the adage is nothing more than routine at this point.

"If only admitting I have feelings for AB was the hardest part, then. He doesn't even— There's never going to be a me and him—even if hockey wasn't a problem."

"Why?"

"Well, disregarding the obvious—"

"What's the obvious?"

"Him making me promise not to fall in love with him? Him swearing off dating? Did you forget about those?"

Maddie waves her hand dismissively. "Oh, that's all for show."

"You've met him one time! How could you possibly know?"

Maddie shrugs. "I talk to Zoe and Reina a lot. Everyone's trying to get him to loosen up on that whole thing. And who better to call off your dating ban for than your maybe Bondmate?"

Matthew raises an eyebrow. "Oh, you've come around to Bondmates, then?"

"Not really. But if that's what it takes to talk you into wooing him, then yeah, I have."

Matthew stares at her, blankly. "You want me to woo AB Cerise."

"You say it like you don't think you can," Maddie says, a challenge in her voice.

"I know what you're doing. But baiting me to prove you wrong won't work here. He barely believes I'm going to stick around, and with my luck he probably thinks I'm only in it for the Bond."

"You've got to be kidding me. There's no way."

"Way. He's just now started to, like, believe me when I say I'm not going anywhere, and he's convinced I'm holding out for a romantic Bond—which he thinks he can't give me. And with my luck, if I was trying to write it off as lingering feelings about a romantic Bond, he's going to do the same thing."

"Trying to convince yourself you're not queer is normal, but it'd be pretty shitty if you told him how you felt, and he wrote you off as confused. Obviously, it'd suck to be nothing more than an experiment, but I hope he wouldn't try to delegitimize your feelings like that."

"Okay, but even if it's not about the Bond, even if he trusts me, I know the media attention is one of the reasons he's sworn off dating. He called it a *hassle*. I can't do anything about the inconvenience of it all. Can I?"

Maddie purses her lips. "So maybe we need a specific plan for the wooing, but we'll get that. I have faith you won't actually have a problem there."

"Your confidence is appreciated, but I think it's misplaced. I don't see how I'm getting around literally any of this. There's too much going against us."

Maddie ignores him. "I think the first course of action with wooing has to be convincing him you're not into him because of your Bond. Even if that's not a hang-up for him, it won't hurt to show him he's the apple of your eye. And to be honest, that's probably the easiest part of the wooing."

"Oh, really? Enlighten me."

"All you have to do is find another True Opposite."

"You say that like it's easy! Like it hasn't taken me this long to find AB!"

"Yeah, because you're a sappy romantic and wanted to find your Bondmate serendipitously! You refused to go on one of those dating apps that links people based on magic! All you have to do is sign up and find another Concealer."

"How is finding another Concealer going to help anything?"

"Look, I know you two had a super-intense initial Reaction, or whatever, but if anything Granny's ever said about Bonding is even remotely true, then you should still have a pretty strong Reaction with any or all Concealers, right? I mean, Aleisha wasn't even a Concealer and you still had a pretty big one with her. And Granny always said if there's a spark, there's a chance. So, if you put another potential Bondmate or two in the mix, and you still stick with him like a lovesick puppy, then how could he say you're not interested in him?"

Maddie has this pleased glint in her eyes and, amazingly, Matthew's mood is slightly bolstered by how contagious her satisfaction is, but he's still not convinced. "You really think it'll be that easy?"

"No, insecurities never are," Maddie says. "But I think it's probably a good idea and worth a shot. At its core, isn't Bonding about cementing an already strong connection between two people? Like, I know it's a fairy tale, but didn't Granny tell us about the two Convenients who barely felt a tug toward each other when they met but they fell in love and Bonded anyway?"

Matthew shrugs. "Yeah, I mean. I've always said it's about the feelings the people have. You're the one who said it sounded too much like fate."

"Whatever. My feelings on this don't matter. You and AB are the ones who need to be on the same page. And if he thinks Bonding is too fate-y, or thinks you're only interested in him as a potential Bondmate, then you have to put more people in the mix you *could* Bond with and still pick him."

"Let me get this straight: you're suggesting I download a dating app to try and meet people I want to be friends with so the guy I *do* want to date will know I'm serious about him?"

Maddie scrunches her nose. "Okay, right. Yeah, we should probably workshop the finding other Concealers thing."

"Probably is an understatement," Matthew says. "But you're forgetting AB's whole fear of people not being able to handle the attention ties directly into me knowing this'll never work because no one in the league is out. How can we possibly get around that?"

"That's step three."

"I appreciate your optimism here. I really do, Mads. But step three sounds a lot like you're suggesting I either change years and years of fucked-up hockey culture or get over it so I can have a boyfriend."

"That's not what I meant," Maddie says. "Step one is accepting you have feelings for a guy. Step two is wooing. Step three is risk assessment, duh."

"Risk assessment?"

"Yeah. Come on; you think Brinkley went his whole career without dating? You think there's no one else in this individuality-stifling league who likes men? You think you're the only man playing hockey who has to think about this?"

"Well, no," Matthew admits. "But I don't understand what you're getting at. Whoever Brinkley was seeing while he was playing was obviously easy to keep under the radar. Low-key isn't really an option with AB. I don't need to assess the risk—I know what it is. If the guys in the Miners' front office decide the attention I get, and in turn the team gets, from a relationship with him isn't conducive to the locker room—or whatever the fuck reasons any team ever concocts to make it look like something other than homophobia or racism or what-the-fuck-ever—it won't matter who our dad is, Maddie. They'll trade me. I highly doubt the goodwill I've garnered from being a Levoie is going to make any difference when it comes to homophobic locker rooms and guys unwilling to change. Some teams barely even try for the You Can Skate Pride nights, and when they do, fans get fucked up over the rainbow tape! How many teams do you think are going to want to deal with the fuss of having the first out guy actively playing and all the individual attention it comes with?"

Maddie's shoulders slump and she sighs, pinching the bridge of her nose briefly. "No, I don't think our name will save you from homophobia. And I don't think a lot of teams would. But you shouldn't have to choose a goddamn sport over someone you like. Over someone you hope to Bond with!"

"Jesus, Maddie. I know!" Matthew says. "If it weren't this way, I wouldn't care at all about the attention hanging out with him could bring. I can handle it when there's no chance of me and AB—when anything people assume *is* untrue. And I could handle it all if hockey wasn't on the table. I could deal with this if us dating never got out and there were no possible ramifications to my career because of it. And I'm getting ahead of myself, especially since there's no chance of this happening, but if the plan is to get me what I want—"

"Which is AB," Maddie interjects.

"Which is AB." Matthew's heart skips a beat, the admission coming a little easier this time around. Still, he's shocked and a little flustered dating a man is something he's even having to consider. Nothing in his entire life has prepared him for being bisexual—if that's even what he is. "Then how exactly do I meet an impossible goal?"

"It's not impossible, Matthew. It's just hard. And it shouldn't be. You absolutely should not have to be standing here debating whether the risk of pursuing this is worth it. That's the risk assessment I'm talking about. I know what you're up against. But at the end of it, you'll have to decide whether or not it's a risk you're willing to take."

"How can you possibly think I can make that kind of decision right now? We're not even dating! He's not even interested in me! It's one thing to decide I can handle some completely false rumors about us dating when there's no chance of it happening. But pursuing it—actually getting it—and having to constantly worry if it'll bite me in the ass? If people will see what's there and believe it. Maddie, I can't decide right now. I don't know."

"It's like you think I'm unprepared over here. Step three-A is plausible deniability, obviously."

"Step three-A," Matthew says. "You can't have come up with all of this on the spot—how long have you been coming up with this plan?"

Maddie shrugs. "I've been workshopping it since you got all moody when AB left. But it didn't come into true fruition until right now. You know how I am; going back and forth with you has really made things clearer in my mind."

"What exactly does plausible deniability even look like in this situation?"

"Okay, here's the thing. Before this, I loved AB. You knew this information, but don't worry; I've decided not to hold associating the greatest love of my life with my brother against you."

"The greatest love of your life?"

"Fine, my teens then. But parasocial bonds are no joke, Matty. That's not the point, though; the point is I forgive you for living my teenage dream."

"Thanks," Matthew says. "I appreciate it."

"You're welcome," Maddie says with a smirk. "But any-way, I've been a fan for a good minute and a half, as you know, so I can count on one finger how many guys the media have suspected AB of dating. And even *then,* they couldn't decide if Heath was AB's or Chloe's guy. And honestly, since Chloe, there's only been a few women he's been linked with. The main players are Heath and his best friend Gabby and then, of course, since he and Chloe are still friends, whenever they get spotted together it's a whole thing.

"But as far as the media goes, they're going to stick to rumors about him and women because...well, because they were the hottest couple there for a while, and everyone loves to forget bisexuals actually like the same gender, too, when they've been linked to a different one. And as for fans who are more prone to thinking he's dating a man—they largely want him to go public with Heath. Like, seriously, Matty, they want this so badly there's conspiracy theories about Chloe being a lie to hide their relationship even though both

Heath *and* AB are out and there would literally be no reason to hide it. It's a wild phenomenon, but since the media is pre-occupied with him and women and the fans are preoccupied with him and Heath, I'm pretty damn confident no one will assume anything if you two aren't loved up in public or out on super-obvious dates. The most the NHL will hear about this, if it even makes it to that circle of journalism, is that you have a famous friend. Which, again, if you're not out partying all the time, I think you'll be fine."

"Okay," Matthew drags out. "I'm confused what any of this has to do with plausible deniability."

"Well, Zoe was telling me AB's going into the studio with Heath next week, and with him in the mix, that'll distract fans from you. And then, I was thinking if you two join up with me, Zoe, and Reina often enough, I could probably throw some heat off you, too."

"So, what I'm hearing is your plan rests on the foundation of *you* being rumored to be dating AB."

"Yeah," Maddie says, looking to the floor for a moment. "It's not a perfect plan since I can't really predict what people will think! But it's there as a contingency plan for *if* it becomes obvious AB is into you once the wooing is under way. Like you said, we're working on very limited data here, so this could all be us doom and glooming. People might not even think you're a thing even when you're dating."

"So then, wooing would actually be step two, wouldn't it?"

"Maybe? Stop being so pedantic." But she gets an intense look of concentration on her face as she contemplates her steps. After a moment, she perks up, saying, "Okay step one: accept you're into AB—check. Step two: prove AB wrong—in progress. Step two-A: find other Concealers—possibly optional. Step two-B: provide plausible deniability for NHL homophobes. Step three: woo AB. Step three-A: see step two. Step three-B: to be determined. Step four: get your boy. Step five: Bond if possible."

"Where, in this very convoluted set of steps, are you accounting for AB being off the market?"

"Don't be obtuse. Getting past the dating ban falls under the umbrella of wooing. Duh."

"Of course," Matthew says. "How could I not know that?"

Maddie rolls her eyes with a groan. "See if I help you next time. This plan is a work of art."

"This plan is...a lot."

"That's why there's steps—only need to focus on one at a time! So first up is meeting new Concealers."

"Which is going to be a lot more work than you think," Matthew says.

"But the payout is going to be great."

Matthew takes a moment, really thinks about everything Maddie has laid out. There's no way he'll have the luck to make it through her steps without any hiccups, but there's a little well of hope forming in the depths of his heart and getting to have the Bond he's always wanted doesn't seem quite as impossible as it did when he woke up. Maddie's right—he's not the only guy in the NHL who's gone through this. And sure, none of them were ever linked to someone as famous as AB, but Maddie's made some good points here. With some careful planning, with a little manipulation of public perception, they could probably keep this a secret until he's ready to come out. It will be hard, but not impossible.

In the comfort of his kitchen, with Maddie there to bolster him, keeping his love life under the radar seems like the easiest part of the list. Everything else though, especially getting AB to reciprocate his feelings, seems unbelievably daunting. In all his childish fantasies about meeting his Bondmate, he never once considered he'd have to work against so much for their relationship to flourish. He never thought of this as fate nor expected love to be instantaneous and guaranteed, but he certainly didn't expect Bonding to be this hard.

"I hope so," Matthew says, and Maddie's face breaks in a radiant smile.

"It will! I'm manifesting it."

Chapter Fifteen

The problem with AB's self-imposed dating ban is Matthew, as Gabby so eloquently put, is damn near perfect. He's smart and athletic and artsy and so infuriatingly tempting. All of this, of course, would be fine if Matthew *is* straight. And of course, Matthew hasn't told AB anything to the contrary. But the evidence is starting to stack up in favor of Matthew having, at the very least, a little crush on AB. Which, if true, is extremely problematic for AB.

How can he ignore these annoying little daydreams about Matthew if there's a chance Matthew might want them too? But still, AB hasn't yet gotten to the point where his fondness for Matthew and his curiosity about magical Reactions has outweighed his commitment to never experiencing the tire fire that was the end of his and Chloe's relationship.

He wishes none of his friends would ever be subjected to the absurd things people come up with for clicks either. But over the years, AB's learned it's much easier to ignore, often downright amusing, when the dating rumors are complete lies about him and his friends. But the way even the truths about his relationships can be twisted into something awful is such a unique challenge for AB. He still can't believe the way a set of pictures of him arguing with Chloe over who was supposed to pack the sunscreen fueled months of breakup rumors. And then, when people don't like them together, if fans think he's better suited with someone else, then it's a hundred times more grueling.

Even though people loved him and Chloe together, dating under a microscope still had its downsides. And of course, public attachment to them as a couple only made the breakup worse. The media had been peddling the same rumor about their mutual friend, Heath Samara, coming between the two of them since the end of last year. Depending on the site, depending on the fan, depending on where they placed the blame for the relationship's failure, all three of them got unsavory things said about them.

But before people loved them, before they couldn't accept the split was amicable and they were very much still friends, before they were each pinned as cheating on the other with Heath, things had been a different kind of hell. At the beginning, before they'd even gone public, certain groups of their fan bases had separate problems with the prospect of them dating. Chloe's fans had grown fond of the chemistry she and her costar had during their recent press tour and didn't want to give up on her and Jackson one day being an item. As for AB's fans, they didn't agree with Chloe being a girl. She was his first, and only, public relationship, and though he'd always been quite openly bisexual, some of his louder fans insisted he should be with a man. The worst of them insisted Chloe was only there to make him more palatable to straight people. They insisted the relationship was a stunt to boost his popularity and distract people from men being his true preference. How people could deny his feelings for Chloe the entirety of their two-and-a-half-year relationship, or still be clinging to the same lie six months after their split, AB doesn't understand.

From start to finish, dating in the public eye is one giant headache. He loves Chloe and he will always look back on their time together fondly, but he can't do it again. Maybe when his fame starts dwindling, he'll give it another go. But this can't work. It won't work.

But see, AB is a reckless, impulsive asshole, and no matter how much he tries, there's a part of him that wants to take the risk anyway. Absolutely unhelpful is the irritating voice in the back of his mind—some amalgamation of Gabby, Reina, and Zoe shouting at once—insisting privacy isn't an impossible feat. Which is an entirely different headache altogether. People still being able to think he and Gabby are secretly dating is proof enough keeping a romantic relationship a secret would be an uphill battle. They wouldn't be able to go on dates; they wouldn't be able to be affectionate where someone might see; AB wouldn't be able to fly home with Matthew at his side; he wouldn't be able to bring Matthew on tour by himself. They'd be limited to time spent out with their friends or secluded to their places where they had the freedom to act as they pleased.

Still, they'd have to be careful leaving AB's house—the paparazzi who frequent his street in the morning could always catch them leaving. And since the only person he's even considered giving up his dating ban for lives with two other guys, they wouldn't even have an alternative for when they wanted to be alone. And then, on top of all the precautions they would take, there would always be the chance people could find out anyway. He and Chloe did all the same things at first and people still found out—who's to say his next relationship would be any better?

Except, he and Matthew have to be careful not to run into each other, given their magic. And it's been so long since the media even thought he was with a man. Hell, there'd been the guy in Paris over the summer, and Steven over the spring, and neither of those made even a blip on his fans' or the media's radar. And it's possible...of course it's possible. But is it worth it? Is Matthew worth it? He can't be sure Matthew won't be the same as Steven—won't use him for experience and then decide his life is too hard to handle. He can't be sure Matthew will even want to be with AB when coming out in sports is hard and keeping secrets is often harder. He can't be sure of anything, which makes it so much easier to not even try.

Unfortunately, AB can't stop thinking about Matthew's beautiful, perfect mouth and wondering if their lips would spark the same as their hands. He's been dreaming of the strength and breadth of their Reaction to each other since he fell asleep to the sound of Matthew's voice in his ears. He's tried to push it out of his mind, but now he's even more curious. Does every inch of their skin have the capability of sparking when they make contact? He knows heat radiates through their skin even with a layer of clothes; he knows they spark if their arms bump, but could this Reaction extend to every part of their bodies? That seems so impractical, so strange.

They're in AB's home studio when AB's brain-to-mouth filter shuts down and betrays him. AB's been staring at the same note on his phone for at least twenty wasted minutes, trying to expand a chorus he'd come up with at the beginning of tour into a full-fledged song, when the idea floods his brain. *They could always test it.* Matthew looks up from his sketchbook for a split second to ask AB how his song is coming along, and AB can't push the thought away.

He's smiling, because Matthew rarely stops smiling, and AB's breath catches a little. There's nothing particularly special about Matthew today—there's a smudge of graphite on his forehead and bags under his eyes—but AB hasn't seen him all weekend and apparently, to his gross, infatuated heart, that's a big deal. Matthew's smile is a soft, sleepy thing, and the dam straining to keep AB's feelings at bay cracks, and like the first time they met, the thought falls out without AB realizing it.

"What would happen if we kissed?"

Matthew drops his pencil and stares. His mouth is slack, his ears and cheeks burning. AB is so embarrassed by Matthew's obvious discomfort he's surprised he's not Invisible. He'd be more impressed by his control if it weren't for the hammering of his heart. Carson was wrong. AB was wrong. They were all so fucking wrong.

"What?" Matthew finally asks.

AB wishes he could take the words back but they're out there now, and there's no way he can twist them into a different meaning.

"Well, I was just thinking," AB starts, but how can he say he was thinking about kissing Matthew without telling him he was thinking about *kissing* him.

"About kissing me?" Matthew asks, the color on his cheeks spreading—soon his whole face will be red.

"Yes," AB admits. Matthew's eyes widen in shock, and AB continues before he can say whatever accompanies his expression. "I mean, not like that."

Matthew's eyes flash with an emotion AB must be imagining. Because Carson was wrong. Because AB was wrong. Because if Matthew isn't straight, he'll have to choose between Matthew and the barely there control of his media he's regained from not dating.

"I don't understand," Matthew says.

"Sorry, I didn't mean to make you uncomfortable—"

"I'm not uncomfortable," Matthew says, but he certainly looks it.

"Okay, good." AB forces a smile. "Good. Sorry to spring this on you with no warning, but I was thinking about our funky lightning magic and if it ever stops. Like, obviously our hands do, our shoulders, too, you know, our exposed skin if we bump into each other. And I know we don't really have to worry about it, but it seems a little impractical for there to be sparks everywhere we touch, don't you think? Say you weren't straight—"

This time Matthew's face clouds over with something complicated, maybe anger, and AB knows better than to continue. "Forget it, Matthew."

"No," Matthew says, the one syllable so much harder than Matthew has ever spoken to him. "Finish what you were saying."

"It's really better if you forget it," AB says.

But Matthew's face softens, and AB cracks as Matthew says, "Come on, Houston; I want to know. Please."

"Fine," AB says, heart beating painfully as he steps to the edge of a cliff he can't un-jump. "I was thinking, you know, if Bonding does end up being real, and we were romantically and physically involved—it'd be a little much to have electricity pulse when we kiss? For a lightning show to happen when we have sex. Don't you think that'd be ridiculous?"

"I haven't really been thinking about that," Matthew says. "But since you mentioned it... None of the women..." He shakes his head. "There was Aleisha whose sparks were yellow, but I only saw them the first time we touched. No one else had any color. At least none they could see, only the neon blue I see around all electricity."

"Are you telling me I'm the only person you've had sustained lightning magic with?"

Matthew smiles, but it's more timid than usual. "Yeah, strange, right? Kind of seems like—"

"Don't say it!"

Matthew's smile grows, his eyes twinkling ever so slightly. "I might win our little bet."

"That counts as saying it," AB says, refusing to acknowledge the nervous swoop his stomach does at the prospect of AB's magic being more Reactive to Matthew's than anyone else's.

"I think," Matthew says, his smile downright devilish now, "it counts as *insinuating* it."

AB rolls his eyes, and the momentary reprieve created by their jokes about Bonding is shattered, leaving them staring at each other in a tense, charged silence.

Matthew bites his lip, and the complicated pained expression from before is back. AB's breath catches as Matthew asks, "Do you want to try?"

"We really shouldn't," AB says.

Matthew bites his lips, eyes boring into AB's. "Why not?"

"Matthew," AB says, gripping the armrest of his spinning chair.

"Come on, Houston," Matthew says, standing up, taking a step to AB. "Do you want to kiss me or not?"

"It doesn't matter," AB says.

"It matters to me," Matthew says, taking another step closer.

How AB was ever foolish enough to think Matthew wasn't interested in him when Matthew is looking down at him with naked desire and unmasked hope, AB does not know.

"My answer will only make this harder."

"I'd like to kiss you," Matthew says. "Do you want to kiss me?"

AB closes his eyes and blows out a slow breath as the dam splinters and breaks.

He's going to have to choose.

Chapter Sixteen

Waiting for AB's answer, waiting for AB to open his eyes and answer him, waiting to find out if Matthew has completely fucked this up when Maddie had a *plan,* is the longest five seconds of his life.

"Don't make me do this, Matthew."

"Make you do what?"

AB's knuckles are white against the black leather of his chair. "You're making this very difficult for me."

"As if the last two months haven't been extremely difficult for me," Matthew says, careful to keep his voice level despite the pain starting to prickle behind his eyes.

"That's why it doesn't matter what I want!" AB's violet rots before Matthew's eyes. "I could *never* ask you to risk being outed before you're ready, and I can't make any guarantees because dating me sucks! Chloe probably wouldn't agree because she's the kindest person you'll ever meet, but it's hard. And going through all of it again? Going through people wondering if I'm cheating on you with Heath? People thinking being in a relationship with one gender means my interest in all others isn't real? Putting up with the way people will talk about you if they don't like you? Dealing with the way things are painted when they end? I don't want to go through any of that again. I told you, from the beginning, we couldn't fall in love! And I haven't changed my mind. I won't!"

"So, what? You're just going to fuck around until you fade into oblivion? Until the tabloids stop being interested in who you're sleeping with? You're going to swear off love because things might end? Because they might be *hard*?"

"That's the plan," AB says. "Yeah."

"That's a terrible plan," Matthew says, taking a step back, needing the distance to keep him from reaching his hand out and brushing AB's hair out of his face, to smooth the furrow in his brow away, to seek the comfort of their magic as his heart explodes.

"But my terrible plan," AB says with a huff of laughter, the color a miserable, dull magenta.

"Let me ask you this. If you weren't famous and I wasn't playing a sport with a deeply fucked up culture surrounding it and we could go out without worrying, would you let me take you on a date?"

AB is wide-eyed and flustered. "Right now?"

"Right now. Tomorrow. Whenever was best for you."

"Whenever is best for you," AB repeats under his breath, smiling at the floor. "You're making this impossible here."

"Answer the question."

"Why? We don't live in that world!"

"Answer the question, AB!"

AB's eyes widen, staring at Matthew like he's never heard his own name, and then he sighs, deflating on the exhale. "Yes."

"Okay," Matthew says.

"Stop smiling!" AB says, voice desperate and pained. "This isn't going to work! We still can't have this. We don't live in that hypothetical world. We live in this one. The one where paparazzi are vultures, and fans are too curious for their own good, and the media preys on their interest for clicks. And you, well, to be honest, I don't know shit about hockey, and I don't know how difficult it'll be for you. But I assume it'll be terrible since straight sports guys don't even want my banner hanging in their stadiums. So how could they possibly be okay with one of their own being queer? It's just easier if we don't even try."

"Then by your same logic it's easier if we aren't even friends."

"Oh," AB says, a spoiled, unpleasant purple. "I didn't— Fuck. Of course, the rumors annoy me, but they do eventually blow over when there's not an actual relationship involved. Or at the very least go dormant when a new, fresher story crops up. But— Shit. I wasn't thinking of the risk you're still taking or the fact you might not be able to wait out the rumors. I didn't realize any at all could be a problem for you."

Matthew is cold all over. He should've kept his mouth shut. "What are you saying?"

"I think," AB says, the sound the horrible, emotionless gray, "you should probably go home."

"And then what?"

"And then you go find yourself another Concealer you don't have to worry about any of this with. One you can have the easy, uncomplicated Bond you've always dreamed of."

"But I don't want someone else," Matthew says.

"But you can't take the risk," AB says, eyes closed off and distant.

"But—"

"But what?" AB says, his voice coming out in sharp, jagged bursts of icy lilac. "Is it not easier for us to no longer see each other? For you to forget this happened? For you to find someone who won't complicate your future?"

AB's words are a sharp knife to Matthew's heart. "You can't actually want— How could you want that?"

"Because two months of friendship, two months of whatever it is we're feeling, is a whole lot easier to move on from than having to deal with knowing we want the same thing while we can't do anything about it."

"But we *can* do something about it," Matthew says, pressing a hand to his eyes. It's really starting to hurt now. "You'd rather us be miserable than take any chance at all?"

"Yes," AB says, a lie if Matthew's ever heard or seen one. "I have experience— I know I can get over this eventually." Another lie. "And if you find another Concealer...if you find a girl you can have a romantic Bond with, and not have to worry about any of this with, then you can get over it too. And then, hey, maybe once you have, we can be friends again."

"Fuck the Bond!" Matthew says. "This isn't about the fucking Bond!"

"Are you sure?" AB says, eyes narrowed, cheeks flushed with anger.

"Yes, you fucking asshole," Matthew says. "I like *you*; I want *you*; there's not a single person I can imagine risking my entire fucking career for, and a Bond with someone else isn't going to change that. I'm here because of *you*."

"You're being serious," AB says.

"Yes."

"We still can't do this," AB says, his eyes glistening. "I'm sorry."

Matthew knows AB is lying. He has the most expressive sound palette Matthew has ever seen, and he knows nasty, gross, rotten purples can't mean he's telling the truth. But he's not going to change AB's mind today. He doesn't even know if he can. All Matthew can do is hope AB will let him know if he does.

"Okay," Matthew says, frustrated and defeated. "I'll be leaving then."

He gathers his things, and with a hand on the door to leave, AB says, "It was nice knowing you, Matthew."

He leaves without saying anything at all.

Chapter Seventeen

Four days have passed since AB pushed Matthew out of his life, and the tight, molten fist clenching around his heart since he told Matthew they couldn't do this has finally started fading to a phantom burn. He has thought of calling Matthew at least a dozen times since he left. But every time he got to the point of dialing, he chickened out.

AB's reasons haven't become irrelevant just because he misses Matthew. But fucking hell does he miss Matthew. Over the last two months, Matthew has become a bright, sunny spot in AB's life. He's been someone AB looks forward to seeing, someone he's started opening up to, someone who's helped him so much without even trying. AB knew Dr. Barnes wasn't lying to him when she said avoidance was making him so much worse, but he didn't expect her to be *so* right. He didn't think being around someone who once made him Invisible on such a large stage could halve his number of intrusive thoughts. He didn't think hanging out with Matthew could propel him so much closer to being able to Divulge to everyone, that their time together would ever get him to the point of viewing the final step in his and Dr. Barnes's plan as a *when*, instead of an *if*.

But AB is there. AB knows he's capable of staying Visible, even at his most emotionally volatile, in a room with someone who's one half of the Spontaneous Invisibility Equation, and he knows he's capable of Divulging. Eventually. But he doesn't need Matthew there to hold his hand as he does it. It would be selfish to drag Matthew into this ridiculous mediascape because he's helped him reach this level of certainty. He can't do it. He won't.

Besides, Matthew deserves someone more than AB. Someone who believes in Bonding, someone who will have faith he won't run away, someone whose existence won't affect his career, someone who is easier to be with. Matthew deserves someone who is not AB, who is better than AB. Someone who isn't a disaster.

He spends the first days after Matthew leaves ignoring Carson, ignoring Gabby, ignoring everyone. But Friday comes, and he has plans. Carson might have been considerate enough to ignore his miserable disposition, but Heath and Derek are not those people. And the bright, exuberant joy he gets when Heath sweeps him up in a bear hug for the first time in too many months isn't enough to cut through his bad mood.

They're not even out of the foyer before Derek pounces. "What happened with Matthew?"

"Nothing," AB lies.

"You're lying," Heath says.

"No, I'm not," AB says.

Heath rolls his eyes, obviously not buying AB's bullshit. "You know I can literally see the color of people's voices, right? Everyone's voice goes particularly wonky at certain times—like when they're afraid or lying—but yeah, everyone's colors are off when they lie. You're no exception, babe."

"You *what*?"

"Is your voice not a sound?" Heath asks, amused. "Can I not see sounds?"

"Well, yes," AB says, his thoughts everywhere at once. This isn't good. This is very much not good. "But I thought it applied to, like, music and animal sounds and I don't know—bird screeching! I definitely didn't expect you to be able to tell I was lying by the color of my *voice*."

Heath holds his hands up. "Whoa, what's wrong? Why are you taking this as a personal attack? I mean, it'd be obvious you were lying in this situation even if I didn't see sounds. But you're acting like I've just learned you're lying about your best kept secret instead of a poorly told white lie. What the hell is going on?"

"You didn't tell him about Matthew, did you?" Derek asks.

"No, he did not."

"I mentioned him," AB says, looking at the floor.

"When?"

"When I asked you if you knew anything about hockey!"

"How is *that* you mentioning him?"

"Matthew plays hockey at Columbia," Derek says.

Heath looks to the ceiling, grumbling. "I have obviously been away too long if you've gotten fucked up over an athlete." He moves toward the kitchen, calling over his shoulder. "I was prepared to dive right into writing, but if I have to deal with your shit, I need some coffee first."

"Knowing what I do about this situation," Derek says, trailing after him, "this conversation necessitates something much stronger than espresso, but since it's ten in the morning, I think a latte will have to do."

"You're catastrophizing!" AB calls after them. "Nothing's even wrong."

"You're lying," they say in unison.

AB can only deny this for so long. He lasts through Heath and Derek making their drinks. He lasts through four flights of stairs and into the studio. He even lasts ten whole minutes tapping away on the piano before their stares from the couch become unbearable.

"Okay," he says, turning his chair to face them. "Matthew and I...for lack of a better term, broke up."

"Y'all did what now?" Derek says.

"We're not going to be seeing each other anymore," AB says, the pain in his chest flaring.

"Why the hell not?" Derek asks, his tone the wrong side of angry now.

"It's not what you're thinking."

"Kind of sounds like the guy who came up to you and insisted you're Bondmates has gotten—"

"Wait!" Heath interrupts. "Back up. I'm missing way too much context here. Someone better tell me who the fuck this Matthew guy is in the next five seconds."

"He's a friend, and when we met, we sparked. He believes in all the legends, and as you know, I do not. But I—he saw me. And I was curious."

"What do you mean he saw you? AB Cerise, did you Display for a stranger?"

Heath's lips turn up in the beginning of a smile before he registers AB's face. "Wait, you really did? You never Display for people."

"Thus, the curiosity," Derek explains.

"But can't you see him Invisible?"

Derek rolls his eyes. "It's different for Immunes. Magic doesn't work on me, so if AB's Invisible right in front of me, he'll look the same as he does right now. Omnivisions have a magic of their own, so they see things differently. Or, well, I assume. AB hasn't really explained what Matthew saw."

"I haven't—well no. I did ask. But we had just met, and he was being all— He was being Matthew and I haven't brought it up again. But he knew I was Invisible, specifically Invisible, and not just a Concealer. So, yes. He saw me. And I was curious."

"An Omnivision?" Heath whistles. "I guess if Bonds ended up being real, this guy'd get one."

"So, if it's not what I think it is—"

"Which is what exactly?" Heath asks.

"That the straight boy got scared off by queer affection."

"Wait—you asked me if I knew anything about hockey for a *straight* athlete?"

"Yes," AB says.

"Again," Heath says. "What happened?"

"A mistake was made."

Heath frowns, his brow crinkling. "What kind of mistake?"

AB turns away again, playing the first few chords of "Dangerous." "We talked about kissing."

"I thought he was straight?"

"It was about an experiment."

"What?" Derek asks. "After Steven—"

"It's not like Steven! Steven was— Matthew's not Steven."

Which might be the worst thing of all—AB knows Matthew is nothing like Steven. AB doesn't think Matthew would use him up and spit him out. He can tell, no matter what happened, Matthew would try. He believes Matthew would give AB as much as he possibly could, that he truly means it when he says this is not about the Bond.

It would be so much easier if Matthew were an asshole like Steven, if he didn't feel Matthew's heart breaking in the depths of his own, if he didn't know Matthew would have stayed if AB didn't push him right out the door. This would be so much easier if AB were the only miserable one here, if he didn't know these feelings were mutual, if he didn't open his big, filter-less mouth and talk about kissing.

"I'll be right back," AB says, pulling out his phone.

"Where're you going?" Derek calls after him.

"I'll be back in a minute."

He makes his way to the roof and screams in frustration before calling Matthew. To AB's utter surprise, he answers on the third ring. He was expecting Matthew to screen his call. He wasn't prepared for talking *to* Matthew. He wasn't even planning on leaving a message.

"Um, hello?"

Matthew sounds equal parts confused and upset which only makes AB crack. "You should've told me you could see the color of my voice."

"That can't be what you're calling me about," Matthew says. "Because I've told you your voice is violet."

"Yes, but you didn't tell me it could *change*, that you could tell if I was lying from it."

"Are you saying you've been lying to me?"

Matthew sounds hopeful instead of upset and—no. They really shouldn't do this.

"You tell me," AB says, because telling another lie might break him completely.

"You've been lying to yourself."

"And you got that from the color of my voice?"

"From your voice, your face, your colors, from the ache in my chest when you told me to leave. You're a very bad liar, but if you're stuck on denying yourself what you want, I can't really do anything about it. If you don't want me—"

"You must know I want you," AB interrupts.

"Does it really count as knowing if all you ever said is we can't do this? That our feelings don't matter because you'd rather be miserable than take a chance? Because that doesn't feel like knowing at all to me."

AB's chest is ripping at the seams, unable to hold this pain anymore. He doesn't want Matthew to be miserable, but all his reasons are still there, rolling around in his head.

AB sighs. "I wish things were different..."

"But they're not."

"No, they aren't," AB says.

"So, we're right back to where we were at the beginning of the week."

"Seems so." AB presses the phone to his forehead.

Matthew begins to say goodbye, and AB's brain-to-mouth filter once again betrays him. "Wait."

Matthew doesn't hang up, but when AB doesn't say anything for a long beat, he sounds flustered as he asks, "What exactly am I waiting for?"

"Me?"

"Excuse me?"

"I'm sorry. I shouldn't ask you to wait for me. I take it back. I'm not being fair."

"Please stop jerking me around, AB. This isn't funny."

"I'm not trying to be funny," AB says, his heart hammering against his ribs. "I truly believe you'd be better off finding someone else to pursue this Bond with. This life isn't something you want to dive into. Dating me is only going to complicate your career—your life. But I like you and I don't want to be your Steven."

"I don't know—what does that mean? Who's Steven?"

AB huffs. God, everything always comes back to Steven. "Steven St. James, a guy who broke my heart several times over. My best friend who kissed me on a dare, a guy who stared at me in a grocery store until I had to run to the bathroom and hide because Invisibility was coming and I couldn't do anything to stop it. He's the source of my obsession about being Known and controlled. He's a guy who didn't speak to me for years, who brought me my favorite flowers and apologized with his words and his body and made me feel special. He's the guy who left me and came back and left me again. He is the source of all my trust issues. And you are not him, and I'm not trying to jerk you around, but I don't want to be someone who makes you feel like you're not worth *trying*."

"Steven sounds like a dick," Matthew says with a hard, protective edge to his voice AB certainly doesn't deserve.

AB snorts. "Gabby doesn't call him Steven Satan James for nothing."

A moment passes, AB's heartbeat fast, but calming. And then, Matthew asks, in a small, hopeful voice, "What do you want from me?"

"Can we ease into it? Can we go back to how things were? I need to reacclimate to—to the way people talk about me when I'm in a relationship, and you really need to sit down and figure out how much you can handle being in the press with me. And we—we really need to think it through before we go on an actual date, before we do anything. Because I don't want to—I refuse to do anything but sit and watch my very delightful baking shows before I can commit to you. I can't let myself be the same type of person Steven was. I can't sleep with you and then run away when everything gets too real and it's easier to flee than it is to stay and see what happens. I know there's no guarantees, but there's a difference between trusting you don't intend to fuck me over and believing whatever happens will be worth it if you do it accidentally. Which is so hard for me but...I like you, Matthew. Like, I'm so grossly fond of you and I want to—god, I don't know. I guess what I'm saying is, if you can give me some time to get my shit together, I'd like to try this."

Matthew lets out a long breath, and AB can imagine his shoulders relaxing as he says, "Of course. I'm a very patient person."

"Yeah, but I don't know how long it'll take, and this time I really mean it when I say I'll understand if you're not as patient as this might take. I know I'm asking a lot."

"AB." Matthew says his name so softly, so gently, AB has to bite his fist not to scream. "All I ever needed was for you to say you want this too."

Chapter Eighteen

The light, buoyant hope Matthew was filled with after his conversation with AB doesn't even last a full twenty-four hours. It's Saturday morning and he's slipping in a little extra studio time before his first full practice of the year when Cam comes up behind him to comment on his work.

"Well, well, well, young Matthew," Cam says over his shoulder. "This doesn't look half-bad." She points to the water-color recreation he did of AB's voice from Monday. "I love this one, actually. I'd ask if you broke up with your muse, but that would imply anything you've done before this was good."

Matthew turns around to look at Cam, who's dyed her hair bright yellow in the three days since he last saw her. "Nice hair."

She runs her fingers through the end of one of her low pigtails and rolls her eyes. "I insulted you and you gave me a compliment. You're trying to deflect, which leads me to believe you *did* go through a breakup or something." She looks absolutely delighted by this prospect, and Matthew groans when she pulls a chair up next to his workstation. "Tell me all about it. Who's the bitch who hurt my soft little Matthmal-low?"

"Don't you have work to do?"

"Oh my god," Cam says. "Does Finn know? He probably does, and I'm not above hanging out with him to get the scoop on you."

Matthew rolls his eyes. "I don't get you two. You look for the flimsiest reasons to hang out just to hook up and start the cycle all over. When are y'all going to make it official already?"

"Oh, Matthmallow." She bops Matthew's nose. "Where is the fun in that? Where is the *thrill*? But really, stop trying to distract me. What's your deal? Who's the girl?"

"There is no girl."

"I don't believe you. I saw you moping in class the other day." She runs her hand over the edge of his work, lips pursed. "This isn't a happy piece, babe. But see, you looked smitten, like grossly heart-eyed, earlier when you were looking at your phone, so I'm assuming things are turning a corner."

"Oliver sent me a video of a dog," Matthew says.

"Even if you were a good liar, I wouldn't believe you." Her gaze lands on what Matthew's working on, the vibrant pink of AB's laugh. "A dog's not what made you feel like this."

"No one said this was based on the dog video."

Cam snorts. "No, but if love's not what you're trying to evoke with this, then you've failed. Miserably."

"Appreciate the feedback."

Cam rolls her eyes. "No problem. If this shit's already seeping into your work, there's no way you'll be able to hold out forever. You're a gusher when it comes to love—you'll eventually burst."

She gets up and turns to head back to her station but then stops, tapping on Matthew's tabletop in quick succession. "I have an idea for your project."

"Yeah?"

"Magic, of course," Cam says.

"What do you mean?"

She rolls her head, looking to the ceiling for a moment, breathing deeply. "You know, for someone who sees the world in a way very few other people can—you never seem to show it off. Might tap into your world view a bit."

"How?"

"I don't know. I don't see what you see. But everything I'm doing this year is related to the manipulation of water. I don't see why you wouldn't use your Vision too. I'm sure you can tie it in with your study of emotions. Or you could give up on emotions all together and do something else. But—" She motions over the pieces inspired by AB again. "—these are good, so maybe stick with their inspiration for a couple more." She shrugs. "I don't know. You figure it out."

"These are—uh, sounds I can see, actually."

Cam arches a brow. "Well look at that; you have been tapping into your magic for inspo without me realizing. Good for you. Push it further now."

"That's a really good idea, Cam. Thanks."

She smiles as she turns to leave. "Yeah, I know. That's why I said it."

Matthew thinks of the colors of the world. The metallic shimmer of the different categories of magic being used and the crisp platinum of Immunes, so different from the warm signatures of all the others. How the brassy sheen of Convenients is as familiar as the golden aura he's always faintly aware of coming off his own person, but the only reason he knows the Immune signature is because he scoured an Omnivision subreddit after meeting Derek on Oliver's birthday to see if anyone else had seen the elusive color before.

He thinks of the white wisps of wind in the air, of the barely there blue of snow landing, of the midnight blue of skates slicing against ice, the neon-red slap of a hockey stick, and the charcoal gray of a puck sliding on ice versus the powder gray of it moving through the air. Of Maddie's warm, vibrant green and the bright, sunshine yellow exclusive to her laugh. Oliver's serene blue and Zeke's champagne gold—the only person he's ever seen whose voice shimmers like magic. And then he thinks about how there's no one he's ever seen with as detailed of a color profile as AB's. How he's never been able to tell so much from someone's sounds—not even with a shared lifetime spent learning all the subtle nuanced changes of Maddie's green. No one is as expressive as AB; no one's colors change as drastically as his, not even when they're shifting between whispering and shouting. Matthew would think it's proof of their potential to Bond—that True Opposites really do have more of a chance—but AB's voice didn't have this much depth in the beginning.

Things didn't start changing until AB got back from tour. With his three distinct colors, AB's palette has always been more intricate than other people's. But since the dinner he first noticed the deep purple Matthew's been chasing ever since, AB's colors have become richer, more expressive than ever. Over the years, Matthew has noticed some things—like lying and anger—work to change the way Matthew perceives a voice no matter how level or controlled the tone is. When Maddie lies, her sound ripples ever so slightly, but the green remains the same. When Derek gets upset, his gold turns flat, the shimmer seeping out like he's lost his glow. When Oliver is angry, his voice goes ice blue whether he's shouting or whispering. Small shifts he's come to understand with time, things he's picked up over the years of being an active participant in their lives.

But AB is different than what he knows. AB's colors don't vary on the same light to dark scale everyone else's seem to. Lately, Matthew has noticed how his base violet—a bright, vibrant color—is prone to drastic jumps and changes. None as obvious as when his voice deepens into the rich, royal purple Matthew loves to see or the sickly green-and-yellow hue his purple takes on when he's upset. He isn't sure, because he didn't think the greater understanding of someone came until *after* the Bond took hold, but the only correlation he sees, the only thing he can come up with, is that his magic is growing as his feelings for AB do. The way their magics React must be transforming the way he *sees* AB—even outside of his Invisibility.

The growing depth of AB's color isn't the only odd development to come from the two of them getting closer. There was the moment where all input seemed to fade, the only thing registering in Matthew's Vision being AB. How Monday, before everything got fucked up, Matthew's usual headache was nonexistent—how for the first time ever he'd been completely ache free without any Healing from his sister or father. But the oddest of all, the thing Matthew hasn't stopped thinking about since, is the searing, foreign pain he'd been pierced with when AB was his most upset.

All signs point to Bonding being real, to his and AB's starting to form, and Matthew should be elated. He should be over the moon with joy. But he can't shake what Cam said. He's terrible at keeping his love for people a secret, and he has no idea how he's going to keep a developing Bond to himself. He's warming to Maddie's idea of plausible deniability; trying to get comfortable with the lengths they'll have to go to keep their names from being linked together in any meaningful way. But what if he does slip up? What if they take every precaution, even now when AB won't commit to anything different, and people still find him out? What if Matthew is *obvious*? What if people don't even think AB is interested in him, but they take one look at Matthew and can *see* how much he feels for AB? What if he falls so hard the results of the crash are visible from space? He doesn't know what makes him sicker, the idea of coming out to the NHL or how much effort it already takes to not accidentally touch AB's skin and how monumental a task keeping this secret will be in comparison.

The reality of this not being a problem if he were another straight guy playing hockey, that the NHL wouldn't give a shit if he was seen in the news looking at any number of women any sort of way, stresses him out so much even the mention of queerness in the vicinity of hockey sends him into a mild panic.

"I've got a good feeling about this year," Finn calls to the room before turning to Matthew with his sharp, teasing smile. "You think you can take five minutes out of your post-workout murder-eye goalie shtick to tell them about the month's hottest party, or do I have to do it?"

"My eyes are perfectly normal after a workout," Matthew says, slapping Finn on the arm with the back of his hand and standing up. The team's in a state of half undress; Matthew himself still hasn't taken his knee pads off, which isn't uncommon, but with everything going on, with his attraction to AB at the forefront of his mind almost constantly now, Matthew is suddenly aware of the nakedness in a way he wasn't before. He gives his head a little shake and clears his throat. This isn't the time.

"So, for those of you new here," he says, looking at the freshmen in the group. "My parents put on this massive, over-the-top Halloween Masquerade charity event every year—and as my father pointed out, Halloween is finally on a Saturday, and no one has to worry about my mom trying to make us get all dolled up on a Wednesday."

At the mention of his father, the new guys perk up a little more and Matthew very dutifully does not roll his eyes—they all eventually see him as Matthew, their goalie, and not Matthew Hellman-Levoie, son of the great and legendary Andre Levoie. "Anyway, every year, my parents rotate between charities and outreach programs for arts and sports. It's usually a pretty fun time, and you're all invited, but don't stress if you can't make it because it's not obligatory. You absolutely won't be offending anyone if you have better plans for a Saturday night."

"Okay, well that's a lie," Finn says. "It's totally a mandatory team event."

"He's not being serious," Matthew says. "Coach isn't going to bag skate you if you don't show."

"I might, though." Finn laughs. Then he stands and puts his hands on his hips. "But seriously, please make a concentrated effort to show up. The Hellman-Levoies do a spectacular job putting this thing on every year and are generous enough to donate on ours and the women's team's behalf, so we get the opportunity to network with a bunch of hella rich and influential people. So, if going to an event held to raise money for a campaign working to better *our* sport isn't enough of an incentive, think of all the famous people you might run into. Wasn't Abigail Hemmings there last year?"

"Nah, that was our freshmen year," Matthew says. "When it was the music therapy thing."

"Oh, right," Finn says. He waves his hand dismissively. "That's unimportant because you still need to show up. It's the night of a game so Matty and I will be going over right after, and if you don't follow, I'll fester on it until Monday, and no one wants that, do we?"

A chorus of nos ripple around the room, lighting up Finn's face. "Besides, it's for a good cause."

"Which is?" Nolan asks. "Neither of you said."

"Oh, uh." Matthew falters, he can't remember. "It's a sport's turn this year. Hockey, specifically, as Finn said earlier."

"God, Matthew," Finn says. "Do you ever read the emails your mom cc's us on?"

"My mom cc's you on emails?"

"Literally every year about this event," Finn says, his put-on surprise morphing into amusement. He turns back to the room. "It's for You Can Skate this year."

Fuck. No. The pain behind Matthew's eyes jolts up, his heart beats erratically. You Can Skate can't be this year. There's no way this is happening *this year*. Shit. Finn's voice is coming from a haze beside him, the chatter growing as the team discussing the event comes across as static, and the only thing Matthew can focus on is *Brinkley* being there. Goddammit.

There's a snap next to Matthew's ear. He turns to see Finn staring at him expectantly. The room's beginning to clear out, the team's focus no longer anywhere near Matthew, but his head still hurts, and Matthew worries if his mind doesn't stop reeling soon someone's going to be able to tell what he's thinking. "What did you say?"

"Are you okay, man? You've been pretty spacey today. More than you usually are after a practice."

"Yeah, I'm fine. Got a lot on my mind."

Finn's brow furrows in concern. "You want to talk about it?"

"Fuck, no," Matthew laughs. "What were you asking?"

"Oh, right. I ran into Cam on the way to practice, and she had some pretty interesting things to say."

Matthew snorts. "As if anything you and Cam do is serendipitous. Until you two sort your shit out, nothing she says about my love life is discussable."

"Then you won't be bringing a date to this thing? You're willingly resigning yourself to a night of small talk with the Rigsbys because you don't want to talk about your new girl."

"There's no girl to talk about," Matthew says. "But who knows, maybe if you get your head out of your ass and ask Cam, I'll find someone to bring."

Finn narrows his eyes. "I don't know if you're banking on me not having the nerves to ask her, or if you think her disdain for all things sports will outweigh her desire to meet your new girl, but either way, we'll see you there, man."

"You won't," Matthew says.

"I might," Finn says, flustered. "The odds are definitely more in my favor than yours. It's been a minute since you thought you found a Bondmate; like hell either of us are missing out on meeting her."

"Who said anything about Bondmates?"

Finn rolls his eyes. "Bro, come on."

"Whatever," Matthew huffs. "It doesn't matter. There's no way you're asking Cam."

"Never known you to set yourself up for failure," Finn says.

"I'm not," Matthew says, the bubbly joy of riling Finn up about Cam making more of a dent in his panic than expected.

But once they part ways, and Matthew is alone, the panic settles back over him. His dad, as usual, is going to want to take him around and introduce him to all the athletes in the room. There's no way to avoid a face-to-face encounter with Brinkley at an event hosted by his dad and for a campaign so important to Brinkley himself. God, will he be able to tell? Will he look at Matthew and recognize himself? Will he see what Matthew's hiding because he knows what it's like? He's going to have a hard enough time keeping his shit together in a room with a man who knows exactly what Matthew is going through without bringing AB. If Finn follows through on the challenge, he's going to have to figure out a way around this, maybe bring someone else, because there's no way Matthew can even be in the same room as AB and Brinkley. He'll take one look at him and be able to tell. Brinkley will know.

But Brinkley isn't going to be the only one who can tell. Cam was right: Matthew is beyond obvious about matters of love—especially when it comes to Bonding. He doesn't know how he expects to be able to tuck AB away from people and be okay with it. How he's even going to keep this growing, magical warmth to himself when all he wants to do is tell people about AB and the way he makes him feel. But Matthew doesn't think he's ready; he isn't sure he'll ever be able to come out—if he'll ever work up the nerve to even tell his dad what he's realized about himself. *Fuck,* Matthew thinks on the train home. *This is a hell of a month to realize I'm into men.*

Chapter Nineteen

By the time he and Maddie make it down to Tribeca for their first-Sunday-of-the-month brunch with their parents, they're late and Matthew's flustered.

"What'd AB send you this time?" Maddie asks.

"Nothing."

"Lies! You're all frazzled, and it's not because we're late," she says, striding out of the elevator and to their parents' door.

"I'm not frazzled," Matthew insists, following Maddie inside.

"Was it a selfie?" Maddie asks. "It totally was. Let me see!"

"How do you know it's a selfie?"

"Because it's always a selfie!"

"It's not important."

Barring the three days Matthew thought he might never see AB again, AB has sent him at least one selfie a day—several of which feature his friends. So, really, Matthew getting a photo from AB on their way here isn't a big deal. Neither is today's photo being one of him and Chloe Lutz. So, what if she's America's darling and AB's ex? Why should it bother Matthew? It's not important. It doesn't matter.

Matthew has his key in the door, but Maddie stalls him with a hand on his shoulder. "Hey, what's actually wrong here? Who're we jealous of?"

Matthew shakes out of Maddie's grip and opens the door "Mom! Dad! Sorry we're late."

Andre looks at his watch as Matthew steps into the living space. "Only fourteen minutes." His gaze flicks to Vivian and then back to Matthew, a wide grin taking over his face. "Two more and your mom would've gotten the first éclair, but alas."

"I don't know how I feel about you two wagering on our tardiness," Maddie says as she leans in to kiss Vivian on the cheek before taking the seat next to her.

Matthew whispers an apology as he presses a kiss against his mother's temple and then sits across from Maddie.

Andre turns to him, a flash of concern clouding his expression as his gaze darts over Matthew's face. For a dreadful moment Matthew thinks he's going to question him about his mood and Matthew is going to be forced to lie straight to his parents' faces about what's weighing on him, but then Andre cracks a smile. He turns to Maddie with a glint of mischief in his eyes and says, "Anything before fifteen is on time as far as you two are concerned. So, technically—" He tips his champagne glass at Vivian. "—your *mother* wagered on you being late. I didn't."

Vivian rolls her eyes and the knot in Matthew's stomach loosens. He can get through brunch with his family. He knows he has nothing to worry about. He knows AB wouldn't tell Matthew to give him time just to get back with his ex... He's still a little queasy about it anyway. But his parents won't assume his mood is about a *guy,* so all he has to do is talk about the masquerade without turning green, and he's scot-free. He can figure out a time to tell them later—he doesn't have to come out today.

Except when the topic of Halloween does come up, his mother surprises him. "So, are you two bringing any plus ones this year?"

Maddie laughs, taking a long sip of her mimosa. "Subtle, Mom."

"I wasn't trying for subtlety. I'm curious about the current state of love in your lives."

"Much to Tristan's dismay—" Maddie starts.

"Wait!" Matthew says, the tension momentarily replaced by shock. "Derek was serious? You've been hanging out with him again?"

"Key word: *hanging*," Maddie says. "It's not unheard of for us to have some of the same classes with the whole 'meeting in a prereq for our same major' thing."

"Are you two getting back together?" Matthew asks.

Maddie furrows her brows, and Matthew realizes he might be using her as an outlet for his Chloe-shaped frustrations.

"Sorry, was surprised Zeke might be right for once," Matthew says. "Carry on, much to his dismay..."

Maddie watches him for a moment, assessing, and Matthew concentrates on pushing a burst of love through their link as another layer of apology. She rolls her eyes but smiles at the gesture. "As I was saying, much to Tristan's dismay—who has not been subtle about wanting to tag along this year—I've actually been thinking about bringing a friend. A girl I've been hanging out with a lot. If that's fine?"

"Yes, of course," Vivian says, absolutely beaming. "Both of you know. You can bring anyone you want."

"A friend? Or something..." Andre's face lights up and he wiggles his eyebrows dramatically. "More?"

"God, Dad," Maddie laughs. "We haven't labeled anything yet. But I think you're going to love her. She's fun. Very, uh, unpredictable?" Maddie's eyes flash with barely contained amusement as she turns her focus on Matthew. "It'll be a real treat watching Zoe interact with your team. She's going to eat Finn and Jamie alive."

"Zoe?" Matthew says, his mouth working faster than his brain. "As in the drummer from AB's band Zoe?"

"Yes," Maddie says. "And honestly, if you don't capitalize on your plus one, I might bring Reina too."

Maddie gives Matthew a look he doesn't understand until his mother asks, "Who's AB?"

"A friend," Matthew says at the same time as Maddie.

"Oh." Vivian smiles. "So more than a friend, then."

"What? No," Matthew says, futilely. He's a terrible fucking liar. "A friend."

Andre's gaze is piercing. "Is this why you've been upset today? Having dating troubles?"

"I'm not upset." But Matthew doesn't sound anywhere near convincing enough.

"Oh, honey," Vivian says. "I should've realized when you barely touched your food." She waves her hand in the direction of Matthew. "This is your forlorn about Bonds mood."

"My what?" Matthew says, managing an actual laugh.

"You are a tad obvious about your love life," Andre says, not realizing how much that fact has been haunting Matthew.

"Where matters of love are concerned," Vivian says, unknowingly twisting this knife. "You wear your heart on your sleeve. An open book, even."

"Mom," Matthew whines.

"What? I don't mean it in a bad way."

"No of course not," Maddie says. "But—uh—"

Matthew can tell she's trying to help, but she's not sure how and Matthew doesn't know either. He shouldn't have mentioned AB in the first place. Especially not in the context of Maddie having someone she's interested in. Of course, his parents would want to know. "AB is—" He swallows hard.

"Not much of a believer in Bonds," Maddie says when Matthew doesn't finish his thought, relief flooding him at Maddie's save.

"Ah, well," Andre says, his eyes only losing some of their questioning sharpness. "That does seem to be your eternal struggle."

"Yes." Matthew shrugs. "But we're making some progress."

"Really?" Andre asks, his pointed gaze giving way to surprise.

"Oh, not so much on the belief thing, but our magics are pretty Reactive so I think—and I know this kills Maddie inside—but I really think Granny's been right this entire time."

Maddie rolls her eyes. "You've always believed her! This means nothing."

"You're just upset I've been blessed with a True Opposite, and you haven't."

"With the headaches you get? Absolutely not! I'll stick with Healing, thank you very much," Maddie says. "Besides, I don't need a magic spark to direct me to people. I'll meet them on Tinder like god intended."

"Speaking of meeting," Vivian says. "When do we get to meet this AB of yours, Matthew?"

"Oh uh—" Matthew can do this. He can skate by this conversation without giving himself up. He just needs to breathe. "I'm not sure we're anywhere near the meeting-the-parents stage yet, Mom."

"Oh, fine," Vivian sighs. "Maybe we can meet her at the gala then."

Matthew closes his eyes for a moment too long, his shoulders tensing.

"Viv," Andre chides gently, looking to Matthew with a small reassuring smile before deflecting on his behalf. "We don't even know how long they've known each other."

Vivian shakes her head, holding her hands up in surrender. "All right, all right. I won't get ahead of myself. I'm just excited about the gala this year! I think this one's really important."

"Yeah," Matthew manages to say through the tightening of his throat—circling back to You Can Skate is no better a topic than AB. "Finn's told the team it's mandatory."

Vivian laughs. "Well, that's unnecessary. Though the sentiment is appreciated."

"To be honest, I'm glad he took that stance as captain," Andre says. "Even if Finn would do the same for this event no matter the charity—being adamantly supportive of this project, in particular, sends a good message to the new guys on your team."

Matthew looks to Andre, shocked by his conviction. "You think so?"

"Yeah, you know what flies out there. You know what kind of environment some of these guys are coming from. It takes more than a handful of guys using Pride tape in warmups to change the culture. We need captains and coaches from top to bottom to send a clear message they won't be tolerating hate of any kind if we ever expect to get to where women's hockey is right now." His gaze lands on Maddie. "I'm so glad you have several women, Olympians even, who you can look up to and show you there is a space for you in this sport."

He turns to Matthew, this fierce, unnerving look in his eyes. "I want the same thing for men."

Matthew's heart constricts. His dad can't possibly know, can he? He wasn't too obvious when his mother assumed AB was a girl, was he? No, she would've caught on, too, if he was. She's way more perceptive. No, this is Matthew being paranoid. He's on edge and thinks everyone can see right into his heart, but they can't. His parents don't know his emotions the way Maddie does. They're just his parents. They have years of experience and instinct to work with, but his dad can't possibly know he's saying he wants a better sport *for* *Matthew*. There's no way.

Andre's shoulders slump as he sighs heavily. "We had lunch with John Brinkley last week—he's been really involved with getting this set up this year. And you know, I didn't think him coming out would change the league overnight, but I was hoping, at this point, we'd be past guys getting suspended for using slurs on the ice."

"Yeah," Matthew says, at a loss for words. "Uh, yeah, we definitely should be past that. Not that, I mean, throwing slurs around on the ice shouldn't have been happening in the first place, but yeah. Guys shouldn't have to worry about their careers being affected if they come out before retirement. They shouldn't have to worry about harassment. But I don't know—" Matthew shrugs. "It seems impossible sometimes."

Maddie catches his eye, and he's hit with a surge of concern and sympathy, the force of the two making him squirm. He hates this. He hates having it laid out in front of him how hard this is going to be for him. How his choices are silently dealing with the casual, and often outright, homophobia guys in the league spew or come out and deal with the same things targeted at him, specifically.

Life was so much easier when he was a straight guy telling other straight guys to fuck off for being a bigot. Being a bisexual—pansexual? queer? don't-have-a-fucking-clue-xual?—guy having to worry about sounding a little too defensive when telling them to fuck off is not where he expected to be in life. Matthew hasn't cried since they got gold at World Juniors, and he hasn't cried because he was upset since knocking his water cup over on a newly finished painting the night before it was due freshman year, but having to decide between the rock and the hard place that is liking men in the NHL has him on the brink of tears already.

Revisiting key pieces of his life with the understanding he likes men has been hell enough. Matthew would've preferred to never unlock the knowledge his jealousy over his

NTDP teammate dating his billet family's daughter had nothing to do with Matthew wanting to spend more time with Katie and everything to do with Tyler not having as much time *for Matthew* outside of hockey. He could've gone forever without realizing his interest in watching his favorite goalies' postgame interviews had nothing to do with goaltending and everything to do with how they looked. But needing to figure out all this shit with hockey and his sexuality is not how he wanted to spend his senior year. Or ever, actually.

He's so worked up about the internal debate that when he and Maddie leave in the evening, his dad pulls him aside to ask, "Matthew, are you all right? You've been super off today."

He goes to put his hands in his pockets but stops—dropping them. Andre notices the nervous tic anyway and raises his eyebrow.

"I'm fine," Matthew says.

Andre purses his lips. "You clearly aren't." He holds his hand up. "It's fine if you don't want to tell me. You don't even have to talk about specifics, but this is about more than Bonding, yes?"

Matthew huffs. "Bonding is actually, funnily enough, the least of my troubles right now. AB is—well, it's nothing and I know it's nothing. But he's out with his ex, and we're not actually a thing yet, and I'm getting worked up for nothing because I don't think they're going to get back together, but I'm feeling a little insecure about it anyway, I guess.

"Did you say he?"

Matthew furrows his brow. "What? No, Chloe is a she."

"Not the ex," Andre says gently, like he's suddenly talking to a caged animal. Matthew's face burns, his stomach drops and his heart ramps up painfully fast.

Is he breathing? Is this what it's like to die? He can't have outed himself to his father in real, actual life. There's no way he slipped up. He must be dying. He'd done so well all day. How did this happen? How did he let this happen? Fuck.

"I'm not—this isn't—" Oh. He's properly panicking now, and when Andre goes to clasp his shoulder in a gesture of comfort, Matthew flinches away. "I misspoke. I didn't mean—"

"Matthew," Andre says. So gentle. So delicate. As if using his regular voice will shatter Matthew to pieces. Which...considering...he might. "You can talk to me."

"There's nothing to talk about," he says, walking backward toward the door. "Really. You know me." He raises his fingers in a peace sign and what? Where the hell did that come from? "Lover of ladies over here. Just an honest slipup. Nothing to see here. Nothing to worry about."

"It *is* nothing to worry about," Andre says. "You don't have to keep this to yourself."

"Come on, Dad," Matthew says, his already fractured veneer crumbling. "You know that's not true."

"You don't want to tell me because of hockey," Andre says, his voice flat.

"There's nothing to tell," Matthew says, hoping his expression conveys how much he needs his father to drop this right now.

"Okay," Andre says.

Matthew turns to go again, ready to run, when his father's words stop him in his tracks.

"If there's ever anything to tell—I'm going to help you in whatever way I can, Matthew. There will be a place for you in hockey."

If his eyes are watering—which they aren't—no one sees. He doesn't look back or acknowledge his father, which he'll be guilty about in approximately seven minutes, and by the time he meets Maddie at the elevator he's pulled himself together.

This is fine.

Everything is fine.

He's definitely not having a full-fledged panic attack.

That's not a thing he has. Nope. Definitely not a Matthew thing.

He's fine.

Really.

Except, Maddie and their goddamn Twintuition never let anything be.

"I take it," Maddie says when they exit the lobby of their parents' building, "this is no longer about whatever AB texted you earlier. But if I'm reading this right—" She motions toward Matthew's tense shoulders and stricken face. "—this is about AB *and* hockey. Which under general circumstances I would understand, but my panic-echo was not this severe when Dad was monologuing about how much the NHL still needs to change. But whatever you two talked about back there took it up to apocalyptic levels. So, what, exactly, happened?"

"Dad knows" is all Matthew manages to get out before a wave of nausea crashes over him.

"What do you mean Dad knows?" Maddie asks. "I know you've been a little skittish today, but there's no way he picked up on—" Her gaze flicks to Matthew, her lips pursing. "—your sexuality revelation. And you were very careful to only refer to AB as AB. Are you sure you're not just being a little jumpy? I mean, I understand worrying everyone knows just by looking at you. But they can't, Matty. They can't actually tell."

He's so tense about this whole ordeal, so petrified of his secret getting out before he can tell it himself, he refuses to answer Maddie's questions the entire way home. But he doesn't stop her when she walks the two blocks past her building to follow Matthew to his.

They don't make it past the entrance of the door before everything comes spewing out.

"I fucked up, Maddie. I fucked up and now he knows. Dad knows! I was talking about AB being out with Chloe Lutz—the selfie he sent me was of the two of them together! Because, of course, the day we're seeing Mom and Dad and talking about You Can Skate is the day I choose to get fucked up over a picture of AB and his gorgeous ex-girlfriend! Because apparently irrationally worrying about AB getting back together with his ex is a thing I do. Which would be a problem on its own but is now barely even the tip of the iceberg. Because the real problem here is Dad knowing. Why is everyone in our family so damn perceptive all the time? I'm surprised Mom didn't get to me first. But he saw I was upset and cornered me before we left, and I was telling him about AB and I slipped up. I said AB was out with *his* ex, and now Dad knows."

"What did Dad say?"

"I told him he misheard."

"Matthew," Maddie says and it's not a reprimand, but it might as well be.

"Yeah, he said the same thing. And then he said if there *was* something to talk about, he'd help me anyway he could. Said he'll make sure there's a place for me in hockey. But how can he say that? He doesn't know. And no one does. Fuck, John Fucking Brinkley doesn't even know. He's spoken, rather recently, about how he doesn't know if the NHL is ready for an out and active player. And I don't know how I'm going to stand in a room with Brinkley knowing I'm going to have to do exactly what he did. I don't think I can take on the massive amount of responsibility and pressure and scrutiny that will come with being the first one to be out while playing in the fucking NHL, and if I can't handle it, then I'll have to sit there and—"

Matthew breathes in, heavy and ragged. "I'm going to have to endure the same sort of shit but directed at opponents or at me but not *at* me. And, to be honest, is that any better? Because then I'll know for certain who will be a problem for me if I ever *do* want to go public with this information. And I'm already tired, Maddie. I've been thinking about this for, like, two weeks, and I'm already fed up and frustrated. How can I—how am I going to do this my entire career?"

"I don't know, Matty. I don't—" She pauses, her lips pursed. His chest echoes with her empathy and concern. "What do you want me to say? Do you want me to tell you to come out? Do you want me to tell you you'll be able to do it? Do you want me to convince you to say fuck hockey and the NHL and be an artist instead? What do you need at this moment?"

"I don't know!" he snaps. "I don't know," he says again, quieter, more level. "How did you decide to come out?"

Maddie shrugs. "It's different in women's hockey. Obviously, it isn't a utopia and work still needs to be done, but it's definitely not the same as men's hockey. You're wading through an absolute cesspool with concrete shoes whereas I was diving into toxic water inhabited by enough other rainbow fish to know I wouldn't be alone. I knew I wouldn't be the first. Knew I wouldn't be taking on the incredibly daunting task of being a groundbreaker. I knew if, by chance, I did have bad experiences I wouldn't have to weather anything silently or alone, and I'd have people who understood me and what I was going through."

"There wouldn't—I wouldn't really have that."

"No," Maddie says, frowning. "I mean—you'd have Brinkley but—"

"But no one in the league."

"Someone always has to be first."

"But it doesn't have to be me."

"No," she agrees. "But Brinkley did pave the way for you in a way. It—" She purses her lips again. "It would be a lot. I won't sugarcoat it. But I think—" Another pause. "You have the benefit of being a legacy."

"You think that'll make it easier? You really think being a legacy will keep me from being harassed? You think it won't make people say ridiculous shit about me tarnishing the family name?"

"No, but people already think we're tarnishing the good name by *me* playing Dad's position, Papa's position, *Great-*Grandad's position, instead of you. They already think you're being selfish by getting a degree before going pro. The problem with being Dad's kid is you're going to be scrutinized more than others, but it also gives you an advantage."

"How? Because you literally just said I'm going to face scrutiny for being a fucking Levoie on top of all the vitriol I could get for coming out, and that doesn't seem like an advantage, Mads."

"No, that's not—" She grimaces. "I shouldn't have said it like that. Let me start over. I'm trying to say that unlike Brinkley, an undrafted fourth-liner, you're a number one draft pick—the first goalie to go first overall in, like, twenty years. Not only are you a fourth-generation hockey legacy, Miners fans have been going absolutely feral over you, you're also disgustingly talented. People want you to play for them! You had Canadians bitching about you being American born the first time you played for Team USA. It won't be easy, and you'll probably face different types of bullshit and harassment because of the family you come from, but I don't think it'll derail your career like it could others."

"Good players get traded all the time. Talent won't stop them from getting rid of me if they think I'm some sort of distraction."

"True, but the Miners would look *terrible* trading you after they've been chomping at the bit to get you for the last three years."

"It's the Miners, Maddie."

"Yes, well—" She shrugs. "—who wants to play for them anyway?"

Matthew huffs. "Are you saying I should come out, then?"

"No, I can't make the decision for you. I'm just saying I think you could do it without the same stress of it ruining your career. But again, it's only my guess. I can't make any guarantees or tell you it won't be harrowing despite any extra job security you have based on your talent and name. Really, what *you* want is what's important here. So, what do you want?"

Matthew snorts. "For this not to be so complicated? For me not to have to worry about homophobia. For me not to worry about coming out. Take your pick, really."

"Well, yes, but we can't have nice things as a general rule of thumb."

"I don't even know what I *am*, Maddie. How can I decide to come out?"

"Okay well, first of all, you don't have to label yourself, and anyone who tells you otherwise can fuck right off. So, jot that down in your guidebook."

"My guidebook?" Matthew asks, amused for the first time since talking to their dad.

"Yes, Matthew's Guide To Being Queer As Fuck," Maddie says with a smirk. "That's the working title at least."

"So, you're saying knowing I like men is enough."

"Yes," Maddie says, smiling more than Matthew thinks the moment warrants.

"Why are you so giddy right now? Am I not having a crisis?"

"I'm proud of you! You could barely say you wanted AB a week ago and now look at you—you're saying you like men. What a phenomenal step to self-acceptance!"

Matthew's cheeks burn. "Shut up."

"Fine. Whatever. No more mush. We're done with the mush," Maddie says, a small grin still tugging at the corner of her mouth. "What do you want to do? If none of this shit was on your mind. If you didn't have to worry at all. Would you want to come out?"

Matthew bites his lip, considering. He shrugs. "Right now, all I want is to take AB out without having to worry about repercussions. But since I don't even know if—"

Maddie rolls her eyes. "Chloe Lutz is dating someone else. Them getting back together is nothing for you to be worried about."

"Whatever. That's not even what I was going to say," Matthew lies, hating how hearing those words loosens the knot in his stomach. "Even if the NHL wasn't a concern—he'd still have his issues."

She looks to the ceiling, and his chest echoes with her annoyance. "You are so—" She glares at him. "Men are so damn dense sometimes. Your biggest hurdle was him giving you a chance."

"Literally how?"

"Because he wants this! And now you're in!"

Matthew raises his eyebrow. "You think that'll make this easy?"

Maddie groans. "Is that what I said? No, it's not! But honestly, you're basically dating already."

"That seems like a leap."

Maddie gives him a flat look. "No, it really isn't! You like him, he likes you, everything else is on the table except sex. So..." Maddie rolls her eyes. "Not to sound like a slut-shamer here, but I can't believe AB has turned you, of all people, into a blushing virgin."

"He hasn't!"

The sex alone isn't what sends his mind reeling. It's the thought of AB being right. They obviously never got to the point of trying, but can they really expect the Reaction to be localized to their limbs? And if Matthew's hand on AB's shoulder burns through him with a layer between, how will his touch feel beneath Matthew's clothes, right there against his skin? Even if the sparks aren't there, the magic will course through them all the same and, really, that's the worst (best) part. All signs point to sex with AB being nothing like Matthew has ever experienced.

"You keep telling yourself that," Maddie says. "But seriously, you don't have to decide today if you want to come out. Remember, plausible deniability?"

"Yeah, and if that's not enough?"

"Then you have to decide what you want, Matty. If you decide you don't want to come out, there's really only two ways this can go." She displays her left palm. "On the one hand you have successfully flying under the radar but severely limiting your alone time." Then her right. "And on the other, you have going out however you want, as much as you want, but risking lasting rumors and any ramifications they breed."

"To be honest both of those sound awful," Matthew says.

"Yeah, but as AB said, you really do need to decide how much media attention you can take. It sucks, of course it sucks, but you've got to prepare yourself for it even if you plan to do your best to stay completely secret. With his astronomical fame, and you not being a complete rando, everything will be harder."

"You're a terrible pep-talker," Matthew says, but somehow, his headache has subsided to its usual dull pressure and overall, dying of a heart attack no longer seems imminent. So...point to Maddie.

Maddie smiles shamelessly. "Absolutely awful, which is why Sara's captain and not me."

Chapter Twenty

@cherrylutz
A KISSING CLUTZ REUNION????? A KISSING CLUTZ REUN-
ION!!!!!!!

@mysweetcerise
MOVE OVER JASON! CLUTZ IS BACK!!!!

@honestlyikes
@mysweetcerise he kissed her on the CHEEK...... don't get
ahead of yourself

@cherrysunset
could Chloe NOT??? Could she PLEASE stop inserting herself between Heath and AB already???

@giggleshrug
oh god here come the love triangle stories.......... have we not
suffered enough

AB knew the four straight days he got to see Matthew
before he went on tour last month wouldn't be the norm. He
knows how to balance hectic schedules and make do with
texting and FaceTime when physical, face-to-face interactions aren't possible. He knows any connection is better than
no connection. But had AB known *how* hard it'd be to coordinate his and Matthew's schedules despite them being in the

same goddamn city, he might have had the forethought to keep his mouth shut.

Much to his and his mother's dismay, AB lacks forethought and a filter and has only himself to blame for his Matthew-less existence. Which, of course, is barely more than two weeks, but the time between The Incident and seeing Matthew isn't awkward, but is a little stilted—once again by his own making—and AB wishes he could go back in time and slap himself. Or, at the very least, not run Matthew out of his house with sheer stubbornness. But time travel isn't real, and AB is a self-sabotaging asshole, and opening the door to Matthew at 10:10 on a dreary Wednesday night while sporting threadbare Christmas pajamas and unwashed hair is probably what he deserves.

"Were you standing outside my door when you called?" AB asks as he lets Matthew in.

He ignores the amused glint in Matthew's eyes as he immediately zooms in on AB's seasonally incorrect sleep attire, focusing instead on the dark circles under his eyes and the smudges of paint on his fingers as they grip the straps of his backpack.

"No, that'd be weird," Matthew says, bending over to pull his boots off. "I was down the street."

"Oh, right, that definitely makes it different."

"It does." Matthew heads straight for the kitchen, not looking back as he says, "I told you on Sunday I might need to crash here this week because Zeke studies out loud and makes it impossible for *me* to focus. But I managed to make it most of the week before I broke. So, did you revoke my open invitation or what?"

"No," AB says, more flustered than he should be by Matthew being in his presence again. "But at the time I wasn't sure you were being serious—that you'd actually take me up on the offer."

Matthew stops in front of the espresso machine. He places his hands on the counter on either side of it and breathes in deeply, shoulders curled upward. He turns, resting a hip against the edge of the counter and meets AB's gaze. "Do you want me to leave?"

"No," AB says. "That's not what I was saying. I just thought you'd give me more than a five-minute heads-up. That's all."

Matthew tips his head back and yawns. He rubs his eyes with the heels of his hands, and when he pulls them away his eyes are brighter than before. He looks exhausted.

"When did you sleep last?"

"It's been a busy week," Matthew says as if it's a good enough answer. He turns back to the espresso machine. "Which is why I need you to show me how to use this thing."

"Absolutely not," AB says.

Matthew whips around. "You've been offended about me not being able to drink coffee this entire time, but when I need it you won't let me have it?"

"How's your Vision right now?"

"Crisp."

"Headache?"

"Better."

AB purses his lips.

"It's a lot better than it was standing outside. It's quiet in here. Not as—" He pushes his hands rapidly back and forth in front of his face, in what AB assumes is some approximation of how he sees the world. "Aggressive."

AB makes up his mind when Matthew's last word is swallowed in a longer yawn. "Sleep and then coffee."

"I need to study—"

"You *need* to go to sleep." AB says. "You've studied enough."

"How can you be so sure?" Matthew demands.

"Because you've been studying since Friday. Because you're disgustingly studious—worse than Gabby—so I know you're prepared. There's no way you're not."

Matthew makes a noise and AB reacts without thinking, stopping him before he can reach the cabinet. Matthew's gaze follows the movement, and his eyes widen as he stares at AB's fingers wrapped around his wrist. "Come on, sleep. Then coffee. Then I will sit here and diligently quiz you on what? French tomorrow, right?"

Matthew doesn't budge. His gaze still resolutely focused on the crackle of electricity around his wrist, and AB's heart stutters as he realizes what he's done. They haven't touched in so long, but this moment would be charged regardless of AB making things weird at the studio. They never touch like this, not after the sparks led to an undiscussed understanding that skin-to-skin contact was off-limits. They have, of course, accidentally brushed into each other within the confines of this house but even with the security of not being seen, they haven't intentionally touched since they shook hands the first day Matthew came over.

Matthew's skin is warm and soft, and AB knows now, why he denied himself this. Not being able to show Matthew the same casual affection he has with everyone else in his life would be impossible if he ever got a taste of it in private.

They've only really been out with each other a couple of times, and it was difficult enough to be aware of Matthew's exposed skin in relation to his own, to be cautious of what could happen if they accidentally sparked in public. But after this? After knowing what Matthew's pulse feels like under AB's touch, not reaching out for him is going to be harder to resist, so much harder not to want.

Matthew looks up, meeting AB's gaze, and AB stares back, unflinching, despite every part of him screaming for him to run—to kick Matthew out before AB takes something as dangerous as taking another step closer to falling in love.

"I should study." Matthew says, his eyes glossy red and his cheeks faintly pink. "I didn't study enough."

AB rolls his eyes. "You *speak* French. You'd scrape by even if you didn't study. Which I know you did."

Matthew's shoulders sag. "You're not going to give me coffee, are you?"

"In a huge turn of events, no."

AB pulls Matthew's arm once more, squeezing ever so slightly when he doesn't budge. Matthew follows then, but AB doesn't drop his wrist until they're in the elevator.

Matthew runs his fingers over the wrist AB was holding and tips his head back, resting it against the wall as they ascend. "I'm not too tired to take the stairs."

"Right," AB says. "I don't doubt you'd take the stairs every time, but I, unlike you, have never done a leg day. Please respect me, Matthew. I don't make a fuss about you always being on the move, do I? That you actually *enjoy* running?"

Matthew laughs, soft and breathy. "Almost all the time, actually."

"Okay, maybe," AB mumbles, stepping out on the third-floor landing and walking into the room on his right, Matthew's attention heavy on his back the entire time.

He turns to face Matthew, and there's this look in his eyes—this soft, open fondness spreading across his face—and something in AB's chest unfurls. He was such a fool to think their paths were ever headed anywhere but here.

"You can sleep here, obviously," AB says after a long stretch of silence.

Matthew looks like he's about to drop, but he still hasn't taken his backpack off or moved to get into bed. He's just staring sleepily at AB like—AB doesn't know what. But it's too much. It makes him fidget.

"But I'll need your backpack."

"What?"

"Hand it over," AB says, arm outstretched. "If you're anything like Gabby, which I've already established you're even more intense, I either take the backpack so you're not tempted to study after I've left, or I sit here and make sure you sleep."

Matthew sits on the edge of the bed, and his fingers curl around the straps of his bag again. "You'd sit here and watch me sleep?"

"No," AB says. "I'd kill my phone's battery playing Wordscapes while guarding your backpack with my life. Obviously."

"Right. Obviously."

"So, pick your poison. You're about to pass out, and I highly doubt sleeping as you are will be comfortable."

Matthew shoulders off his backpack and hands it to AB. "What's to say I won't come up and take it once I know you've passed out?"

"Because you're falling asleep as we speak. Duh."

Matthew lies back on the bed, fishing his phone from his pocket. "Set alarm 3:00 a.m."

"Oh, absolutely not," AB says, grabbing the phone from Matthew. "I'm taking this. I'll wake you up at five."

"You can't take my phone," Matthew says, peering up at AB with heavy-lidded eyes. "You won't wake up."

"I'll wake you up, Matthew. I promise."

Every part of him is singing with energy; there's no way he's even going to fall asleep. He's tried so hard not to let Matthew in, to not *care* about Matthew, but here in this moment, with Matthew seeking him out for a small stretch of quiet when Maddie's place is two blocks away, AB knows—like he knew the day they met—he's going to need more than his usual fortitude to keep Matthew out.

Matthew grabs AB's wrist as he moves to go, and the touch is no less shocking the other way around. Matthew's fingers are strong against AB's wrist and AB *likes* that. He likes the spark of their touch and the warmth of Matthew encircling him.

"Thank you," Matthew says, quietly, barely more than a whisper.

"You can sleep here whenever. It's not a problem."

Matthew's eyes are shut, and his breathing is evening out, but he hasn't let go of AB's hand. AB starts to pull out of his grasp, but Matthew's fingers twitch, tightening against his skin.

"Not that." Matthew opens his eyes, slowly resting his gaze on AB, and despite his state, despite the exhausted sprawl of his body, his eyes have never looked so alive. They're fiery as he says, "For giving me a chance, Houston."

"Matthew." His name catches in AB's throat.

His eyes slip closed again, and for a moment, AB thinks he's finally fallen asleep, but then Matthew says, "I'm not going to hurt you. You just have to trust me, and I know I can show you that you can. If you give me the time to."

The sparks around their skin burn brighter, hotter, and a ripple of warmth unrelated to their point of contact courses through AB's chest. Matthew covers his heart with his free hand, and not for the first time AB thinks Matthew might feel it, too, that this magic of theirs might be growing. The warmth in AB's chest flares as he realizes he wouldn't mind if Matthew's absurd, fairy-tale dream of a thing ended up being true in some way. A small part of him might even be hoping it will be.

Fuck.

If love were a living thing it'd be ivy, and Matthew planted the seed that could overrun his walls in a blanket of green weeks ago. AB isn't sure of the exact moment. It could've been when he brought him those art supplies, or the flustered look he got when he saw AB's lingerie, or the way he's sent AB a photo of a flower every day since he left for Houston.

Or maybe, Matthew planted the seed the moment they met, and every day since, Matthew has tended to it and watered it with kindness and care and an earnestness AB is so unused to. He and his friends show love with teasing barbs and easily given physical affection, only serious when the moment truly demands, while Matthew's feelings are upfront and unfettered. He has made AB feel so much, want so much, ache so much, without giving him the physical intimacy AB craves above all else.

AB comes to the horrifying realization as he settles into his own bed, restless and unsleeping, he's already given Matthew the means to break him. If he left tomorrow and never spoke to AB again, it would hurt as badly as any breakup. Despite his best efforts, the only thing keeping AB from completely shattering if this thing fails is them not being physically entangled.

His weakest wall fortifying him against heartache is not indulging in his favorite affection of all, but it really is all he has left. The warmth and rush accompanying their skin pressing against each other is intoxicating, and if AB gets used to it, if AB was allowed to chase the thrill as much as he wanted, he's not sure he'd ever want to give it up.

But the problem is even if AB wasn't at risk of wanting something he could never find outside of Matthew, which seems to be the case, and even if he wasn't consumed by the anxiety of another one of his breakups splashed across the headlines, AB isn't sure he could give Matthew what he wants right now.

Because Matthew looks at AB like he wants forever, and while it doesn't make a lick of sense paired with his unshakeable fear of good things ending, AB doesn't know if he can commit to something so big. He doesn't know if he can allow himself to want the same thing—to hope for the same thing.

But that's the problem with Matthew, AB hasn't known a goddamn thing since the day they met. He's wanted Matthew and not wanted Matthew with equal measure, and his only guiding force through this entire situation has been his inability to *stay away*. He's nothing but a contradictory mess when it comes to Matthew, and after a sleepless night of reflecting on weeks of indecision, the urge to *do something* wins out.

Years ago, after AB ate an entire Halloween's worth of candy in one sitting without getting sick, his mom told him he wouldn't always be so lucky and one day his lack of impulse control would get the best of him. But AB's always thought he had just enough self-preservation, just enough forethought, to prevent him from doing anything truly reckless. But now, standing in his guest room at five in the morning sipping coffee as he waits for Matthew to register what's been said, AB finally understands what his mother meant.

Because accosting the guy he likes, the guy he's failed miserably at pushing away, with a backpack to the side and then blurting out they should go out for real definitely counts as his impulse control getting the best of him.

Matthew pushes the bag off the bed and rolls over on his back, rubbing his eyes. "You didn't tell me my wakeup call would be so violent."

"You were dead to the world. It was this or my coffee," AB says. Relief and disappointment roil inside him as Matthew not hearing his proposition settles over him. Maybe this *won't* be the time his own impatience leads to his downfall.

Matthew sits up, crossing his legs in front of him. He's sleep rumpled and adorable, and it makes AB want to scream. Matthew shouldn't be appealing with the impression of a pillowcase crease on his cheek, but here AB is, endeared. AB is a goddamn disaster, the same as ever.

Matthew turns his head to catch AB's eye and smiles. "You'd never waste coffee."

"Probably not."

He closes his eyes, a confused look flashing across his face. He presses his fingers against his temples then smiles, small and skeptical as he looks back at AB. "My headache is completely nonexistent."

"See, I told you—you just needed to sleep! Do you think maybe you were overreacting about how much you needed to study as well?"

Matthew stands, waving his hand in the air, dismissive. "Probably. Yes. But that's not the point right now."

"It's not?" AB raises an eyebrow. "Because I'm pretty sure me being right is always the point."

"Whatever. I'm still making you run through flashcards with me. I can't get cocky."

"You're saying we could still be sleeping, but you're going to force me to help you study for an exam you're completely prepared for? This seems like torture to me."

"It *is* why I came here. I'm only following through."

AB hides his smile by sipping at his coffee. "No one is going to think you're a quitter if you go back to bed."

Matthew tips his head to the side, assessing. "Do *you* need to go back to bed? You look like you didn't sleep at all."

"I didn't," AB admits.

A wrinkle forms between Matthew's eyebrows. "Why not?"

"Was thinking," AB says.

"About what?"

"It's not important," AB says into his coffee mug.

"Come on, Houston," Matthew nearly whines. "We've gone over this—your colors have changed."

AB huffs. "What an inconvenience your magic is. To me. Personally."

Matthew laughs, but it's not nearly as delighted as AB likes it to be. "It does have its drawbacks. But come on, I came over here in a mild panic—" AB snorts. "Okay, maybe a full panic. Whatever. That's still not the point."

"I thought the point was your headache."

"My nonexistent headache, yes. But that's no longer the point."

"It isn't? Because I'd like to go back to that point, actually."

"You're trying to distract me," Matthew says.

"Is it working?"

"No! Because you're being weird. And I can tell you my headache is entirely gone—not even a dull ache like I always have—and still be concerned about you."

"You have a headache *every day*," AB says.

"Yes, but that's not the—"

"Actually, no, that really is a point I'd like to discuss."

"Why?"

"Uh, because daily headaches sound fucking miserable. And maybe we should figure out what's so special about this particular night of sleep, so you don't live like that anymore?"

"I've gotten used to it."

"You're being dismissive."

"And you're deflecting!"

"It is a thing I'm known to do."

"You're infuriating!"

"One of my finer qualities, actually."

Matthew huffs. "You helped me last night when I was worked up. You insisted I reset even though I didn't want to, and I can't—"

Matthew huffs again, like the aggressive sigher he is, always blowing his frustration out. AB really hates how he recognizes Matthew's tells.

"I can't help you if you don't tell me what's wrong. And this should be a mutually beneficial relationship. We should both help each other. It's not symbiotic if we don't, and we don't want that, do we?"

AB can't help but smile. Who even thinks like that? Who thinks about symbiosis in a situation like this? Matthew is so damn ridiculous. "I assume we don't?"

"Right." Matthew nods. "We don't."

AB laughs. "You're not going to let us focus on your headaches until you know what's wrong, are you?"

"I'll stand right here until you tell me if I have to."

"Oh really? You'd skip your midterm? Your practice?"

Matthew's nostrils flare; he's trying not to smile. "I will stand here until I have to leave, and then I'll come right back and stand here until you break."

"Fine!" AB rolls his eyes, really trying not to laugh. "Fine. I'll tell you!"

Matthew has out-stubborned him, which he'd be impressed by if it weren't so damn irritating.

"I was thinking about restaurants. Or restaurant-like places."

"How are you—?" Matthew looks utterly confused. "How have you learned to lie so perfectly in the space of ten minutes?"

"Are you calling me a liar?" AB says, touching his chest in feigned offense.

"What could possibly be so important about restaurants it kept you up all night? Are you starting a restaurant I don't know about? Because I feel like, and don't take this the wrong way, that's not very you."

"You think I can't run a restaurant?" AB asks, laughing in kind now.

"No? Yes. What I was getting at is you seem more like a coffee shop kind of guy?"

"That would be more up my alley," AB says. "But no, I'm not planning on opening a restaurant or a coffee shop."

"So, you were just stressing about food?"

"No, Matthew." AB smiles. "I wasn't stressing about food."

"You've lost me."

"I was thinking about my news coverage lately and how—" AB takes a deep breath; apparently, he does want Matthew enough to take this risk. What a terrifying conclusion to come to before the sun's risen. "Been writing with Derek and Heath the last couple weeks, and I think Heath might be right. All this ridiculous buzz around me, him, and Chloe coming back up might provide the perfect smokescreen for us going to dinner."

"Wait, what? Are you asking me out on a date?"

AB's pulse quickens. Matthew doesn't look pleased. He looks confused. This is *not* how AB imagined this going. He expected at least a smile.

"Uh, yes? I thought—" He takes a sip of his coffee. "Is that not still on the table?"

"I thought I was supposed to be—to be—"

Matthew's cheeks are so rosy, AB thinks they must be hot to the touch, and his fingers itch to reach out. But now is definitely not the time for that.

"Do you no longer want to go to dinner with me?"

"Of course, I want to go to dinner with you!"

"Well, excuse me if this reaction isn't convincing me!"

"I'm sorry, but it's the crack of dawn, and I've barely slept all week, and I had a plan! There was a plan! I was supposed to be wo—goddamn it, Maddie has poisoned my mind, and I can't stop saying this fucking word—woo! I was supposed to be wooing you with flowers and pastries and, like, weird statement rings. Didn't you say you needed time? I feel like time generally means more than two weeks."

"I changed my mind."

"You changed your mind," Matthew repeats. "Just like that?"

"What can I say? You won me over with your sleepiness."

Matthew's cheeks flush. "No, I did not—shut up."

"You're quite cute when you're trying too hard to stay awake, actually."

The redness of Matthew's cheeks fans out, but he's wearing the goofiest grin AB's ever seen, and the reward to this risk is already so much greater than AB imagined it to be. He's warm and happy all over and nothing's even changed between them. Not really. Not yet.

Chapter Twenty-One

The Three Muskequeers

Thu, Oct 15, 10:37 AM

Are either of you up?

Heath

It's nearly eleven babe

And?

Chloe

And even you're usually up by now so we definitely are

I'll have you know I've been up for hours

And I was only trying to be COURTE-OUS

Heath

Are you about to have a crisis?

Is it always that obvious?

Chloe

You rarely make sure we're both up before dropping in with anything random so yeah, this has to be a Deal

Heath

That and you're always having a crisis

I am not!

Heath

I love you dearly and will walk by your side through any and all crises imaginable but you have a crisis when retiring a pair of your jeans. You are literally always having some sort of a crisis

Chloe

He's right you know

Okay so you two are the worst and I'm texting Gabby next time

Chloe

As if Gabby wouldn't give you ten times the shit as us!

Can y'all let me have my crisis in peace then

Chloe

On a scale of that time you couldn't find your palm tree swim trunks and insisted it would ruin our trip to the Bahamas, and you actually Concealing on stage how big of a crisis is this?

> Uhhhhhhhh it's a where do you take a first date crisis

Chloe

I'm sorry, what? Did you ask Matthew out?

Heath

You???? asked him???????????????????

> Can y'all take the surprise down five notches and help me or not

Heath

Yes but I need info first. When did this happen? I literally had dinner with you LAST NIGHT

> I made a rash sleep deprived decision this morning
>
> Then I took a nap when he left
>
> And now I'm trying to figure out where to take him before I freak out and cancel

Chloe

Babe, you can't cancel! Matthew seems to be an extremely patient man but being asked to wait and being canceled on are awfully different. I don't think you'd recover from bailing on him.

Heath

Also, he left this morning???? AB I swear to god if you don't give me some details I'm walking out of this meeting and coming to your house to interrogate you

Chloe

YOU'RE IN A MEETING??

> Tbh Chloe I'm surprised you're surprised

Heath

Only technically

> Apparently Zeke is a loud studier and Matthew needed peace and quiet thus my predicament

Heath

When is this date? Is it dinner? What are we planning here?

> I was thinking dinner but I'm not sure anymore

If I knew what sounded good I wouldn't be texting y'all in a panic now would I

Heath

Tell me you at least know when

I was thinking tonight??

Chloe

It's been a long time coming but day of plans does limit you to places that won't need reservations

I'm trying to avoid anything like that. I don't want it to SCREAM first date in case someone sees us

You know how it is

Heath

What'd you and Chloe do before you went public?

I'm not sure that's the best tactic since people still speculated

Chloe

If you can keep your heart eyes in check for a night, all the speculation flying around about us rekindling our romance should work in your favor

Heath

You're asking so much of him here babe

BUT we were photographed together at our dinner last night so you might get away with the heart eyes if you REALLY can't control yourself

We're deep in the love triangle revival

Chloe

The absolute disregard for Jason in all this is astounding.

OMG DID YOU TIP THE PAPS OFF

Heath

No but I DID tweet about the restaurant we were at and let the world do its thing

Gotta get my best boy laid etc etc

Also sorry Chloe but love triangles get more clicks than budding romances

Send our condolences to Jason and tell him he's free to take my spot in this love triangle at any point in time if he'd like

And Heath I'm not going to take him where I had my first date with Chloe that's weird

Heath

I didn't mean the exact place! I meant what
sort of things did you two do

Chloe

So many zoos

SO many zoos

Heath

Then do a museum and get food on the way
home? Or order in after?

Chloe

Oooooh! Do the met!! He likes art, you like
pretty things, it's a win-win all around.

AB has a date. A real, honest-to-god date with someone he
likes, and he's absolutely out of his mind with nerves about
it. He spends an inordinate amount of time figuring out what
to wear—trying to distinguish tonight as new and different
than before without broadcasting to everyone he's trying to
impress someone. He goes with black jeans, a baby-pink
sweater, and his favorite black jacket—the leather biker one
with pink floral embroidery and silver studs lining the seams.
He pairs it with a thin black choker, pink vans with matching
floral details, and a dusting of pink glitter across his cheekbones.

While he waits for Matthew to arrive, he paces around
the kitchen, rearranges his rings several times, drinks a shot
of espresso, runs upstairs to brush his teeth, rapidly shakes
his knees as he sits on the patio wondering why he thought it

was a good idea to drink coffee when he was already so riled up. And by the time Matthew rings the doorbell, AB has convinced himself this was a huge mistake. That he wasn't ready to take this step. That he's not prepared to dive into the media storm an actual, real, futilely denied relationship creates. That try as he might, Matthew doesn't know what he's getting into here, and he can't possibly be prepared for the rumors he'll be part of.

As he heads to open the door, the whirlwind of anxiety causes the tell-tale tingle of Invisibility to flare up, but it isn't accompanied by the dreadful thought of someone doing this to him, as if finally, his mind has realized it holds all the keys to this specific hell. And when he checks his hand—because checking may be a compulsion when he's anxious and there is no tingle, but in its presence, he thinks even Dr. Barnes would allow it—he is still perfectly Visible, perfectly there, and he's not even compelled to count to ten to *really make sure* his Visibility remains intact before opening the door. When he does, Matthew is standing there with his head ducked and his hands in his faded jeans pockets, rocking back and forth on the balls of his feet, and something slots into place when Matthew glances up. AB might be a ball of nerves, but this is Matthew's first date with a man, and AB refuses to ruin this experience by being a disaster.

He takes a deep, calming breath and pushes the ripple of magic beneath his skin down until all he feels is the hammering of his own heart. This isn't much different than every other time he's seen Matthew. He can do this.

Matthew is tall and beautiful as ever, but his eyes shine with a new sort of mirth, and he looks so devastatingly soft in his thick gray cable-knit sweater it should be illegal.

"Hello, Matthew. Was I right or was I right about you being prepared for your exam?"

Matthew's smile grows. "You were right. But it never hurts to be overly prepared."

"Except when you're dead on your feet and can no longer read because your eyes hurt."

"I guess that could be counterproductive," Matthew says.

"I guess," AB mocks, rolling his eyes.

Carson walks out and AB locks the door behind them as Matthew and Carson exchange hellos. AB wishes he could leave Carson behind, but the last time he and Gabby tried to go off on their own they'd been cornered outside an ice cream shop by a group of aggressively handsy fans. Without Gabby's Calming ability they would've been there forever, and in the end, having Carson as a shadow is much more agreeable than having his date disrupted.

While they explore the Met, Matthew touches his elbow, his shoulder, his upper back anytime he wants to get AB's attention or direct him to another work, and Carson's presence slips from AB's mind entirely. Despite the layers, every press of Matthew's fingers sparks right through him, each one leaving him increasingly warm and electric. It's a bunch of seemingly inconspicuous gestures, but each one is such an obvious delineation from their norm it must be deliberate.

"You're doing this on purpose," AB says, as Matthew cups his elbow to pull him toward another case of jewelry.

"Showing you all the lavish things I know you'll be interested in?" Matthew asks, the devilish glint in his eyes is answer enough.

"Yes, that's exactly what I meant," he says, curling his hand around Matthew's arm to turn him toward the exit.

Matthew's arm twitches against the touch, and AB leaves his hand there for a breath longer than needed, satisfied he caught Matthew off guard. "Ah, you did know what you were doing."

"I don't know what you're talking about," Matthew laughs, following AB as he works his way toward the main hall. "Where are we going?"

"I don't know about you, but I'm *hungry*," AB says, which is true, but mostly he needs to get into the crisp fall air before he burns right up.

"You want to stop at that waffle stand before we get take-out, don't you?" Matthew asks.

"Oh my god," AB says. "I forgot, but yes, absolutely. You know me so—"

"Incoming," Carson interrupts, sidling up behind them and making AB jump.

AB whips his head to the side. "Can I put a bell on you? How are you so quiet?"

Carson's mouth twitches. "I'm still in stealth mode."

"Ah, fuck," Matthew mumbles, and before AB can ask, he's greeting the people Carson must've been talking about. "Cam! Finn! You two on another one of your not-dates?"

AB steps back, giving them room, as the curvy petite woman with pale skin and a messy yellow bun answers. "I'd call this a tradeoff, actually. One you should be pretty interested in."

AB watches curiously as Matthew's posture tenses and his tone turns wary. "What do you mean?"

The guy with auburn hair and striking auburn eyes answers. "Cam here said she'd go to the gala if I took her to dinner and the Met. So here we are. And you know what that means."

"You've got to be fucking kidding me," Matthew says, sounding shocked and a little hurt, which only confuses AB.

"Man, I told you she'd want to meet your new girl more than anything else."

"I can't believe you two," Matthew says, his tone from before gone and replaced with a warm exasperation. "You'll do anything but commit."

Cam shrugs, a playful smile spreading across her lips. "We are who we are."

Finn's gaze slips to AB, his eyes widening for a moment, but then he turns his attention back to Matthew. "Have you asked her yet?"

"No," Matthew says, fidgeting with the sleeve of his sweater. "I haven't asked."

"What is with you right now?" Finn asks. "You're usually bursting at the seams talking about Bonding. Never known you to be so secretive."

Matthew doesn't flinch, but AB thinks it's a near thing. "I never said it was about Bonding. You assumed."

Cam's gaze settles on AB for a long, searching moment, and then she asks Matthew, "There really isn't a girl, is there?"

Matthew goes rigid, and he clenches his jaw so hard AB wants to stretch his own.

"I told you there wasn't," Matthew says after a tense moment.

Finn furrows his brow, seemingly unperturbed by the growing tension between them all. "Really? Cam's not usually wrong. Though, her being wrong is almost as rare as you being tight-lipped so..." He shrugs it off, mischief welling in his eyes as he turns to Cam. "Deal's already been made, though. You're stuck with me on Halloween."

"I'm a woman of my word," she says. "Now, please, I've been trying to keep my cool sense we saw you, but *how dare you*—" She punctuates it with a backhanded swat to Matthew's arm. "—not tell me you're friends with this guy!"

She turns her attention to AB, talking a mile a minute. "I love your last album. I love your outfit. I love how soft your hair always looks. I love you. Thank you for existing."

"You're welcome?" AB says with a nervous laugh.

AB's not always the best at fielding compliments from fans, but he's much more adept at it than he is at watching as one of Matthew's friends seemingly realizes what she's interrupted.

"No, seriously," Cam says. "When I came out to my grandmother, I was worried she'd be one of those pick-a-side people, or worse 'cause she's old as shit, but she was like, 'Oh, Cameron, good for you. You're like that beautiful boy who always has such nice manicures—the one that sings that song I told you about?' Funnily enough, she's how I got into your music."

"Your grandmother sounds like a real treat," AB manages to say through his tightening throat. He'll never get used to people telling him he helped them in some small way with coming out—his eyes will always start to prickle.

"Oh, hey," Finn says, like he's had an epiphany. He directs his attention to AB. "Speaking of LGBT acceptance, you should totally come to the gala with Matthew since Cam got my hopes up for nothing."

"The what?" AB asks as Matthew snaps Finn's name.

"What?" Finn demands. "When you have rich celebrity friends, it only makes sense to invite them to your parents' charity events." He turns to AB with a smile. "Not to boil you down to your money or anything."

AB can't help but laugh. "Of course not." He glances at Matthew who looks absolutely mortified. "I *do* like to throw my money at charities, though."

"Perfect. You should definitely come, then," Finn says.

"Finn," Cam says. "You can't demand people you don't know come to charity events." She looks to AB with a warm apologetic smile. "You'll have to excuse him—he's embarrassingly invested in all things hockey."

Finn looks appropriately chastened. "Sorry, I got ahead of myself. Would you be interested in coming to Matthew's parents' Halloween Masquerade to benefit You Can Skate and their draconian task of ridding hockey of homophobia and making the game an accepting and welcoming place for every-one under the rainbow?"

"Finn!" This time Matthew says the name with a little more warmth, a little more affection, but when AB glances over, he still looks at risk of cracking his jaw.

"What? Is that *not* what we're trying to achieve here?"

"No, it is," Matthew says. "You should call them up and pitch that as their new mission statement."

"I just might!" Finn says, beaming at Matthew. His gaze flicks back to AB, his smile as bright as the sun. "So, will you come?"

AB looks to Matthew again, trying to glean how he should answer, but he and Cam seem to be in a silent conversation of their own—AB's answer obviously not a priority.

"I'll have to check my schedule," he says, unable to commit to anything before he knows what Matthew wants.

"Perfect," Finn says. "You can help keep the twins safe from everyone's favorite snob, Allison Rigsby."

Cam leans in, rising on the balls of her feet so she can slip a hand around Finn's neck as she whispers to him. The gesture speaks to familiarity, and AB's heart aches for the same thing with Matthew.

Cam settles back to the ground, curling her fingers through Finn's, and he nods, the softest of smiles gracing his face. "Apparently Cam needs to see one last thing before the museum closes."

He reaches his hand out to shake AB's. "It was nice meeting you. Really hope you can make it to the gala. It's always a fun time."

Matthew says goodbye to his friends, telling Finn he'll see him tomorrow and Cam not to give Finn too much hell for bringing up hockey on their date. She rolls her eyes, but assures Matthew Finn loves it when she gives him hell and they all laugh. But the tension in Matthew's posture doesn't bleed away until Cam leans in to tell Matthew something before walking away.

"Sorry about that," he says. "You'd think Finn was part of the planning committee with how hyped he always is for this thing."

"He seems very enthusiastic," Carson says.

"You don't know the half of it," Matthew says, hesitating as he reaches out for AB like he has so many other times tonight. He curls his hand into a fist at his side, his brow furrowing before he sets his shoulders and wraps his hand around AB's wrist.

His hand is dangerously close to the edge of AB's sleeve, to brushing AB's skin, and the brief tug of his wrist sears through AB like nothing else from the entire night.

Matthew lets go after one step, but the heat lingers.

"I'm going to get you back for this."

Matthew feigns innocence. "I don't know what you're talking about, Houston."

"Of course, you don't," AB answers, entirely too pleased with being teased again. "You'll understand later, though."

"Oh, will I?" Matthew asks, heat flashing in his eyes.

"Mm. But you're going to have to wait. You owe me waffles!"

"What exactly do I owe you waffles for?"

"For being right, obviously."

"Obviously," Matthew deadpans. "How could I forget?"

"Beats me, babe," AB says.

Chapter Twenty-Two

As far as first dates go, running into two close friends who assume he's newly involved with a woman while he's out with AB is not ideal. But it doesn't compare to the mood killer that AB having a bunch of invasive questions hurled at him about his relationship with Chloe Lutz and Heath Samara turns out to be. The walk from the Met to AB's place seems unbearably long as he keeps pace by AB's side as they're followed by flashing cameras and shouted questions.

Carson shoulders between AB and the photographers, and neither of them so much as flinch when AB is asked whether he's now the other man in Chloe's relationship or if the frequency with which Heath has been seen leaving his house since Blue Sunset came back to New York City is any indicator they're finally going public with their indiscretion. But Matthew can't tell how affected AB is until the photographers start to slow their pace and one demands to know if there's any truth to what people are saying about AB only being into men. His pain and anger blooms in Matthew's chest like a festering wound, and even when the questions cease, the silence between them lingers. By the time they make it back, any hope Matthew had left about salvaging this date from the sheer panic he experienced running into Finn and Cam is gone.

AB goes straight for the stairs, and Matthew pauses with his hand on the rail, not sure if he should follow or give him some space, before deciding AB would've told him to leave if he no longer wanted him around.

"I see we're mixing it up tonight," Matthew says as he finds AB lying on the floor in front of an empty fireplace in the den he never uses, instead of lounging on his over-pillowed living room couch.

AB turns his head, eyes muted as his gaze lands on Matthew. When Matthew sits down, cross-legged on the ground perpendicular to him, AB smiles. "I don't expect you to wallow on the floor with me."

His color is dull like the light in his eyes but not the murky, greenish-purple Matthew was expecting to see.

"Are we wallowing?"

"Maybe for a little bit," AB says, looking to the ceiling before closing his eyes. He sucks his bottom lip between his teeth and angrily furrows his brow. Eventually, he breathes out and says, "When I saw them, the paparazzi, I was flustered. I'm always flustered when they get tipped off to where I am. But we'd just seen your friends and—"

"I panicked," Matthew says.

AB crosses his arms behind his neck, turns his head to rest against his arm, and looks at Matthew. "I was going to say you looked wildly uncomfortable, actually."

"Wildly," Matthew laughs. "That's a good way of putting it. But Cam won't tell. That's what she was saying when they were leaving. Not that—I mean, I didn't confirm anything. But," he sighs, "I trust her with the truth. I just hadn't—"

"Told her yet," AB finishes for him.

"Yeah, only my roommates and Maddie know. Well, no, that's not true. Technically, my dad knows. But I'm not counting him."

AB narrows his eyes. "What do you mean?"

"Oh, uh." Matthew rubs a hand over the back of his neck, embarrassed. "I *might* not have reacted so positively to the photo you sent me a couple weeks ago of you and Chloe—"

AB arches an eyebrow, but Matthew barrels on. "And my dad is too damn perceptive, so when he was asking me about my mood, I was trying not to lie—to give him some of the truth."

"How'd it go?"

"Terribly!" Matthew's embarrassment mixes with relief as he finally talks about this with someone other than Maddie. "I spent an entire afternoon not referring to you by anything but your name—because you know, Maddie mentioned Zoe at brunch and then I, of course, like an ass, blurted out she was in your band and then Bondmates came up—"

"Oh," AB says, biting his smile. "You were having quite the conversation."

"Yes," Matthew says, pleased, at least, the life in AB's voice is coming back. "Anyway, I managed not to gender you all the way up until the very end, but then my dad cornered me before leaving and asks me about my mood and I'm telling him about your selfie and my irrational jealousy—don't look at me like that—and I go and say *his* like a buffoon."

"Your misplaced jealousy aside," AB starts.

"Okay, to be fair to me, Chloe Lutz is a fucking bombshell, and you have a history, and everyone wants you to get back together and—"

AB's smile is sunshine bright when he reaches out and brushes his fingers against Matthew's hand. "I was only fucking with you. Though, I am interested to hear more about you thinking she's a bombshell." He touches his hand to his heart. "Should *I* be jealous?"

His voice is bright purple and teasing, but Matthew still blushes all the same, mumbling, "Shut up."

AB sits up, situating himself right in front of Matthew to where their knees knock. The warmth of contact between the layers of their jeans is as good as ever but doesn't distract him from AB reaching out and swiping his thumbs across Matthew's cheekbones, fingers splaying over his neck. The spark of his touch is a warm caress and makes the heat within Matthew simmer.

AB's eyes twinkle as he pulls away. "I've wanted to do that for a while now. Especially at the museum. Your skin is *so* warm, like, more than a usual blush, I think."

Even without AB's skin against his own, Matthew is burning. But AB continues like he hasn't done anything to Matthew—as if he hasn't fuzzed Matthew's brain out with desire. This must be what payback looks like.

"As I was saying before," AB says, laughter filling his voice as Matthew curls his hands into a fist and then flexes his fingers out against his thighs. "How exactly are you not counting your father knowing when he explicitly knows?"

"Oh." Matthew waves his hand in the air. "I told him he misheard."

AB's mouth goes slack. "You what?"

"It wasn't one of my finer moments, but I was *not* ready to have that conversation."

"And you haven't addressed it since?"

"I've screened every one of his calls," Matthew says, only slightly ashamed.

"Matthew!"

"It's fine. I'll— I mean, we're guaranteed to see each other on Halloween. So, I'll— I guess I have to acknowledge the whole thing before then but for now— He was supportive, all 'if there's something to tell, if I didn't mishear, blah blah blah, I support you,' and more emotional things about helping me feel safe and accepted in hockey if coming out is what I want. You know, usual caring parent stuff."

"That's good; that's really good," AB says. "Is the gala going to be—" He pauses, thinking. "—challenging for you? All things considered."

"I am absolutely freaking out," Matthew admits. "Brinkley—he's the only guy who's ever come out who played in the NHL."

"Oh, really? There's an out guy?"

"Yes, but he's retired so—" He shakes his head. "No one has ever been out while playing—I don't know. It's different and also absurdly terrifying for me to think about. And before all this, before I accidentally came out to my dad, we would've gone around together and talked to all the hockey people at the thing, and even now, there's no way I can get out of the mingling. Like, we're the hosts. And there's no way I can avoid talking to him when this event is all about making it to where we have more guys like him. I don't know, it sounds absurd to say it out loud, but what if—" He takes a deep breath. "I don't want him to look at me and, like, know I'm him. Or think I'm too much of a coward to do what he did."

"Matthew," AB says, his voice firm. "Do *you* think *he* was a coward for not coming out while he was playing?"

"Well, no—"

"Then why would he think you are?"

Matthew shrugs. "Maddie says being elite, and a number one draft pick, and from a legacy family will give me more cushion than Brinkley had—and I—maybe he'll think I should do it. I don't know."

AB knits his eyebrows together, frowning. "Are you saying Maddie is telling you to come out?"

"What, no? She just said if I wanted to, if we ever—if *I* ever wanted to go public with someone instead of trying to keep my relationships a secret, she doesn't think it'll completely ruin my career."

"And what do you think?"

Another shrug. "She's usually right about these things, and I mean, even without all that, the league is so goddamn white I know I'll have the benefit of not facing racism on top of any homophobia, and like, I don't want to sound like I don't know I'm already incredibly privileged here but none of it really makes coming out any less terrifying to me."

Another brush of AB's fingers against Matthew's hand. This time the electricity comforts. "Being the first to come out is an incredible thing to shoulder on your own, and I don't think a man who's gone through that, regardless of the privileges you have, could ever think someone in his same situation is cowardly for staying in the closet."

"No, I guess not." Matthew presses his fingers to his eyes until they burn. "You Can Skate, the project my parents picked to fundraise for this year, can do a lot from the bottom, I think. They can teach the players at a young age that the toxicity their coaches were used to, the stuff they and older guys might've contributed to, isn't acceptable and they need to do better. But it's just...so fucking ingrained at the upper levels. Like, the NHL is trying—kind of; they have Pride nights, and You Can Skate ambassadors, but none of it has actually stopped anything. And neither did Brinkley coming out.

"And yeah, it's not all going to stop overnight, and it *is* better than it used to be. But there's so much vile shit still accepted and ignored as part of the culture that it seems like they're fighting a massively uphill battle. And on the one hand, if I did come out my team probably wouldn't act the same; they'd probably drop the slurs and casual homophobia that passes as locker room talk. But on the other hand, opposing teams, and opposing fans, and hell, even my own team's fans are going to do whatever they want. And choosing between suffering in silence or being blatantly harassed isn't easy. And none of that takes into account how my team could cut the shit in the locker room but never actually accept me, how I could still be alienated from my own team, left out of group shit.

"I've lucked out here at Columbia because our coach has always been real supportive of You Can Skate and doesn't allow anything to slide in the locker room. And if a guy comes in that's used to that kind of thing, thinks he can get away with it here, he's taught otherwise on his first day with the team. We make it clear we're not about that. But it's a whole different thing in the NHL. I can't guarantee the room will be like it is here. I can't guarantee it won't sidetrack my career—

even with everything I have going for me, coming out, being with another man specifically, could still throw it off track."

AB nods. "That makes sense. But you don't have to decide now, do you?"

"No, but I do eventually have to make a decision, don't I? Especially when we're—I mean, I assume getting spotted together by paparazzi is going to be a little different than us getting photographed by fans and them getting passed around on Twitter?" AB nods, frowning. "Yeah, assumed so. And I'm not, I don't want to be freaking out, and I *have* thought about it, you asked me to think about it, and eventually I do want to. I do want to come out and not have to worry about a rumor getting started because, honestly, I think a high-profile rumor about me being involved with you would do almost the same thing as coming out. Once the seed's been planted, it's only a matter of time until it's turned against me."

AB groans, flinging his head back, and Matthew tries to focus on the moment. He tries to stay present in their conversation and not get distracted by how incredibly turned on he's been all night. But the bob of AB's throat is doing nothing for his concentration, and really, what's the point of talking when they could be touching?

"Existing in the public eye is so fucking exhausting," AB says, bringing Matthew back to this soul-wrenching moment.

"Yeah," Matthew sings. "I liked it better when the most I had to worry about was if people were saying I was washed up before I even played one professional game."

"Do people say that?" His voice is a shocking neon purple.

"Of course, they say all sorts of things."

"What do you want to do about being photographed with me?"

"Is there anything we can do? Don't we kind of just have to wait and see how people will interpret it?"

"Basically, but I more so meant going forward. As we already established, you know, when I was being an ass and pushing you away," AB says with this self-deprecating laugh that turns the magenta of the sound a little browner—closer to maroon. "I'm used to the rumors and waiting it out, but that's not really the case for you. So, I'm putting the reins in your hand, here, Matthew. What do you want to do? Do you want to keep going out or...?"

"I do but—" Matthew hates this. He hates not being ready. He hates how he's spent his life preparing for hockey, and absolutely no time figuring out how to navigate this situation. There's no class, no workshop, no activity he could have done at any point that would have prepared him for getting involved with a famous man far more visible than he'll ever be. Nothing could prepare him for having to choose going about the Bond he's always wanted however he pleases and being cautious for the sake of a sport that doesn't want men like Matthew and AB anywhere near it.

"I'll understand if you think this is too much of a risk," AB says, but this time his voice is the normal violet. He really means it.

"I don't know what I want," Matthew says after a moment. "I want to do this again, but I'm nervous. I haven't even told my own teammates, or my grandparents, or even my *parents*. I—I'm sorry."

AB purses his lips. "You have nothing to apologize for."

"But I don't want you to think I'm running off."

"I don't," AB says, placing his hand on Matthew's knee, rubbing his thumb over the seam of his jeans. The steady violet of AB's voice and the warm magic rushing through Matthew work wonders for his nerves.

"I'm invested in this," Matthew says.

AB leans in closer, and Matthew's heart skips at the proximity of AB's face to his own, and the way AB's voice turns the rich, midnight purple Matthew loves so much when he says, "I believe you."

"I want to keep doing this," Matthew says. "If you don't mind, uh—"

"I don't mind holding off on more one-on-one public time," AB answers. "Not only can I lean into my own ridiculous press to take heat off you coming in and out of my house all the time—"

"You really think Heath always being around will be enough of a distraction?"

"Possibly," AB says, leaning out of Matthew's space but not removing his hands from Matthew's knees. "For a while at least...you know, it'll give you enough time to get your head together, for us to decide on a better game plan. But for now, I really don't mind if we have to stick to here or your place; like, I don't know if you noticed, but I'm a terrible sharer and wouldn't mind having you all to myself. At all."

Matthew is so relieved AB's not upset, he's dizzy. "Can we reevaluate after the gala?"

"Of course," AB says, as he tiptoes his fingers up Matthew's thigh. "I like you quite a bit, Matthew, and I know I'm notoriously impatient, but I'll be patient for you."

He leans in, bracing himself with his hands on Matthew's thighs. AB blinks and the glitter on his cheekbones catches in the light, and everything fades away again—nothing but AB and his blue-green eyes, and the twinkle of light on his cheekbones, and the devilish smirk forming as he leans in closer, bracing himself against Matthew's thighs, as he says, "That is, if you'll still have me after I get my payback, of course."

"I think I can handle the payback," Matthew says.

"You think so?" AB asks, cupping his hand around Matthew's neck, stroking the edge of his jaw.

Matthew nods, unsure opening his mouth would end in anything other than an embarrassing sound, and that's all AB needs before he presses his mouth to Matthew's.

AB's fingers curl tighter against his skin, the bite of AB's nail amplifying the heat across the back of Matthew's neck. Every inch of Matthew is on fire, and when AB's tongue moves against Matthew's lips, he burns brighter than ever before.

Chapter Twenty-Three

@TheDailyCerise
#ABSeen: leaving The Met

@cherryrings
@TheDailyCerise is that the guy AB went to dinner with a couple weeks ago???

@mysweetcerise
@cherryrings yeah I think he's the twin of the girl Zoe's been seeing

@timothyjimothy
@mysweetcerise @cherryrings he's Andre Levoie's son Matthew!!!! How'd I miss this????? HOW'D Y'ALL NOT TELL ME MADDIE AND ZOE WERE DATING??? THAT HE AND MATTHEW ARE NOW FRIENDS WITH EACH OTHER??????

@theotherzoe
saw @abcerise carrying @brightsunzoe on his back this morning at the zoo. They looked like they were getting smoked by two blonds in a piggyback race but it was adorable lmao

@timothyjimothy
I know rich and famous people make friends all the time but how can I accept my favorite hockey family now being intertwined with my favorite pop star??????? This is too much for a bitch to handle

On Sunday, Matthew calls his mother to see if it would be all right to come by for lunch. As expected, she says of course. But at the end of the call, she gently tells him he won't be able to avoid the conversation his dad's been attempting to have with him. Matthew assures her that's what the lunch is for, and she *ahs* like everything is starting to fall into place. Maddie offers to come with him for moral support, but Matthew insists on going alone. She wraps him in a bone-crushing hug and tells him everything will be fine, and even though he knows they love Maddie, even though he knows his father said he'd help Matthew carve a space in the NHL, even though he *knows* this part of coming out will, in fact, be fine—the gesture warms him all the way through.

The warmth and knowing lasts all the way up until the end of lunch when they're sitting there in front of empty plates and dread chills him to the core. He can't do this. He can't tell his parents. How can he tell his parents? How the *hell* did Maddie do this? How did she come out to them before knowing, without a doubt, they'd accept her?

"Honey," his mother says after a tense moment of silence. "Did something happen? Are you in trouble?"

"Define trouble," Matthew says without thinking. He should've brought Maddie. He's fucking this up.

His mom sucks in a sharp breath, but his dad puts his hand over hers on the table and squeezes. "He's not in trouble, Viv." He turns to Matthew, an inquisitive arch to his brow. "Unless there's been a new development since you began ignoring me."

Matthew dips his head in guilt. "No." But that's not really true. So much has happened in the last two weeks. "At least nothing not related to that thing you misheard."

"Okay, someone's going to have to tell me what's going on," Vivian says.

Andre looks to Matthew. "You're up."

"You really didn't tell her?" Matthew asks.

"You told me I misheard," Andre says, like it's that simple.

"Thank you," Matthew says. He looks to his mother and back to his father. Andre smiles encouragingly. "Well, uh." Matthew stares at his mother's shoulder, rapidly tapping his fingers on the table. "I'm bi, now." He snorts. "I mean, I've realized I'm bi now. Meeting AB—" He looks up at his mom. "He's a he, by the way."

"Ah." A soft smile forms on her lips. "I see."

"Meeting him has brought a few things into perspective."

"Thank you for telling us," Vivian says. "And I'm sorry I assumed when you were telling us about him."

"Don't worry about it," Matthew says. "It came as a real shock to me—so how could you know?"

"Still," she says, her lips pursed.

"I'm glad you felt comfortable telling us," Andre says. "Are things going better with him now?"

"Is that why you feel like you're in trouble?" his mother asks. "Because they aren't?"

"No, things are going really well," Matthew answers. "Really well."

Thursday night replays in his mind. AB's lips on his. A night's worth of teasing AB boiling over into his own desperation. His hand hesitating under AB's shirt, unsure of where to go and worried about disappointing. How fucking relieved he'd been when AB placed his hand atop Matthew's, stalling him as he asked, "Do you want me to show you what I like?" How his own nervous uncertainty was quickly overshadowed by the hot pleasure running up his spine every time AB told him what to do. How intense even the smallest of touches was with the magic burning between them.

"Then what is—?" She blows out a breath, her temper rising. "Hockey."

"Bingo," Matthew says.

Vivian tilts her head. "How can we help you, Matthew? What do you want to do?"

"I want to come out eventually, but..." He pinches the bridge of his nose, groaning. The idea alone still ramps his headache up tenfold. He doesn't know how he's ever going to be able to do *it* if he can't even think about it without panicking.

"You don't have to make up your mind right now," Andre says. "You have so much time ahead of you to make the decision on when is right for you."

Matthew grimaces and Andre's nostrils flare, his voice taking on a hard edge. "Matthew, is this boy pressuring you to come out?"

"No! God, no. The complete opposite actually."

Twin expressions of confusion cloud his parents' faces, and Vivian asks, "Okay, then why don't you think you have plenty of time to come out? Do you want to get Brinkley's info? He might help you feel more comfortable taking your time. He did it his entire career—I'm sure he can offer you some insight we can't."

The thought of telling anyone connected to the NHL other than his dad he likes men, that he's *dating* a man, makes Matthew unbelievably queasy. But he knows his mother is right. Brinkley could offer him so much advice, could prepare him better for what he might face in the locker room before he's out, for what it's like to have people's opinions of him shift on such a large scale.

"Yeah, that'd be—helpful. But..." Matthew swallows. He can't believe he picked a world-famous pop star with astronomical media attention to have his bi awakening with. This is *not* what his grandfather meant when he said he and Maddie needed to constantly challenge themselves. "The problem is AB's famous."

"Oh," his mother says, falling back a little in her chair. "That does change things a little."

Andre rubs a hand over his stubble, a pinched wrinkle forming between his eyes. "I was going to say it's not unusual for guys to be single or silent about their relationships—so it'd be manageable to date AB in private without your teammates batting an eye. But him having his own media attention is going to make it more difficult."

"How famous are we talking?" Something clicks for his mom before he has time to answer. "You mentioned the girl

Maddie's bringing to the gala is in the same band as him—is it the type of band people want to know about their relationships? Are your dates going to be a whole publicized thing?"

"Uh." Matthew laughs, nervous energy bubbling over. "You know AB Cerise?"

"Your sister's favorite pop star?" Vivian asks.

"Yup," Matthew says. "The one and only."

Andre lets out a low whistle. "Unbelievable. How the hell'd you manage to pull this one off?"

Matthew laughs, pure and unguarded. "Are you saying he's out of my league?"

"No, I'd never," Andre says, a large playful smile crinkling his eyes. "But I am wondering how your paths crossed. Let alone long enough for Bonding to come up."

"I actually, uh—" Matthew rubs his hand over the back of his neck. His parents aren't traditional about Displaying by any means, but Matthew has no idea how they'll react to this. "We were trying this new brunch place over the summer, and when I was washing my hands, he walked into the bathroom and went Invisible."

"You saw him *Display?*" Vivian asks.

"Viv, it sounds like he *made* him Display."

"Is that possible?" Vivian asks, excitement brightening the baby blue of her voice. "How is that possible? Matthew!"

"I don't know! All we know is he didn't do it on purpose, and the same thing happened at a concert of his I went to. We think it was our magic Reacting."

Andre slaps the table, his smile growing and his voice bursting like cherry-red fireworks. "You're really going to do it! You're going to Bond."

The knot in Matthew's stomach unwinds. With his mother smiling at him, gently shaking her head at his luck, and his father rosy red around the cheeks from laughing joyously at how Matthew never stops surprising him, the stress of coming out slips away. So much of what he and AB are up against is out of Matthew's hands but in this moment all he can think about is his parents' love and the incandescent happiness seeping through his every cell as his sexuality, and his belief in Bondmates, is embraced with delight.

He rides the high of this moment with his parents all the way up until their game on Friday night. Nothing—not the acceptance from his parents, or finally getting a compliment on this year's art from his professor, or the progress of his relationship—could soften the blow of losing their opening game because Matthew let in the only goddamn goal scored the entire night. He's so furious with himself his Vision goes berserk.

There's no difference between sounds—whether it's the white of a pad being taken off five stalls down or the golden-retriever yellow of Finn asking Matthew if he wants to get a drink before calling it a night—every color appears as if it's happening right in front of Matthew's face. He closes his eyes and buries his head in his hands, propping himself up with his elbows on his knees, trying to steady his breathing and calm the fuck down. Except, nothing works.

Not the breathing exercises Maddie taught him, not re-minding himself this is only one game, not even sitting with his eyes closed until the entire team has cleared out and he's alone. He's so overwhelmed, so sensitive to light and sound and the mixture of the two, he stuffs gauze in his ears in a desperate attempt to eliminate as much input as possible. He can't bear the thought of getting on the subway, so he calls himself an Uber, barely opening his eyes as he meets the car outside, and on a hunch, heads to AB's house.

AB opens the door, and Matthew could cry as his Vision clears and his headache slips away entirely.

"Matthew? Are you okay?" AB asks. "What are you doing here? Was it that bad of a game? You didn't say in your text."

Matthew steps inside, dazed, and the quiet click of the door shutting doesn't appear at all. "You make my headaches go away."

"What?" AB asks, reaching out to brush his thumb against the shell of Matthew's ear—the touch like warming his hands by a campfire. "Do you have earplugs in? And what do you *mean* I make your headaches go away? Babe, I'm not a Healer."

Matthew places his hands on either side of AB's face, crashing with every passing second.

Before Matthew can explain, AB's eyes widen in shock. "Matthew, what the fuck happened to your eyes? They're basically all pupil."

"Houston, AB, babe," Matthew says, brushing his thumbs across AB's cheeks, delighting in the crackle of light and the heat seeping through him.

AB's smile grows, fond amusement brightening his face. "Matthew, you're babbling." He circles his fingers around Matthew's wrist, pulling his hands away. "And getting distracted by my face."

"It's a nice face."

"Thank you, and as pleased as I am by your attention, you're acting a little...loopy?"

"Sorry," Matthew says, trying to focus on what he's realized but he's loose and tingly. The rapid release from the pain makes him feel like he's floating, grounded only by the touch of AB's hands against his wrists. "We lost."

"I'm sorry," AB says, still confused.

"Unimportant now," Matthew says, surprised by how much he means it. "My headaches, though." He pulls his right hand free and waves it in front of his face. "From everything I see, gone—" He snaps his fingers. "—just like that. Right when I saw you."

He reaches up and pulls the gauze from his ears, the muted veil dropping and leaving the pretty magenta of AB's breathing as clear as can be.

"I don't understand," AB says, an adorable wrinkle of confusion forming between his eyes, his nose scrunched.

Matthew's steadier, the disorienting rush from the pain leveling out, leaving him content.

"I've been noticing, since I slept here before my midterm, that my headaches are kind of going away for longer periods of time. And I think you're the reason. Or, well, your magic balancing mine out or whatever. I don't know the specifics, but it's you. I'm sure of it."

AB drops his hand, crossing his arms against his chest. "How's that possible?"

"I have no idea. I don't pretend to understand magic here."

AB purses his lips. "But I'm still not a Healer? How could I even—?"

"All I know is I was two seconds away from vomiting from pain, and then you opened the door and it all disappeared."

"That explains your mood. Rush of endorphins and all that." AB smiles, thinking for a moment. "Is the pain the only thing different?"

"What do you mean?"

"Like, are you still seeing too much like you would when you get these magic migraines—okay, that's a perfectly apt name, Matthew!"

"It is," Matthew agrees. "And no, everything's faded back to normal."

He narrows his eyes, thinking. He turns around to face the windows, listens as the noise of the street filters in, but he doesn't see anything but the room itself. When he concentrates, he can bring up the colors of the hustle and bustle outside, but unlike the other times he's noticed the absence of his headaches, he's not having to concentrate on dimming anything. Everything is right at the edge of his Vision, not quite there but not quite gone—like his nose. "Actually, it's better?"

AB touches his fingers to his forehead, eyes downcast. When he looks up, he's smiling, but begrudgingly so. "Okay, if we're conducting magic experiments all night, I need coffee. Come on."

"Who said anything about conducting experiments?" Matthew asks, trailing after him.

"Me, obviously."

"Oh yeah? What do you have in mind?"

"I'm not sure. But I'm absolutely suing the universe if your shit gets balanced out and I don't get better at this Invisibility thing. You know I can barely hold on to it for more than half an hour?"

"Really?"

"Dr. Barnes says not accessing it enough has left me with shitty control—which is probably true. But what about how *long* it takes me to go Invisible? I mean, it comes in handy for all the times I've gotten so anxious I couldn't help it, gives me enough time to find privacy. But what about when I *want to*? I've looked around, checked out some anonymous Invisibility groups, and pretty much everyone says it takes a while to *go* Invisible—that they've had to work years to get it anywhere close to instant. And honestly, what's the fucking point if I can't do it at the drop of a hat? Why must I *practice*?"

Matthew huffs. "Definitely feel the same way about not being able to filter out all the sounds. Like, do I *really* need to be able to see the wind every single day? Must I try so hard not to be lost in a sea of colors?"

"No! You don't," AB laughs. "You really, really shouldn't have to."

Matthew watches as AB fiddles with the espresso machine, the sting of their loss muted by AB's intrigue. "You've come a long way on this Bonding thing, huh?"

AB looks at him over his shoulder, smirking. "Who said anything about Bonding? I certainly didn't say anything about Bonding!"

"You used to think people were lying about having Reactions to each other! And now you want to see how far our Reactions go. You're totally coming around."

AB turns, resting against the counter as he looks at Matthew and blows on his coffee. "Well, I *am* a curious being, Matthew. And I've only ever gone Invisible in under a minute twice in my life. Both times because of you. So maybe a True Opposite"—his smile is so ridiculous as he makes finger quotes with his free hand—"is the key to faster Invisibility."

"Yeah, yeah," Matthew says, waving his hand in the air. "You totally think we're going to Bond."

AB blows on his coffee one more time. Then he takes a sip, licks his lips, tilts his head. He blinks one, two, three times and then grins, visibly repressing his full smile. His eyes are twinkling, and when he speaks, Matthew's breath catches at the sight of the deep, majestic purple. "We'll see."

Chapter Twenty-Four

AB spends the whole night Invisible, never slipping once no matter what Matthew does to distract him. They lie on their backs on AB's bed listening to music as Matthew tries to dissect what he hears into one single color instead of a multicolored burst of fireworks. AB closes his eyes and tries to imagine the things Matthew describes—the black of the drums, the red of the guitars, the neon green of the bass, the twinkling blue of the keys. He's falling asleep to the laughter in Matthew's voice as he explains how *frustrated* he'd been the first time he saw fireworks as a toddler and the sound of the booms were their own bright purple no matter what the color of the fireworks when Matthew asks.

He shifts next to AB, brushes his fingers over the dip of AB's collarbone, and when AB opens his eyes, Matthew is staring at him with an intense single-minded focus.

"What's that look for?" AB asks, despite the warm flutter in his chest wanting Matthew to keep looking.

"I know things went a little sideways and we...didn't talk about it after we ran into Finn but...the gala is going to be really difficult for me, and I know we can't go *together* but—"

He breaks eye contact, gaze falling to his hand still on AB's chest, and blows out a breath. AB reaches out and lifts Matthew's chin. "Are you asking me to go to the gala?"

His heart beats uncomfortably as he waits for Matthew's answer—afraid of what he wants to hear. "I know it's a lot to ask."

"Not really," AB says. "Not if you want me there."

"I always want you there," Matthew says, dangerously sincere.

"Then I'll go," AB says. "But are you sure you want me there? It's a charity event hosted by a friend's parents and Zoe and Maddie are essentially dating, so I think we'll probably not have to worry about any rumors starting about who I'm there for. But it's not really my risk to assess."

"I want you there," Matthew says, his eyes fiery like the warmth blooming through AB's heart. "Besides, we have a game that night, so we couldn't arrive together anyway."

"As long as you have everything thought out," AB says. "Then I'll be there."

Matthew's smile is so genuine, so radiant, and his happiness bursts in the middle of AB's chest. AB's heart is a pulsing sun, warming him all the way through, leaving him giddy in an unfamiliar way, and for the first time, AB is *positive* this is Matthew's emotions manifesting inside him.

The warmth of Matthew's happiness and AB's desire to not only feel it again, but to be the cause of it, is how AB finds himself donating enough money to the Hellman-Levoies' gala to cover the entrance cost of his entire band three times over. It's how he weathers Kimbra's and Anita's griping as they insist a week's notice is nowhere near enough time to coordinate six black-tie masquerade outfits. It's how, an hour after Matthew and Finn arrive at the gala, he finds himself riding an elevator to the third floor of the New York Public Library with Carson. It's how Carson, who can convincingly pass as event security, ends up patrolling the hall near the men's restroom to make sure their coast stays clear as AB slips inside the bathroom to meet Matthew.

"Took you long enough," Matthew says.

"Look who's being impatient now."

"Me, obviously," Matthew says, turning AB's laugh into a groan as he crowds him in the corner next to the door.

Matthew trails his fingers down the center mesh panel of his black jumpsuit's bodice, stopping when he reaches the cinched waist, momentarily resting his fingers on the gold floral belt.

"I take it you like my outfit?"

Matthew finds the mesh panels on AB's hips, his thumbs digging in at the bone, and when Matthew meets AB's gaze, his eyes are intense, heated. "You knew I would."

"I had an idea," AB says, thinking back to Matthew's reaction to the lace underwear. "But I couldn't have known you'd like it *this* much."

"I—yeah." Matthew licks his lips. "So much."

AB sweeps a falling strand of Matthew's hair to the side, rests his arms on Matthew's shoulders, and links his fingers behind his neck. "You don't look too bad yourself."

He nods, gaze dropping to AB's mouth. "Thank you."

AB presses a kiss to the corner of Matthew's mouth, delighted when Matthew makes this displeased little sound as AB pulls back.

Matthew's eyes fall shut, his grip tightening against AB's hips as he gently rests his head against AB's forehead. "Kiss me, please."

He and Matthew have only seen each other a handful of times since their first date, but AB has noticed how Matthew does this. He waits for AB to kiss him first, and if AB waits too long, if Matthew gets impatient, he *asks,* and every time—especially right now—it sends a thrill up AB's spine. He pulls Matthew in as close as he can, tips his head up, and meets Matthew's lips for a kiss.

There is a desperation to this encounter of theirs. From the minute AB walked inside the bathroom, there's been a charge in the air, their magics apparently ramping up the Re-actions with their growing arousal. Matthew waits for AB to kiss him, to lick into his mouth, to pull back and nip at the spot Matthew likes so much—the juncture of his jaw and his neck, right below his ear. But from there, Matthew sets the pace.

The kiss is rough and needy, and when AB pulls away for air, Matthew's mouth is red, red, red, and AB wants so fuck-ing much. He drops his head on Matthew's shoulder, his frustration escaping in a huff of laughter. Fuck. "We are *not* having sex in a bathroom."

Matthew takes a deep breath, and when he lets it out, AB can feel it against his cheek.

"Of course not."

AB straightens up, pushes Matthew back to where they're an arm's length apart, and pouts. "That was more for me than you."

"Right. Yeah."

Matthew's pupils are blown, and his lips are still too ob-viously kissed, but his suit is surprisingly unaffected. AB smooths his hands down Matthew's lapels, anyway, smiling back at Matthew. "You can probably leave this room soon without bringing too much attention to yourself. But how do I look? Do I look presentable?"

Matthew grins. "Definitely presentable."

"Perfect. This has been a very successful mid-gala ren-dezvous, but I think if we stay in here any longer, someone's going to notice you're gone, or I'm going to crack on my no-sex-in-bathrooms rule. So."

"Why is that a rule you have?"

"For situations like this, obviously!"

"Right," Matthew says, the flush of his cheeks subsiding faster than the red of his mouth. "Obviously."

"We just have to get through, what, forty-five-ish minutes? Maybe an hour more of this?"

Matthew nods.

"I think we can keep our hands off each other for an hour, don't you?"

Matthew nods again. "Our time without far surpasses our time *with* touching, so it should be a piece of cake."

But the look in his eyes when AB drops his hands to his sides screams otherwise, and AB must agree. Before their kiss, before their date, before they dove right into this, AB wanted to reach out for Matthew more than anyone else, both his magic and his heart demanding a contact he couldn't have but never stopped imagining the allure.

But now AB has touched Matthew's skin, now he knows how the crackle of warmth feels as Matthew trails his hands over his arms, his chest, his back, now he knows the wet, hot sting of their lips meeting and has experienced the absolute white-out bliss of sex with magic burning through him, and it's excruciating not being able to chase a fraction of those feelings by brushing their hands together in passing.

He and Matthew are nothing if not versed in the torture of denying themselves each other, so what is an hour or so under their belt? At least now they get to indulge in, and slowly explore, how different and intoxicating this magic of theirs makes even the simplest of contact. And after a night of keeping track of Matthew in his peripheral as he flits around the room making small talk with the guests, after Matthew's sheer panic bursts through AB as Matthew met Jonathan Brinkley for the first time, after fighting off his own anxiety and not Displaying in front of everyone as he met Matthew's parents for the first time, after a night of Finn watching him with this knowing smile, indulging is exactly what he and Matthew do.

Chapter Twenty-Five

Is AB Cerise Finally on the Rebound?

@cherrysunset
Who the FUCK is this guy and where the hell is Heath?????

@siemprecerise
@cherrysunset RIGHT?? I did NOT suffer through years of bearding for AB to not date heath????? Wtf

@houstoncryptid
@cherrylutz and you thought clutz was getting back together riiiiiiip

@cherrylutz
@houstoncryptid But is he dating Heath??? Didn't think so!

@princecerise
Since when is hockey even on AB's radar??? He must have it BAD for this guy

@mysweetcerise
@princecerise isn't Zoe dating Maddie Hellman-Levoie? AB was probably there for them and to hang out with the rest of his band who he adores. Do we even know if AB knows this guy outside this event????

@TheDailyCerise
#ABSeen: Attending the Hellman-Levoie Foundation's fund-raiser for You Can Skate 📷: @allisonrigsby

@pinkpinkcerise
@thedailycerise oh my god I DEFINITELY saw AB at a bar with this guy a couple months ago

@princecerise
@pinkpinkcerise @mysweetcerise what were you saying about AB not knowing this guy???

@cherryrings
@timothyjimothy on a scale of one to literally six feet under how dead are you over AB going to the Hellman-Levoies' Halloween event??

@timothyjimothy
@cherryrings I'M TWEETING FROM THE BEYOND

★

The morning after their first date, Matthew left AB's house for the second day in a row wearing the same thing he'd arrived in, and nothing came of it. They were far enough removed from AB's brunch with Heath and Chloe that the paparazzi were no longer camping outside AB's house trying to get a shot of an apparent walk of shame like they were the first week. But since interest in who AB might be dating hadn't fizzled out enough to no longer photograph Heath arriving to work on AB's album, they'd needed to make sure he left before Heath and Derek's arrival to make sure Matthew didn't get caught in more paparazzi photos.

Matthew was lucky no rumors came from their first date, especially when someone had recognized him as the same guy who went to dinner with AB nearly a month ago. So that Sunday, when AB offered his rooftop as a space for Matthew to fling paint and dried flowers around, without worrying about the mess he'd make, Matthew left a couple of spare clothes in AB's closet just in case.

He knew then being photographed leaving AB's place in the morning, whether in last night's clothes or not, would present problems, that Zoe and Maddie dating could only link him and AB together so much. He knew leaving AB's house with neither Maddie nor Zoe in tow would probably make people wonder. But even so, the only risk-free way to date AB would be to never actually see him, and Matthew isn't willing to do that.

But the morning after the gala, Matthew begins to understand just how unpredictable strangers interpreting AB's interactions and body language can be. How even the most obvious things can be overshadowed by snapshots that tell the wrong story. How plausible deniability is good in theory but dreadful in practice. How confusing it is to want his luck to run out just so people will know *he's* with AB and not someone else.

Matthew spent the night asking AB for what he wanted, being given the sweetest gifts in the form of AB's mouth and AB's hands, discovering how enjoyable giving a blowjob is despite his nerves. Halloween is a night of new sensations and experiences, and he wakes up with the same contentment he'd fallen asleep with, unaware fans and media alike had latched onto *Oliver* as AB's new boyfriend.

Allison Fucking Rigsby—stuckup Team USA center, daughter of his dad's biggest rival, girl who had the audacity to show up to *this* gala as if she didn't call Maddie a slur in high school when she made captain—posted a picture of AB online that ultimately got picked up by one of his several fan accounts. And honestly, if his family didn't have such a history with hers, Matthew wouldn't even be that mad about it because the picture was nothing. Just a shot of AB handing Oliver a glass of champagne. But their fingers seemed to be touching and Oliver was leaning in to be heard, and paired with the shot of Oliver and Zeke arriving with AB and his band and the sequence of photos of Oliver and AB righting each other after AB tripped into him on the way out, it was all enough to spark a rumor of its own.

The fervor was so bad AB's street was peppered with paparazzi the same as the week of his brunch with Heath and Chloe, and the only reason Matthew made it to his brunch in time was because AB pressed a spare key into his hand and then walked to breakfast with Carson. Now, as he catches his breath in the locker room Monday afternoon, Matthew can't stop thinking about their luck so far and the inevitability of the truth getting out. Yeah, their inability to touch in public is doing a lot more work in keeping their secret than Matthew realized, but eventually, they're going to be caught in a situation that can't be solved by AB luring the photographers away.

Eventually, people will start to notice Matthew spends far more time with AB than Oliver does; his proximity to AB won't be able to be explained away by being Maddie's twin. No matter what safety net their lack of touching has created, soon the part of Matthew deeply aching to be seen as AB's, to be recognized, in some small way, as important to him, will surpass the part of Matthew wanting to avoid coming out, will overrun his ability to keep this secret to himself. Soon enough, Matthew will have to decide what to do with this growing need to let people know what AB means to him.

So, when Finn flops down next to Matthew after their weight training, Matthew isn't surprised by the way his Vision whites out entirely, and he freezes for a brief, panicked moment, as Finn looks up at him and asks, "So you and AB, huh?"

"Me and AB what?"

Finn rolls his eyes. "Oh, come on, we're the only ones in here. You can tell me the truth—if you want."

Matthew sinks down on the bench next to Finn, throat tight as he asks, "What do you think is happening?"

Finn shrugs. "I'm not sure. Something. But see, on Halloween I was thinking: 'How could I miss this? How did I not see this when we ran into them at the museum?' But then, I'm checking Twitter earlier and my sister's retweeted this article about AB and Oliver—your Oliver!—being a new item with a ridiculous slew of crying emojis and well...either you're about to steal your best friend's boyfriend, or I'm missing some key details here."

"You can tell Georgia you know for a fact Oliver isn't AB's new boyfriend," Matthew says, managing a smile.

Finn nods. "And you and him?"

Matthew dips his head, runs both hands through his hair. "Yeah—" He meets Finn's eyes. "—a couple weeks now."

"Yeah?" Finn's smile is incandescent, his joy spilling over into laughter. "You took him to the Met as your first date, didn't you? Oh my god. I'm so pissed I didn't realize when we ran into y'all."

Wiry tension uncoils in his chest. "He took me, actually."

"Ah, he's got it bad, then," Finn says.

Matthew raises an eyebrow. "Oh, so you've got it bad for Cam?"

"Fucking gone for her, man."

"Does her taking you to her sister's wedding mean you're finally an actual couple or what?"

"You'd think so!" Finn laughs, and Matthew expects the color to be muted, but it's brighter, more vibrant. "She says she's got three weeks to decide how she'll introduce me to her mom. Says we'll both find out what she's decided at the same time."

Matthew laughs. "You guys are so fucking weird."

Finn shrugs. "If it works, it works."

"I guess so. I'm happy for you, man."

"How about you?"

"Yeah, I'm happy," Matthew answers.

"But?"

"You know." Matthew gestures around the locker room.

"Have you—" Finn stops. Thinks. "Do you know what you want to do about the league?"

"I'd *like* to not have to worry about it but—I'm fucking terrified, to be honest."

"Do you want to—" He rubs the back of his neck, a pinched expression clouding his face. "I can't begin to tell you what to do here, and I don't want to bullshit you about people being super homophobic, but I think, if you wanted a place to start, this team could be an accepting place for you to begin."

Matthew is unsure if he's even ready to take that step but knows he can't be Brinkley. He knows he'll crack if he tries to keep this to himself his entire career. He won't survive. There's no way.

"I'll keep that in mind."

★

R.I.P Matthew's Heterosexuality

Mon, Nov 2, 3:17 PM

Oliver

Did you know I have better cheekbones than Heath Samara?

Zeke

You do

Oliver

Yes but even @cherrysunset agrees

> Is that supposed to mean something to me?

Zeke

She's The Most intense samarise tinhat, so it's HIGH PRAISE considering Oliver's 'stealing' Heath's man lol

> What the fuck is a samarise tinhat?

Zeke

Samarise is Heath and AB's ship name and a tinhat is someone who thinks they're legit together but keeping it a secret. Come on Matthew, keep up!

> Right, these are the people who think Chloe was a beard then?

Zeke

AGGRESSIVELY SO

Oliver

Which is why I'm confident the next time they're seen together I'll be old news.

> And if it doesn't play out like that?

Oliver

Might use my newfound attention to become an influencer

Zeke

That'll be an EMBARRASSMENT so let's hope it does blow over

By the end of Tuesday, Twitter user @cherrysunset has gone viral with a thread of "evidence" on why Oliver *can't* be AB's actual boyfriend. To Matthew's absolute delight, her thesis seems to hinge on Oliver dating Zeke. When Zeke brings it up over dinner a couple of days later, pleased in the way he only gets when Oliver gives him attention, Oliver's cheeks flush, which Matthew notes as a new development.

Friday morning, in the announcement of his charity Christmas concert benefiting the Trevor Project, AB posted a picture of himself in a fluffy green sweater and antler ears, looking up at a sprig of mistletoe while he was kissed on each cheek by Heath and Mary Ann Ramirez—the rest of the night's lineup—and like Oliver said, the news of the event and the fan fervor over the photo was enough to push Oliver out of the news and off people's minds. Because as Maddie said so long ago, Heath is a fan favorite, and if AB isn't in a confirmed relationship, he's the default. Which works for keeping Matthew's secret, but not for Matthew's growing need to tell people what AB is to him—what he is to AB.

So, Friday night, when he climbs into the back of Carson's SUV after his game against Quinnipiac, he's caught somewhere between terror and elation when AB tells him he's thinking about coming to tomorrow night's game, thanks to Tanner Ross and his infuriating doe eyes.

Apparently, while Matthew and Maddie were being whisked around the room with their parents to schmooze with their guests, AB was being convinced by Tanner it was *unacceptable* he'd never been to a hockey game (correct) and he *had* to come to one of theirs (one day) and it should *definitely* be one of the ones this weekend (absolutely unideal, all things considered).

"And you're coming?" Matthew asks once they're back in Matthew's room.

"It's up to you, but I was thinking about it."

AB's sitting on Matthew's bed for the first time ever, picking at the frayed quilt his granny made him years ago, and Matthew can't believe neither of them thought of AB Concealing to come to his apartment unnoticed before now. Their schedules weren't conducive to it earlier than this, but with the attention on AB skyrocketing, AB being able to sneak up to and out of Matthew's place without them worrying about stoking rumors will be extremely useful.

But still, his elation over AB in his room, on his bed, making himself comfortable in his home, can't mask his apprehension about AB coming to the game.

"If you think it's a bad idea, I won't," AB says after Matthew doesn't respond.

"No, I want you to," Matthew says. Because he does. He wants AB to be able to come to his games without either of them worrying. But... "Who will you go with?"

"I have a plan," AB says, pleased with himself.

"Oh, yeah?"

"Yeah. Emily—"

"Tanner's girlfriend?"

"Yup, that's the one."

"Oh, my god. How much bonding did you do at the gala?"

"What can I say? People love me."

"They do," Matthew says, joining AB on the bed, the warmth of their knees knocking soothing his growing nerves.

"I got her number, actually."

"Of course, you did." Matthew smiles.

"She offered it to me! Tanner was very insistent about me going—"

"Of course, he was. He invited you to go to Barry's with us after the game, didn't he?"

"He did!"

"Classic Tanner."

"Anyway," AB says, smoothing out the quilt only to start picking at it again. He's nervous. "Emily said I could sit with her and her friends. So, I was talking with Heath earlier—"

"You want to bring Heath?"

"He likes hockey."

"Really?"

AB grins. "Doesn't seem the type, does he?"

"Not really, no."

"He's a decent enough explainer. I might actually understand what the fuck you're talking about by the end of it all."

"Emily can help too," Matthew says, forgetting for a moment he should be nervous about this. "You're fine with this?"

"Why wouldn't I be?"

"Won't hanging out with Heath outside of writing make people talk more?"

"Yes, but that's the point," AB says.

"I don't understand," Matthew says. "You don't— I know it bothers you when people refuse to believe you and Heath aren't involved, yet you're willing to have it happen to come to my game?"

"I made a commitment, and I don't want to flake," AB says, shrugging one shoulder. "Besides, it's not a *burden* to come watch you. I hear you're pretty good."

"I am," Matthew says.

"Then let me come."

Matthew's chest aches with how close this is to what he wants and his head spins at the thought. A clingy desperation flares up in him, encasing his heart with a need he can't identify.

"Okay."

"Really?"

"Don't sound too surprised," Matthew says. "I did say I'd reconsider things after the gala, and Heath will be there as a buffer and—"

"You want to show off for me," AB says, a wicked grin forming.

"I said no such thing," Matthew mumbles, before pressing in for a kiss and swallowing AB's smug little laugh.

But AB's not wrong. Matthew does want AB there to watch him play. Which is how he ends up celebrating a shutout, and the season's first win in regulation, against Princeton at Barry's with half his team and two of music's hottest artists.

They're all crowded together in the back, spilling over from their two booths into surrounding high-tops. Emily and AB are giggling as they dance in the middle of their group. AB's had two shots of tequila, and the pink of his cheeks is the same as the pink of his laugh as he twirls Emily around. Her drink splashes on his shoes which only makes them laugh louder, Emily's fingers curling into the front of AB's shirt as she leans into him.

"I can't believe he came," Tanner says, turning his attention back to the table.

Matthew does the same. "You're the most persuasive person I've ever met."

"Yeah," Finn laughs. "There's no way I'd have a lion tattooed on my ass if you didn't."

Jamie chokes on his beer. "Excuse me?"

"When he made captain," Matthew explains. "Tanner talked him into it."

"Oh no." Tanner slaps at Matthew's arm. "You picked the lion out! You can't blame this all on me."

"I'm not sure Finn following through on what is basically a dare counts as Tanner being persuasive," Nolan chimes in. "Finn would swim the Hudson if you dared him to."

Finn tips his beer toward Nolan. "You might be right there."

"See," Nolan says. "Though I'm glad everyone other than Matthew finally had a good fucking game."

"Hey, speak for yourself there, bro," Finn says.

Nolan rolls his eyes. "Whatever, we've been a mess. And it would've been so damn embarrassing to lose again after Tanner talked us all the way up on Halloween."

"Hey, we finally won the night of the gala," Tanner says.

"By the skin of our teeth," Jamie says.

Tanner shrugs. "Still counts."

"Two overtime wins is still a mess when we've had maybe ten shots on goal each game," Nolan says.

"That's an exaggeration," Finn says.

"Whatever, what matters is we *did* look better tonight," Jamie cuts in. "But most of the credit still goes to Matty over here. Never seen you so fucking focused, man."

"Yeah," Matthew says. He mastered playing with the dull ache behind his eyes a long time ago, gotten used to the pain surging after a particularly loud crowd response, but with AB there, he was able to filter everything out in a way he couldn't before, to where there was nothing but the puck and the direction of its sound without anything else coming in the way.

"Maybe AB's our good luck charm," Jamie says. "Tan, you and Emily should bat your eyes at him again and get him to come to the Harvard game."

"Don't think I can take all the credit for it," Tanner says before taking a sip of his beer. "Matthew probably had a little to do with it. You know, with Maddie dating the drummer in his band and everything."

"Wait, what?" Jamie asks, distracting the table from Matthew's shock. He didn't think anyone other than Finn knew they were hanging out. He didn't think any of the guys on the team would know he was connected to AB at all before Halloween.

"Dude, come on," Tanner says. "Have you ever paid attention a day in your life? They were all over each other at the gala."

"I didn't know she was in a famous person's band though!"

"She was literally talking about how excited she was to be going back on tour!"

"Okay." Nolan snorts. "Maybe it's not that Jamie doesn't pay attention—which you don't by the way—but that you're an eavesdropper."

"Does it count as eavesdropping if I'm standing right next to the conversation happening?" Tanner asks.

"Oh, whatever. That's not the issue here. The issue is you—" Jamie motions at Matthew with his drink. "—have been holding out on us!"

"About what?"

"Your famous friend, bro!"

"What makes you think we're friends?" Matthew asks.

"Because you and Maddie are best friends and there's no way you haven't met him before if her girlfriend's in his band."

"And," Nolan interjects, "there's not a single person you've met that doesn't love you, so you're bound to be at the very least *friendly.*"

"Yeah, you could say we're friendly," Matthew says, careful to keep his face blank but his gaze slips to Finn, who's barely containing a smirk, and by the curious expression on his face when he turns his attention back, Nolan noticed.

"You should bring him to more games, then," Nolan says. There's an intense ripple in the mahogany of his voice, and surprisingly, the prospect of another teammate recognizing the obvious doesn't make Matthew want to throw up. It actually fills him with a warm relief—maybe he can come out to them. Maybe he is closer to making this decision. Maybe he *can* handle the pressure of being the first to come out before his career in the NHL even starts.

Chapter Twenty-Six

@bret714
Have I entered some sort of twilight zone where my school's hockey team is friends with AB Cerise and Heath Samara?? What the fuck is happening here??

@TheDailyCerise
#ABSeen: at Central Park Zoo with a group of friends, including Blue Sunset's Heath Samara and Mary Ann Ramirez.

@TheDailyCerise
#ABSeen: leaving a recording studio with Heath Samara and Mary Ann Ramirez.

Nothing Can Tarnish This Friendship: AB Cerise, Heath Samara, and Chloe Lutz Caught Enjoying Time Together at the Zoo

@cherrysunset
If I see Chloe fucking Lutz's face anywhere near AB's one more goddamn time I'm going postal

@smallsucculent
@cherrysunset they're literally friends CHILL OUT

@cherrysunset
@smallsucculent she was literally his beard and as long as she's around there's enough people who will believe the bullshit love triangle management keeps pushing over the obvious truth of samarise dating

> Night Before Blue Sunset Tour Heath Samara Seen at Raiders Game With AB Cerise. Could There Be Any Truth to Dating Rumors?

> What Is the Deal with Chloe Lutz and AB Cerise? Are They Really Just Friends?

Three weeks have passed since he fell into Oliver and people started talking. Two since the narrative started shifting and attention was back on Heath being AB's secret lover. A week and a half since it became achingly obvious to AB, Matthew needs something he doesn't quite know how to ask for and AB can't quite figure out. It's been six days since he was once again seen with both Heath and Chloe and five since a syndicated morning show host said he was flitting between Heath and Chloe like a confused puppy, unable to choose his favorite toy.

Three days have passed since he and Heath joined Matthew and Finn for a hockey game and the indecipherable feeling AB's been experiencing deep in his chest while Matthew's around quiets into something soft and pleased when Finn refers to Matthew as *AB's* boy. It's been twenty-six hours since he came home from Matthew's to a street unperturbed by flashing lights or shouting photographers and thirteen since he left again, still no photographers, to spend the day getting pampered with Reina and Chloe.

And in approximately forty-five minutes, Matthew will be back in his house for the first time since the beginning of the month. While he waits, AB takes a long, meticulous shower; then he lies on his bed with sizzling, pent-up energy coursing through him. His skin prickles with anticipation like this is the first day Matthew visited his house, like this is the first time they kissed, like this is their first date.

They've spent the last three weeks in Matthew's apartment, restricted by the thin walls of his room bordering the living room. Spent their nights together sharing heated kisses and taking each other to the brim with hushed foreplay in the middle of the night, only pushing each other over the edge with exploring fingers and wet, hot mouths late into the night once Matthew's roommates were asleep. But AB wants more. He wants to be able to give Matthew what he needs, wants to pull every sound out of Matthew he's had to swallow down the last few weeks.

AB wants Matthew in a way he hasn't had him before, in a way he hasn't with anyone since Steven.

"You're late," AB says as he opens the door, his chest aching with nerves and his skin burning with desire.

"Sorry. Overtime," Matthew says.

He quirks an eyebrow as his gaze narrows in on AB's lips, and AB's stomach twists anxiously—he knows this look. AB knows it means his voice has gone strange and Matthew is trying to gauge what the change in color means.

"Did you win?" AB asks, thankful Matthew isn't questioning him.

Matthew takes his coat off, watching AB the whole time, eyes sweeping over AB's body, assessing. He only answers after he's hung his coat up, taken off his boots. "We did."

"Oh, good," AB says, clasping his hands behind his back, bouncing on the balls of his feet. "Good, good, good. Y'all've been winning a lot lately."

"Five-game win streak," Matthew says, following the fidget of AB's hands. "I'm crediting you, which means Tanner is crediting himself for inviting you, and Nolan is crediting himself for telling the team not to embarrass him in front of a celebrity."

AB nods, finally finding his legs to move out of the foyer. "Glad I could help."

He trips over his own feet at the elevator. The words were on AB's tongue when he opened the door, but now he can't even think them. With getting what he wants right there at his fingertips, he can't bring himself to vocalize it. He has no idea how Matthew's been giving himself over to this—how he's been able to ask for what he wants without being embarrassed.

Matthew places his hand on AB's shoulder, his fingers curling in as he turns him around. AB doesn't make eye contact, gaze darting all over the place, until Matthew gently cups his hand around AB's neck.

Matthew's hand is still cool from outside, and the chill of his skin, combined with the spark of electricity, is too damn much on his already hot skin.

AB inhales, sharp, almost a gasp, and Matthew tips his head to the side, curious, a flame of hunger flickering behind his eyes. "You're a bit jumpy tonight, babe."

"I—" He turns, presses the call button, asks the elevator because he can't ask Matthew, "What are my colors saying?"

The doors open. Matthew steps in after him. He twines his fingers through AB's, pressing into AB's side so they're shoulder to shoulder. "That you're nervous."

"And?"

"Is there an and?"

AB feels Matthew's gaze on him; he turns toward it. "You tell me."

The doors open. Matthew doesn't answer. The walk to his bed is seemingly endless.

AB sits at the edge. Matthew stands in front of him, hand on each shoulder, the smallest sliver of each thumb pressing into the juncture of exposed shoulder and neck, the touch excruciating in AB's state. His eyes flutter shut, and Matthew laughs, but maybe it's a groan.

It's that desperate feeling of Matthew's flaring up again that gives AB the push he needs. "Tell me what my colors say, Matthew."

Matthew swallows hard, Adam's apple bobbing. He runs his fingers through the hair above AB's right ear, follows the curve of his neck with his thumb, wraps his fingers around the back of his neck, thumb pressing in near the dip of his collarbone. Every point of contact is a flickering flame.

"You're incredibly turned on."

"Unbelievably so," AB says.

"But what I can't figure out is—what's made you so shy? I'm usually the one too nervous to ask for what I want."

"True," AB says.

"Then what's different this time?"

"Because I've quite enjoyed giving you what you want and going at your pace."

"Oh," Matthew says, cheek burning.

Zeke once told him AB brings blushing out of Matthew, but AB's not sure he believes him—he's never met someone who flushes as much as Matthew.

AB pulls Matthew down by the collar and kisses him, the heat and prickle of their mouths slotting together as tantalizing as always. The familiarity of it—the way AB knows he'll never find this again, that it's his and Matthew's alone—bolsters AB.

He pulls back from the kiss, trying not to get distracted from the point when Matthew moves to his jaw, presses him back against the bed, tugs at his earlobe with his teeth, nips at the skin above his collar, breath hot against AB's neck, and asks "What do you want?"

"How do you feel about trying something new tonight? Something along the lines of you inside of me?"

Matthew stills with his hand under AB's sweater, pulling back to get a look at AB's face.

Matthew nods. His cheeks are flushed, his mouth is red, his pupils are blown wide. His warm brown eyes are almost entirely black before they flutter closed, and when he opens them again, AB isn't surprised by what Matthew asks for. "Can you ask me again? I want to see it."

"Matthew," he says, firm and slow.

AB doesn't have the words for Matthew's expression when AB says his name during sex—heated and soft and wanting all at once—and it calls to something deep and hidden away in AB's heart. Still, it pales in comparison to the way Matthew looks at AB when he acts on the hunch he's had since Wednesday.

"My, *my* Mattycakes," he says, noting the way Matthew's eyes burn brighter as AB emphasizes "my" and his own satisfaction Matthew's so affected he can't even muster his petulant little pout at being called Mattycakes in this moment.

AB can't help making Matthew wait a bit longer so he can savor the look. There's fire in Matthew's eyes and AB isn't sure Matthew realizes, but AB doesn't miss the way the echo of Matthew's desperation clawing at AB's heart has turned content, manifesting like the warmth of morning sunlight. And as Matthew stares at AB, patient and pleased to be called AB's, the thing AB promised not to do, the feeling he's been so careful to guard away, reaches out for Matthew like a sunflower.

"How do you feel about fucking me tonight?"

AB's colors must be another level, because Matthew hovers over him for a beat, staring down at his mouth like it's the best thing he's ever seen, trapped in a moment AB's not privy to.

"Well?" AB asks, amused. "Is that a yes?"

Matthew nods, and AB's grin grows as he's manhandled up the bed. Matthew's eyes flashing golden as his gaze sweeps over AB's face, but when his hands move to the hem of AB's sweater, he forgets to wonder what it could mean—too caught up in being given what he wants.

Matthew is quick to undress them both. But his hands are sure and steady, the nervous energy usually present in Matthew's movements as they try something new absent as he sweeps his gaze across every newly revealed stretch of AB's skin. Every shift of Matthew's eyes is the strike of a match against AB's skin, and by the time Matthew's undressed himself, AB's a million tiny candles burning as one.

Then something different and remarkable happens. Matthew walks his fingers down AB's sternum, the delicate touch producing glittering, golden light. Matthew lays his palm flat against AB's chest, watching as the sparks crackle around them like petals in the wind. Their eyes lock and there's that feeling again, spilling out, twisting around the warmth of Matthew's own like ivy.

Matthew's face is soft, unguarded and surprised, and so, so wanting, and when their bodies meet again, everything melts into feelings and sensations. There is only the heat and crackle of their magic surging in and around them, Matthew's wide-eyed wonder as AB slowly sinks down on him, the desperate grip of Matthew's fingers on AB's hips as AB begins to move on top of him, Matthew's hand on AB's neck pulling him down for a sloppy kiss, their sweat-slick bodies and Matthew's full-body shudder as they catch their breath after, and the truth settling over AB that maybe forever isn't so overwhelming after all.

Chapter Twenty-Seven

@TheDailyCerise
#ABSeen: Celebrating an early Thanksgiving at CeCe Flowers's apartment with the rest of the band. 📷: @flowersintherain

@pinkpinkcerise
@TheDailyCerise is that OLIVER??????? So much for him only being a friend of the twins

@cherrysunset
@pinkpinkcerise he IS a friend of the twins & he's been all over CeCe's Instagram since the gala so there's nothing to worry about

@pinkpinkcerise
@cherrysunset lol who said I was worried? I'm just curious if they're dating

@cherrysunset
@pinkpinkcerise are gay men not allowed to have MALE FRIENDS? This is as ridiculous as saying AB's secretly dating Matthew because they hang out together too. They're obviously friends he's met through the people he loves.

@pinkpinkcerise
@cherrysunset I sure hope you're saying gay as an umbrella here and not erasing AB's bisexuality! And you know what! Maybe he IS dating Matthew?? They're together a lot more than he is with Oliver and Heath

@cherrysunset
@pinkpinkcerise you can't seriously think AB is dating Matthew! Look at him! He's as straight as they come.

@pinkpinkcerise
@cherrysunset well I hadn't thought about it until now but you've made me wonder. But lol I'm done talking to someone who thinks you can tell someone's straight based on a handful of photos

@cherrylutz
Chloe and AB will always own my ass but I saw some people talking about seeing AB getting coffee with Matthew after CeCe's and.......maybe @pinkpinkcerise is right

@pinkpinkcerise
@cherrylutz YES JOIN ME GIRL! At first I was joking but I've been going through one of the update accounts and AB IS with Matthew a lot so maybe @/cherrysunset stumbled upon the truth for once

AB hasn't felt homesick before leaving on tour since his very first one, but as he lies in bed with Matthew curled up next to him, the melancholy of being gone pulses through him already. Matthew's alarm will go off soon, half an hour earlier than usual, so they can have breakfast before his practice, the last time they'll see each other for three weeks. It's only a few days longer than the last time AB left, but this time three weeks and several time zones apart seem monumental. AB wasn't accustomed to Matthew's physical presence then. He didn't know the heat of Matthew's mouth, or the warmth of his body in AB's bed, or the unbearably soft smile Matthew gets when he opens his eyes to find AB there next to him.

The last time he left New York City, AB barely thought of Matthew as a friend, still scared he'd run away and leave, still deep in denial, trying not to want what they have right now. But he has it now, he knows the joys of Matthew's attention, the depths of his earnestness, the overwhelming warmth he gets from making Matthew happy, and AB can't imagine a world without it. He doesn't want to *miss* him.

Matthew's alarm goes off, and he stirs next to AB, his skin beautiful in the soft light of dawn filtering in through the blinds. The alarm doesn't even get a second chance to ring before Matthew turns over and silences it, situating one arm under his pillow as he looks up at AB with the soft, sleepy smile AB loves so much.

"You're up early," Matthew says, his voice groggy with sleep.

AB brushes his fingers over the cluster of freckles across Matthew's shoulder, down his arm, watching curiously as the sparks that were a golden sunbeam hours ago have gone back to their regular form—fire and lightning dancing together.

"I've been up for a bit," he says, still watching the sparks.

"Not like you to wake up early," Matthew says. "Couldn't sleep?"

AB shifts his gaze back to Matthew, still trailing his fingers up and down Matthew's arm to feel the heat at his fingertips. "Will you water my plants when I'm gone?"

Matthew blinks a couple times, his nose scrunching up with confusion. "Is that what kept you up?"

"Yes, nightmares about coming home to zombie succulents if they don't get fed," AB says.

Matthew grins. "Would the zombie succulents eat your brains? Or suck the water out of your blood?"

"They're not vampires, Matthew."

His smile grows, the edges around his eyes crinkling as he tries not to laugh. "Right, of course. Silly me."

"So, will you water them?" AB says after a beat.

"I'll need a key," Matthew says, and then he narrows his eyes, his sleep-fogged mind finally catching up to the flutter of AB's chest that must be echoing against Matthew's ribs. "Is this your convoluted way of giving me a key to your place?"

"Perhaps," AB says, as an incandescent happiness bursts through him.

AB covers his heart with his hand, watching as Matthew's gaze follows the movement. "I take this as a yes."

This is the first time either of them has acknowledged the mirror into each other's hearts they have, at least out loud, and Matthew's responding smile is magnificent—even the light burning in his chest pales in comparison.

"Yeah, AB, I'll water your plants."

★

AB misses Matthew's art exhibition, but as he and the band are boarding their second-to-last plane on the Cerise World Tour, Finn sends him a slew of pictures of Matthew's work. AB has caught a couple of glimpses of what Matthew's been working on over the semester, saw him diligently gluing flower petals to giant colorful canvases, adding another layer of texture to the representation of how he sees the world. He's seen him morph delicate golden wire into these twisting forms that make AB think of manic flowers overrunning a meticulously kept garden.

But all together, they paint a beautiful, dynamic picture of growth. On the left, a putrid mix of purple and green, scattered with gnarled wires and dead leaves; to the farthest right, a bright, lush canvas full of layers and layers of yellows with wire flowers bursting forth, overgrowing into the space beyond. The middle canvases gradually shift between the two opposites, reminding AB so much of the murky space he resided in when he was still denying his feelings for Matthew, trying so hard not to let his guard down long enough to catch real feelings.

Not being there to tell Matthew how much he appreciates his work doesn't help AB's early morning irritation, but to AB's surprise his intrusive thoughts don't ramp up as they're known to do on long plane rides. AB knew Matthew's presence was helping him. The growing fiery rush of their magic beneath his skin is similar enough to the crackle of electricity right before Invisibility takes hold that when AB's tired—when he's had a bad day, when he's read another thing about how he's lying about dating Heath—he's prone to mistaking them for a quick, heartbeat-doubling moment. While fleeting, the panic still settles over him like ice water, and he finds himself checking his hands, checking to make sure he's not Invisible. But still, he'd estimate he's gotten the incessant buzz of his obsession taking over his brain to less than once per day since Matthew's been around.

His months with Matthew have been the furthest thing from the beginning when AB felt like a guest in his own brain. The year before Dr. Barnes should have been the best year of his life, the experience of opening for the hottest band in the world, having his popularity skyrocket the longer the tour went on, getting to live his dream should have been enough to cast out the obsessive thought of *what if anyone who Knows can control me, pull me in and out of Invisibility like their personal plaything,* but it hadn't been. Even now, more than five years after his first session with Dr. Barnes, he has a hard time recalling a single moment from that tour without remembering the painful claw his obsession had in his brain, strong enough to bring him out of any moment of elation.

AB has felt completely free inside his mind over the last couple of months, each thought an unwanted, angry knock on the door of his mind—rattling to experience but easy enough to push away—each one an obvious intruder instead of the owner of the house. It's been good to have control of his mind, to not constantly feel like he's one unwanted thought away from a debilitating dive into obsession, but he was convinced he'd revert back to where he was before Matthew came along the longer they spent apart.

But three weeks have passed, and each day has felt the same, no matter how tired or cranky or ready to be home he is. Even now, four hours into a nine-hour flight, with his legs jittery from sitting, and his heart aching for his own bed, AB is still in control. He still feels like himself and knowing it isn't Matthew at his side, but AB's own mental process, his own acclimation to being next to a trigger, his own fear slipping away and leaving space for confidence in his own ability that's gotten him here is enough to push the gloom of a travel day aside.

"I think I'm going to Divulge," AB says.

Zoe's more asleep than he thought and doesn't answer. She only shifts closer to him in her sleep, her hair tickling his ear.

But CeCe and Lupe are wide awake across from them.

CeCe cocks a perfectly pink eyebrow, and Lupe says, "Yeah?"

"Yeah, think so," AB says.

"What changed your mind?" CeCe asks.

"Matthew? Me? Using my magic more at home? Dr. Barnes? I don't know," AB says. "All of it probably. It's hard to explain, but I feel good."

Lupe raises an eyebrow this time and AB laughs. "Okay, I'm emo as shit right now, specifically, but crying over spilled coffee aside, I feel good. These last couple weeks have really driven home how right Dr. Barnes has been about the progress I've made."

"It's great you can finally see what we can see," CeCe says, her smile warm and kind.

"There's still a little—prickle?—of anxiety, I guess. But I think that's how it'll be for the rest of my life—or god forbid, until another obsession takes hold—but I really think I can do it without going insane. That I'm not going to be walking around on the verge of an anxiety attack just because I'm Known."

"AB, I am disgustingly proud of the progress you've made," Lupe says; then her smile turns into a smirk. "And I am thrilled to see how much of a nuisance you're going to be to Carson once you've shed your one inhibition."

AB barks out a laugh, and Zoe shifts against him, grumbling. He smothers his laugh with his hand, the last hook of anxiety dissipating, fading into a whisper of a worry in his veins.

"Now all I need to do is figure out how to do it. Can't really tweet 'LOL. I'm an Invisible.' That'd be so underwhelming after years of evading the question."

"Well," CeCe says, her smile taking on an edge like Lupe's smirk. "If you're feeling a little reckless, I've got an idea."

Chapter Twenty-Eight

Matthew doesn't mean to come out to the guys; it just sort of...happens.

They've just finished their game against the women's hockey team—an unofficial thing they've done every semester before finals since Finn and Sara were both named captain. For once, Matthew stopped *all* of Maddie's shots, and despite their loss, Matthew is ecstatic. In part because he's taken the lead in the ongoing competition spanning all aspects of his and Maddie's lives, but mostly because AB will be home Sunday morning. They don't have any set plans, but with AB's key having a new home on Matthew's key ring, and AB's invitation to stay as much as he pleases while he's gone, Matthew always planned to be there when AB got home.

Matthew misses AB like nothing ever before. He misses his smile, the warm, sweet taste of light weaving between their lips when they kiss, the bright, bright magenta of his laughter bursting through the air. Matthew misses hearing his voice from right next to him, the giddy joy he gets from seeing the contradiction of AB's color when he tries to downplay his feelings for Matthew. He misses his playful taunts about tea being inferior to coffee, the teasing way he makes a complete mockery of the rules when they're watching a hockey game despite Matthew knowing Heath's taught him well, the satisfied cackle he lets loose every time he puts on one of the same baking shows he and Matthew have seen a thousand times by now. Mostly Matthew misses the inflection, the shape, the deep, deep purple of the word *my* coming from AB's mouth right before he says Matthew's name and the contentment that washes over him the moment the word registers.

It's embarrassing, really, how AB figured out this desperate, needy thing inside him before Matthew did. Even more embarrassing is how he's never felt this way before, how AB has tapped into a deeply buried desire that only grows more unbridled each time AB refers to Matthew as his. The soft satisfaction he gets from it doesn't make sense, and with anyone else, Matthew would be too afraid to explore it, to want it, to need it, but with AB, Matthew knows he can ask for anything. Matthew can be whatever he wants with AB, can ask for whatever he needs with no threat of judgment, and Matthew's never had a relationship like this one.

He's so distracted by AB's impending return, his mind full of possibilities and lost time, that when Jamie smacks him with a towel to get his attention, asking what's got him so preoccupied, Matthew answers with the truth.

He doesn't think his voice carries enough for those at the other end of the room to hear, but a hush falls over the locker room all the same.

Jamie rubs a hand over the back of his neck, laughing, not quite uncomfortably but not completely natural either. "Cool. Thinking about introducing him or just...preoccupied with his existence?"

"What?"

"We were talking to you, and you weren't paying attention," Nolan says. "Jamie asked what was on your mind, you blurted out—"

Nolan's gaze flicks around the room, and that's when Matthew notices everyone who wasn't part of their little group staring at him with curious, expectant expressions. "Uh, I'm not actually sure if you meant for everyone to hear. So, the floor is yours?"

"'The floor is yours,'" Finn says. "Jesus Christ, what is wrong with you?"

"Hey! I'm trying to give him some semblance of control over this situation, you dickhead." Nolan motions to Matthew, the mahogany of his voice rippling like a lake. "Does this look like a man who meant to say what he just said?"

Matthew stands, and despite whatever his face is doing to make Nolan think he's panicking, an eerie calm has settled over him. There's a slight prickle of pain behind his eyes, and his heartbeat has doubled, but Matthew's Vision remains the same, unchanged by admitting to a room full of people a fact he hadn't planned to reveal yet.

He rocks back on his heels, wishing for pockets to hide his hands in. "So, uh, yeah, I'm bi and have a boyfriend now?"

"Are you asking us or telling us, Matty?" Tanner asks after a beat of silence, his doe eyes twinkling with mischief, his smile sharp and devilish.

"Goddamn it," Nolan starts as Finn turns his glare on Tanner.

But it's such a Tanner way of reacting, so ridiculous and irreverent that it startles any remaining discomfort right out of Matthew, replaced by relief and laughter. "I'm telling you."

"In that case, I hope he wants one of those shirts the girlfriends have. Because Emily's going to lose her mind and make him one regardless of if he'll wear it."

"I'm sure he'd wear one," Matthew says.

There's a lot of nodding after his best friends' responses, a lot of awkward uncertainty as the guys navigate responding to what is so obviously the first of their teammates coming out. Once past their initial shock, most responses are short but supportive—much like Jamie's "cool"—but Peter and Justin react far less seriously, immediately wanting him to settle their argument over who's hotter. David, on the other hand, offers to set him up with his gay cousin if he finds himself single again, to which Benji insists Matthew would need to be *desperate* to take him up on since Stan is insufferably dull all the time. It's not perfect—not that Matthew knows what perfect would look like here—but Matthew finds solace in none of his teammates' colors belying their words of acceptance and how a rich and emphatic rainbow erupts through the room when Matthew tries to make a joke about this getting out to hockey media and they immediately shut any of his concerns down.

The room slowly clears, leaving only his closest friends on the team. Matthew flops down on his stall bench, heaving a sigh. "That's certainly not how I meant to come out."

Jamie shrugs. "Served its purpose, though."

"Yeah."

"I think it went well," Finn says, clapping Matthew on the shoulder.

Matthew doesn't miss the relief in his voice, though. Matthew knows Finn had faith in this team, but neither of them would ever dare to hope unanimous support was a sure thing.

"I've got some con-crit for you though," Tanner says with the same devilish grin.

"Oh, yeah, what's that?"

"I just think, as far as recipients of your spur-of-the-moment self-truth goes, Jamie is the worst option. I mean, come on, Nolan was right there!'

Finn barks out a laugh and Matthew dips his head to hide his smile as Jamie says, "Fuck you! Like you did any better."

"Which is why I offered Nolan up, duh."

Finn snorts. "What're you talking about? Mr. The-Floor's-All-Yours over here didn't do too well either!"

"You're very stuck on that," Nolan says.

"Because who *says that*?"

Nolan shrugs. "Whatever. There are more important things to discuss here."

"More important than me coming out?"

"Yeah." Nolan raises one eyebrow, his expression an uncanny mirror of Tanner right before he asks a smart-ass question. "Who's this nameless boyfriend?"

"I think you know," Matthew answers, heart beating against his ribs as he remembers the night at the bar and the intensity of Nolan's voice when he'd said he should invite AB along more often.

"Maybe," Nolan says. "But the floor's all yours."

Nolan bites down on his grin as he looks to Finn, his eyes glinting with the smirk he's trying to hide.

"You're an ass," Finn huffs, crossing his arms over his chest.

But before Nolan and Finn get caught up in their bickering or Matthew has time to answer, Tanner asks, "So, it's AB, right?"

"Yeah," Matthew says. "It is."

"Yeah, Em's definitely going to lose it; she's been dying for him to come to another game."

"Wait, *what*?" Jamie asks. "How the hell'd you come to that conclusion?"

Conversation shifts to Jamie's absolute obliviousness after, but Matthew doesn't participate much as they leave the locker room, too overwhelmed by the warmth of happiness spreading through him. He's been holding this secret so close to his chest, worried for so long no men in hockey besides Finn and his father would accept him, that he can't fully process how relieved he is to be accepted by his team, how comforted he is to expand the circle of people who know the truth about him and AB.

And later, when Nolan texts him *"I am too,"* an overwhelming swell of camaraderie washes over him, and Matthew starts to think he can bear coming out to the league sooner rather than later.

Chapter Twenty-Nine

@TheDailyCerise
#VIDEO of AB and CeCe playing the keys together while Displaying

@abc123bbUnMe
@thedailycerise really not trying to sound like a traditionalist here but WHAT THE ACTUAL FUCK

> Traditionalists Call for Boycott of AB Cerise After He and Bandmate CeCe Flowers Display on Stage

> After Years of Mixed Messages and Avoided Questions AB Cerise Displays Himself as Invisible on Last Stop of World Tour

@TheDailyCerise
#ABSeen: celebrating the end of the Cerise World Tour in Dubai with his band, Dawnovan, and various other crew members. #PHOTOTHREAD

★

The thing about having a twin who's also dating someone on tour is that Matthew's anticipation and impatience is only amplified by Maddie's own. Matthew attempts to pass the time before AB gets back studying for his finals, but the intensity of the emotional reverb between him and Maddie makes it nearly impossible to concentrate. The closer their arrival gets, the more overwhelming their link becomes. Despite their apartments not being in the same building, or even on the same street, Maddie's jitters rattling around inside him lead to a terrible, terrible headache, and Matthew's left with no choice but to strain their link with even more physical distance.

He escapes to AB's house early Saturday afternoon, and the closer he gets to the Upper West Side, the more his and Maddie's emotions detangle. It isn't perfect—Matthew's frustration with time moving so slow doesn't allow his Vision to fully stabilize, but the peace and quiet of AB's living room gives him the environment he needs to study. Or it does until AB starts texting him, and the loose tether he has on focus is lost completely. He knew AB was getting closer to the point of Divulging, but the swell of pride is more than Matthew thought possible, and it mixes with Matthew's awe at AB bucking tradition and Displaying in front of tens of thousands of people in an utterly distracting way. Matthew studies as best he can while AB sporadically texts him during his night of celebrating his own achievements and the end of the tour, but by the time AB goes silent, his night dwindling into the wee hours as Matthew's afternoon turns to evening, Matthew has lost all traces of focus. In an attempt to reset his concentration, he goes to all AB's favorite bakeries to pick up all the sweets he loves best, but once he's back, he still can't keep his mind from running astray.

He spends the rest of the night painting in the little studio AB set up for Matthew in the sitting area outside his bedroom. There's half a dozen of AB's paintings tacked to the wall, each done in watercolor—a skill AB picked up quickly despite being abysmal in all other mediums he tried—with a dried bloom of the flower depicted to the right. Matthew paints them all, and then when he's still too eager to see AB to focus, he paints them all again. By the end, he has a portrait of AB peeking out through a dozen of his favorite flowers. It's not his best work, but he leaves it on the easel for AB to see because the frenetic brush strokes remind him of the spark of their touch and the fevered emotion that courses through his chest when he so much as thinks about AB.

He sets an alarm, but instead of waking to the annoying shrill of his phone, he wakes to the spark of AB's fingers running through his hair.

"Houston?" Matthew asks, disoriented by sleep.

AB climbs in the bed next to him, chest flush with Matthew's arm, the last dregs of sleep vanishing with the fiery touch of AB's hand traipsing over his flesh. He gently runs his fingers across his collarbones, down his sternum, over his ribs, and Matthew doesn't know what's more beautiful, what makes his heart flutter more: the awe written across AB's face as he watches the golden light dance between their skin or the way the sparks contrast with the deep, alluring purple of AB's "Good morning, Matthew."

"Morning, Houston," Matthew says, reaching out and stilling AB's hand, holding it to his chest. "I meant to be up when you got here."

"Figured as much when I turned your alarm off," AB says, his voice a beautiful purple tinted by the magenta of his laugh. "Weird for you to oversleep, though. Did you have a bad night?"

"No, just restless," Matthew says. "Missed you."

AB leans down for a kiss, and Matthew's surprised when AB licks into his mouth to deepen it.

When AB pulls away, a smile spreads across his face as Matthew parrots his words. "Weird for you to kiss before teeth have been brushed."

AB grins, runs his fingers through the front of Matthew's hair. "Missed you too much to wait."

Their magic burns Matthew up, fills his veins with a lovely warmth. "I got all your favorite desserts for breakfast and everything."

"Oh, you did?" AB asks, eyes twinkling. "Someone was feeling generous."

"Only for you."

"Lies," AB says, leaning in, their faces so close. "You're the most generous person I know."

Before Matthew can respond, AB catches his mouth in a long, languid kiss. When he pulls away, he drops a kiss on Matthew's nose and rolls off the bed.

Matthew sits up, slinging his legs over the edge. "Where're you going?"

"As much as I'd love to spend the rest of the morning in bed with you," AB says, "the decorators are coming to transform this into a winter wonderland, and I need to not smell like I've been on a plane for half a day."

"Ah, right, it's time to go full Christmas. I remember now."

"Yes, *we*," AB says, stepping into Matthew's space, their knees knocking as AB clasps his hands behind Matthew's neck. "I'm putting you to work this week."

Matthew quirks an eyebrow. "What kind of work?"

"Fun kind, I promise," AB says, removing his hands from Matthew and stripping off his chunky knit sweater, dropping it at their feet. "And I'll tell you all about the things I have planned after I shower."

"Or," Matthew says, standing and dropping his hands to AB's waist, reveling in the way his eyes flutter shut at the petal light caress of golden heat spinning around their skin, "you could tell me about them *while* you shower."

AB grins. "You make a fair point here, Mattycakes."

They don't do much talking in the shower. But after, as they sit in the kitchen, waiting for the interior designers to arrive, AB tells Matthew all about his grand plans—none of which require much work from Matthew.

"You want me to pick the dessert for your Christmas baking competition?" Matthew asks, flustered by the request for no good reason.

"Well, you stuck around a lot longer than I thought you would, and since you can't be there for it—" AB shrugs, but the rich purple of his voice contradicts the casualness he's trying to project. "—it's the least I could do to reward you for proving me wrong."

"I'm a big fan of positive reinforcement, obviously. But your idea of a reward could use a little work. This is *stressful*. What if I choose something too hard?"

"That's quite literally the point," AB says, rising from his seat. "Besides, Gabby told me our moms are being *secretive*, and since they're judging this year it only serves them right."

"You're a little too excited about potentially serving your moms terrible, maybe even inedible, dessert," Matthew says.

"I told you this is a cutthroat competition, babe," AB says over his shoulder, going back for another shot of espresso.

Matthew groans. "I can't believe I'm going to miss it."

AB turns around, crossing his bare ankles in front of him as he leans against the counter. But instead of the small frown he wore when Matthew originally gave him the news, the one Matthew expected to see again, AB's mouth quirks in a sly grin. "I guess you'll have to last another year, then."

"And what will I get if I do?"

AB raises one eyebrow. "Other than my affection?"

"Yes, other than your affection."

"If I remember correctly, we still have an outstanding bet on our Bond," AB says.

"We do," Matthew says, as warmth bursts in his chest.

"I'd hate to have two outstanding promises," AB says, reaching back for his espresso.

Matthew joins AB at the counter. He takes AB's mug out of his hand and sets it aside despite AB's quiet sound of protest. "Oh, would you?"

"I would, but for you I can make a concession."

"Very kind of you," Matthew says, leaning in and kissing AB

Matthew intends for the kiss to be quick, but AB, apparently, has other plans. He places his hands on either side of Matthew's face and pulls him in closer, deepening the kiss immediately. AB kisses Matthew with a desperation that wasn't present before, and the heat of their mouths moving together sears right through Matthew, each swipe of AB's tongue alighting the fiery sun that's been growing in his chest.

When AB pulls away, a minute, a month, a year later, Matthew's breath catches at the intensity in his eye as he says, "If you make it to next year, Matthew, I'll give you anything you want."

A million things rush through Matthew's mind at once, but he's saved from having to decide which is the best by the doorbell ringing. AB presses one more kiss to the corner of

Matthew's mouth before darting away to answer the door, leaving Matthew in the kitchen breathless and awestruck. Matthew touches a hand to his chest as the moment washes over him. Tendrils of warmth, with a touch as soft as their sparks, entwine the beating star that is now his heart, and Matthew knows, despite neither of them saying it, this is what their love feels like.

Chapter Thirty

Three years ago, to make up for the absence of their traditional holiday flare, AB hired Grace Atman's design firm to transform his house for his and Gabby's very first Christmas away from Houston. Mary Ann was the one who recommended her, and Grace did a magnificent job, but even beautiful, well-crafted materials expertly placed can't make up for the fun he and Gabby always have decorating each of their moms' houses with increasingly more ridiculous items. He, Gabby, and their moms have collected a truly impressive haul of tacky, over-the-top holiday decorations over the years, and even though Christmas in New York City will never be the same as it is at home, AB made sure to start a collection of his own after the first year, so the parts of his house untouched by Grace Atman would be shining with dollar store decorations like home.

He has a couple boxes of things set aside for him, Gabby, and their moms to do when they get here on Saturday, but after the trees are delivered and the designers unload their supplies, he and Matthew get to work. They spend the rest of the morning, and a good portion of the afternoon, stringing tinsel garland from every possible surface, hanging the tackiest wreaths he was able to find from every door in the upper half of his house, framing the bookshelves with bright, colorful lights, and dusting them with glittery fake snow.

They finish right as the lunch he ordered for everyone is supposed to arrive, and before they head back downstairs, Matthew twists a strand of extra garland around AB's neck like a shiny boa and presses a kiss to his mouth.

"Matthew," AB whines, wanting so much to sink into his kiss. "I cannot go down there with another clearly kissed mouth. People will get the right idea."

"Would that be so bad?"

AB's heartbeat kicks up. "No, of course not, but you're—"

"I've been thinking I should come out," Matthew interrupts.

AB blinks, confused. "Um. *Should*?"

Matthew rubs his hand over the back of his neck, cheeks turning red. "I told you I came out to the team."

"Yes, but—"

"And that night one of the guys came out to me, and I think—I don't know. Someone needs to be the first. Why not me?"

"But do you *want* to come out?"

"Yes." Matthew swallows, like the word physically hurts to say, and anxiety claws through AB's chest.

He takes Matthew's face in his hands and kisses him until the foreign nerves unknot, and Matthew smiles against his lips. "Okay. I think maybe we need to talk about this—or you need to talk about what's going through your mind, and I need to listen."

Matthew nods, his anxiety flaring inside AB again.

Then, the doorbell rings and what they were previously doing crashes back into focus. AB tips his head back, blowing out a breath. "Okay." He looks back to Matthew, brushing one thumb across his jaw to elicit a smile. "I'm going to go be a good host for a second, tip the delivery guy, get us some food, make sure no one needs anything. And then we will talk about this. Promise."

Twenty minutes later, AB comes back upstairs to find Matthew passed out in his bed, and the exhaustion AB's been trying to stave off since he got off the plane finally wins out. When he wakes up, the sun has set, and Matthew is sitting beside him studying star charts.

"What time is it?"

"Almost eight."

AB sits up, panicked. "But Grace and the—"

Matthew pushes his charts away. "I saw them out, thanked them all profusely for doing such a phenomenal job—which they did. Your house is basically Santa's workshop now, though it lacks some of the charm the decorations we put up have, if I do say so myself."

"I knew you'd come around to my aesthetic eventually. But you could've woken me up. You didn't have to fill in for me."

Matthew flicks his wrist, dismissive. "I don't mind. Besides, from the impression I got from her assistant, most of their clients aren't around while they work. She thought I was your assistant."

AB laughs. "Did you correct her?"

"No, I didn't have to." AB raises an eyebrow in question, and Matthew explains. "The intern recognized me. Apparently, she and her family are big fans of my family."

"No!" AB pouts. "I can't believe I missed that. Did she ask for a picture? Tell me she asked for a picture." Matthew's cheeks blush adorably, and AB swats at his chest. "You should have woken me up!"

"You're far too excited about this."

"I can only hope one day someone interrupts our dinner and asks me to take y'all's photo. Only then, will I know pure joy."

"You're so weird," Matthew says, but he's smiling.

Silence settles between them, and AB bites his lip. This is as good a segue for the topic as he's going to get, but he's not sure how to bring it back up. Luckily, Matthew starts the conversation before AB has to.

"I do want to come out, you know."

"Okay."

Matthew turns to AB, his gaze heavy with emotion. "But I'm still a little freaked out about it all."

"Yeah, I can tell," AB says, the mention of their growing magic eliciting a small smile. At any other moment, AB would tease him for being so predictable, but right now he's just glad it worked. "You don't have to rush into a decision."

Matthew wrings his hands together. "I know, but I'm afraid if I don't rip the Band-Aid off soon, I never will."

"Okay."

"Stop saying okay."

"Okay," AB says, dodging the pillow Matthew tries to hit him with. "If you want to come out, I obviously support you. But I don't want you to think you *should*—like you have to because it'll benefit other people in your sport. You need to be the priority in the decision, babe. Yeah, being the first guy in the league to come out before retiring is going to make massive waves, probably going to make a lot of people confront their homophobia more than what y'all have right now, but you have to put yourself first here."

"I just think this is the push I need. If I tell myself I *should,* it'll help me take the risk. It'll make it easier for me to do what I want—especially if everything goes to hell and I ruin my career."

"Matthew."

He huffs, fiddling with his star chart, and when he speaks, his voice is so fragile it breaks AB.

"I thought you'd be excited about this. I thought you'd be happy we wouldn't have to sneak around anymore."

"Hey, look at me." Matthew does. "If this is what you want, this is what I want. But please don't come out because you think it'll make me happy. I'll wait as long as you need me to. I will do everything I can to keep this private, so you don't get spurned in the process. Don't doubt that."

Matthew tips his neck back, skull knocking against the headboard. "I know you will. But this is so fucking *hard,* AB, and I don't want to keep worrying about who's seeing us and what people are saying and whether it's going to make its way to some sports reporter." Matthew's eyes are desperate and imploring when he returns his attention to AB. "I want to take you out. I want to go on an actual date with you again. I want to stay here this week for my finals without having to worry who might see me leaving in the morning."

Matthew ducks his head, rubbing at his temples.

"Does your head hurt?" AB asks, concerned this conversation is upsetting Matthew enough to counteract whatever balancing effect AB's magic has on Matthew's.

"Yes, but not in a magical migraine way, in an 'I'm fucking stressed' way."

AB moves to sit in front of Matthew, knocking his hands away so he can massage his fingers over Matthew's scalp—some-thing they accidentally discovered was an instant relaxant for Matthew weeks ago when AB washed his hair for the first time. AB works his way down Matthew's skull, to his neck, across his shoulders, until Matthew is loose and relaxed again.

"I have an idea," AB says.

"What kind of idea?"

"What if we could do all the things you want to do without having to come out first? Would you like that?"

"That'd be ideal, but I don't see how it's possible. If we ditch our friends and start going on dates, if I start leaving your house every morning, people are going to talk. It's inevitable."

"Then let them talk," AB says, ignoring the rapid beat of his own heart. "Reins tells me we've got ourselves some shippers already. How do you feel about that?"

Surprisingly, the news brightens Matthew's expression. "That people think we're together? Or that people want us to be together?"

"A little bit of both," AB says.

AB feels Matthew's warring emotions echoing around, feels the moment Matthew's desire to be seen with AB wins out. "I'm pretty okay about it."

"So why don't we ease into it? We reevaluated after Halloween—you know, started going out and getting photographed together—so, what if we reevaluate now? We can go on dates and let people think what they want without confirming anything. We can see how people react, and then go from there. See how you feel when people *really* start talking before you make a final decision."

"That's a pretty good idea," Matthew says.

"I am known to have one or two a year."

"I guess your first good idea this year was taking me out."

"I was going to say it was when I decided to do a charity concert, but taking you to the Met could be a runner-up."

Matthew's responding smile is as radiant as the sun, as warm as the feeling spilling out and over every single wall AB tried to reinforce the very first day he set his ground rules with Matthew. He's known for a while, but it's undeniable now—AB broke his own goddamn promise and fell in love.

@lalalani
My family's been a fan of the Levoies for decades I literally can't wait to tell my dad I met Matthew before he met Andre

@hockeybruja
@lalalani omg lani!!!! I thought you were working today DID YOU SERIOUSLY GET TO DECORATE THE LEVOIES' HOUSE FOR CHRISTMAS?????

@lalalani
@hockeybruja no I'd absolutely die if that was the case but I'm not actually sure if I can say whose house we're working on?? But Matthew was just here! In the house when we arrived! I guess they're friends???

@dayshiftbitch
She won't say but I'm pretty sure this hockey fan I follow who's interning for Grace Atman's design firm met Matthew Hellman-Levoie while decorating AB's house. @houstoncryptid doesn't this look like his kitchen in the background?

@houstoncryptid
@dayshiftbitch omg I'm pretty sure IT IS 👀 uhhh not to jump ship but I wouldn't be opposed to them dating

@dayshiftbitch
@houstoncryptid LITERALLY WHAT I WAS THINKING

@siemprecerise
@cherrysunset what do you think about ppl speculating AB is dating Matthew? :(he was at his house the day AB got back from tour & now ppl are saying they hear him in the background of the countdown video he posted this morning

@cherrysunset
@siemprecerise I'm unbothered by AB having male friends. If that was Matthew filming the video it doesn't change my stance on AB and Heath being a couple. Their love is RIGHT THERE for everyone to see.

@houstoncryptid
@cherrysunset @siemprecerise idk guys that video was clearly filmed right after AB woke up!! How do you explain Matthew sleeping over?

@cherrysunset
@houstoncryptid @siemprecerise you're acting like AB's friends aren't always in and out of that house at all hours of the day

@siemprecerise
@cherrysunset @houstoncryptid idk :((it's been almost a year since the split with Chloe. AB's super famous on his own now and they're both loudly bisexual so why would they still need to hide it? Even if he's not with Matthew I'm starting to think we were wrong about samarise

@TheDailyCerise
#ABSeen ice skating at Bryant Park

@cameauxron
@TheDailyCerise "skating" is giving him way too much credit

@ABCerise
@cameauxron @TheDailyCerise like you were much better than me!!!! Finn caught you a million times

@TheDailyCerise
#ABSeen shopping at Grand Central Holiday Fair

@princecerise
@TheDailyCerise lmaaaaaaaao at all of us thinking AB was dating Oliver when Matthew's with him all the goddamn time

As a general rule for his mental health, AB avoids Twitter at almost all costs, only going on to cross-post the occasional Instagram photo. But with their new plan to no longer try to hide their relationship, AB has spent a couple minutes each morning after posting his countdown covers scrolling through his mentions to see what people are saying. And somehow, despite what AB believes to be a pretty flagrant display of *dating,* his fans can't seem to agree on whether he and Matthew are or not. As for gossip in the media, not even the usual tabs have begun to speculate about the very obvious double date he and Matthew had with Cam and Finn two nights ago.

But AB has more pressing concerns today than the gossip about him. He and Zoe are meeting Matthew and Maddie's parents today, and as much as Matthew reminds him that they met at the gala, it's just not the same. They met in *passing.* They barely even said ten words to each other the whole night. He thinks he made a good impression—Matthew swears he did—but shaking hands with his boyfriend's parents will never be as stressful as joining them for their annual end-of-the-semester cookie-decorating session. Finding out this tradition dates back to when Matthew and Maddie were in kindergarten and not *once* has anyone outside the four Hellman-Levoies been present only makes the whole afternoon they have planned even more headache-inducing for AB.

"Good afternoon, Matthew," the doorman says as he lets them through the building, his genial smile and familiarity with Matthew providing a nice reprieve from AB's ridiculous nerves.

"Hey, Todd," Matthew says. "Haven't seen you in a minute. Your wife finally had the baby?"

Todd beams. "She did!"

Matthew makes a one-eighty turn, walking backward so he's still facing Todd as they head to the elevator. "When I'm not running late, you'll have to show me pictures!"

As the elevator doors close, Matthew takes AB's hand. "My parents are going to love you."

AB huffs.

"My parents *already* love you."

"I barely spoke to them!" AB says, flustered by Matthew's confidence.

"I'm touched you think an afternoon with my parents is more nerve-wracking than, like, playing at the Grammys or skydiving—"

"Are the Grammys your parents though? Are your parents some randos whose opinions I don't really care about?"

"Look," Matthew says. "Not only would my mother not have invited you and Zoe here if she thought you were anything but great, but my dad actually thinks we're going to Bond."

"You didn't tell me that," AB says, the news pulling at his heart strangely. "I thought he was an even bigger skeptic than Maddie."

Matthew beams at AB, his delight coursing through AB as he says, "He is. He was. That's what I'm saying."

"Huh," AB says, trying to keep his face neutral. "That's something."

Matthew laughs as the elevator door opens. "It's adorable how you're still trying not to broadcast your emotions when you know I can feel them."

"Shut up," AB grumbles. "I'm supposed to be mysterious."

"Literally no one thinks you're mysterious," Matthew says as he fits his key into the door.

As they step inside, Zoe's voice rings from farther in the condo, "Finally! You two are way late!"

"Not even," AB calls back as he rounds the corner with Matthew. "We're very comfortably in the fashionably late window."

"Way late," Zoe says again, before turning to Maddie with unchecked glee. "Now that the gang's all here, do we get to eat some cookies? I know this is a decorating thing, but you can't put me around so much sugar and not let me at it."

"You'll get your sugar, I promise," Maddie says, patting Zoe's cheek with a soft, amused grin before turning her attention to Matthew. "Mom and Dad are handling a Granny-sized disaster at the moment. From the sounds of Mom's shrill voice when we got here, it's a real doozy."

"Oh god," Matthew groans. "You think she tried to invite another one of her boyfriends to Montreal for Christmas?"

"We can only hope," Maddie says with a conspiratorial smile.

Not even five minutes pass before Matthew's mom comes strolling around the corner. Unlike on Halloween, her golden-brown hair cascades down her back, so much longer than AB expected, and even with the pinched quality around her eyes, she is just as radiant in worn jeans and an oversized Columbia sweater as she was at the gala.

Vivian stops at the edge of the coffee table, her focus darting between her children on opposite couches before she drops her gaze and pinches the bridge of her nose. She takes a deep breath and fixes Matthew with a look somewhere between sympathetic and hopeful. "Looks like you won't be missing the bake-off after all, Matthew."

Her gaze flicks to Maddie. "We'll be hosting your grandparents here this year."

"Um, what?" Maddie says. "We never have Christmas here."

"How'd Granny manage this?" Matthew asks, an amused smile on his lips despite the echo of disappointment churning in AB's stomach. "Did she lose her passport again?"

Vivian blows out a breath. "Worse. It's expired. There's no way around it. We either do it here or not at all. Your dad's on the phone with your grandfather arranging all the new flights. But Christmas is next week, and I doubt we'll be able to get everyone here by Monday evening like we planned to be there. But we'll definitely have them here for Christmas morning, though. Promise."

"Is Papa blowing a gasket?" Matthew asks. The amusement takes over the disappointment in AB's chest and, not for the first time, AB wonders how different an actual Bond could be from what they already have—or if they've somehow missed the moment entirely. But that can't be it, can it? Can magic know their hearts better than they do? Can this thing form between them before AB can even say those three words to Matthew?

"Surprisingly enough, he's excited to come down for the holidays. Nana, on the other hand, is devastated because—"

"No pond painting—" Maddie and Matthew say at the same time.

"Exactly," Vivian says. "But you know my mom—she's going to go above and beyond to make it up to her. I'll be surprised if she doesn't try to buy out one of the rinks for a night while we're all down here."

Maddie snorts. "Don't tempt her."

"Now," Vivian says, with a mischievous glint in her eyes so similar to Matthew's. "Who wants to watch six-year-old Maddie and Matthew singing Christmas carols?"

"You wouldn't," Maddie says.

"Please don't," Matthew begs.

Zoe's eyes twinkle, her mouth curling in a sickly sweet smile. "I, for one, could not think of a better way for us to pass our time before cookie decorating. What do you think, AB?"

"Absolutely same," AB says, matching Zoe's conspiratorial tone. "But hear me out here: What if we do an updated version after? Who doesn't love a 'then and now'?"

"Oh! What a brilliant idea," Vivian says, face lighting up. "What do you say, Maddie? Matthew?"

Maddie purses her lips at Zoe, who only smiles wider, and then turns to Matthew with a defeated expression. "We should've known better than to put the three of them together."

Matthew rolls his eyes, but AB recognizes the undercurrent of Matthew's amusement radiating through his veins as Matthew says, "Fine. Let's get this over with."

Chapter Thirty-One

Not long after his mom syncs her phone to the television, his dad joins them in the living room with news that the flights are settled, and everyone will arrive by the morning of Christmas Eve. Matthew is relieved his grandma's absent mind hasn't shaved off too much of their family time, but a cold dreary panic settles over him at how this changes his plans of coming out to his grandparents. The sense of dread only lasts a moment because even with the promise of immediate sugar neither Zoe nor AB can be swayed away from watching Maddie and Matthew—gap-toothed and dressed as elves—singing Christmas carols atop a coffee table stage, and soon there's only room in his mind for nostalgic embarrassment.

Matthew's sure AB was counting on Matthew's (and Maddie's) inability to back down from a challenge when he suggested they do an updated version of one of their songs, but Matthew's also sure AB wasn't banking on the snowball effect one ridiculous holiday song would have. Which is how one enthusiastic performance by Matthew and Maddie leads to them demanding Zoe and AB partake in this foolishness which leads to Zoe and Maddie serenading a hysterically laughing AB with "Santa Baby" which leads to Maddie sitting at a piano for the first time in years while their dad and AB sing a surprisingly good (on Andre's part) rendition of "Jingle Bell Rock."

More than an hour passes before they get to the cookies, but when they do, AB's cheeks are flushed adorably from laughing and the echo of his nerves Matthew felt on their way here are long gone. His parents take to Zoe and AB like a house on fire, and the latent anxiety he had about his parents not knowing how to interact with AB as Matthew's boyfriend is eliminated the moment Andre extends an invitation for AB and Zoe to join them at a Raiders game on New Year's Eve.

Matthew shares a look with Maddie, her shock only amplifying his own. His parents have opened their arms and their pockets to several of their friends over the years, but they've never invited any of their significant others to a game. They've footed the bill for plenty of his and Maddie's group outings to a game before, but attending a game with them *and* their father is a treat only ever extended to two of their closest teammates. Adding in their grandfather's presence, Matthew can't believe what he's witnessing.

Matthew is almost as surprised by the offer as he is by the sincerity of Zoe's words when she says she can't because she'll still be in California with her parents. He's so thrilled with his dad wanting AB's presence in his space, his dread about coming out doesn't emerge until they're back at AB's place. He probably has nothing to worry about, but AB going to a hockey game with his family means there's no way to put off coming out to his grandfather. He's been planning to tell them over Christmas, but coming out and introducing his boyfriend are vastly different things.

What if his grandfather isn't as accepting of Matthew dating a man as he is with Maddie dating women? What if he's of the mind it's fine—maybe even expected—for women in hockey to be queer but it's unacceptable for Matthew to be bi too? What if he doesn't *like* AB? The thought of disappointing his grandfather makes his heart constrict painfully, and the prospect of someone he loves, someone he looks up to, not embracing AB infuriates him.

"Okay," AB says, dragging Matthew's attention away from the rerun of the *Holiday Baking Championship* finale they're watching. "Did I make a mistake by saying I could go to the game with your family? I can always say Gabby still being here is a reason I can't go. It's super considerate of your parents to extend the invitation to her, too, but I don't mind saying she's not into it. I mean, I think she's going to love Maddie, but she's also planning a girls' night with Reina, CeCe, and Lupe, and I don't think any of them are going to object to partying together for the New Year."

"It's not that," Matthew says.

AB looks skeptical.

"It's not. I swear," Matthew says, his eyes prickling with a pain that's become unfamiliar. "It's just, well, I wasn't planning on having to introduce you to my grandfather yet."

"Ah," AB says, sitting up to where his feet are no longer propped against Matthew's legs.

The loss of contact and the twist of AB's nerves in his stomach only worsen Matthew's mood.

"I don't know how I thought I could come out in the fucking NHL if I'm freaking out over telling my own goddamn grandfather."

AB purses his lips, thinking for a long moment, but when he speaks, his words are muddled purple. "If you want me to go, I'll go, but I need to know if you're going to be treating me like a friend or your boyfriend. I'll understand if you don't want to introduce me as your boyfriend, but I need to know what to expect going in."

"I'm not going to *lie* about you, AB."

"Okay. Then why don't I just skip it? If it'll be easier to tell your grandfather you're bi without having to introduce me, then let me say I can't make it."

"You don't understand! This is so—my dad has *never* asked any of my or Maddie's significant others to come to a game with him. This is like—not only is it a big deal for my dad to like you enough to do this, but if you're there my grandfather's going to know you're important to me. Which you are. And I'm not going to hide that. I don't want to hide that. I'm so tired of hiding this from people."

"Okay. Then, I'll go. I mean—wait, what are you doing?"

Matthew is standing, with his phone to his ear. "I'm calling him."

"You're calling him? Your grandfather? Right now?" AB's words come out as sharp bursts of purple, the shape reflecting his shock more than the change in his color. "Matthew! It's late."

"Not really! It's not even ten. He'll be up—

"Hey, Papa," Matthew says, before mouthing *I told you* at AB.

His grandfather's voice is as gruff as ever when he asks, "What's the matter, Matthew? Did something happen?"

"Oh, no. I just wanted to tell you something."

Papa laughs and the sound of his genuine amusement soothes Matthew's nerves. "And it couldn't wait until we got to New York?"

"Uh, no?"

"You don't sound so sure."

Matthew grimaces at AB, who's staring at him in utter disbelief.

"Okay, well it *could* have waited, but it's easier to tell you over the phone. Is Nana up? I want to tell her too."

"Did you get some girl pregnant?"

"What? No! Of course not!"

"Helen!"

Matthew flinches at the sound, the shout not muffled enough, and AB's concern hits him like a brick, but Matthew waves him off.

"Matthew," Nana says after a moment. "You're on speakerphone now. What's got you calling us so late? I was about to go to bed."

"Sorry, Nana," Matthew says, genuinely apologetic. "I just need to get something off my chest real quick, and if I didn't tell you literally right now, I might chicken out, and I didn't want to chicken out, and see now I'm rambling because I'm nervous about your reaction, so here goes. I'm bisexual now. I mean, like, I've been bisexual, but I've now realized it, and, uh, I have a boyfriend, and I needed y'all to know before you got here." He takes a deep breath. "So there."

There's a beat of silence, and then Papa asks, "Your boyfriend from the south, Matty?"

"What?"

"I've never heard you say y'all once in your entire life."

Matthew blinks, shocked by how unexpectedly his grandfather is taking this. "Yes, he's from Houston."

"That's in Texas, right?" Nana asks.

"Yes. Is that really all either of you have to say?"

"Of course not," Nana says, her gentle voice filling Matthew with a newfound warmth. "I'm glad you wanted to share this with us."

"Yes, that," Papa says. "Have you told your father about this?"

"Yes, of course."

"Have the two of you talked about coming out before you sign?"

"Marc!"

"No, it's fine, Nana." Matthew says, appreciating the way coming out hasn't changed his grandfather's straightforwardness. "Only briefly. But I don't want to— I can't wait as long as Brinkley did, Papa."

"And you shouldn't have to," Nana says.

"No."

Matthew's heart jackrabbits in his chest as he wonders where this conversation is headed.

"No, I don't think you should wait until you retire. I'll be fucking damned if the league our family gave so much to tries to alienate you for who you love."

Matthew can't help the blush creeping up the back of his neck, but he doesn't bother correcting his grandfather— He's right, after all. He does love AB.

Instead, he asks, "What're you going to do—fight every sports reporter out there for their shitty hot takes?"

Nana's laugh is light as a wind chime. "Don't tempt him."

"I'll throw my name behind you—that's what I'll do. My support and your father's will be worth something. And it doesn't hurt that you're more talented than Brinkley was. The two of them combined should alleviate at least some of the fallout. Which, I'm sorry, Matthew, but there will be. We won't be able to shield you from it all."

"I know," Matthew says, the support of his grandfather making the pill slightly easier to swallow. "But Maddie said the same thing—about me having some privilege with coming out in the league."

"She's always been a smart one," Nana says. "She's good at reading a situation. But—" His grandmother sucks in a sharp breath, the color of the sound far more grating than it usually is while tinted blue. She's frustrated. "I don't want you to think I doubt your strength, but are you sure you can handle this? Are you sure you can take on the extra weight of being out while you're playing? You already have so many eyes on you, sweetie."

"I think so, I mean, I, uh—" Matthew looks to AB, taking solace in his presence, gaining strength from his grandparents' acceptance. "I still have to figure out how I want to release the information, but yeah, I think I can handle it."

And if he can't...well, at least he has the support of the most important people in his life.

★

@TheDailyCerise
#ABSeen: Getting dinner with Matthew Hellman-Levoie and Heath Samara
: @samebutlupe

@disasterbisexual
@TheDailyCerise @samebutlupe I smell a new love triangle brewing

★

"I can't believe you turned down going to see Blue Sunset's sold-out show to hang out with Zeke before he leaves for Boston," Oliver says as he flops down on the couch next to him.

Zeke kicks at Oliver's legs, barely grazing him from the chair he's in. "Why do you pretend you don't adore me?"

"Because I don't," Oliver deadpans, but for the first time Oliver's words cloud with a lie instead of darkening with teasing affection.

"I'm meeting AB's moms tomorrow."

"What does that have to do with the show?" Zeke asks as Oliver's face scrunches in confusion. "Also, doesn't he only have one mom?"

"Oh yeah, but Gabby and AB think of each other's moms as their moms too," Matthew says, remembering Oliver and Zeke aren't as close with AB as they are with CeCe and Derek and how years of being fans doesn't make them privy to all the same information he is.

"Makes sense," Zeke says. "When I first got into his fandom, I really thought he and Gabby were twins."

"Oh, same," Matthew says, thinking back to all the pictures of her in AB's house. "Well, sister. But still."

"Absolutely none of this gives me an explanation as to why you're here and not out with AB," Oliver says, steering them back on course.

Zeke snorts. "He has a point. I'd do anything to be in the same room as Jason Steel and Mary Ann Ramirez."

"Yes, well, I don't think I could handle all the noise tonight."

"I thought your growing Bond with—"

Matthew cuts Zeke off. "We haven't Bonded!"

"Are you sure?" Oliver asks.

Matthew takes a long pull of his beer. "I think I'd know if we Bonded."

"Would you though?" Zeke asks. "I've never seen anyone describe the process."

"Since when have you done any reading on Bonding?" Matthew demands.

"Since you stopped getting headaches."

Matthew's attention snaps to Zeke. "Wait, really?"

"Disappearing headaches is a little more than a magic Reaction," Zeke says.

"Yeah, well, it isn't foolproof. I got the usual pain behind my eyes last night when I was freaking out about introducing my grandfather to AB."

"Wait," Oliver says, sitting up a little straighter. "You're taking AB to Montreal with you?"

"What? No," Matthew says. "Oh god, right, I forgot to tell y'all. My grandma forgot to get her passport renewed, so everything's been switched around. We're doing Christmas here this year."

"Look at you two," Zeke says. "Meeting each other's entire families. Adorable."

"Next thing you know," Oliver adds, "Andre's going to invite him to a game."

Matthew chokes on his beer.

"No fucking way," Oliver says. "He didn't."

"He invited him and Zoe yesterday."

"Oh my god," Oliver laughs. "This is amazing. First cookies and then a game. They've basically been declared marriage material over here."

"Shut up," Matthew says. "It's not *that* big of a deal."

"It is!" Oliver insists.

"What am I missing?" Zeke cuts in. "What's so special about all this?"

"Let's put it in perspective," Oliver says. "I've known Matthew and Maddie since kindergarten, and I've never been invited to either of these things. Ms. Viv's big on family time, so cookie day has always been *just* their thing. And how many people have you or Maddie brought along to watch live hockey with your dad?"

Oliver and Zeke look at him expectantly and heat creeps up Matthew's neck, the first sign of a headache taking hold as his nerves ramp up. "Only Sara and Finn."

Oliver's smile turns smug. "Oh, *only* Finn and Sara. Your best friends on the team. People who know hockey. People who love hockey. Funny how it's never been someone you two have dated."

"Really?" Zeke asks. "In your entire life? Only those two people?"

"Whatever," Matthew grumbles. "It doesn't mean my parents think he and Zoe are *marriage material.*"

"Oh, okay," Oliver says. "You keep telling yourself that, Matthew."

"I will!"

Zeke wrinkles his nose. "How are you balking at the idea of marriage when you're literally trying to Bond with the man? Are you not planning to spend the rest of your life entwined with him?"

"But that's different."

"How?" Oliver and Zeke demand at the same time.

"I don't know! It just is!"

Zeke rolls his eyes exaggeratedly. "Whatever. What were you saying about your headaches coming back? You think the actual Bond will wipe them out completely or what?"

Matthew shrugs. "I don't know. I mean, I didn't expect any of this stuff to happen until after the Bond. But maybe. All I know is I'm stressed as *fuck* over meeting his mom and Gabby and I know I wouldn't be able to handle the noise of a concert. God, if Gabby doesn't like me, it's over—"

"Gabby's going to love you," Zeke says.

"Hopefully."

"She will," Oliver assures. "Besides, with the way your magic has been developing, I don't see a scenario where you not making the best impression—because even at your worst you're still likeable—"

"Truly," Zeke interrupts. "It disgusts me."

Matthew snorts. "Love you, too, bro."

"What I was saying," Oliver stresses, "is your magic seems to support Bonds being real, and Bonds being real would mean you're both in love, and being in love usually means you're not going to flee when the person makes one hypothetically bad impression."

"That word has not been used," Matthew says.

"Yet," Zeke says.

"It's really only a matter of time before you crack," Oliver says. "It's on the tip of your tongue all the time, isn't it?"

"No," Matthew says.

"Lies!" Oliver and Zeke both say.

"Maybe half the time," Matthew says, thinking over all the ways their magic has grown—the golden sparks of their touch in their most intimate moments, the way AB's handprint has been flickering to gold when Matthew allows himself to think about the possibility of being in love, the growing sense of *right* he's felt manifesting in his heart every time they're together.

All signs point to Matthew's feelings being mutual, but he wishes AB would say the words first—that Matthew wouldn't have to bare his heart first.

Chapter Thirty-Two

@TheDailyCerise
#ABSeen: Attending the Blue Sunset concert with Chloe Lutz, Jason Steel, and Mary Ann Ramirez : @pastelpansexual

@TheDailyCerise
#ABSeen: surprising Heath Samara on stage with Mary Ann Ramirez : @ztuleolhc

@annabanana
Currently sitting behind @ABCerise's mom on this flight hoping AB will meet her at baggage claim and I can have my very own meet cute

★

Matthew gets to AB's place half an hour before his family is supposed to arrive, and when AB answers the door, his eye bags are darker, more pronounced than usual, and Matthew is hit with a wave of restless energy.

"Oh my god," Matthew says, shoving the double mint macchiato he stopped to get into AB's hands. "You didn't sleep."

AB takes a sip, lips curling behind the lid of the cup. "Thank you. Also, no. Too excited. It's been so long since I've seen them."

"You're going to be exhausted at your own show," Matthew says, as they head upstairs.

"Taking a nap at the venue is literally part of my preshow ritual—I'll be fine."

Despite his insistence, AB falls asleep curled up in the corner of the couch as they wait, the sound of his breathing a gentle, soothing wash of pastel magenta doing wonders on Matthew's nerves.

As the minutes tick down, he repeatedly reminds himself of AB's nerves when he met Matthew's parents and how that day went great. There's now a video of AB singing with his dad on his mom's phone that Matthew's sure will join her Christmas carol rotation. This will be fine. He can do this. He can make a good impression on the three most important people in AB's life. Really.

And he believes it too. At least until he hears the front door open and an unfamiliar voice, muffled by distance, calls out, "How dare you not meet us at the door! What if I didn't remember my key?"

He nudges AB's shoulder, shaking him awake. "Houston, they're here."

AB bats at his hand. "Five more minutes."

Matthew would laugh if the growing reality of facing Matthew's mother for the first time while he's, at the very least, half asleep weren't making his heart race.

"AB!" the voice calls out again, closer this time.

AB grumbles, kicking out his legs. "Fine, Gabby! Fine! I'm getting up."

"You were asleep?" Gabby says, sidling up next to Matthew. She spares a smile for Matthew before giving AB a derisive look. "I sent you our flight itinerary *and* texted you when we landed."

"I was expecting more traffic," AB says as he wraps her in a hug. "And I'm *tired*."

"I can tell." Gabby pulls back and cups AB's face in her hands, shaking her head. "We're going to spend this entire trip listening to Eloise talk about sleep hygiene and iron supplements! I can't believe you'd subject poor Matthew to your mother's wrath."

Matthew blanches and AB snickers, swatting at Gabby's arm. "Don't scare him. He's already nervous."

Gabby is a head shorter than both Matthew and AB, but when she turns to give Matthew her full attention, he feels the need to cower.

"Oh, the moms are going to love you. Don't sweat it." Matthew sighs in relief, but then Gabby's smile turns to a smirk. "Unfortunately, babe, you're now the newest ear for Eloise's concerns about AB's health. And the iron deficiency is the number one offender."

Eloise and Lily join them in the living room before they make it downstairs, and Matthew quickly learns Gabby wasn't exaggerating. The first thing Eloise does upon seeing AB is ask about the iron pills she sent him home with. AB grumbles about her obsessing, but Matthew doesn't miss the burst of affection aching around his ribs. Matthew stands on the outskirts as Eloise and Lily reunite with AB, his heart beating rampantly in his chest, worried what the two of them will think of him once they've gotten their fill of hugging AB. But then, Gabby comes to stand next to him and a sense of calm washes over him in an instant, making the waiting much more bearable.

Matthew knows they aren't biological siblings, but he sees so much of both Gabby and AB in the two women before him. Gabby has the height of her mother, the two of them much shorter than AB and Eloise, and the same striking green eyes and soft, round face. But where Lily is soft and round all over, Gabby is lithe like Eloise, with the same gently curling hair and freckles. Lily has warm, tan skin and sleek gray hair with brows suggesting it was once as dark as AB's is now. AB is the palest of the four, so far from Lily's tan skin, but like her, he has smooth, unfreckled skin save for the three moles framing their mouths—Lily's on the right, AB's on the left. They have the same dimpled chin and dimpled cheeks, and Lily's soft, measured voice is the same exact shade as AB's voice when he's not speaking to or about Matthew.

Everywhere there is something of each child in each mother, as if the magic of the world conspired with genetics to make the four of them as much a family in appearance as they are in practice. They are so obviously a family unit, moving around and reacting to each other with such ease and familiarity Matthew would feel like an intruder if it weren't for how easy they make it to be part of what they have. When Eloise and Lily get enough hugs, Lily turns to Matthew with a smile so much like AB's, then stands on the tips of her toes to hug him as she says welcome to the family.

Matthew locks eyes with AB over Lily's shoulder. He gently rolls his eyes, but AB's fondness bursts through Matthew all the same. There's an underlying unease breaking through the calmness Gabby seems to radiate, one he doesn't understand until Eloise knocks his hand away, going in for a hug like Lily did, and AB lets out the most relieved sigh, nearly laughing, as he says, "Oh, thank god. I thought this was going to be super weird and y'all were going to spark too."

He wipes his brow exaggeratedly. "We dodged a bullet there."

Gabby, thankfully, takes pity on him and explains. "Oh, Eloise is a Concealer too."

"Camouflage," Eloise adds, mouth quirking a little. "Matthew, have you ever Reacted to another Concealer before?"

"Uh, just one other."

"She was a lesbian," AB says.

"And I had a girlfriend at the time," Matthew says.

"And he didn't believe in the power of friendship and never wanted a platonic Bond before me," AB says with a self-satisfied smile.

Matthew is about to chide AB for getting too cocky, but then Lily throws them both for a loop by asking, "Have you two already Bonded?"

AB chokes on thin air. "Lily!"

She dismisses him with a wave of her hand. "Why are you Lily-ing me? It's an honest question! My dad used to tell me you stopped Reacting to people once you Bonded. So, I'm curious."

Eloise looks between AB and Matthew, intrigued. "Have you?"

"Not that we know of," Matthew answers as AB says, "Unsure."

"Interesting," Gabby says. "Ten bucks it's already happened, and you just don't know."

"How, exactly, could you win that bet if neither of us know?"

Gabby pulls a face. "It's a *saying*, AB. But, if you want to be pedantic, I'm betting ten actual American dollars it happens before the year is out."

"Should've gone higher," AB says as he reaches out to shake on it. "I already owe Matthew a whole *fifty* for when he wins our bet."

Gabby and AB go on bickering, pulling their moms in on the bets and configuring more and more ridiculous payment all while Matthew's heart flutters away. One day he'll stop reacting to AB acknowledging their Bond's inevitability—but today is certainly not that day; tomorrow probably won't be either. Not when each time looks and feels like an admission of love. When they first met, AB's voice was murky and muted when he spoke about Bonds, so clearly full of disbelief, but now it's a dark, vibrant, beautiful purple and the words resonate deep in Matthew's chest, turning his heart into a warmth of light and his ribs into a trellis for AB's willowy lighting to entwine through.

★

@honestlyikes
How Matthew is having lunch with AB's entire fucking family and some of y'all are still swearing on your mothers' graves he's fucking Heath I have to laugh

@cherryredlips
@honestlyikes okay fair but do you actually think AB's dating Matthew? He's SUCH a bro I just don't see it

@honestlyikes
@cherryredlips a gorgeous bro tho!

Being back in the place his and AB's journey began is strange. Three summers ago, an electric heat crackled beneath his skin, amping him up and agitating his Vision. But this time, the heat is the gentle, comforting warmth of a fire, familiar as the kiss of the sun. The word he's been trying to hold back, the one he's had on the tip of his tongue for weeks, begs to be said. The truth of how he feels for AB blooms through him like untamed wildflowers—vibrant and beautiful and demanding attention.

AB must be experiencing the same thing. They're watching Heath perform from the side of the stage with Mary Ann when the echo of AB's feelings gives him a split-second heads-up to AB pulling at his sleeve to drag him away with frantic, hurried steps.

He expects AB's frenetic pace to subside once they're safely shrouded from view in the privacy of a quiet, empty room, but it only increases once they're alone.

The only thing AB says before pinning Matthew to the wall with a searing kiss is "Alma will kill us both if you mess up my hair."

Matthew has just enough sense to keep his hands at AB's waist as he tries to take Matthew apart with his lips alone. The spark of their magic is no longer a tickle of electricity, nor is it quite the same as the skittering petal of golden light they've been periodically producing. The heat of their lips meeting starts the same, gentle and warm, but the longer AB's mouth moves with Matthew's, the hotter the sparks become—as if amplified by whatever it is AB is leaving unsaid.

When AB pulls away, the sparks linger far longer than they usually do. The golden light dancing against AB's bottom lip, reflecting in his eyes, and the word presses against Matthew's lips with new life.

But before it can break through, AB says, "I have a question."

"I might have an answer."

"You will," AB says.

The searing heat of their kiss does not subside as their bodies adjust to the space between them. Instead, the sparks rage through him, lighting up every one of Matthew's nerve endings until he's dizzy and wanting. "You picked a horrible time to kiss me."

AB shrugs, coy. "I was overcome."

Matthew tries not to smile. He fails as always. "What's the question?"

"Well, it's kind of a surprise," AB starts, his nerves barely making an appearance through the heat within Matthew. "But I was thinking, and I want to— I want to reference being in a relationship on stage—"

"Okay."

"Without actually saying your name, of course," AB barrels on, unhearing. "And I'm—is that fine? I know we're easing into being out without coming out, but this would bring more attention to it. Once I say this, it might be harder to shake the paparazzi for a bit. I want to make sure I'm not making a declaration you'd be uncomfortable with."

Matthew grabs AB's shoulders, stopping his spiel. "I said okay."

"Wait, really?"

Matthew doesn't have to think about it very long. He wants this. He wants to be out. He wants people to start talking. His stomach still spins uncomfortably at the thought of coming out, but after telling his grandfather, after telling the last person he was worried would react poorly, confirming rumors seems so much easier than...releasing the information himself.

"Yeah. I mean, if you want to tell me right now so I can verify that I am, in fact, okay with it," Matthew says. "So, you don't second-guess yourself, I can do that for you."

"It's a surprise!" AB says, beaming at Matthew.

And once again, the word almost cracks through him. But he holds out until AB takes the stage, beautiful and radiant as the first time Matthew saw him. Tonight, he and the band are coordinating with crushed velvet. Zoe and Lupe are stunning in bloodred; Derek and CeCe glow in gold, while AB stands apart in deep, lush green. He's wearing a slim, strappy jumpsuit over a sheer white shirt embroidered with snowflakes and chrysanthemums, with an embellished, glimmering poinsettia at the center of his collar like the world's most festive bow tie. Each one of them has an ungodly amount of glitter in their hair, and their outfits are adorned with an enamel Pride pin—bi for Zoe, Derek, and AB, pan for Lupe, and a heart-shaped pin split between the trans and lesbian colors for CeCe—and when the light catches in their hair, Matthew realizes each one is sporting a different color of the rainbow.

Everything is loud and vibrant, but unlike the last time, Matthew isn't overwhelmed by the sounds of thousands of people manifesting around him. All his Vision is focused on is the sounds of AB, and when the dancing violet of his voice bleeds into the glittering blue of his singing, the words fall out.

"I love him."

"Have you told him?" Maddie asks.

"No."

"You should tell him." But this time, the voice is Gabby's.

His attention snaps to his left; he's surprised Gabby even heard him.

She shrugs. "He doesn't like to go first on shit like this."

Matthew is afraid she might be right, that AB took the one risk he was willing to take with his heart by asking him out on a date. But AB is patient with Matthew despite impatience running through his veins; AB thrives on attention, but when they're together, especially when they're sleeping together, Matthew is always AB's main priority. AB has a surprise planned for him tonight. AB has been surprising Matthew since the day they met—maybe he'll surprise him on this front too.

Midway through the show, the band exits the stage, and AB shows Matthew how full of surprises he actually is.

AB takes CeCe's seat at the keyboard; he runs his fingers over the keys soundlessly, speaking into the mic. "I have a secret to tell y'all."

There's a loud uproar around Matthew, but all Matthew can see is AB's smile, the small, shy one Matthew so rarely sees.

"The last time I was here," AB says, after the room has quieted some, "something remarkable happened."

Maddie looks to Matthew, one eyebrow raised, and Matthew shrugs—Matthew doesn't know what he has planned either. Despite the heads-up, all he knows is the feeling in his chest is exploding.

AB starts playing a little melody as he talks. "I didn't know it at the time, but there was someone in the crowd that night who'd go on to turn my world upside down. Someone who's made me reexamine my view on love, someone who's made me *want* to be as risky with my heart as I am with almost everything else, someone who's shown me how magical this world truly is. I didn't know it then, but I could feel it."

AB stops playing the melody and looks out into the crowd, only for a moment, and though they're nowhere near each other, Matthew can feel the weight of his attention as if he's right there next to Matthew. He can feel Maddie and Gabby staring at him, too, can sense Lily's and Eloise's attention behind him, but he can't take his eyes off AB. He's mesmerized by the way AB's voice shifts from his standard purple to that of his voice for Matthew, the way even the color he's grown so fond of takes on new depths. As the color of AB's voice turns stormier, more celestial, the love in his chest vibrates with a new intensity—making him dizzy.

"There was an electricity in the air that night. It seeped into my bones and exhilarated me," AB says, the color of his voice mixing beautifully with the pink of the piano melody. "At the time, I thought I was excited to be home, excited to be here, excited to perform, and all those things were true, but I really had no clue what I was in for. I didn't know I'd ever experience the same electricity again, let alone how important its presence under my skin would become to me."

AB turns back to the crowd with his disarmingly beautiful smile. "I know y'all know I've been in the studio." Another loud uproar. "But this song was not part of those many, many writing sessions. This song is about diving into the unknown for the sake of love and taking a chance on someone despite your own fears, your own history, your own neurosis. I wrote it on the plane home from Dubai, with Zoe dozing off on my shoulder and CeCe playing this melody from her phone. And while I hope y'all enjoy it—my boyfriend's opinion is all that really matters."

The gold of AB's handprint glows golden, pulsing in time with Matthew's heart, and he would laugh at the dramatics of AB saying *I love you* in a song in the middle of a concert if he wasn't so happy. Matthew would laugh if he weren't so pleased AB keeps surprising him, if he weren't so grateful AB keeps guessing what Matthew needs before he can place it himself, if he weren't so in love.

Chapter Thirty-Three

@honorarytexan
HOLY SHIT DID AB JUST ANNOUNCE HE HAS A BOY-
FRIEND BY DROPPING A BRAND NEW SONG AT THIS
CONCERT??????? IS THAT WHAT HAPPENED RIGHT IN
FRONT OF MY EYES???

@pnkchrryblssm
The song has to be about Matthew right???? Who else
could this boyfriend be????
@wingstomars
@pnkchrryblssm maybe Oliver? Idk if Matthew was there
but I remember after the gala someone found pics of Oliver at the msg show way back

@awfulalot
Thank you Maddie for using insta so much and document-
ing your time at AB's last msg show! Matthew WAS there
and it has to be him the song's about cc: @pnkchrryblssm
@pnkchrryblssm
@awfulalot absolutely agree! Oliver was there too but
WHEN was the last time they were spotted together? He
and Matthew have been attached at the hip this week! He
met HIS MOM ffs

@abcherry
Please god HOW is @cherrysunset going to get around this song not being about Heath when AB clearly said it was about someone AT his msg show and Heath was all the way across the Atlantic

@sintonskisses
Caught somewhere between absolute ELATION Matthew Hellman-Levoie might be dating AB Cerise and absolute TERROR at how hockey Twitter will react

@rainbowpuck
I will ABSOLUTELY sucker-punch a man who dares to talk shit about Matthew Hellman-Levoie's sexuality

@timothyjimothy
BRB compiling a timeline of Matthew and AB's relationship

@spacefacegrace
Lmao I know we're all preoccupied with AB saying he's got a boyfriend but are we all just ignoring his hand GLOWING like the entire last half of the show last night???????

@dannibby
@spacefacegrace Ok right WHAT WAS THAT?? How prone is he to the Frits?? Unless he's an Illusionist too?? But come on AN M4??????? Is that even possible

@spacefacegrace
@dannibby I literally have no idea but maybe??? Though he performed an entire song while Invisible with CeCe Morphing her hair in tune with it so this would be a truly underwhelming way to let us know about his other magic

@dannibby
@spacefacegrace Okay true! Doesn't seem like his style. And it's like OKAY AB I get you're in love and all but I've got some questions about your magic that I'm gonna need the answers to!!

★

Before Matthew, AB had no experience with magic Reactions and knew next to nothing about Bonding. He was under the impression it was some sort of fate thing, that the world was thrusting him and Matthew together and saying, "Make it work." He assumed he had no say in any of this. But now, months into his and Matthew's magic growing and Reacting in unimaginable ways, AB is no closer to understanding what exactly Bonding entails. To be honest, he might have even less idea what's going on between his and Matthew's magic now than he was when this whole thing started.

Last night AB did the unimaginable. He dived right back into the tumultuous sea of giving parts of himself to the public knowing they'll take and twist and morph it to fit the version of him they want to be true. He went on stage and announced he was in love with his boyfriend and came off stage indescribably happy—elated to be sharing even the slightest piece of the joy Matthew brings him with the world.

AB *thought* Bonding was about mutual love, that every bit of their magic growing was leading up to the Bond. But AB walked off the stage knowing the strange light and warmth working to break down all his walls as it grew in his heart was their magic's manifestation of their love. So, when he met Matthew in the dressing room after the show and Matthew greeted AB with, "I love you too," and kissed him softly, so damn sweetly, AB thought, if anything, he'd have an inexplicable knowledge the Bond was complete.

But no, he's no surer of Bonds being a real, achievable thing than he was at the beginning. Maybe love and a magic distinctly their own is all they'll ever have; or maybe there's still another level of intimacy to be achieved before it solidifies; or maybe they *have* Bonded, and they don't know it. All AB really knows is their magic is unpredictable, so when it Reacts in a new and inconvenient way right before the real fun of the baking competition begins—AB can't truly say he's surprised.

He and CeCe have just finished their truly miserable attempt at recreating the mirror cake Matthew picked for them; Zoe and Lupe are heckling them for having an even uglier cake despite finishing a full fifteen minutes after Gabby and Derek. Reina and Maddie try their hardest to remain impartial judges even though Carson, Oliver, and their moms have already picked a favorite on looks alone.

"*How* did this turn out *so* matte?" AB whines at CeCe. "There is literally *no* shine."

CeCe shrugs, Morphing her short hair to a glimmering silver that twinkles against her black skin. "Here's your shine, babe."

AB laughs. "If only either of us were Modifiers. We'd have this in the bag."

"I bet you regret giving me the job of choosing the dessert," Matthew says, coming up beside him.

Matthew's eyes are twinkling, his mouth quirking in an infuriatingly smug grin that should irritate AB, but only fills him with giddiness instead. Because Matthew is here. Matthew has made it to one of his most cherished traditions—something AB was sure he wouldn't be around for—and AB loves him. He loves him a ridiculous amount, and he knows it's selfish, he knows he shouldn't be glad Matthew's own holiday plans got mixed up, but he is.

"I don't know what you're talking about," AB says. "Are you saying our cake's ugly? That it's going to *taste* bad?"

"I'd never," Matthew says. He presses his mouth into a hard line, but the smile breaks at the edges. Matthew is so useless at concealing his joy.

"Good thing your sugar crashes aren't a problem anymore," AB says. "Now you don't have an excuse to not eat the entire piece of cake I give you."

"You wouldn't," Matthew says.

"Wouldn't I, though?"

Matthew's facade slips fully, his smile shining as bright as the internal radiance of his happiness bursting in AB's chest.

AB can hear the commotion behind him, can tell the routine of this competition is going on as planned around them, but the light in his chest makes succumbing to tunnel vision easy.

"You're a mess," Matthew says after a beat. "How'd you even get icing in your hair?"

Matthew reaches out for the icing, and so much happens at once.

His heart overflows with emotion, no longer capable of holding the warm light love has built, and Matthew seems to glow with it.

Glass shatters.

Matthew's fingers brush against AB's scalp, hand grazing against the shell of his ear. The gentle lick of heat against his skin is familiar, even the golden sparks registering in his peripheral aren't entirely new, but Matthew standing in front of him like he's made of the sun is a brand-new phenomenon.

"What the actual fuck," Zoe says, snapping AB's gaze away from Matthew's glowing, semitransparent form.

"Can you see this, too?" Violet bursts out of AB's mouth along with the words.

Zoe's gaze skitters around. "Babe, I'm not seeing anything except light. You're Invisible." Periwinkle splashes through the air.

"What? No, I'm—" He looks down, expecting to see pale skin, or the usual purple of his Invisible form, but what he sees is breathtaking. "Mom, close your ears—what the *fuck*? Matthew—are *you* seeing this?"

Matthew has his hand held up, turning it from side to side with awe in his eyes. "Am *I* Invisible right now?" Matthew's words are a sunny marigold.

"You are," Lupe says, topaz flying out from the table where her and CeCe are watching this unfold like a perfectly normal occurrence. "But kind of like...glowing? It's hard to describe."

"It's like looking at a lens flare in real life," Reina says in burgundy.

"Except more like if you took the lens flare and then edited out the center," CeCe says, neon pink. "That's what it looks like."

"How is this even possible?" AB asks. "It sounds like you're describing our sparks, but that doesn't make any sense. We're not touching."

"Are you two Bonding *right now*?" Maddie asks, the laugh in her voice brightening her green with yellow.

"It appears so," Oliver says, perfectly chill, perfectly casual, perfectly blue.

"I guess this explains the glowing hand last night," Eloise says, her voice a mix of awe and amusement.

"Wait, *what*?" AB says, finding his mom behind him sweeping up a shattered plate.

"You could see that?" Matthew asks.

"We all did," Gabby says.

"All of you?" AB asks the room, surprised when he finds Derek staring at him curiously. "Even you?"

"Going to be honest," Derek says in forest green. "I took a bathroom break while you were professing your love last night, but I'm seeing this."

"And it's not how you usually see AB?" Matthew asks, the sunny color of his voice perfectly capturing everything Matthew makes AB feel.

"Nope, I'm seeing y'all the same as I always see him. But you're both glowing a little? Like Lupe said, it's hard to describe. But it's kind of like a gentle ambient light? Kind of an aura?"

"That sounds like how I see people's magic."

Derek huffs a laugh. "Leave it to love magic to break through Immunity."

"That should be impossible," Carson says, whiskey brown like his eyes.

Derek shrugs. "I don't know, I can still get burnt by an Elemental's fire. Or hit by a Telekinetic's books."

"Yes, but those are real things," Oliver says.

"Magic is a real thing," CeCe says.

"But he can't see Illusions," Lupe counters. "Or be Healed."

"But I can see their gold sparks."

"You can?" AB asks, his head starting to hurt.

How is he seeing the color of people's voices? How has he made Matthew Invisible? *How* can Derek see the light they're producing?

"Well not before," Derek says. "But I can see them when they're gold."

"I'm sorry, *what*?" AB asks. "Why would the color of the sparks change your ability to see them?"

"Wait," Maddie cuts in, green. "You two have been sparking *every* time you touch this entire time? I thought that went away."

"What do you mean? Why would you think that?" Matthew asks.

"Because I haven't seen it? You two were bumping into each other all over the place on Thursday and nothing happened."

"Wait, no," AB says. "That's not possible. How is any of this possible? You're saying before—when they were yellow and purple—none of you could see them?"

Everyone who could've seen them, who's ever been in the room when AB's let his guard down and allowed himself to touch Matthew outside the privacy of their homes, nods. AB might cry. "You mean we've gone through all this to not even graze each other's hands *for nothing?*"

CeCe grimaces. "Seems so, babe."

"I hate this," AB mumbles. "I hate this so much."

"I don't understand," Matthew says, his confusion muting the golden yellow of his voice as it flares in AB's chest. The color makes his heart twist, but Matthew not understanding either settles him in a way. Everyone else around them is taking this in stride, but at least he knows Matthew is as unnerved too. "How could AB see it, then?"

"I think," Lily says, her gentle, melodic voice, the same color as his, "before now, the sparks might have been part of your combined magic—a bit like how you can still see yourself in some way when you're Invisible, AB. But now it seems like y'all've produced a physical thing."

"Which would be why I can see it—because the light is actually there now instead of, like, altering my perception of things."

"Okay, now you've lost me," Zoe says.

"Yeah, I don't really get what's happening here either," Gabby says, midnight blue.

There's a chorus of *sames* throughout the room, which does make AB feel a little better—this is incomprehensible.

"Immunity is, like, a barrier of sorts," Derek says. "It stops Clairvoyants and Empaths from being able to pick things up from me; a Healer can't mend my broken skin—magic can't be *used* on me. But things magic has physically changed or controlled can still affect me. Like, an Elemental could drench me with lake water, but they couldn't manipulate the water in *my* body. Or I can see CeCe's hair because her magic has changed it in reality, but I can't see you when you're Invisible or see an Illusion because those are more of an altered perception instead of you changing the physical properties of your body. Does that make sense?"

Yes," Matthew says while AB says, "No."

They look at each other, and AB laughs, barely holding on to his composure. "God bless your Ivy League education."

"So, before the sparks were purely magic, but now they're an actual source of light," Oliver surmises. "Is that what you're saying, Derek?"

"I can't say for sure, but since we're all standing in a room with two Invisible people but seeing light coming off them, I would think yes. It's the only thing that makes sense."

Carson snorts. "I think we can safely say Bonding has rules none of us understand."

"Yeah, because none of this explains how *Matthew* is Invisible even if they've produced actual light," Reina says.

"Can you and Matthew ever tap into each other's magic through your link?" Zoe asks Maddie.

"No," the twins answer together.

"But maybe you can with a Bond?" Gabby says. "That'd be kind of cool."

"No offense, AB," Lupe says after the room falls into a tense, confused silence. "But can you make y'all Visible again? This light is kind of starting to hurt my eyes."

AB was so distracted by the absurdity of it all he didn't even try, but now that he has, a chill cuts through the warmth of their light and panic spikes in him. "No, I can't. I'm trying and nothing's happening!"

Everything goes cold, but the pressure of Matthew's hand, the warmth it radiates, breaks through the icy grip of panic enough for AB to think.

And then, it's easy to push back against the incessant buzz of his obsession, the viscous little wasp carrying *someone's controlling you because you're Known* on its wings, ready to inject its venom into the crevice of his brain with one sting. His mind is clear enough to counter the thought.

No one can control his magic. Not Matthew. Not the paparazzi who frazzle him. Not the people who Know. Only AB can make himself Invisible.

The wasp stings, the thought seeping through him like acid. *But you're Invisible now and you didn't do this.*

"AB, are you with me?" Matthew asks.

His voice is calm, level, his face carefully neutral, but AB can feel Matthew's concern coiling around his ribs, can see how the brightness of his yellow has seeped away.

"Sort of," AB says, because everything's a little hazy, but he's not untethered by the thought. "Give me a second."

It's like the Frits.

Reactions are a wild and unpredictable thing the same as the Frits. Reina's cousin couldn't stop the frog Illusions, and AB can't stop the Reactions. But that's not a failure of his own, or a power of someone else; it's a testament to the magic in and around them operating by rules they barely understand.

No one but AB and magic can control his Invisibility.

This is not a failure of his. This is not his thoughts coming true. This is different, and he doesn't need to panic.

He takes a deep breath, squeezes Matthew's hand, focuses on the warmth of magic rushing through his veins, breathes out.

"Okay," AB says. "I'm better."

"Are you sure?" Matthew says.

"Yes, I was having a little freak-out—"

Gabby snorts, and AB whips around to face her. "You know just because you can't see me doesn't mean I can't *hear you!*"

Gabby hides her smile in her hand. "Sorry, sorry. Matthew, what does his face look like right now? Is this actually a *little* freak-out?"

Matthew's concern is still there against his ribs, but Matthew smiles, soft and surprised as he, presumably, concentrates on untangling AB's emotions from his own. After a moment, he sweeps his gaze over AB's face, smile growing. "You know, I think this one's tiny, all things considered."

"And you thought I was a liar!" AB says, vindicated.

"Okay, I'm glad you're not freaking out here, babe," Lupe says with a laugh. "But you two are burning my eyeballs. Can you, like, stand in a corner while we do the judging?"

CeCe digs through her bag and produces a pair of heartshaped sunglasses. "Take these; they're only getting brighter."

Matthew looks them over, then sweeps his gaze around the room, his mouth thinning as he notices the way everyone's averting their eyes from their brightness. He turns back to AB, a sad twist reflecting in AB's heart. "I'm sorry Bonding ruined your day."

"Who said anything's ruined?" AB asks.

Matthew wrinkles his nose. "You mean, we're seriously still doing this? Even though no one can see us and Lupe's having to wear sunglasses inside?"

"Oh, bless you, Matthew," Lupe says.

Derek nods sagely. "Rookie mistake."

"Nothing stops this little shindig," CeCe says to an equally perplexed Oliver.

Zoe shakes her head, laughing at Matthew. "You think a little glowing is going to stop these two?" She points between AB and Gabby. "Last year a pipe burst while we were doing this, and I had to eat wet pie because they're that stubborn."

"You're joking," Maddie says.

"You'd think!" Zoe says. "But, unfortunately, no."

AB looks to Gabby. "Come hell or high water," AB starts.

"A winner will be chosen," Gabby finishes.

"They take this thing *very* seriously," Carson fills in.

"Too seriously," Lily adds, but her voice is laced with fondness, the violet of it glittering like a kaleidoscope.

"Take your time," Reina says, with an exaggerated flip of her bangs. "I'm in no rush to try either of these atrocities."

"Well in that case," CeCe says with a devious grin, "I think you should get the first slice, Reins."

There's a chorus of groans throughout the kitchen as Gabby and CeCe serve up slices of each cake, but AB is confident his and CeCe's at least tastes decent—they didn't waste those fifteen minutes. Really.

Lupe wrinkles her nose as she looks at her plate. "At least they get *paid* for *Nailed It*. Why are we doing this again?"

"For the thrill of watching Gabby and AB out brat each other," Zoe says.

"Now is the time to admit which one of you switched out the other's sugar with salt," Carson says. "I do *not* want a repeat of those Oreo cupcakes."

"No salt switching," AB and Gabby promise.

CeCe grins at Derek. "No promises."

"You didn't!" Derek says.

There was no salt switching but there *was* sabotage. CeCe successfully put hot sauce in Derek and Gabby's mirror glaze while AB distracted them with a feigned attempt at a salt switch. As a result, he and CeCe should be a shoo-in, but Gabby's a master saboteur and managed to switch out their glaze's water for vinegar *and* sprinkled pepper on the tops of their cakes when she put theirs in. The whole thing is an absolute shitshow, and AB loves every second of it.

He's so caught up in the joy of this tradition, the way Oliver, Maddie, and Matthew fit right in, he doesn't notice the way Matthew's concern has transformed into uncomfortable nerves until they're alone again. After everyone tires of goading each other into eating more and more of the atrocious cakes, the group of them filter out far sooner than AB planned.

They leave in groups. Derek, Oliver, and Zeke go first. Then CeCe and Lupe drag Gabby off for last-minute shopping while Reina, Zoe, and Maddie head out with these mischievous glints in their eyes AB doesn't even *want* to know about. And though AB protests, even Lily and his mom insist they need time alone and head out with Carson.

Matthew rocks back and forth on his feet, hands flexing at his sides, and the full breadth of Matthew's unease seeps through AB. He's wary and on edge, hyperaware of every twitch Matthew makes.

"Why're you nervous?"

"I'm not," Matthew says, the sunshine of his voice rusting in front of AB

"Lie," AB says, stepping forward and taking Matthew's hands in his. "Even if you weren't resisting the urge to hide your hands in your pockets—"

"I'm—"

"You are," AB says, eyes lingering on the golden smear AB's touch leaves across Matthew's molten skin as he removes his hand. That's new too. "But even if you weren't— and even if I couldn't feel it bubbling up inside me—I now know what it's like to see a lie. It's unpleasant."

Matthew stops rocking. "What?"

"Seems we've melded powers," AB says, but for some reason that only makes Matthew more anxious.

"Do you think we're actually Bonding? I mean, look—" AB takes one of Matthew's hands and draws a little smiley face with his finger, amused by Matthew's shocked expression as gold stains his hand. "This is new too."

And for a moment, Matthew's discomfort softens into mesmerized appreciation as he brushes his thumb across AB's bottom lip. "Gold looks good on you."

AB's mouth twitches. "Will you focus?"

"I'm trying," Matthew whines. "But you're so beautiful like this, and it's distracting."

"And yet," AB says, placing a hand over Matthew's heart, "you're still anxious. So not distracting enough. Tell me what's the matter."

"We're Invisible."

"I'm aware."

Matthew purses his lips. "And we've been this way for way more than an hour."

"Yes, I know. Look, if this is about my almost panic attack—it's fine. I got through it, didn't I? Quite efficiently, if I do say so myself."

"Yes, but..."

"But what, Matthew?

"But aren't you worried this will happen again?"

AB shrugs. "Not really."

Matthew takes a step back, untangling their hands. He rubs one hand over his face, and AB notes the light emanating from Matthew's hand doesn't leave a trace of gold on his skin like it did AB's.

A flood of regret washes through AB, and AB realizes what this is—what horrible conclusion Matthew has drawn today.

"You have got to be fucking kidding me," AB says.

Matthew's gaze snaps up, and AB can't believe this is happening. AB does a horrible job of masking the hurt in his voice, not that it matters with the way things are. "You don't want to Bond."

Matthew steps back farther, face twisted like he's been struck, hand against his heart. "You're upset?"

"No—"

"Lie."

"Fine!" AB snaps, giving up on trying to underplay his emotions. "Maybe I'm a little upset! I don't understand how you're changing your mind *right now*. When we're here like this! We're sharing powers, Matthew! It's kind of late to decide you don't want this."

"I do want this!"

"How is that true?" AB demands. "I can feel your regret. I can feel how much you hate that it's happening right now."

"Because, AB!"

The sick, twisted yellow of his name takes AB aback. He doesn't want to hear what follows, but he needs to.

"I don't want to make your magic unstable! I don't want to make you deal with this. I don't want to be the reason you accidentally Display! *Again*! I don't want to be part of the reason you doubt the control of your own magic. I don't want this when it fucks with you."

And like a candle being snuffed out the glow dies, and the molten color of Matthew disappears. He's normal, Visible, beautiful Matthew again, but this is wrong.

AB's empty. Cold. He can't feel the light in his chest or Matthew's emotions rattling around his ribs.

"What did you do?"

"I didn't do anything!"

"Then why can't I feel you anymore? I can't feel—" He touches his chest, his heart aching for what's gone. "There's nothing anymore. It's like before I met you."

Matthew's fingers dig in where his hand is over his heart, scrunching up his sweater, and AB doesn't need the echo to know how crushed Matthew is—it's written in the lines of his face, in the wetness of his eyes, the sorrow of his voice. "I don't know."

AB grabs Matthew's hand, knowing it won't spark when he does, but still gutted by the confirmation. "Matthew, I already Displayed. People Know."

Matthew pulls back, narrows his eyes. "Doesn't mean you don't still have those thoughts about people controlling you, of Displaying without your say, does it?"

"No but..." AB sighs, rubbing circles into his temples. "Matthew, that's never going away. I'm going to be like this for the rest of my life. We talked about how being around you and knowing this could happen again was good for me."

"I know," Matthew says. "I know! But I still worry! The last thing I want to do is make your life harder. To put more stuff on your plate."

"You like the sun, right?"

"What?"

"You heard me," AB says, not smiling. Because Matthew looks about two seconds away from crying, or walking out of his house, and AB's not trying to be a dick; he's trying to calm him down the best way he knows how. But Matthew's mouth turns down in a frown, and AB thinks he failed.

"Yes, I like the sun."

"Right, and you like to go running, even in the summer, correct?"

"Yes," Matthew says slowly, still not understanding.

"Right, but you can get the Frits from that. And you still do it anyway."

"Yes, but how does that have anything to do with this?"

"Babe, you're supposed to be the smart one here," AB says.

"*Maybe*," Matthew says, a crooked little grin forming. "If you were making any sense, I could be."

"I'm trying to say you don't stay home all summer even when you know getting overheated is the leading cause for getting the Frits! That's what this is. The Frits and Bond magic and my own neurosis are the only things that can affect my magic other than my own concentration. And I know it sounds bananas, because it is, but I've never worried about the Frits, which is a legit way I could've Displayed before Divulging, the entire time I've been obsessing over being Known, and that's how I got myself out of my little panic earlier. I told myself this was like the Frits, and I felt better; the thought went away. It was fine."

"Are you comparing Bond magic to a literal illness?" Matthew asks, his smile falling flat. He's still upset.

"No, I'm saying you're the sun."

Matthew smiles, the apples of his cheeks burning red, but it doesn't last long enough. He stuffs his hands in his pockets, rocking on his heels. "You really would have been okay with a Bond if today was always a possibility?"

"I've been doing it the last four months, haven't I?"

"Yes, but that was—" Matthew is flustered. "Four months isn't forever."

"No," AB says, stepping closer to Matthew. "But I think I remember someone saying we could tell each other to fuck off and that I could have New York if this went south."

Matthew's smile grows. "I think I said we could negotiate New York."

AB takes another step closer, wraps his arms around Matthew's shoulders. "Before today, I hadn't had one of these thoughts since I landed, since one popped up with the first click of the camera. That was the test—there were people shouting at me about Displaying, and I was nervous, and it was there, burrowing into my mind saying, *This is it, one of these guys is about to control you, about to make you Conceal.* But it didn't happen. No one controlled me, my emotions didn't get the best of me, I got through the ultimate test, my number-one-fear scenario, without losing control. If I could do that, I knew I could take anything this magic threw at us."

When AB starts running his fingers through the hair at the base of Matthew's neck, his eyes flutter shut, and he moves his hands to AB hips. Matthew sighs, and the tension in his shoulders ebbs a tiny bit.

When he opens his eyes, they're wide and full of regret. "I'm sorry I ruined everything."

"And I'm sorry I didn't tell you, like, *really* tell you how much better I've been. How much I haven't been worrying about this. But I hate my brain, and I don't like talking about it."

"I understand," Matthew says. "But I'm still sorry. I think I broke our link by saying I didn't want this. I guess at least one of us has to want to Bond for it to stay."

"You can't be serious right now," AB says, caught somewhere between irritation and guilt. "You can't possibly believe I wasn't on board with Bonding!"

"No, of course not!" Matthew says, an adorable pinch of confusion at the corners of his eyes. "But I thought it was more of you wanting it because I'm into it, not because you actually had any real desire to Bond on your own."

"I literally said I love you *on stage* last night!" AB says, stepping back into Matthew's space.

Matthew's hands twitch against AB's hips. "Yes, but love doesn't require a Bond."

"No, it doesn't," AB says, taking Matthew's face in his hands.

AB kisses Matthew, slowly, gently, until every bit of tension has bled from his shoulders and he's melting against AB. Then Matthew's fingers tighten against AB's hips, pulling AB flush against him, and the kiss turns desperate, like Matthew's trying to reignite the magic with the passion of a kiss.

Nothing changes. There's no searing dance of light against his skin or the heat of a campfire burning through his chest. But Matthew's mouth is wet and hot, moving with familiar intensity, taking AB's breath all the same.

When AB pulls back for air, Matthew's mouth moves to his jaw, to his neck, his shoulder. AB sucks in a sharp breath as Matthew scrapes his teeth against skin, and it's not the same—it will never be the same—but it burns him up just as good.

"But I wanted to Bond anyway," AB says, the words electrifying him all the way through.

As quickly as it left, the glowing returns—so much brighter than before—and for an instant Matthew is a raging flame, and AB is a neon bolt of lightning. They are two independent sources of light pushing against each other, and then like the crash of a wave on sand, they meld together.

They are a sunset lightning storm, a dazzling blend of all their colors, and then they are Matthew and AB, standing in his foyer, awestruck and confused as the handprints on their palms burn gold one last time before fading away.

"Wait—" Matthew says, and when the palm of his hand touches AB's cheek, the familiar dance of light heats his skin and golden light reflects in Matthew's pupils. "Did we just Bond?"

"I think so," AB says, a hysterical laugh bubbling out of him.

"What the *fuck*," Matthew says, his laugh only slightly less hysterical than AB's. "How is this possible? How did—? I don't understand."

"Babe, literally none of this has ever made sense."

Matthew wrinkles his nose. "Okay, but this makes even less than no sense."

AB shrugs, giddy to have the crackle of heat back between them. "I guess we both had to want it."

"But then—"

Matthew shakes his head, and the confusion is no longer a feeling flopping around his chest, but an innate knowledge as intrinsic to AB as his own.

"Shouldn't it have happened before? If we both did, in fact, want it? "

"I guess we had to communicate the desire?"

"Like we had to choose it?"

Neither of them will ever know for sure—there's no guidebook for any of this—but AB likes the sound of a Bond being a choice.

He chose to stop running.

He chose to take a chance.

He chose Matthew.

Chapter Thirty-Four

Matthew's and AB's magics have been charged and Reactive since the day they met but never as intense, never as volatile as they've been the last few weeks. The stronger their feelings, the stronger their magic grew, and in a way, Matthew was expecting the Bond to make their shared magic even more wild, even more intense. And while their magic is the strongest it's ever been, there is nothing volatile about it anymore. Instead of a bubbling, physical sensation, AB's emotions flicker in his mind like one of his own—a fully formed piece of information with no interpretation required. And when their skin touches, the spark is a hot kiss of sunlight, always glittering gold, seeping out from the synchronized stars beating in time with each other in their chests. Like every moment leading up to this was them being forged together, their magics melted and molded into something perfect and balanced, their hearts a filament for the Bond's power, their bodies now vessels to reflect the light it creates. And later, when they're taking advantage of the empty house, they learn sharing magic wasn't a one-time thing exclusive to the Bonding process.

AB paints Matthew's body gold with his mouth, teases Matthew until he wants to cry just to see light run across Matthew's body, takes him in his mouth and brings him right to the edge before pulling off. He kisses him and kisses him and kisses him, and when Matthew can't take it anymore, when Matthew finally says please, finally vocalizes what AB knows he wants, he presses inside Matthew for the first time and takes him apart with slow, delicious thrusts.

As the heat of their bodies and the light in their chests gets right on the edge of their peak, AB asks, "Do you want me to leave a mark this time?"

AB anticipated this need of Matthew's before Matthew even knew what it was. Matthew still doesn't understand why he gets such pleasure from AB referring to Matthew as his, or why a mark on his skin soothes the restless, frenzied thing in the corner of his heart, but he does and AB knew it first.

So, AB doesn't need to ask. He already knows the answer. But AB likes when Matthew asks, and Matthew doesn't mind. AB gives him so much; Matthew can give him this.

"Please do," he says, and then AB's sucking a bruise against Matthew's collarbone and their bodies are a supernova and all Matthew knows is gold burning behind his eyelids and the pressure of AB's all around him.

After, AB links their hands together, and when Matthew turns his head to look at him, AB brings their hands to his mouth. AB's lips meet the back of his hand, and they transform into the same shimmery light of their touch.

"Huh," AB says, dropping their hands back to the bed, gaze heavy on the golden, transparent form of their linked hands. "This is new."

As AB talks, Matthew notices how all other input falls away. How other sounds aren't even showing up in a subdued, barely peripheral way. There is only AB's violet voice and the undercurrent of magenta AB's voice has when he's amused but not yet laughing.

Then AB's squeezing his hand again, and the only warning before the two of them are entirely Invisible, a beautiful golden wisp of sunlight, is AB saying, "Watch."

"We don't spark like this," Matthew says.

"I just made us both Invisible, like entirely fucking Invisible by sheer force of will, no accident, and your first thought was about the light we don't produce? Get your priorities straight, babe."

Matthew rolls his eyes. "Yes, because it's not like it was before, in the kitchen. Kind of seems this is closer to what everyone else was seeing earlier, but like, our bodies instead of a glow. Are you sure we're even Invisible?"

AB pulls his hand out of Matthew's, reaching over to find his phone on the nightstand. He thumbs open the camera but doesn't take Matthew's hand again. Instead, he presses their shoulders together as he holds the phone out in front of them, and this time, Matthew feels the electric current running through his veins as the Invisibility slips over him. And on the screen, there is nothing but their rumpled pillows.

"Okay! Now do me," AB says, swatting excitedly at Matthew. "I want to see how my new album looks."

"I thought you weren't done yet?"

AB's cheeks color. "Yes, well, technically, I was done."

"What does that mean?"

AB blushes furiously this time. "I obviously have new things to write about."

Matthew sits up suddenly—the dark, majestic purple of AB's voice finally clues him in. "Did you write an album about me?"

"No," AB grumbles, hiding his eyes with his arm. "Possibly."

"And now you're going to write more about how great a boyfriend I am," Matthew teases.

AB pulls his arm away from his eyes, looking at Matthew with a poor attempt at scorn. "More like an all right boyfriend. A passably decent partner."

They spend what little time they have left before AB's family comes home listening to AB's complete, but not quite finished, album. Singling out certain sounds isn't as easy for Matthew while they're sharing, but AB doesn't seem to mind.

AB watches the sound coming from his computer with such awe Matthew has to look away. Not that the dark purple of what is unequivocally AB's Matthew Voice bleeding into the blue of his singing is any less overwhelming to him. So, he shuts his eyes, allowing AB the thrill of seeing the Technicolor beauty of his music, while Matthew counts the beat of his heart to keep his own emotions at bay. Because nothing about making art inspired by other people could prepare him for the strange, exhilarating, crushing experience of listening to AB's feelings for him unfold in song.

He leaves AB's place emotionally spent and worn out from the exertion of sharing magic for an extended amount of time, and despite the cold, Matthew is warmed by the ever-burning ember of heat he's come to believe is the physical manifestation of their magic—their love. And though Matthew enjoys all the new wonders of their Bond, Matthew doesn't realize until Christmas morning how phenomenal this thing between them is.

Houston

Fri, Dec 25, 10:14 AM

GUESS WHAT VERY IMPORTANT VERY UNEXPECTED BUT ALSO KIND OF INEVITABLE VERY EXCITING NEWS I JUST GOT

Eloise and Lily are engaged?

Literally HOW could you know that

I have no fucking clue but I had a hunch??? I was literally about to text you to see if I was right when I got your message. And I knew kind of like how I know what your emotions are instead of feeling them???

Ngl that's pretty cool

But does this make it impossible to surprise each other?

Omg what if I want to surprise you with something ridiculous and extravagant because you never let me be ridiculous and extravagant and all the information about it JUST POPS INTO YOUR MIND

> Did you or did you not send everyone an edible arrangement because our Bonding got in the way of your regularly scheduled Christmas bake-off plans?

Is that supposed to be an example of ridiculous and extravagant

> OBVIOUSLY

You do realize you've just activated my deep psychological need to prove people wrong, right?

AB's idea of proving Matthew wrong ends with Matthew and his entire family standing on AB's roof as he unveils several cans of paint and at least fifteen different pairs of rollerblades.

Maddie looks to Matthew with an eyebrow raised, but Matthew has no explanation to give. Despite knowing AB was over the moon as he, AB, and Gabby had one last lunch with their moms before they headed home, whatever it was that gave Matthew insight into the engagement did not extend to the specific knowledge of AB's surprise—no matter the proximity.

So, when AB tells them this is his attempt at a substitution for the pond painting they're missing by being here in New York, Matthew is as shocked as the rest of his family.

Matthew knows AB's tics by now, so he doesn't need the Bonded knowledge to know he's nervous. He can tell by the way he clasps his gloved hands behind his back, by his cold, rosy cheeks burning even brighter in the waning sunlight, by the way he sucks his bottom lip between his teeth before he says, "I know this won't be the same as on the ice, but I hope it's at least a little fun. And I hope I have enough skates to eliminate the possibility of no one having the right size. I didn't want to ask Matthew and clue him in to what was going on."

Maddie squeals beside Matthew, her excitement bursting through him in a whirlwind, making him dizzy as it mixes with his own while the knowledge of AB's pride settles through him. He forces his gaze away from AB—beautiful and laughing as he and Gabby work with Matthew's dad to set up their concrete canvas—to reorient himself in the now. His grandmothers have gone misty-eyed, while his mom seems to be stuck in a perpetual state of disbelief, fingertips touched to her smile as Granny babbles excitedly about how she knew AB was a keeper.

"Mom, AB could be a certified loser and you'd like him for proving you right about Bondmates," Vivian teases.

Granny flicks her wrist in the air, but her smile is unbelievable, and her words are bright with delight. "Yes, but he's *not* a loser."

"No, he is quite wonderful," Nana says. "This was very kind of him to set up for us."

Matthew only manages a nod, still unable to process how AB remembered this when he was half asleep the night Matthew told him about it.

"Oliver and I were talking the other day," Maddie says, gently knocking her shoulder with Matthew's. "AB is so much better, so much lovelier in person, than we ever imagined he'd be."

"He's pretty great, huh?"

"Yeah," Maddie says. "And he brought me Zoe, so I owe him a fruit basket or something. Probably expensive coffee with how he is, actually."

Matthew presses his finger to his lips. "Shh. Don't let him hear you. He'll take that as proof sending everyone a gift basket wasn't excessive."

"Thoughtfully excessive," she says, as if being thoughtful makes it any less ridiculous.

AB joins them after a moment, linking his arm through Matthew's as he asks, "How's this for ridiculous and extravagant?"

"You really did outdo yourself," Matthew says. "Though, should I be offended this only came about because you wanted to prove to me you could be more ridiculous?"

AB grins so hard both cheeks dimple. "Oh, babe, I've had this planned since I found out you'd be here for Christmas."

Matthew's heart swells with affection, the light in his chest burning brighter. He knows AB isn't lying, but he asks anyway, "Seriously?"

AB nods, bashful and a little embarrassed.

Then his mouth twists in a devilish grin, and he presses in close to whisper, "When I rent out the library for a private event just so we can have sex in that bathroom just like you wanted—then you'll know how extra I can be."

AB's breath hot against his ear is enough to send a shock through Matthew's system. "You wouldn't."

AB pulls away, eyes dancing in the low light as he walks backward to the roof's exit. "Don't dare me, Matthew."

His ears burn, and for the second time tonight, he must avert his gaze—now is not the time to be thinking about AB naked. Instead, he watches as his mom and Maddie dip the front wheel of their skates in puddles of paint—bright green for his mom, pink for Maddie—before heading off in opposite directions, only to come back and twirl in the middle.

He's moving to join in the fun when the door to the inside opens, bringing his attention back to AB. "Where're you going?"

"Inside. We don't want to intrude."

"You don't have to go. This is literally your house."

AB starts to speak, but then Maddie skates over and takes Gabby's hands in hers. "Matty tells me you're the artist in the family. Come, show me what you've got."

Gabby giggles as she follows Maddie. "But I don't know how to skate!"

"Well, that won't do," Nana says. "Grab yourself some skates. You've got three generations of hockey players here; someone's bound to be able to teach you."

Nana easily folding AB and Gabby into their family is confirmation AB made a good impression, but when his grandfather beckons AB over, Matthew knows how much AB has endeared himself to Matthew's family. Pond painting is yet another thing in their household outsiders have never been included in, and his grandfather, the most family-oriented of them all, insisting AB is part of the family and has earned a place to participate in this event of theirs makes Matthew's chest ache with contentment.

He wants so badly to be able to tell the world he and AB are together, and as he lies in bed that night thinking over how well AB got along with his grandfather, Matthew wonders if hockey's reaction to him coming out will be better than he expects. Because really, if AB can make his grandfather, a man known for taking hockey a little too seriously, bark out a laugh by saying he knows fighting is bad on an intellectual level, but he still hopes he gets to see two hot dudes duke it out at the game on New Year's Eve, then how bad could the rest of the sport take it?

Chapter Thirty-Five

@NYRaiders
No better way to end the year than playing with the Levoies in the house! Add in @ABCerise and we've got ourselves a good thing this New Year's Eve!

@kyle99
@NYRaiders @ABCerise NOT AGAIN.............I guess I'm rooting for the puffs tonight

@mtritt286
@NYRaiders @ABCerise I was hoping this friendship wouldn't last. Being friends with a musician like AB is really not the kind of distraction Matthew needs right before he signs

@r_jones6
@NYRaiders @ABCerise this is your second strike. Please don't start riding Cerise's ass like y'all did with Bellamy

@asmitty
@r_jones6 @NYRaiders @ABCerise lol he'd probably like that

@TheDailyCerise
#ABSeen: on the jumbotron with Marc Levoie (famous hockey player and coach) at the New York Raiders game tonight

@rainbowpuck
@TheDailyCerise LOSING IT over "(famous hockey player and coach)"

@timothyjimothy
Can't believe I'm at the same game as the entire Levoie family AND AB Cerise my mind literally can't process the fact he and Matthew might actually be dating let alone that he's already chill with his entire family

@rainbowpuck
@timothyjimothy we gotta protect Matthew if they are because men are already losing it over AB being at a game

@timothyjimothy
@rainbowpuck ugh ofc they are! God forbid us gays love hockey too

@TheDailyCerise
#ABSeen #Video of AB at the New York Raiders game tonight

@spacefacegrace
@thedailycerise okay can we PLEASE talk about AB's magic now??? This is the second time we've seen this happen and I refuse to believe it's the Frits. I know we saw him turn invisible??? BUT WHAT IS THIS

@rainbeau
@spacefacegrace right like is he OR IS HE NOT an M4 Illusionist??? Please AB I'M DYING OF CURIOSITY

★

Multiple Videos Show Bursts of Light Around AB Cerise's Hands: Could He Really Be an M4?

AB Cerise Spends NYE with Hockey's Biggest Family Before a Night of Partying with the Hellman-Levoie Twins, Childhood BFF, and Band

Timeline Suggests Matthew Hellman-Levoie Could Be AB's Cerise Mystery Man

As Speculation Surges Around M4 Potential, This Expert Says It's More Likely AB Cerise Was Experiencing a Strong Magical Reaction

★

It's the eleventh day of the New Year. Which isn't important, but Matthew hasn't stopped counting since AB was caught on television with his family at the game. The broadcast showed AB's hand grazing Matthew's, and the light of their touch lasted long enough to thrust their relationship to the forefront of people's minds. It's been ten days since Matthew made the mistake of reading the replies under the Raiders' tweet about AB being at the game and got his first taste of what might be in store for him when he comes out. Nine since Matthew's anger overwhelmed him so much even the natural balance his and AB's magic brings couldn't completely stop his Vision from dialing all the way up and giving him a massive migraine. A week since practice resumed and one of the freshmen asked if it was true he's dating AB Cerise and Matthew couldn't find his voice.

Five days since he sat down with his dad and truly discussed how he should come out to the league. Three since getting a shutout in their first game of the new year was overshadowed by one of their opponents calling Finn a homophobic slur as they crashed into each other behind the net. Two since he finally reached out to Jonathan Brinkley for advice.

One hour since he and AB arrived at Brinkley's home in Chelsea.

From their brief encounter at the gala, Brinkley seemed like a kind man with a good head on his shoulders. But their fleeting conversation about advocacy at his parents' charity event, and the interviews he watched of Brinkley talking about his experience coming out, couldn't prepare Matthew for Brinkley inviting him and AB into his home for dinner and a side course of frank conversation about the realities of being queer in the NHL.

"I guess first," Brinkley says, after the conversation has stalled, and the reason they're all here stretches taut between them, "I need to know if you're trying to get advice on how to keep this a secret, or if you're here for me to talk you into coming out."

They're sitting in Brinkley's absurdly cozy living room now. Brinkley and his husband, Travis, aren't close enough to be touching, but their bodies seem to bleed into each other anyway, a stark contrast to the stiffness in Matthew's posture. The fire blazing next to them dances in the gold band on Travis's rich brown skin, and Matthew thinks of a wedding, of gold light running around his and AB's hands as they dance, of what it'd be like to leave this nervousness behind and introduce hockey to AB as his husband. It's such a silly thought to have in a moment like this, when he's still working himself up to coming out, but he thinks back to his conversation with Oliver and Zeke before Christmas, and how AB really is marriage material.

"Not really talk me into it. More like," Matthew says, trying to focus on the now, instead of a future he hasn't found the nerve to make possible yet, "convince me it won't be any harder than trying to keep my very famous boyfriend a secret."

"I'm not sure I can really do that. They'll be two distinctly different experiences." Brinkley shrugs, directing a sheepish smile at AB. "I also never dated anyone with your star power while playing."

AB furrows his eyebrows, looking to Travis. "Aren't you on Broadway?"

Travis's eyes light up at AB's recognition. "Yes, but Johnny and I met when I was still way, way off Broadway. And let's not kid ourselves," Travis says, his smile growing. "I still don't have your international appeal."

AB ducks his head bashfully. "Right."

The cyan of Brinkley's voice clouds over as he continues, "I actually didn't have many steady relationships while playing. Not necessarily because of needing to be secretive, but because the dating pool vastly shrinks when the closet meets long distance."

Matthew must grimace because Brinkley huffs out a laugh. "But you two have practice with the long-distance thing already—so that shouldn't be a problem."

Matthew glances toward AB again, their joint realization buzzing through him, irritating and dreadful. Edmonton is so fucking far, and they haven't really broached the topic at all. Though, now that he's thinking about it, AB being able to travel to Edmonton as much as he pleases without raising suspicion over Matthew's sexuality would probably make managing long distance significantly easier.

Matthew's tongue is sandpaper in his mouth. Figuring this out is so much harder than he wants it to be. "I wish I wasn't so nervous. That I could just—" He throws his hands out in frustration. "—tell people. It's starting to take a toll on me. But I'm unsure if I'm mentally prepared for the fallout. I'm constantly going back and forth between thinking I'm ready and thinking I'll never be."

"I understand that feeling," Brinkley says. "As you might guess, I always came down on the line of not being ready yet. But with it all said and done now, I wish I had come out while I was playing. Because once I did, you know, I got a lot of support from former teammates who I saw be casually homophobic in the locker room and on the ice. And it's not an excuse, and it's not up to us to put ourselves on the line so these guys can really examine the way this culture of ours has warped what they think is okay to say about their opponents or, let's be real, to their friends in the locker room, but I do think a lot of my inner turmoil coming from my own teammates could've been mitigated if I had been up front. But again, you shouldn't need to come out so your locker room isn't hell for you. And I wish I could say my own coming out made a significant push for change, but I'm sure you know—"

"It's barely made a dent," Travis says, his voice cutting.

Brinkley squeezes Travis's knee. "A sizable dent when you consider what we're working against. But, yes." He turns to Matthew. "You'd still be taking a monumental step. Especially if you're thinking of doing it right before you start in the NHL."

Matthew scrubs his hand over his face, heart beating rapidly, the slightest prickle of pain behind his eyes. The whole thing is so mentally taxing—he doesn't think his career would survive being in the closet. But he's not sure his Vision will fare any better coming out either. What a fucking disaster.

"I— How would you say the response you got coming out was compared to keeping it a secret for so long? Like, how it affected you mentally, I guess? Because my—" He swallows. "I know it's not unique to have a bad game because your head's not in it, but when you throw in my magic, my game can get *really* messed up if I'm having a bad day. And I'd kind of prefer not to fuck up my entire career by being in my head all the time."

Brinkley mulls it over for a moment. "I know what it's like for your game to be fucked up by someone else's words, from the weight of being surrounded by people who are hurting you without even knowing it. That's a unique sort of hell you've only just begun to understand. And I can't tell you for sure what it'll be like to go into the NHL as an out man, but I know every message I get from a kid who plays, telling me I've helped them, even in the smallest of ways, makes everything else worth it."

"Do you get a lot of those?" AB asks.

"Enough," Brinkley answers.

"I think he'd get more if he was on social media," Travis adds. "Easier to reach out when they don't have to track down an email."

AB nods. "Yeah, I get a lot on there too." He looks to Matthew, the upturned corner of his mouth betraying the neutrality he's been trying to project all night. "Knowing I've helped other people see themselves reflected in what they love gets me real emo. But like, in a good way."

Brinkley and Travis nod, an experience they all share. Then, Travis raises an eyebrow. "How'd your family take the news? Do you have their support?"

"Yes." Matthew huffs out a laugh. "Recently sat down with my dad to figure out a game plan, and my grandfather was here over Christmas. I was, admittedly, a little worried about him, but he's been really good."

"So, you've got the support of two hockey greats?" Brinkley asks. "That's going to make this easier. The more reputable sports outlets aren't going to want to go on record being outright homophobic to Hall of Famers' family."

"Yeah, Maddie's been saying that from the beginning."

"Look, Matthew," Brinkley says. "This is a hard decision to make. It can, and often is, hard before you even add in the public opinion aspect. But not only will you be making a difference for guys in the league—which, believe me, you and I are not the only ones—you'll be making it so much easier for kids to come out during development. And I think, I mean, that's how we're really going to change this shit. We have to build from the bottom up. But on top of that, the two of us have an incredible amount of privilege in the league just for being white men from North America."

"And on a personal level," Travis says. "On a 'this shit hurts me' level, privilege and your daddy's name and your unbelievable talent aren't going to protect you from homophobia, aren't going to make any of it sting less. But all those things will contribute to people's willingness to accept you, to support you, to make room for you in the league, in a way guys who look like me wouldn't be granted."

"Right," Matthew says.

"But no matter how much cushion you have, no matter who else you'll be benefiting, no matter what good intentions you have for other people and your sport, you have to want it for yourself," Travis says.

"I do," Matthew says, more confident in the words than ever before.

AB looks at him, this content little grin on his face, and Matthew knows he finally believes Matthew wants this for himself more than anyone else.

Chapter Thirty-Six

Is the NHL Ready for an Openly Gay Player?

The response to growing rumors sur-rounding the sexuality of Edmonton's star prospect, Matthew Hellman-Levoie, shows there is still a lot of work to be done. But in the three years since Jonathan Brinkley came out on the heel of retirement, the NHL has ramped up its inclusivity efforts, so acceptance isn't entirely hopeless.

Matthew's pacing again. He's not reading the article on his phone like the last time he was trying to wear through AB's floors, but AB knows he's thinking about it. The knowledge is a splinter in the middle of his brain, and the more Matthew's stress eats away at him, the heavier AB grows. Their Bonded emotional link isn't the same as before; it's no longer the echo of a rapid beating heart or a twisting stomach; there's no longer an uncertainty to what the echo means, but there is still a certain physical presence to the knowledge.

Matthew knew about his mom and Lily, and AB knew right as Matthew started reading the Sportsnet article. The story and Matthew's panic as he read it flashed in AB's mind hours ago, the sensation under his skin, the weight of it boring down on his mind, growing more frantic with every minute since Matthew got home from practice.

Matthew stops, whipping around to face AB, shoving his hands in his pockets. "Let's go to a hockey game."

"Okay," AB says, not tracking how this has to do with the article.

Matthew pulls his phone out, wrinkling his forehead in concentration, as a sense of nervous anticipation worms its way into AB's mind.

"Wait," AB says, sitting up. "Do you mean tonight? Matthew, it's almost six!"

Matthew's gaze snaps back to AB, his eyes wide, pleading even. "Yes, which is why I'm seeing if I can even get tickets."

"Is there even a game tonight?"

Without looking up, Matthew answers. "Two actually. Sailors vs Aeros and Raiders vs Storm."

"Can you get tickets to either?"

Matthew looks up. "Got a preference?"

"Not sure I want to go all the way to Brooklyn tonight. But who's got better seats?"

Matthew grins. "When'd you turn into a seat snob?"

"We don't all have supervision, babe."

"You're in luck," Matthew says, fiddling with his phone again. "Found some pretty decent ones for the Raiders."

And then the knowledge of what this is about hits AB like a brick. "Coming out at a hockey game is much more my speed than yours."

Matthew beams at him, his satisfaction at AB knowing— of their magic working like this—sweeps the jitters away for a brief, buoyant moment.

"I guess you've rubbed off on me," Matthew says, smirking.

"Mind out of the gutter," AB says, as his mind follows.

"I think," Matthew says as he slinks up the bed, "we could use a little stress relief."

AB arches an eyebrow. "Yeah? What do I need stress relief for?"

Matthew answers by straddling AB and tipping AB's chin up for a kiss. A moment, a day, an instant, a year later Matthew pulls away. AB chases after his mouth for one more kiss, and Matthew indulges him. He licks into AB's mouth, fingers tugging at AB's growing hair when he tries to speed up the kiss. AB groans. He'd hate how much Matthew loves slow, teasing kisses if it weren't so good, if Matthew weren't drawing weeks of pent-up frustration out of AB with his mouth alone, if this slow, careful way Matthew takes him apart didn't thrill him so much.

This time, when Matthew pulls away his lips are cherry red, face splitting into a grin. "And you said you weren't stressed." He drops one last kiss to AB's mouth, satisfaction dancing in his eyes. "You only like kissing like that when you're stressed."

"We kiss like that all the time," AB says.

"No," Matthew says. "*You* kiss *me* like that when you want to torture me—"

"Torture," AB snorts.

"Shush," Matthew says, his cheeks flushing as the last time they'd gone as slow as AB could bear flashes through his mind. "You're never patient enough until I want it, or you're stressed."

"Perhaps," AB says.

"Definitely," Matthew says, expression growing serious. "But really, I know you're prioritizing my stress, but I also know how much you're bothered by people talking about your magic again."

AB rolls his eyes. "They think I'm a boring Illusionist!"

Matthew grins. "That's not quite what they think."

AB huffs. "Okay, so they think I'm an M4, which, fine, cool enough, but what they *really* think is that I'd be boring enough to not even *try* with the Illusions."

"God forbid anyone thinks you're boring."

"Exactly."

A wrinkle forms between Matthew's eyes. "What do you want to do about it?"

"Haven't decided yet. There was that article about Reactions, and I'm a little worried that'll lead to discussions of a Bond. And then it's either correct them and let the Bonding rumors happen or ignore it and die a slow, painful death because people think I'm an amateur light Illusionist. After Displaying on stage in the middle of a show, you'd think people would know I'd do more than *this*—" He grabs Matthew's hand for full dramatic effect. "—to show I can do Illusions too."

Matthew shakes his head fondly. "You're ridiculous, and I love you."

Then he shifts, balancing himself more on the heels of his feet than on AB's lap, and Matthew ignores his pout, too lost in contemplation. "You know firsthand how unlikely it is for people to consider a Reaction being anything other than magic behaving the way it's known to do."

"Yes, but if they *do*, we're facing another layer of speculation. And there's only so much the public will put up with before they decide we're dating without any sort of confirmation."

"Good thing I'm coming out tonight. And it won't matter what people say, right?"

"Right." AB cups his hand round Matthew's neck, brushing his thumb against the stubble on his jaw. "But you don't have to do this tonight, if you don't want."

"I know, but I'm never going to find a perfect time to do it. And I want to get it over with already. Do it in a way I want before I put it off too long and the decision is taken out of my hands."

"Okay, if you're sure," AB says. "Let's go be gay at a hockey game, then."

Matthew raises his eyebrow. "How gay are you thinking?"

"This is your show, babe."

"But?"

"It's not really a but," AB says. "I will literally make out with you on the jumbotron if that's how you want to play this. But I don't really want to have to confirm what the sparks mean. And I don't know if we could get away without addressing them. Or how much longer I can deal with people thinking I'm boring."

"They don't think you're boring," Matthew says, pressing in for a quick kiss before AB can refute the claim. When he pulls back, he's beaming. "But as I was saying before, most people aren't going to jump to Bonds after they see a Reaction, and I'm thinking, once we confirm we're together and people realize we're True Opposites, they'll be more inclined to believe we're having such an intense Reaction, you know? But even if people do start talking about Bonds, we don't have to address it; we can let them think it's a Reaction until they move on to another topic."

AB takes in the gentle curve of Matthew's smile, the thoughtful look in his eyes, the acceptance settling over AB, and says, "You're really okay with not telling people we're Bonded, aren't you?"

"Yeah, as you're always saying, it's okay to not let everyone have every piece of us. We don't have to lay ourselves bare. It's okay for this to be just ours," Matthew says, his smile growing. "And, you know, like, all our friends and family."

AB's mouth quirks in a smile. "You've changed a lot on Bonding, too, you know. Summer-Matthew would've been shouting this from the rooftops by now."

"Yes," Matthew says with a huff of laughter. "But Summer-Matthew knew nothing."

AB pulls Matthew back into his lap. "Winter-Matthew only knows, like, four more things, though."

"Wow, rude," Matthew says, his laughter bright and happy.

"Shush," AB says, trailing his hands down Matthew's arms.

The slow creeping heat of his touch turns the laughter in Matthew's eyes to fire, his gears shifting in an instant. Matthew lifts his arms when AB goes for the hem of his Henley, goes pliant as AB takes it off him, and then lets out a soft, satisfied groan, as AB presses him back against the bed and mutters, "I believe something of mine was due for some destressing."

Chapter Thirty-Seven

@TheDailyCerise
#ABSeen at New York Raiders game with Matthew Hell-man-Levoie

ABCerise Love & Hockey

mhl21 Date night with this guy

@timothyjimothy
This is fine this is fine I'm TOTALLY fine but MY TWO FAVORITE MEN ARE DATING????? Is this real life??? How have I been so fucking blessed

@sunsetred
Someone check on @cherrysunset there's approximately five minutes until she goes scorched earth on us all

AB Cerise #Confirms Relationship with Matthew Hellman-Levoie

Matthew Hellman-Levoie, Miners Star Goalie Prospect and Youngest in the Levoie Family, Comes Out at Raiders Game

@outathletics
Three years after Jonathan Brinkley became the first NHL player to ever come out, Matthew Hellman-Levoie announces he has a boyfriend months before entering the NHL. He will likely become the first athlete to play an NHL game while out.

@mtritt286
@outsports coulda kept that to himself

@mi_ers
@outathletics cool but can he sign already I'm tired of waiting

@stormsurgesteve
@outathletics incredibly brave for him to do before his career has even started. Wish him well.

@bret714
@outatheltics I guess this explains why a pop star's chummy with my college hockey team

@adam829
@bret714 bro came off private to announce he's bagging a celebrity, gotta respect that energy

@bret714
@adam829 right? Dunno if I could've kept it a secret this long

@rainbowpuck
HOCKEY JUST GOT GAYER I'M LITERALLY CRYING THANK YOU MATTHEW FOR SHARING THIS WITH US

@rainbowpuck
@abcerise show your boyfriend this tweet since he's not on Twitter please and thank you

@sintonskisses
Do I have to root for the miners now??? I don't really look good in orange.....but I will ABSOLUTELY fight every single homophobe in Matthew's honor

The response to Matthew coming out is a mixed bag—far more positive than his worst fears assumed it could ever be, but negative enough to rattle him. He runs on autopilot the first week after. The days pass in a haze as Matthew tries to ignore a bunch of guys he doesn't know hypothesizing about Matthew fucking up the team dynamic, suggesting a locker room can't be a comfortable place when there's a guy checking the others out. He has a dull, dull pain in his eyes going into the weekend—the Bond not impervious to the roiling emotion of strangers judging him on his sexuality—and the first games back aren't his best. He's sloppy, but he still makes the saves. They don't lose. It's fine.

He's fine.

Except, it's Sunday evening and AB's standing in front of him with his hands on his hips, lips pursed. "Matthew."

"Yes?"

"Don't *yes* me! You know what you're doing," AB says. "Your shit's affecting me, which is then affecting *you*, and now we're in an endless loop of agitation. You've got to stop searching your name on Google. It isn't healthy—which I'm sure you remember telling me before."

"I was wrong," Matthew grumbles.

"No, you were not," AB says, coming to join him on the couch. "I wish so much that I could silence everyone who's making you feel this way. But unfortunately, I don't think it would be very ethical to sic my fans on your naysayers."

"Your fans?" Matthew says, lolling his head to the side to look at AB. "How would you even do that?"

"Babe, you should see the shit some of these fans say when I get a bad review on an album. If I quote tweeted one of these guys telling them to shut the fuck up, it'd have a snowball effect. Especially since we've got some crossover among our fans who are absolutely rallying my solo fans to get on the Matthew defense squad."

"Shut up, they are *not*."

"It's cute how you have a built-in lie detector and still try to disagree with me when you're embarrassed by the truth," AB says, a smug smile dimpling his cheek. "Some of them like you more than me, which I think is rude, but whatever."

Matthew snorts. "How do you even know all this? Have *you* been searching my name on Twitter?"

AB puts a hand to his chest, dramatic. "You think I'd do that? After how unhealthy you've told me it is? After how much you've *nagged* me about it?"

Matthew's lips twitch despite his effort not to. "Obviously."

"Well, well, well, my darling Mattycakes, you're in for a real shock," AB says, smiling as Matthew arches a brow. "Maddie's been filling me in on the deets. Duh."

"Of course, she has. She might be worse than you."

"Ah, to be a boy not emotionally linked to his two favorite people," AB says.

"Mighty presumptuous of you, Houston," Matthew says, cracking a smile for what feels like the first time in days. "Definitely a top five, but I don't know about top two."

AB smiles, eyes dancing as the buoyancy of his joy settles into Matthew and lifts his mood. "I guess I need to step my game way up. I was willing to concede first to Maddie, because twins, but you know I hate losing."

"I'm scared to see what stepping your game up would look like," Matthew laughs.

"Ridiculous and extravagant certainly," AB says, with a small, soft smile. Then, he wraps his arm around Matthew's shoulders and pulls him against his side, kissing the top of his head. "Sorry again. I hate that you're having to deal with this. That coming out, especially a high-profile one, can't just be met with complete acceptance and positivity."

Matthew huffs. "It hasn't been all bad."

"Yeah, I read the new *Outathletics* article about you. Not only do they love you, quite a few of the comments were about how much hotter you are than Brinkley. Which, no offense to Jonathan, but they are correct."

Matthew snorts. "The flattery is nice. But I was mostly thinking about the kids who've told me what this means to them."

AB starts brushing fingers through Matthew's hair, scratching ever so slightly on every other stroke through, and Matthew absolutely does not make a sound of contentment.

"Yes, well, those *are* the most important bits. But let's not kid ourselves here; we all love to be called pretty."

"No one as much as you," Matthew teases.

"You got me there," AB laughs, continuing to pet Matthew's hair.

"Thank you," Matthew says after a quiet moment, AB's fingers in his hair and the dual beat of their magic in his chest improving his mood monumentally. "For getting me out of my head. And I'm sorry I've been making you feel like shit."

"That is not what I said," AB says. "It's just strange. You're rightfully upset, and I'm upset because you're upset because, like, I empathize with you, but then I'm extra upset because I'm literally sharing your emotion? Which only makes you worse and it's... I mean, there are several plus sides to the Bond, as we are well aware, but I'm hoping we get better about this part."

Matthew sits up, not liking this feeling of AB's washing over him. And sure enough, AB's frowning, as he says something Matthew hates, very much. "But if it's always like this, I'll totally understand if you need a break from the emotional reverb and want to go home for a bit."

"This is my home," Matthew says, without thinking. The only thing cluing him into the words falling out of his mouth is the shock on AB's face and the warmth of their magic burning stronger. "Wait, I mean, no look—"

"Don't you dare complete that thought," AB says, grin bright and dazzling. "You haven't slept at your apartment in more than a month. I gave you a key! I always have to correct myself in my head. I'm definitely not bothered by this."

Relief floods Matthew and AB swats at his chest, rolling his eyes. "I can't believe you were worried about *that*. Especially since you'll need a place here once you relocate to the great white tundra that is Edmonton. Well actually, is it cold there? I have no idea, but it *sounds* like a forever cold kind of place. But whatever, what I'm saying is you can obviously stay with me when you're here."

"You inviting me to move in?" Matthew says, trying for flippant but failing on all counts.

"Can it really be called an invitation when you've had a key for months and basically live here already?"

"Yes," Matthew says, throat tightening with emotion. "It can be."

"Then yes, Matthew, I am asking you to move in for re-alsies. Now, once your lease is up, whenever pleases you."

"Okay." Matthew nods, repeatedly. "Yeah. Definitely. Let's do that."

"Someone's excited," AB says, but there's relief moving through Matthew, betraying the nerves AB was trying to hide.

"Yeah, you."

"Yeah," AB says, surprising Matthew with the lack of sarcasm. "I am."

Chapter Thirty-Eight

The overall positive response to his coming out, and Matthew's hope everything will, in fact, be fine, hits its first bump on the cold, dreary bus ride up to Union.

Finn's in the aisle seat beside him, fishing for ideas of what to get Cam for Valentine's Day.

Nolan snorts next to Matthew. "Doesn't Cam think Valentine's Day is for suckers?"

"Yes, but as she always reminds me, I'm a sucker." Finn shrugs, grinning. "Besides, everyone loves gifts. *And* she dyed her hair bright pink. She's definitely about the sappy love day this year."

"Oh, are you two in *love* now?" Matthew asks.

Finn blushes, and Nolan huffs out a laugh. "You still haven't told her."

"Actually," Finn starts. But then his phone rings in his hand and his eyes light up, like maybe he's expecting a text from Cam, only to dim as his face falls, mouth pursing, brow furrowing.

"What's that face for?" Nolan asks, and when Finn's expression sours as he flicks his thumb across the screen, eyes darting as he reads, a cold dread creeps through Matthew.

His bad feeling is only justified when Finn looks up, eyes sort of panicked, sort of furious. "Some guy from

MineCountry wants to know if your magic has ever gotten in the way of your game," Finn says, the color of his voice a sickly yellow.

Matthew sits up straight, heart pounding. "Well, this isn't a good sign."

But Matthew doesn't find out just how bad a sign it is until Monday morning.

The first article is about whether or not Matthew was a wasted first pick. Whether the Miners made a mistake going for a goalie when they could've had a powerhouse like Axel Nilsson, only for Matthew to opt out of signing immediately and doing four years of development in the NCAA. How waiting around four years could backfire on the Miners now that they know Omnivisions can be so erratic. MineCountry, of course, didn't get comments back from anyone who *knows* Matthew, let alone any past or present teammates, but they did get a former major juniors' goalie in his sixties on record saying he's an Omnivision, and he's surprised Matthew's made it this far, considering how hard the noise of a hockey game is to manage and how it often leads to sensory headaches. Andre fumes when Matthew tells him about it, throwing his hands in the air, nearly shouting, "That's proof enough you're elite!" But the writer, and Miners fans, don't seem to agree. They think he's a *liability* now. That NHL games are louder, more intense, more stressful, and can Matthew really manage all the new pressure on top of a magic that can give him headaches? Omnivision is already widely seen as a hindrance—not a benefit like other Big Fours restricted by the Enhancement Cap each team must deal with—and do they really want to risk making the transition between a veteran goalie to a rookie with headaches possibly compounded by the high stress level of professional hockey he's so unused to?

The next is about Matthew being a twin. About the link being remarkable but just as much of a distraction, if not more so. They have anecdotes from twins all over who've felt anything from a hangover to their twin's arm breaking despite the distance between them, to the truly traumatic story about a twin who felt his brother die in a car accident. Matthew thinks a line was crossed bringing the last one into all this, and plenty of people agree, but it doesn't stop the people from questioning how reliable Matthew is. Because can the Miners really rebuild with such a faulty piece, with someone who could be taken out of the game if their sister got hurt in her own career? Can they really have any faith in Matthew as all these issues stack up against him?

Then there's the editorial piece about how Matthew prioritizing his education is commendable but doesn't really mesh with the team-first mentality being fostered in the locker room. And of course, no one in the press ever comments on his bisexuality being a problem, specifically, but there's the one reporter who points to Matthew refusing to comment on what label he uses as a sign he's stubborn and uncooperative. There's the one who points to AB's star power, and his proclivity for partying, as yet another distraction. The one claiming Matthew dating someone he Reacts to so strongly is as much a liability as being a twin. And Matthew's not naive—he knows the real reason for this.

He's seen how this plays out, how star players get targeted and torn down, presented as bad seeds all before the inevitable trade. He's certain his career with the Miners is over before it's even begun; he's accepted his fate, but despite the emotional toll, despite people who know nothing about being an Omnivision insisting Matthew's magic is a detriment to his play, he and the guys are having a remarkable season. They've clinched the Ivy League title, and with four games left in the season, they're leading the ECAC in points. Matthew refuses to let the prospect of a trade ruin his last season of college hockey.

But then, his phone lights up with an Edmonton number while he's lying on his couch being pelted by little pieces of Zeke's straw wrapper while Oliver and Maddie bicker about takeout options in the kitchen, and he's not so sure he's ready for the call.

Because really, there could only be one reason for an Edmonton number to be calling him.

He bolts upright, head piercing for one sharp moment before he gets ahold of himself and filters out all colors. A faint pain lingers, but he doesn't think he's going to vomit. Which is good. Because the person calling answers Matthew's greeting with "Hello, Mr. Hellman-Levoie. I'm glad I caught you. I'm calling on behalf of Jared Dell, the marketing manager for the Miners. Do you have a moment?"

"Uh, yeah," Matthew says, unsure. He doesn't see why marketing would be reaching out to him about the trade, but what else could this be about?

"As I'm sure you know," this clipped, nameless voice says, "February is You Can Skate month, yes?"

"Yes." Matthew nods, realizing belatedly the room around him has gone completely silent. He glances to Zeke, only to find Maddie and Oliver standing behind his chair, looking equally concerned.

He mouths, "Miners' marketing," but it does about as good explaining the call for them as it did for Matthew.

"Well, our Pride night is this Saturday, and I understand this is all terribly last minute, but we'd like you to film a video for the jumbotron. To go alongside our ambassador's segment."

"It's Thursday," Matthew says, tongue too thick.

"Indeed, it is. We have, of course, made arrangements for a cameraman to meet you at your rink tomorrow afternoon after your pregame skate. All you have to do is be there and give a little statement on why you came out, the support you've received, anything really. It's one thing for us to have a player up there, as an ally, talking about the league striving for inclusion, and if you can skate, you can skate, but it really opens the door to how much we mean it when it comes from you—someone who's living it."

Despite the uneasy churn of his stomach, Matthew finds himself saying okay, and when he hangs up after being told he'll be emailed with the exact details, Maddie is the first one to speak.

"What was *that* about?"

"They want me to film something for their Pride night."

Maddie snorts, her eyes burning with fury, mimicking the uneasy anger growing in his chest. "I don't like the sound of this, Matty."

"Neither do I," Matthew says.

This should be good, this should ease his concerns, this should show him he's supported, but it doesn't. It does absolutely nothing to ease his mind—it only ramps it up.

"I don't understand," Zeke says, looking between Matthew and Maddie. "Why do you both look so...angry? Isn't this a good thing?"

"It should be, but..." She looks to Matthew, a mix of concern and protectiveness echoing around Matthew's chest. "I have a bad feeling."

"You think this is a gimmick?" Oliver asks.

Maddie makes a frustrated noise. "I don't know! But it sure seems like one. It feels like they're covering their asses after nearly three weeks of concocting enough reasons to get away with trading him. Slip him in at the trade deadline so it might get lost in all the hubbub."

Zeke purses his lips. "Can they do that when you're still a prospect?"

"It's not unheard of," Matthew answers. "I guess we'll see soon enough. The trade deadline's on Monday."

"Okay, I know I'm not the most informed here," Zeke says. "But do you two really think they'd deal him out at the deadline? What the hell kind of trade could they even come up with? Haven't they been waiting for you to be the starting goalie?"

"They have," Maddie says, "They'd probably have to give up at least a forward if they wanted to get a goalie they could reliably bring in as a replacement to the piece they've been very vocally waiting on. Don't really see how they could say this was about anything other than you dating a man if they traded you for some draft picks or a one-for-one with a mediocre goalie."

And she's right.

She should be right.

And when Austin O'Brien calls after he's filmed his video, he starts to believe her. Because welcoming him to the team, saying his sexuality doesn't matter, assuring him he won't be left out in the locker room, could all be empty platitudes, but they sound true in his deep, even voice and the color is a rich, forest green even through the neon tint of blue and Matthew believes O'Brien too.

Then the trade deadline hits, and Matthew's world turns upside down.

@EdmontonMiners
Goalie Leon Koskinen acquired from Carolina @Storm for Matthew Hellmann-Levoie and conditional first round draft pick.

@stormsurgesteve
@EdmontonMiners @Storm can't believe y'all are giving up on such a talent because homophobes are pushing the narrative he's a distraction and a liability. But I'm glad we got him! Can't wait to see him play his first game.

@johnson1276
@stormsurgesteve @edmontonoilers @Storm don't make this about his sexuality when everything points to Koskinen being more reliable

@stormsurgesteve
@johnson1276 lol you can't possibly believe that

mhl21 Date night with this guy

vsvenningsen Can't wait to have you in Raleigh bro! Brady and I have a bunch of places to show you when you finally get your ass down here

A week and a half has gone by since he was traded, and despite the initial devastation, despite the lingering anger, Matthew *is* relieved to know he won't be playing in Edmonton. To his surprise, Matthew gets a call from both the Storm's captain *and* the GM and they sound sincere. Matthew believes them, but after what happened with the Miners, his doubts linger. But when Viktor Svenningsen, the Storm's star forward, and likely future captain, calls, Matthew starts to believe they really are trying to be allies. Svenningsen has no one's expectations telling him to reach out to Matthew, but he did anyway, and it does far more to bolster Matthew's faith in the organization than anything else.

After talking to Svenningsen, Matthew thinks being traded before his professional career even begins isn't going to be the worst thing to happen to him, that maybe the Storm is what he needed. Not only has their fanbase been significantly more accepting of his sexuality but, as Maddie reminds him at least once a day, who the fuck wants to waste away in Edmonton anyway? And he would've never said it before, but she's right. He's seen the way Edmonton has sucked the joy right out of so many of their first overall picks, and he'd hate the same thing to happen to him. So even if they did it for terrible reasons, it benefited Matthew in the end.

"How was Victor?" AB asks, not looking away from his computer, as Matthew steps back into the living room.

"He seems nice. He and Brady Thatch are very loud, though," he says, tapping AB's legs so he'll lift them long enough for Matthew to sit down with him.

Over his laptop, AB looks at him with a curious smile. "Was it a conference call?"

"No, Brady was in the background yelling about looking up gay bars for us to check out when I finally get down there."

AB coughs out a laugh. "Well, he's my favorite. I'm going to buy his jersey. Wear it to all your games next year."

Matthew smacks AB's leg. "No, you won't."

AB smirks at him. "You should know better than to dare me."

"I do," Matthew says, his face flushing at the thought of Valentine's Day and AB's commitment to proving Matthew wrong. "What're you looking at anyway?"

"Houses," AB says, like it's obvious.

"What? You love this house!"

"Not for here," AB says, turning his laptop so Matthew can see.

On screen is a strange brick tower of a house, tucked away from the street, surrounded by lush trees and a back-yard bleeding into a lake.

"Where is this?"

AB rolls his eyes, but his face is soft with fondness and the ball of heat in his heart surges with love. "Raleigh, obviously."

"No," Matthew chokes out. "Not obviously."

"Wait," AB says, face falling, nerves splintering through Matthew's mind. "Do you not want to share a house there too? Did I misunderstand?"

Matthew's chest is bright and full and overflowing with joy.

"You didn't misunderstand," Matthew says. "But I didn't think you were planning to do more than visit. I didn't know you'd want to do more than visit."

"Matthew, my dear, sweet buffoon," AB says, his voice filled with laughter.

The color is the beautiful vibrant purple of his Matthew Voice, with a bright burst of magenta through the middle to reflect his laugh, and Matthew had been wrong before—this bright, beautiful amalgamation of AB is Matthew's favorite color of all.

AB pats Matthew's cheek in a way that should be condescending, but with AB's radiant smile and the magical light warming Matthew all the way through, it just feels like love.

"Of course, I'm coming with you," AB says, his eyes dancing. "They say *y'all* there."

Matthew's mouth twitches, but he stops himself from laughing. "The only valid reason, really."

AB pushes his computer away, the mood turning electric as AB climbs into his lap, and his smile is sharp and teasing as he looks down at him. "You're a pretty solid runner-up in reasons, though."

AB cuts Matthew's laugh off with a kiss, the heat of his mouth and the burn of their magic working together to steal his breath away—pushing out all thoughts about the future, leaving him with nothing but this moment, with AB, and the love bursting in his heart.

Epilogue

Nine Months Later

It's been almost a year since he and AB fully Bonded, and after years of playing hockey with a dull headache, after years of tracking the puck through the wisps of colors the sticks and skates and crash of bodies produce, Matthew relishes playing hockey with no added sight at all.

Tonight is his first game against the Miners, and he's gotten all the way to overtime without using his Vision, without letting the buzz of the narrative the press has been pushing about this game get under his skin. And while he knows seeing the sound a puck makes doesn't help him stop it, that the color trails behind instead of bursting out, that it doesn't give him any advantage in tracking its movement, seeing the charcoal gray the puck makes against the ice soothes him in a way. So, as overtime starts, and his heart ricochets in his chest, and the idea of losing against this team settles into his bones, unnerving him for the first time all night, Matthew filters in the color of the puck.

The charcoal-gray streak of a puck bleating out under his glove takes on a whole new beauty when he stops McDonnel's five-hole shot fifteen seconds into overtime. But still, it doesn't compare to the stunning firework of sound erupting at the other end of the ice two minutes later when Brady wins the game. Or even the bright, bright red of Sven's laugh as he skates up to him and congratulates him by yelling, "You fucking showed them, baby! Liability my ass!"

Nothing compares to the feeling his and AB's Bond creates, but the flare of vindication and pride ripping through him as he steps off the ice is almost as good. He got his first shutout of his rookie season against the team who did everything to justify his trade, who went after his magic and his link with Maddie and his relationship far after the trade was done. He'll keep this feeling and everything leading up to this exact achievement with him forever.

Matthew isn't the only one excited by the circumstances of the win, so it's not surprising when the first question he gets asked in his scrum is: "How's it feel to record your first shutout against the team that traded you under such questionable circumstances?"

"Oh." Matthew smirks. "Was that the Miners?"

There's a ripple of laughter.

"You know, O'Brien actually reached out to me to express his support after I came out. Wanted to let me know he and the team would have my back. So, as far as the guys on the team go, I hold no ill will for them in that regard. And if things panned out differently, I'd like to believe I would've been as welcomed and embraced there as I am in this locker room, but yeah, it does feel good. It's great to show the front office they were wrong about me."

"What Matthew means to say," Sven says, pushing his way through the reporters to sling an arm around Matthew's shoulder, jostling him as he laughs, "is that it felt fucking fantastic!"

He's so glad to be on a team with guys who truly support him, playing for a team that chose him, for a front office that isn't glaringly homophobic, for an outpouring of queer fans now feeling verifiably accepted in this arena.

"Yeah," Matthew says, his vindication melting into elation. "What Sven said."

Index

Let's Talk About Magic!

Because it never hurts to refresh your memory every once in a while.

By Kim Martinez

Magic of Immunity

The rarest magic of all magic. Immunes disrupt the magic of others, making them impervious to it.

Magic of the Heart

- **Empaths** can read and impact the emotions of others.

- **Healers**—you guessed it!—heal living things.

Magic of the Mind

- **Omnilinguals** can read, understand, and speak all languages.

- **Omnivisions** have perfect vision, will never need glasses, and can see the unsee-able—which ranges anywhere from the wind to the magic surrounding us.

- **Instacognition** lets Instacogs master any and all skills immediately after being told/shown/ taught them.

- **Clairvoyants** can glimpse the future through sensory-triggered visions that come to them in dreams or flashes of sounds and images while wide awake.

- **Telekinetics** can move things with their minds.

Magic of the Body

- **Concealers** come in two varieties.
  - Those who are **Invisible** are totally see-through.
  - While those who can **Camouflage** perfectly mimic their surroundings to hide themselves.

- **Strength & Durability** is so self-explanatory even I feel a little condescending reminding you that S&Ds are significantly stronger and significantly less likely to get injured than the rest of us.

- **Shifters and Modifiers** can both change their bodies at will but differ in what they can change their body *to.*
  - **Form shifting** is the ability to take on the properties of nonhuman things, both living and inanimate.
  - **Self-Modification** is the ability to change your body into other bodies.
  - This one can be tricky, so for clarification: a Shifter could turn into a table or a cat,

but not your best friend Jill, and a Modifier could turn into a carbon copy of your sister, but not a chair or a bird.

Magic of the Exterior

- **Elementals** have the ability to control the elements. (Another pretty self-explanatory one but! Did you know Elementals are often more attuned to one element despite being able to manipulate them all?)

- **Illusionists** can create Illusions that range anywhere from unreal firework shows to meticulously detailed virtual realities full of characters you can interact with, but not touch—no one's *that* good.

- **Object Manipulation** allows Manipulators (seriously, we couldn't have come up with a better shorthand here?) to manipulate the form of inanimate objects.

Magic of Convenience

The most common magic of all. Convenience is a catchall for anything that falls outside the parameters of the Big Four and Immunity. What Convenients can do ranges anywhere from never losing anything (an actual convenience) to having contagious enthusiasm (a tiny fraction of Empathy) to always hearing birdsong (a truly useless and annoying ability I've only found appealing three times in my entire life).

Now, those are the six Categories and everything that falls under them, but there's still one more thing for us to go over—the ever-elusive **M4s** who allegedly hit the jackpot and have magic from multiple Big Four categories. And look, I'm not saying they're not *real*. I'm just saying having multiple Conveniences isn't exactly common, having Big Four magic *and* a Convenience is downright rare, and Multiples with *two* Big Fours from the same category are almost entirely unheard of. So no, I'm not saying they're fake; I'm just saying there are about as many reliable sources supporting an M4's existence as there is of Bonds being real.

So, there you have it, babes! Hopefully you'll remember it all this time, and if not—that's what bookmarks are for.

Acknowledgements

First, this book would be nothing without the endless support and encouragement I received from my friends and family over the last three years. I owe so much to Kim, my constant cheerleader. To Kenny, who patiently listened as I worked through building an entire magic system and ultimately disregarded 90% of his suggestions. To Emilie, who was always open to answering even the most frivolous hockey and hockey-adjacent questions. To Jazmin and Jim, who helped do the final sweeps of this book. To Kat, the one-woman hype machine who helped me find the artist for this book and encouraged me to follow through when I thought asking would be too much. To everyone who lent me your names and your handles as a blueprint to spoof, who gave input when I needed help carving out the tiny details of this story.

Second, I am endlessly grateful to Raevyn and NineStar Press for stepping outside of their standard format and working with me to publish this illustrated novel. To Victoria, who brought my characters to life so beautifully, who took the idea of a man and turned him into AB, who gave him a face when I couldn't pin down one reference for him in three entire years. To Barb, who worked tirelessly with me to make this book the best it could be.

And finally, to anyone and everyone who ever contributed to the Wikipedia pages of Shawn Mendes' and Taylor Swift's tours—you are quite literally the backbone of this book.

About

Stephanie writes romance novels with a magical twist. She lives at the intersection of Crying Time and Excited Screaming and tells stories that blend the melancholy of self-discovery and self-acceptance with the delights of friendship and falling in love. She's a plotter with plot-commitment issues who lives and dies by chaotic bisexuals and happily-ever-afters.

Twitter
_stephaniehoyt

Website
www.stephanieahoyt.com

Tiktok
www.tiktok.com/@stephanieannwrites?

Tumblr
stephaniewrites.tumblr.com

Other NineStar books by this author

Love Blooms

Also from NineStar Press

Love Blooms by Stephanie Hoyt

Nico Hamurişi is the one and only son of Santa Claus. All his life, Nico has known he's expected to fall in love and find life-long commitment by the Christmas of his thirtieth year—like every other heir before him. But knowing and accepting are vastly different things, and as the final countdown begins, Nico has yet to embrace his fate. His once great enthusiasm for eventually becoming Santa has been dimmed by uncertainty over how the Santa Line will be affected when he marries a man.

With only a year left, will Nico have time to find love and commitment all while learning how magic will transform the family line to accommodate who he is and who he loves?

Connect with NineStar Press

www.ninestarpress.com

www.facebook.com/ninestarpress

www.facebook.com/groups/NineStarNiche

www.twitter.com/ninestarpress

www.instagram.com/ninestarpress

Made in the USA
Monee, IL
16 June 2022